Their Half of The World

B. H. Nelson

ISBN: 0-692-62338-8
ISBN-13: 978-0-692-62338-1

DEDICATION

For my mom who always told me to dream big

CONTENTS

ACKNOWLEDGMENTS

Words cannot express my gratitude for my sister Samantha, who wanted more when this book was just a half thought out dream and a few scribbled pieces of paper. I'd also like to give a special thank you to Taylor and Jeannie for waiting months at a time for me to finish the next chapter of the first draft. I'd also like to thank my husband for the immense help he's been in polishing the final manuscript and the cover.

CHAPTER 1: THE END OF EVERYTHING

Claire touched the gold chain attached to the locket around her neck and felt the cold metal between her fingertips. She heard a rustle of leaves outside her tent. Startled, she let go of the chain but it was only the wind.

She wasn't sleeping well. A reoccurring nightmare plagued her dreams, and the startling images haunted her well into the waking hours. The dream started in a dark forest clearing with Claire standing barefoot in wet, coarse grass. As the sun rose, Claire glanced down to find the grass soaked scarlet with blood, her blood. In the trees next to her she heard dark laughter. With difficulty her eyes picked out a man in a dull blue uniform approaching her. As the sun melted the shadows that obscured him, Claire noticed flecks of scarlet on his clothes. In his hand he held the locket. Blood dripped from the pendent and splashed against the growing pool around her feet. Claire screamed as she turned to run, only to jerk awake in a cold sweat.

She wanted to tell her husband, Leon, about the dreams, but she didn't want to burden him. He had found everyone a small clearing to spend the night in, and after all the tents had been set up, he'd left on a patrol. That was a few hours ago.

She paced back and forth in the small thread worn tent and felt a twinge of sadness as she surveyed the humble dwelling. The log cabin she grew up in seemed very far from her now.

She jumped as someone pushed his way inside the tent.

"Sorry, I didn't mean to scare you." Leon pulled her into a tight hug and kissed her forehead.

He was a sturdy man with ash blonde hair and dark gray-blue eyes that reminded her of a misty spring morning. A large bow was strapped to his back with freshly made arrows in a pouch at his side. His perpetual lack of sleep had caused the bags under his eyes to become a permanent addition to his features.

Their daughter, Mimie, had fallen asleep on top of a pile of tattered blankets. He reached for her and cradled her small frame in his arms. Mimie stirred and wrapped her thin arms around his neck, her face resting on his shoulder. Her cheeks were rosy from sleep and her lips were pursed in a slight pout at having been awoken from her nap.

"You're not going to leave again are you, Daddy?" she asked in a bell-like voice. "I was trying to wait up for you."

"Only for a moment, sweetheart. I'll be back before you know it."

"Okay," she yawned. He eased her down onto the blankets and tucked the edges around her shoulders. Leon straightened up and rubbed his eyes. "Will you take a walk with me?"

"I don't want to leave Mimie by herself. I'd feel more comfortable if someone looked in on her while we're gone."

"Already taken care of, love. Xander is waiting just outside." A man with a wild beard and kind eyes poked his head in.

"Don't worry, Claire, I would die before I let anything happen to that little girl."

"Thank you, Xander." Claire looped her arm around Leon's and followed him through the tent flap. "Alright, husband, where would you like to go?"

"I don't know yet," he admitted. Claire fell into a comfortable pace at his side and leaned her head against his arm. He traced circles across the back of her hand with his thumb. "I woke up the men for the second patrol, they should be leaving soon. I don't know how, but every one of them got up without waking his wife."

"Don't feel bad, I'm a light sleeper."

"Hardly, you wake up at my slightest shift and wrap your arms and legs around me in a death grip."

"Well, that's my way of ensuring you say goodbye to me before you go."

A grinding sound caught her attention. One of the watchmen was sharpening his sword with a whetstone. His eyebrows were furrowed into a deep-set line, and he cast an anxious glance toward the trees as if able to see right through them to the danger within. Claire huddled closer to Leon as they walked past the last of the tents on the edge of the pine trees. Leon settled down with his back against a lichen-covered boulder, his eyes fighting sleep.

"Have the patrols seen any sign of Max?" Claire asked, sitting down next to him and laying her head against his chest. The familiar pain twisted through her stomach as she said her brother's name.

"No." Leon closed his eyes. "If they had, you know what would happen. He attacked you and tried to steal the key. We can't make exceptions just because he's family."

"I know, but you know how he feels about us sealing the gate," Claire reminded him.

"That's not his choice to make, it's yours."

"Do you think I'm doing the right thing? By sealing humanity out of the magical side of the world, I mean. I want to keep the gate open, but with the Zanties getting more powerful, it's just too dangerous."

Claire took the locket out from under her shirt and worried the chain between her fingertips. Zantie greed and cruelty toward magical beings was the reason the wall had been created in the first place, countless generations ago. The Zanties sought to steal the key from her to regain access to the magical side of the world, Kolanna. Claire pushed those thoughts from her mind.

A buzz of electricity raised the hair on her arms as she slid her fingers down the chain to the pendent hanging from it. She studied the strange engraving in the gold metal and for the millionth time tried to open it, but it wouldn't budge. Leon gently took her hand away from it and pulled her in close again.

"It's not going to open, and even if it did, it would kill you to channel that much magic on this side of the world."

"I hate not being able to use my powers. I can't wait until we get to the other side of the gate."

"I know. I'd love to see my family again."

The skin on the back of Claire's neck prickled as if someone was watching her. A guard was dozing at his post, another was focused on cleaning the underside of his nails with a knifepoint. She hugged Leon tighter, hoping it would make her feel safe. She listened to his heartbeat and used the steady rhythm to try and calm her nerves.

A commotion coming from the direction the patrol had gone, caught her attention. Claire jumped to her feet, hiding behind Leon's exposed blade. He ran toward the guard and shook him from his daze.

"Get everyone out of here!"

The guard stumbled toward the tents and grabbed a large bell. The sharp clanging cut through the silence that had fallen over the morning. Claire curled her fingers into the fabric of Leon's shirt, walking with him as he shouted orders.

He broke her grip and placed both hands on her shoulders. "Take Mimie and run." Claire kissed him firmly on the lips, and knocked his restraining hands aside. She embraced him and tried to find the resolve to let go.

A crack split the air, making her jump. She watched in terror as a red flare arched over the trees in the distance.

"Claire, go!" Leon's words snapped her out of her daze. She turned and sprinted toward the tent. Panic raced through her as she heard the sound of pounding hooves. There had never been this many before, how was she going to get Mimie out before the clearing was surrounded?

Mounted figures thundered out of the trees. It was hard to see through the confusion of clashing metal and screams. Leon had disappeared. She backed into the shadow of a tree and tried to work her way around the perimeter to avoid being discovered by the

Zanties. She grimaced as she watched men fighting to protect their wives and children. They were so outnumbered their efforts were feeble against the advancing army.

She froze when she saw a mounted figure with a torch approaching her tent. She was too far away; she'd never make it in time. The blaze licked across the thin fabric and a child's screams could be heard from inside. Her legs blurred as she raced to Mimie's aid.

An old woman emerged from the trees and darted toward the blaze. Claire paused, gasping. The old woman pushed her way inside the tent and reappeared seconds later. She was coughing and her clothes were singed, but Mimie was held firmly in her arms. Claire nearly choked on her relief.

"Mom?" Claire said, recognizing the old woman. She hadn't seen her since the first raid over a month ago.

Her attention was diverted as a Zantie lunged toward her. She ducked out of his reach and cast a panicked glance at Mimie before sprinting into the trees. She heard a commotion behind her and turned to see Leon tackle her pursuer to the ground. The Zantie threw Leon off and grabbed for his sword, but Leon was faster. He rolled to the side, drew a knife and stabbed the point deep into the smaller man's neck. He didn't withdraw it until the light dimmed in the Zantie's steel-gray eyes. Leon wiped his knife on the ground and took Claire in his arms, holding her tightly.

"Are you ok?" he demanded.

"Yeah. I saw my mom; she saved Mimie and ran off with her into the forest."

"I knew the old bat was still around. Mimie is safer with her than anyone; her cloaking magic is incredible."

Claire still felt uneasy. She and her mother's relationship hadn't been the same since, Orient, the Zantie leader, had found them. Mom wanted to go into hiding with Mimie, but Claire hadn't liked that idea. After what almost happened tonight, though, she saw the wisdom in her mother's words.

She saw something in the corner of her eye and ducked just as

Leon shoved hard against her side. He drew an arrow and shot it into the bushes. Leaves rustled as the Zantie fell to the ground.

Claire heard a pained grunt and saw Leon sink to his knees.

"Oh God," she whispered. A knife hilt was protruding from his side.

Leon closed his eyes and touched the hilt with a trembling finger. Claire helped lower him to the ground and cradled his head in her lap. She couldn't breathe. He placed a hand on her arm. She tried to focus on his face through her tears.

"Shhh…" he muttered.

She wanted to tell him she loved him. That she would always love him, but she couldn't make her mouth form the words.

"Claire—" He coughed on the blood filling his mouth. "Get away from here." He could barely get the words out.

"No." She used the hem of her shirt to wipe the blood from the side of his mouth and stroked his hair. She hummed the lullaby he'd written for Mimie. His lips twitched as though to speak again, but his body fell still, and he stared unblinkingly past her. "I love you," she choked out, but he gave no response.

He was gone.

With shaking fingers she closed his eyes and stroked his face, buckling under the pain of her grief.

She heard footsteps running toward her and glanced toward the approaching Zanties with a feral snarl. The closest one grabbed her arm and dragged her away from Leon. A weak crackle of electricity add a hum to the air around her as a Zantie grabbed Leon's body and dragged it toward the bushes.

"Get away from him!" Claire clawed viciously at her attacker's hand in an attempt to break free. She watched Leon's body disappear from view and gradually fell into hiccupping sobs as the Zanties dragged her from the forest. It was over; the world was lost. The Zanties released her, and she fell hard onto her side.

"Is this her?" a cold voice asked a man standing next to him.

"Yeah. She's the one you're looking for," a familiar voice replied.

Claire glanced up and saw her brother, Maxwell, standing next to Orient. It only took her a few seconds to put the pieces together.

"You told him where we were!"

"That's right, love," Orient said in a low tone.

"How could you?" Claire recoiled from the sight of her betrayer.

"I won't let you lock the humans out." Max knelt down in front of her, his eyes begging for her understanding.

"Leon is dead because of you!" She ripped a knife from his belt and stabbed it into his foot. He howled in pain and stumbled backward. She lunged for him, but two Zanties pinned her down.

"Let her go," Orient said quietly. The Zanties instantly released her. "Give me the key, Guardian."

Claire trembled as she rose to her feet and put as much hatred and defiance into her glare as possible. "No, you'll have to kill me first." She braced herself, but the death blow didn't come. She opened her eyes and saw that he was staring at her, trying to decide what to make of her comment. The screams and the flicker of fire faded from Claire's vision. It was just her and death staring eye-to-eye waiting for the other to make the first move.

"Give me the key," he said more forcefully, taking a measured step in her direction. She spat in his face with a continued glare of defiance. He wiped it off with his hand in disgust. He nodded to the Zantie behind her, and she felt an agonizing pain in her lower back. Her legs buckled and she fell to the ground, unable to process what had just happened. Something warm and sticky spread across her side and she fought the urge to be sick.

Orient slowly knelt down until he was a foot above her face and took the chain from around her neck. Claire was too weak to stop him. He smiled at his prize for half a second then straightened up and put it in his pocket.

"No survivors," he said to his men. The Zanties pulled out their swords and walked toward their group of captives.

Screams filled the air. They sounded far away to Claire, and oddly distorted.

Orient studied Max coldly. It was clear in his eyes that his informant had outlived his usefulness.

"Wait!" Max exclaimed, but his pleas were cut off as Orient drove a sword through his chest.

"Fool," Orient muttered under his breath and turned to the Zantie next to him.

"Find the girl. If she survives, she could ruin everything." The Zantie nodded and headed toward the trees. Orient trailed behind him more slowly.

"Murderer!" Claire screamed, finding new strength in the hatred she felt toward him. It gave her the resolve to crawl toward the trees, but she only made it a few feet before she collapsed again.

The pain was fading. She would be with Leon again soon; his arms were waiting to take her home. It soothed some of the hot fury that coursed through her veins like poison. Mimie would be alone now. Claire felt tears fall from her eyes; Mimie was too young for the responsibility that would now rest on her shoulders. She was the new Guardian, and she was the only hope to save all that had been lost.

***

Hugging close to the shadows of the forest, Gram retraced her steps to the tree hollow where she had told Mimie to hide. It had been almost eight hours since the Zanties left, but she wanted to make sure they were a safe distance away before she removed the cloaking magic from Mimie's tree. The basic enchantment had left her drained, but there was no time to rest.

It took her longer than she expected to find the tree again, but once there she removed the illusion that hid the hollow and found Mimie curled up in a ball inside. Tears cut lines through her dirty cheeks, and the burns on her arms had turned an angry red color.

Gram knelt down next to her and gently shook her awake. Mimie sat up quickly and threw herself into Gram's arms, fresh tears streaming down her face.

"Where's Mommy and Daddy?" Gram didn't reply and felt her lower lip tremble. She closed her eyes and took a deep breath. She knew there was only one way she could keep Mimie safe from the

Zanties. They had to go somewhere far away where Orient would never think to look for her, only then would she be safe from the grim fate that had befallen her parents.

CHAPTER 2: SOMEWHERE BETWEEN TIME

Nearly fourteen and a half years had passed since Gram had disappeared with Mimie. It had taken a while before Gram felt safe staying in one place for more than a few days. When they stumbled across a sleepy town buried in the heart of the forest, she decided it was finally time to put down roots.

The village had changed little in the time they had spent there. The collections of log cabins, though plain, were sturdy as ever. The people there were unchanging as well, they knew what to expect from every day, and lived their lives accordingly. Mimie found the monotony boring. This place was her home, but it was also her prison.

Mimie tucked her arms behind her head and stared at the charcoal sketches that covered her ceiling. Most of them were scenes she'd seen in the woods: a chipmunk holding an acorn, a deer peeking out from behind a tree. There was another drawing that was half finished sitting on her desk. She'd started it last night, but had given up on it halfway through.

She kicked off her blankets and shuddered as her toes touched the cold wood floor. Yawning, she arched her back to stretch out the stiffness from sleep. Her tangled hair tickled her nose and she pushed it out of her face. She grabbed a brush and used it to return order to her hair. The only mirror she had was lying face down on a shelf collecting dust. She liked it that way. Her childhood burns created unattractive reddish patches on her skin. There was one on the back of her left hand, another on her forearm, and one more by her right elbow. Her fingers itched to grab a long sleeve shirt to cover them.

Without enthusiasm she wandered toward her chest to dig out the dress Gram had made her. She heard a sharp knock and jumped as Gram impatiently swung the door open.

"Are you ready?" Her eyes flicked up and down as she looked Mimie over with a frown. "You don't even have your dress on yet! Get moving. We leave in five minutes." She closed the door, and her hurried footsteps disappeared into another part of the cabin.

Gram was a sweet woman; this day was just stressful on her. In truth, it was stressful on Mimie too. Birthdays were supposed to be fun, not this mad dash of ceremonies and dances. It was a custom of the town, though, so she had no choice but to comply. It made her sad that Gram was more excited about her eighteenth birthday than she was. She forced a smile on her face and tried to keep it there, but the edges eroded away until her expression was blank again. She pulled her nightgown over her head and tossed it to the side. She pulled on the dress and frowned when she saw that the hem brushed the floor. It suddenly occurred to her that this was the first time she had worn the dress since Gram had given it to her over a week before. It was pretty; the hem was embroidered with lace and it was made from blue silk, but it was too tight. Mimie never wore anything this tight. It would show how bony she was.

Her shoes were shoved in a corner; she grabbed them and put them on her feet. She lifted up the hem of her dress and walked into the front room. Gram was waiting for her there; she beamed at Mimie proudly, but frowned when she noticed the bottom of the dress.

"You didn't tell me the hem was too long?" She let it go with a defeated expression, and followed Mimie out the door. Gram seized her arm as though she were afraid Mimie would make a run for it, and half led, half dragged her toward the forest.

They headed toward the caves, a place where all the ceremonies in the village took place. Mimie's was a womanhood ceremony; it was where she was formally accepted into adult society and given a symbol. The symbol was supposed to tell her where she belonged and what she was meant to do with her life. Mimie thought a more likely explanation was the town elders just wanted another excuse to be able to control everyone. Sometimes the symbols ran in families, but Gram had always kept hers hidden. She was secretive like that.

Elder Lenten was waiting for them outside the mouth of the cave. He was a short man with thin stubbly hair perched on his head like burnt weeds. His robes were a fading blackish gray and hung from his shoulders like old rags. Of all the members on the town council, he was the one she disliked the most.

"Good morning," Gram panted.

"Same to you, shall we proceed?"

He motioned Mimie to follow him and then disappeared into an underground tunnel. Mimie glanced back at Gram anxiously, and after seeing that she would receive no help, reluctantly entered the dark hole. She sighed, resigning herself to her fate.

The temperature dropped as she walked into the cave entrance. The thick cavern air had a strong mineral smell to it. The farther she followed Elder Lenten into the tunnel, the darker it got. After the first turn, Elder Lenten stopped to light a torch, and they continued toward the ceremony room. Mimie glanced at the huge crystal spikes hanging from the ceiling and winced as some of the gathering dew fell and splashed against her cheek. The dress she was wearing was impractical for this kind of environment; it already had flecks of mud on it and they'd only just gotten started.

They passed beautiful underground lakes but Mimie was too distracted by how all the rocks seemed to resemble food to notice. More than once she stopped to examine a rock she could have sworn was a huge piece of bacon. She pushed all thoughts of food from her mind once she entered the ceremonial chamber. The walls sparkled with the light from hundreds of moonstones and shone so brightly they didn't need the torch.

Elder Lenton walked to the center of the room where there was a small tree stump. Mimie followed more slowly and stared at it with a raised eyebrow.

"Come here," Elder Lenten motioned. She walked over to him. "See that tiny little hole?" He pointed at the center of the ceiling. A small beam of sunlight streamed through it and fell directly on the tree stump. "Hundreds of years ago, a seed fell through and took root in the soil." He pointed at the stump. "See the green stem growing on the side?" She leaned in to examine the new branch.

"Yes."

"Even though someone cut off the rest of the tree long ago, it is still alive and growing," he told her. "Sit and feel the energy of its life coursing around you." This is stupid, Mimie thought, but she sat down to humor him. Her stomach dropped as a pillar of light fell across her face. She blinked a few times as it registered her surroundings had changed.

"Mimie..." a soft whisper called.

"That's creepy." She crossed her arms warily. "Who's there?" she shouted at the surrounding trees.

"Mimie," the voice called again. She spun around; and found a woman standing behind her. She screamed and fell off the stump.

"Who are you?" Mimie demanded. She scooted away from her and tried to regain her composure. The lady didn't respond; instead she turned around and disappeared into the forest. Mimie blinked a few times, and then for some reason she'd probably never understand, she followed her.

Now that the shock had worn off, Mimie heard a stream trickling somewhere nearby. Everything had a strange glow around it as if this were all a crazy dream. The trees linked their branches to make a leafy canopy, and through the gaps yellow streams of sunlight drifted toward the ground.

"Where am I?" Mimie demanded.

"Somewhere between time." Mimie narrowed her eyes; she'd never heard of something like this being part of the ceremony. She studied the woman carefully and found, to her confusion, that she was just as faded and indistinct as everything else. The woman was tall, slender and wearing clothes made expertly from plants. She had long bronze hair that fell in light curls down her back and an almost inhuman grace about her. When she spoke, the sound was like wind blowing through leaves.

"Who are you?" Mimie finally asked.

"I am Naowa, a tree spirit. I was sent here to wait for you, to tell you of your true identity."

"If my choice means anything, I'd prefer to be a seamstress like Gram. If you assign me to the garden I might kill everything and we'll starve."

A smile pulled at the corner of Naowa's lips, and her eyes crinkled in amusement. She sat down on a fallen log carpeted in moss and patted the spot next to her. Mimie humored her. She sat close enough her arm nearly brushed Naowa's, but she felt no heat coming off her skin. It was like sitting next to a ghost.

"How much do you know about your family's history?" she asked.

"Not much, Gram doesn't like talking about it."

"I see. That's a shame; your ancestors fought in a war many generations ago and helped secure the freedom of those on the other side of the wall."

"What wall? What are you talking about?" Mimie demanded. Maybe she'd been drugged, and all of this was a crazy hallucination.

"There is a wall that divides the children of magic from the children of men. The two could not coexist peacefully, so the wall was created to end the bloodshed." Naowa grabbed a leaf from a pile of litter on the forest floor and turned it in circles between her fingers.

"If what your saying is true, and my ancestors knew about the magical world, why didn't anyone tell me about it?"

"Your Grandmother hid the knowledge from you, to protect you, but the time has come for you to know the truth."

Mimie shifted uncomfortably and got to her feet, avoiding Naowa's gaze. Her whole life she'd wanted to know what secrets Gram hid from her, but now that someone was offering answers, she wondered if it might be better leave the questions unanswered. She chewed her bottom lip as she tried to decide what to do.

"Why now? What's changed?"

"You weren't ready before, and knowing the truth might have put you in danger."

Mimie leaned against a tree and set her shoulders. "Alright, tell me."

"A golden gate was forged in hopes that one day humans would be able to reenter Kolanna, the magical half of the world. Your ancestors were entrusted with the key and were told to open the gate when they deemed humanity worthy to live amongst us again."

"Who told them?"

"The four founding fairies."

"Where's the key now? Does Gram have it?"

"No, it was stolen from your mother by an ancient organization who used it to infiltrate Kolanna. The Zanties swept across the land like a virus and built and empire on top of the chaos. Their leader, Orient, was the one who killed your mother."

Mimie's chest tightened. So, her parent's death wasn't a senseless act of violence after all. That didn't make losing them any easier.

"You are a Key Guardian Mimie. It is your responsibility to retrieve the key from Orient and use its magic to force the humans back to their half of the world."

Mimie swallowed hard against the lump that had formed in her throat. Several questions whirled through her mind and she couldn't decide which of them to ask first. Naowa motioned for her to sit down, and gave her a moment to collect her thoughts.

"How do I learn to use magic?"

"You will need to travel to Kolanna and study with the fairies. The magic it will take to defeat Orient will not be easy to learn. It will take you years of study to prepare yourself. Once you cross into the magical world, find Luna, she can tell you where the fairies are."

"Ok, how do I get to Kolanna?"

"There's an old space fairy ritual I can teach you, it will transport you where you need to go." Mimie tried to stop her hands from shaking. She'd spent her life being kicked around and bullied by others. If she couldn't stop them, how was she supposed to stop someone as powerful as Orient? Still, Naowa was offering her what she'd always wanted, a way out of this place. She'd be a fool not to take it.

"Ok, how do I perform this ritual?"

"Magic on your side is bound by rigid rules. You will need to follow what I tell you in exactly the order I say, or it won't work. Do you understand?"

"Yes." She hoped Naowa was ok repeating herself a few times.

"Take a Moonstone from the wall in the central chamber and find one of the cave springs. Drop the Moonstone into the pool and wait until it turns the water silver, then take it out and hide it. Wait 24 hours. Set the Moonstone on the ground and spit on it. It should start to glow bright blue and give off misty smoke. Step through the smoke and you will be transported where you need to go."

Naowa had her repeat the instructions several times to make sure she had them memorized. Mimie continued to say them to herself as a cold wind swept through her. She squeezed her eyes closed and a second later the steady drip, drip, drip, and musky smell of wet rock confirmed she was back in the cave.

"Mimie? Mimie!" She opened her eyes and found Elder Lenten staring at her. "Are you alright?"

"Yeah, I'm just a little nervous is all."

"Why weren't you answering me?" He crossed his arms in irritation.

"Sorry, I spaced out for a moment." She tried not to let her private amusement at this answer show on her face.

"May we continue, or is it too hard for you to pay attention?"

She flinched at his harsh tone. "I'm ok now."

He cleared his throat and went on about how Mimie would have more chores and responsibilities. Mimie tuned him out as she tried to think of a way to get a Moonstone without him seeing her.

"Are you ready to receive your symbol?" Mimie turned her attention back to him as he walked toward the back wall. He picked up a large bowl and quickly returned. As he got closer, Mimie saw a faintly glowing stone inside. "Lift up your left sleeve please," he told her.

She obeyed and watched him dip two fingers into the water and trace a circle on her arm. He lifted the glowing Moonstone from the water and touched it to her skin. The glow changed from white to dark blue and small cracks appeared on the surface. Elder Lenten pulled the stone away from her skin and put it back into the bowl of water. The cracking noises grew louder while the bright blue light grew more intense, blue smoke rose from the water and wafted toward her. When it touched her skin, a glowing shape appeared, and the burn intensified as the smoke consolidated on her arm. Elder Lenton gasped and backed away from her in shock. The light faded leaving behind a delicate dark blue crescent moon with a broken five-prong star near the bottom point.

"That mark..." he gasped. "You should go. Do not show that mark to anyone, do you understand? Not a soul. I have to go talk with the other council members." He turned and disappeared into a side tunnel.

"Wait I don't know how to get out of here!" Mimie exclaimed, but he was already gone. Mimie pushed herself to her feet and walked toward the cave wall, grumbling to herself in irritation. She plucked off a loose Moonstone and cautiously approached the mouth of the tunnel she had entered through. The light from the Moonstone seemed to illuminate the entire passage with its pure silver light. As she pushed forward, Mimie felt the enormity of what she knew she had to do weighing on her shoulders. How could she leave Gram? She could be stern sometimes, but she was the only family Mimie had left.

She heard a soft trickling sound coming from one of the smaller tunnels. The tunnel branched off the main one she was standing in and ended in a wall with a large crack in it. She slipped through the broken section, trying to rein in images of it giving way and crushing her.

Once inside she held the Moonstone out in front of her to illuminate the small chamber. A pool of water occupied most of the floor space. If was fed by a drizzle flowing down the wall from a hole near the ceiling. Holding the Moonstone in her fist, she lowered her hand into the cold depths of the pond and watched the Moonstone drop to the bottom.

Oily looking silver swirls appeared on the surface. Mimie waited for them to become more pronounced, then reached in and pulled the Moonstone out again. The sound of water dripping on stone rang softly through the chamber. She dried the Moonstone off on her dress and squeezed back into the passageway. The stone was different, a swirling mist was contained inside, and it was heavier.

The main tunnel branched off in different directions, and wound through vast chambers, but eventually she found her way out. Intense relief washed through her as she spotted sunlight pouring through a narrow opening. She climbed over some broken rock and paused only to tuck the Moonstone into her bra.

Gram was waiting for her on a log near the entrance. She had kept herself busy by embroidering an elaborate design into one of the dresses she was working on. She must have gotten bored and gone back to the cabin for it. She set it aside when she saw Mimie and pulled her into a tight hug.

"How was it?" Mimie pulled away from her and started toward the cabin.

"It was fine." Gram frowned, catching on to her mood.

They walked to the cabin in silence. Gram opened the door for her, and she walked wordlessly to her room. Once the door closed behind her she threw the Moonstone into her wooden chest. She changed out of her ridicules dress, and collapsed onto her bed. Gram opened her door a crack and peeked inside.

"You can't be tired already? The fun stuff hasn't started yet." Mimie didn't reply. "Can I come in?"

"I guess." Mimie kept her gaze fixed on the ceiling. Gram pushed the door open and sat down on the edge of Mimie's bed.

"What's wrong sweetheart? Are you unhappy with the mark you got?" Mimie let out a short laugh in response.

"What does your mark look like, Gram?"

"My mark is nothing of any particular interest. What's gotten into you?" Mimie clenched her teeth together and ripped her sleeve out of the way so that her tattoo would be visible.

"So it doesn't look like this!" Mimie yelled. Gram suddenly looked much older.

"This is exactly what I was afraid of." She pinched the bridge of her nose. "How much do you know?"

"I know you've been lying to me." Mimie's tone was more level now; it was hard to stay angry with her when Gram looked so tired and frail.

"I was trying to keep you safe, Mimie. Keep you away from all this dangerous nonsense. I couldn't lose you the same way I lost your mother. I hoped that with the key gone you wouldn't be marked as a Guardian. You can't beat him Mimie, what's done is done, and if he finds out you survived..." She swallowed hard.

"I want to be alone right now." Mimie pushed passed her and headed toward the front door. She crossed the narrow clearing and trudged into the woods beyond. She stepped around fallen debris irritably, paying little attention to where she was going. She didn't need to; this was a path she had well memorized. She looked up and found herself in front of an ancient oak tree. She walked toward the frayed ropes tied to a flattened stick and sat down. This was a private place few people knew about. Shrouded in the trees she felt protected from the noise of everyday life.

She kicked her legs out and started to swing, the old rope groaned under her weight. She glanced up at the remnants of a tree house she had tried to build years ago. The first time a storm had blown through her progress had been smashed to pieces. Now, only small portions of the foundation remained. She knew she'd have to face Gram soon enough, but for now she was content to hide in her own little world.

CHAPTER 3: DEPREDATION

←← ←← →→ →→

Mimie watched the shadows lengthen. There was a party planned for her that would start soon. Gram would be worried if she didn't show. She knew she had to go, but forcing her feet to move in that direction was a struggle. She dragged them across the ground to slow the swing and stood up. Music drifted toward her, freezing her muscles. The feast had already started, where had all the time gone?

She weaved her way through the forest until her path intersected the trailhead she was looking for. She broke into a run, but after a few minutes a stitch in her side forced her to slow to a walk. She didn't push as hard after that, not wanting anyone to catch sight of her sweaty and out of breath. The town square wasn't big enough for this sort of thing so the celebration had been moved to a large clearing outside of town. After twenty minutes or so she caught sight of it, amazed to find that most of the townspeople had showed up. It wasn't so much that they cared about her birthday; it was more they wanted an excuse to get drunk and eat until they passed out. Still, not wanting to be caught late to her own party, she snuck in by the people dancing.

"Mimie, there you are," a voice behind her exclaimed. Mimie jumped and turned to face the speaker. It was her friend Zarin, she recognized his trademark shoulder-length brown hair and hazel eyes. His appearance had changed very little since the days when they used to run around as kids. Mimie smiled at the memory. The other girls were jealous of her easy friendship with him, but they'd cooled off when it became apparent that nothing was going to happen between them. Mimie simply didn't see him that way; she had too many memories of him eating dirt and putting slugs on people. He was what made this place bearable.

"Hey, how's it going?" she asked.

"Fine. This is quite the party, for those of us that have been here anyway." Mimie bit her lip.

"Don't tell Gram, please."

"I won't, don't worry." A sly gleam entered his eye. "On one condition."

"What's that?"

"Dance with me, just one song," he prefaced, watching the way she was eyeing the food table.

His light mood and carefree demeanor unwound some of the tension from her shoulders.

"There, see, that's the smile I've been looking for!" His eyes crinkled as he spun her around. He lowered her into a quick dip, seeming pleased with himself. The song ended, and Mimie stepped away from him, panting. "See you around, happy birthday!" He waved goodbye and drifted back into the crowd.

Zarin's happy nature had earned him a lot of friends. As a consequence, Mimie had been pushed to the periphery. He still cared about her, his large volume of friends just made it difficult to give each of them individualized attention.

Her stomach grumbled as she grabbed a bowl. The food table was filled with huge platters of fruit, roast duck, and a steaming pot of stew. She grabbed a small bushel of wild grapes and poured herself a bowl of soup. She sat down at an empty table and popped one of the grapes into her mouth, then sipped at the stew. The warm, flavorful broth pooled into her stomach, and she was reaching for more before she realized her bowl was empty.

When she was full, she decided to go back to the dance floor and see if Zarin was still there. He seemed busy socializing, so she glanced around to see if there was anyone else she wanted to talk to.

Her eyes fell on a small form sitting in a dark corner by the trees. She looked closer and recognized Anna. Anna saw her staring and glared at her, then turned her head away and wrapped her arms around her legs. Mimie walked toward her in concern.

"Anna, what's wrong?" Mimie said, sitting beside her. Anna was another one of her longtime friends. They weren't as close as she was with Zarin, but Mimie still cared about her.

"Zance is talking about breaking up with me." Fresh tears streamed down her face.

"I'm sorry."

"No, you're not, you hate him!"

"You're right, I do, but I'm sorry you're hurting." Mimie had seen the bruises on Anna's arms. She deserved better; she deserved someone who actually cared about her.

"It's your fault he's leaving me. Why couldn't you just keep your mouth shut!" Mimie looked at her in shock. She had told the town council what Zance was doing to Anna, but she'd asked that her identity be kept private. Somehow Zance must have figured out who tipped them off.

Well, at least he'd have to be more careful when he abused people in the future. It was high time someone stood up to him.

"What he was doing was inexcusable, I don't understand how you could defend him after how much he's hurt you," Mimie tried to keep her voice level.

"Get out of here, ok? I want to be alone!" Anna tucked her face into her knees, and her shoulder shook with grief.

Mimie stumbled away from her and returned to the crowds. She tried to focus on the people around her. Everyone seemed happy; they had a place to be and people to talk to. She thought about walking up to one of the groups, but she didn't know what to say. It was lonely, always looking from the outside in. She found a quiet corner and sat down, watching some of her friends laugh with one another and talk. This was her party; she should be enjoying herself, not feeling miserable. She watched as the sun went down; her expression empty.

It was late when she finally stood up and decided to walk back to the cabin. She approached the edge of the forest and paused; it was too dark to see the path and the fire had gone out. She couldn't make a torch. It was foolish of her to wait this long. Now there was no one to walk her back. She shrugged and pushed into the trees regardless. Progress was slow, and she had no idea where she was going. The hair on the back of her neck stood up as a stale odor filled the air. She walked into the ring of light cast by a fire and saw a boy there who was a year older than her. He was sitting on a log taking a long drink from a glass bottle he kept at his side.

"You lost, baby?" This was a dumb thing to do. Mimie turned to leave and muffled a frightened squeak when she ran into Zance, who was standing behind her.

"Town is that way." Her chest tightened as she registered the dark gleam in his eyes. She kept her head low as she hurried in the direction that he'd indicated.

The trees seemed darker to her now, more menacing. Sweat accumulated on her palms as she worked her way through the darkness. A rustling sound behind her indicated that someone was following. She picked up her pace, nearly breaking into a jog. She ignored the brush tearing at her clothes. Her heart pounded behind her ears as the rustling drew closer. A root caught her ankle. She rolled down an incline and lay sprawled at the foot of an oak tree. A few boards were draped over some of the lower branches, frayed rope swayed in the wind. Mimie grabbed a stick and jumped to her feet. In the moonlight, she saw a shadowed figure leaning against a tree.

"Stay away from me!" Mimie threatened.

Zance took a step toward her. Her grip on the stick tightened.

"I mean it, stay away!"

"Someone needs to teach you to mind your own business."

He charged at her and wrenched the stick from her grasp, bark bit into her palms. She turned to run and felt his arms lock around her waist. They fell to the ground.

"Stop it!"

The leaves crackled underneath her as she struggled to roll out of his grasp. He grabbed her leg and pulled her back to him. She screamed, though she knew no one would hear. Zance forced her onto her back and tried to pull her jacket over her head. She struggled to lock her arms in place, her strength failed. The cotton sweater ripped as he wrestled it off her, exposing her bare arms to the cold night air.

He leaned down and his sour breath swirled around her face. She shook her head trying to shake him off, but he tangled his fingers in her hair to keep her from moving. The other hand slid across her stomach toward her chest. She screamed again, thrashing uselessly. He reached for the button on his pants and started to remove them. She kicked him away from her with all her strength, but he over powered her.

She just wanted it to end, but it didn't, not for a long time.

Mimie opened her eyes and squinted. The bright sunlight hurt her eyes. She sat up and felt her sore muscles ache from the movement. Her throat was raw from screaming.

It was cold; every inch of her was frozen. She grabbed her sweater and pulled it to her chest, wanting to be less exposed. Dark purple bruises had formed on her wrists and along her arms. She brushed the dirt off her front and looked for her bra, finding it a little ways away. She tried to put it on, but her shaking fingers were too weak to grip the fabric. She gave up as tears welled over. Happy birthday, she thought bitterly, happy birthday indeed.

She pulled her clothes back on and picked bits of leaves out of her tangled hair. Stiffly, she pushed herself to her feet. Her swing swayed gently in the breeze. She glanced up at the oak. Its branches, which had once seemed to curl around her in an embrace, now seemed indifferent. The refuge of her childhood had become the stage of her worst nightmare. Why had this happened to her? She stumbled back toward town, barely registering where she was going. She tried to hide behind a smile, but the best she could do was not cry. She opened the door to Gram's cabin and headed toward her room.

"Where have you been?" came Gram's concerned tone from the kitchen. "I've been worried sick!"

"Sorry." Mimie tried to keep her voice even. "I got lost in the woods and had to sleep out there." Gram laughed and peeked around the kitchen wall.

"That's a new one. How was it?"

"Cold."

Mimie knew the mask was going to crack at any second. She turned away and headed toward the bathroom. She turned the knob on the tub, letting the hot water pour out and added some bubble soap. She held her clothes away from her as she took them off and threw them to the side. Once she was free of them, she climbed over the edge of the tub and sank up to her neck in hot water, trying to forget. It didn't work. The harder she tried to overlook what happened, the stronger the memories were. She curled into a ball and made no effort to stop the fresh wave of tears.

Eventually, she accepted that she couldn't soak away her problems and pulled the plug, letting the water drain out. She sat in the empty tub and let cold air blow across her body. She had to get out of here. If she had any doubts about leaving before, they were gone now.

Her towel was draped over the side of the tub. She grabbed it and wrapped it around her as she got out. She picked up her dirty clothes and carried them into her room. Not wanting to look at them, she dropped the dirty bundle on the floor and kicked it under her bed. She put on fresh clothes, just pants, and a loose-fitting long sleeve shirt; then grabbed her brush and started working it through her hair. She wasn't sure she would ever get the tangles out.

She studied her reflection in the small mirror and noticed a small cut on her lip, but didn't see any other injuries that would give away what happened. Of course not, Zance was far too careful for that. She tossed the mirror on her bed tried to find her deerskin travel bag. It was shoved in a corner by the door. She picked it up and dropped it on the floor in front of her wooden chest. She dug out as many pairs of traveling clothes as she thought she could carry and shoved them in the bag. She hid the Moonstone at the bottom and walked into the kitchen looking for some dried meat.

"Are you going somewhere?" Gram asked with a frown, looking her over carefully for the first time. "What happened to your lip?"

She put the knife down she was using to slice up vegetables and put her hands on the sides of Mimie's face, turning it back and forth in concern.

"I'm okay." Mimie pulled away from her. "I tripped while I was walking last night. Don't worry about it."

"You always were accident prone." Gram let it go.

As much as Mimie wanted to tell her what happened, anyone who knew the truth about Zance was in danger. It wasn't worth the risk to Gram's safety.

"You didn't answer my question though. Are you going somewhere?" she asked again. Mimie felt her shoulders sag in defeat. She tried to think of something to say, but the words kept getting caught in her throat.

Gram massaged her forehead tiredly as if, somehow, she already knew what Mimie was going to say.

"Are you sure you want to do this? You're barely more than a child; you still have your whole life ahead of you."

"I'm old enough to make my own choices," Mimie said firmly. Gram saw her conviction and sighed, knowing there was no way to change her mind.

"Well, at least take some food with you." She rushed into the root cellar and reappeared a few minutes later carrying a leather pouch. Mimie saw something that looked like dried carrots poking out.

Her bag was already full, but with some effort she was able to make the pouch fit in as well. She tried to keep her emotions level as Gram led her toward the door.

"Come home soon."

"I'll try." Mimie didn't mention that this place would no longer be home to her by the time she finally got back. If she got back, there were no guarantees at this point.

She waved goodbye to Gram and headed toward the trees.

Her destination was the cliff by the riverside; it was supposedly haunted so she doubted anyone would disturb her there while she worked. The local legend was that a man named Mernie had committed suicide there, and his skeleton could still be seen at the base of the cliff. If anyone leaned too far over the edge, Mernie's ghost would push them off. Multiple people who had disappeared over the years were rumored to have died that way. Mimie doubted any of this was true and assumed the people had merely left in search of a better life. The legend was a ghost story to discourage children from going there and playing too close to the edge.

"Where are you off to this early in the morning?"

Mimie jumped and almost hit her head on the low-hanging branch of a passing tree.

"I'm not going anywhere Zarin, just looking for some fresh air."

"You're awful jumpy today, is everything ok?"

"Yep, everything is good." He didn't look convinced, but he dropped the subject. "Don't you have to do something for the blacksmith? I thought apprentices weren't supposed to have any free time."

"Brog gave me the morning off," Zarin shrugged.

"How come?"

"He accidently broke my hand with a hammer." Zarin showed her his thickly bandaged left hand.

"I'm so sorry."

"It's ok. Do you mind if I come with you? I think I could use some fresh air as well."

Mimie shook her head with a half-smile and led the way. Truthfully she was glad for his company. She hadn't been overly excited to venture into the trees again on her own. She felt better knowing Zance wouldn't dare try something with Zarin around. She put her hands in her pockets and looked at the ground. Even though she'd taken a bath and scrubbed herself clean she still felt dirty. It angered her that she hadn't been strong enough to fight Zance off, and that she'd left the party late enough to put herself in danger in the first place. She was so ashamed of what happened she was worried she might start crying again.

"Zarin! Hey!" called a boy to her right. He emerged from behind a tree with a dead squirrel in his hand. There was a second boy to his left holding a trap. "We were going to go down to the swimming hole. Want to come?"

"No you guys go ahead; I'll catch up with you later."

Mimie scowled after them. The Avery brothers were notorious bullies, especially towards her. Once, when she was eight, they pushed her into the pond when they knew she couldn't swim. They laughed while she desperately tried to pull herself out again. She'd never gone near there again.

"Why do you hang out with those idiots?" Mimie growled, her dark mood returning.

"The Averys? They're not so bad; they've matured a lot over the years."

Mimie heard them snickering as they walked away. Her cheeks warmed.

"Ignore them, they're just joking around," Zarin said, rolling his eyes. Mimie nodded numbly, and kept walking. They didn't say anything for a long time. After a while, she heard a stream and walked toward it. She knelt down and splashed some of the cool water on her face. It was crystal clear, with small fish swimming around on the gravelly bottom. The liquid mirror reflected the forget-me-not blue of the sky and the emerald green of the trees. The wind distorted the image as she caught sight of a dark shape reflected in the water on the opposite bank. She heard a low growl.

Zarin reached for his knife. Mimie looked up, expecting to see a bear, and felt her heart jump into her throat. Watching them with lethal stillness was a beast she had never seen before. As a matter of fact, it was a beast she was sure no one had ever seen before.

It had a huge round body covered in shaggy black fur that was supported by stumpy legs as thick as tree trunks. Its arms were long and skinny, with thick three-inch long claws. It had more claws for toes. Two pointy horns rested on top of its massive head. The creature's mouth gaped wide, opening to half the size of its body. Each tooth was bigger than her hand. Its beady eyes were locked on her face. It crept into the water, its cruel claws outstretched.

"Run, I'll hold it off," Zarin yelled. He tried to step in front of her. Mimie bolted to the side and rushed into the water.

The monster was right behind her. She crawled onto the opposite bank and stumbled to her feet. The monster swiped at her and missed by inches. Zarin was screaming something at her, but she couldn't hear what he was saying over the monster's roars. She sprinted forward and weaved quickly through the trees. She couldn't tell if Zarin was following her, but she hoped he wasn't. She didn't want him to get hurt. The monster wasn't fast, but its size allowed it to stomp over the low growing plants that caught on Mimie's clothes and slowed her down. At any moment she expected to feel its claws rake across her back. A sharp pain in her side threatened to make her stop, but she kept going.

Suddenly the ground disappeared, and a hundred-foot drop loomed before her. Mimie jumped to the side and caught a tree that was growing near the edge of the cliff. She swung over the side but didn't let go. The creature didn't see the edge until it was too late. It let out a fearsome roar that hurt Mimie's eardrums. The impact shook her tree. She gripped it tighter and dared not look down, the height made her feel sick. Using her feet she tried to work her way back on to the cliff edge, but her grip on the tree was slipping.

"Need a hand?" Zarin asked. She gave him her foot, and he pulled her back onto solid ground.

"Thank—" Mimie started to say, but Zarin stopped her.

"Don't thank me yet, I think it's still alive." Mimie peeked over the edge and shrank back when she saw movement. A grinding sound echoed its way back to them; the monster was clawing its way back up the cliff.

Mimie scrambled away from the edge and fished through her bag for the Moonstone. It seemed hollow with a swirling mist caught inside. She glanced over the edge and saw the monster had already climbed a fifth of the way up. At that rate, it would reach the top in minutes.

"What's that?" Zarin asked.

"It's a Moonstone. Listen, I need you to run back to camp and warn them about the monster. There might be more of them out here."

"What about you? I can't leave you alone with that thing!"

"Don't worry about me," she said with a reassuring smile.

"Please be careful." He gave her a tight hug. If any other male had tried that she would have flinched away from them, but Zarin was like a brother to her. He'd never hurt her. Zarin looked her over sadly, then backed away and disappeared into the trees. Mimie put the Moonstone on the ground, ignoring the tightness in her chest. She was going to miss that boy.

She glanced over the side of the cliff. The monster was halfway up. How could something with such skinny arms climb so fast? She gathered spit into her dry mouth and spat it on the stone. Panicking, she prayed it would hurry up. A small stream of smoke drifted from the moonstone. At first Mimie was afraid it would blow away, but it stopped just beyond the edge of the cliff.

After a painfully long minute, Mimie could just make out a faint picture inside the swirling blue mist. She heard the monster's breathing and its claws scraping against the rock. A few more seconds and Mimie saw a beaver's dam as though she were looking at it from the top of a tree. Beside her, a pair of claws grabbed the top of the rock. The monster heaved itself up until its small black eyes were glaring at her from over the ledge.

The image was right in front of her. If she walked through it now, she'd be safe. There was only a slight problem. The smoke had gathered in a way that Mimie would have to walk off the cliff to get through it. There was no time to think, the monster was almost up and the image was fading. With a deep breath, she stepped through the image into the open air. The monster roared as it jumped after her, but she'd already disappeared. The monster fell, and this time when it hit the bottom, it didn't get up.

Mimie closed her eyes; she was falling. She tried to scream, but the wind tore the sound from her lips. When she finally hit the ground, the impact knocked the breath out of her. Whether she was still in one piece, she wasn't sure, but she'd made it. Somehow, impossibly, she'd made it.

CHAPTER 4: THE BEAVER'S DAM

←← ←← →→ →→

Mimie half opened her eyes and blinked a few times. Her body felt heavy, weak. She lay there in the sweet smelling grass for a long time. She heard a river splashing nearby, and birds chirping in the distance. She thought of Zarin and wondered if she was ever going to see him again. Her old life seemed very far from her now, although that wasn't entirely a bad thing. Suddenly, she heard shuffling footsteps approaching, and stiffened, waiting for something to attack her. Maybe the monster had followed her in after all. She opened her eyes, and found a large brown nose an inch away from her face.

She jumped back. The nose belonged to a beaver; there were two of them, a male, and a female.

"Ern, you fuzzy idiot!" hissed the female. "Look what you've done! Scared the poor dear half to death." She hurried toward Mimie. Mimie backed away in alarm.

"You're talking! How are you talking?" Black spots appeared around the edge of her vision, and the world swirled up to meet her as everything went dark.

Mimie rolled onto her side and felt a soft blanket beneath her; maybe this had all been a crazy dream. When she opened her eyes, she would find that Zance hadn't attacked her that she wasn't in a strange world with talking beavers, or magic, or any of it. Maybe things could go back to being simple. The soreness in her limbs told her otherwise. A crude wooden door opened and one of the Beavers walked in.

"Poor dear, she's been through a lot today. It was nice of Koren to carry her in for us. I hope we didn't scare her too badly."

"I'm sure she's fine dear, just give her a little while to adjust," Ern said, walking through the doorway and dropping a pile of sticks on the table.

"It was nice to see him again, he seems a little happier now, less broody," Martha commented. She glanced in Mimie's direction and jumped a little when she saw she was awake. "I hope you're feeling better," she said, keeping her distance this time.

"I'm fine." One of these days she hoped to say that and have it be the truth. She stiffly pushed herself into a sitting position to get a better look at her surroundings. The floor was a single pad of hard stone, and the walls were alive with different plants. The vines were so twisted around each other Mimie could hardly see any of the logs making up the frame. The female beaver saw her studying the walls and said,

"The plants are what make the difference. We put aquatic plants in the mud on the dam. As they grew bigger, the roots worked their way down and strengthened it. I reckon it's the best idea we've ever had. So we decided to do the same thing with the lodge. Anyway, where are my manners? Would you like anything to drink?"

"Yes please," Mimie said.

"Ern!" Martha yelled.

"Yes dear," he replied tiredly.

"Go out back and fetch some wood for the fire." Muttering, he shuffled out the door. "Lazy old coot."

Mimie hadn't realized how interesting a beaver's lodge could be. On the opposite side of the door was a water basin, and four small cabinets. On the other side of the room was a nest just the right size for two beavers, made from woven grass and twigs. In the middle of the floor was a fire pit, and just above it, a smoke escape that was black with soot.

The oddness of the situation still hadn't sunk in by the time Ern came back with the wood. He dropped it into the fire pit and started a fire by striking two stones together. Mimie didn't realize she was cold until the warmth of the fire reached her. She pulled her knees up to her chest and put her arms around them. Martha put a few small stones in the fire and filled a small bladder bag with water from the basin. There were some leaves in a basket on one of the cabinets that she took out and sprinkled in the bag. They smelled good, like mint and honey. As the stones heated up Martha fished them out with a long stick, and picked them up with some cloth before adding them to the bladder bag. When the stones cooled off, she removed them and replaced them with hot stones from the fire. She did this until the water was steaming hot. She added the leaves and then set the bag off to the side.

"I wasn't sure what you would like dear, so I just made Koren's favorite, I hope that's ok?"

"It smells wonderful, thank you." The smell reminded her of home, and Gram. Gram had always loved tea. When it was ready, she poured some of it into a wooden cup and hesitated before handing some to Mimie, not wanting to scare her again by coming too close. Mimie reached for it gratefully and took a quick sip. The water had absorbed the soothing flavor in the leaves, and pooled warmly into her stomach. "This is perfect," Mimie said with a smile.

"I'm glad you like it." Martha beamed, and returned to the fire to pour a cup for herself.

"So, how did you know I was coming?" Mimie wondered, hoping she didn't sound rude.

"You don't want to hear that story," Ern told her with an amused gleam in his eye. He sat down next to Martha and poured some tea for himself.

"What happened?" she wondered.

"Well..." Martha threw a sly look in Ern's direction. "A few weeks ago Ern and I were in here, sitting by the fire when a spirit appeared to us. Poor Ern was so surprised he fainted, and I had to pull him to safety before his fur ignited."

"Ignited?" Mimie laughed.

"Yep, he fell over into the flames."

"My fur still has singe marks," Ern grumbled into his tea.

"Anyway, the lady told us to watch out for you and give you a place to stay for the time being."

"What about Koren?" Mimie asked her. She felt bad for taking up space when there was already so little.

"Don't worry about him dear, as one of the forest Guardians he's hardly around nowadays. It will be nice to have someone living with us again after so long." Mimie guessed the pad she was laying on belonged to him, but it seemed much bigger than the nest the Beavers had in the corner for themselves. Koren had also carried her in from outside, so either he was a large beaver, or he was something else. The image of a talking, furry animal running around the forest with a spear made her smile. "It will be a busy day tomorrow so rest up," Martha advised.

"Ok," Mimie yawned, pulling one of the blankets around her. They had a refreshing, earthy scent to them, as if whoever slept here last spent more time outside than inside. "Where's Koren now?" Mimie wondered, it was a strange name for a beaver, but then again what did she know.

"He's out in the forest somewhere. He was here today to warn us about slave catchers in the area, but I imagine he's long gone by now." Was that pain she saw in Martha's dark eyes, Mimie wasn't sure.

Martha wandered away toward her nest to take a nap and was soon dozing peacefully next to Ern. Mimie closed her eyes and tried to do the same, but memories of Zance's face hovering above her soon brought her back to consciousness with gasping sobs. She gave up on sleep and decided to go for a walk. She pushed herself to her feet and walked quietly toward the front door. It squeaked a little when she opened it, and she held her breath, not wanting to wake the Beavers. Martha grunted softly but otherwise didn't move. Mimie turned, slipped out the small door, and stepped into the strange world beyond.

A little bridge connected the lodge to the shore. After closing the door behind her, she crossed it quickly, not entirely sure it would hold her weight. She walked up the sandy shoreline to the thick grass growing beyond and took in her surroundings. The sky was a deep shade of indigo blue, and the forest a rich, inviting green with tangled branches. She noticed a small trail winding its way through the meadow, and couldn't resist. She walked toward it and followed it into the trees. The branches swayed in the light breeze above her while colorful birds chattered excitedly in the treetops. She stopped when she came to a small moss covered rock and sat down. She caught movement out of the corner of her eye and saw a small reddish, gray squirrel scurrying around the base of a tree.

She was still close enough to the beaver's lodge to see the meadow and noticed a figure walking toward a small dock a little ways upstream from the lodge. The trees mostly obscured him, but she could still make out a rough outline. Experience had taught her to be wary of strangers, but for some reason she wasn't afraid of him, only curious about his identity. The stranger sat down on the end of the dock and took off his boots, then rolled up his pant legs, and let his feet hang over the side into the water. He had a bow strapped to his back, along with a quiver, and arrows that had long silver feathers on the ends. She slid off her rock and edged through the trees to see better. Was this Koren?

He was looking out over the water with a faraway expression. He seemed to sense that someone was watching him and glanced over his shoulder. She ducked behind a tree and held her breath, hoping that he hadn't seen her. She peaked out between two branches to see if he was still looking and saw that he'd gone back to staring at the river. He had gentle features, with messy blondish-brown hair and green eyes. Even from this far away she could tell that he was handsome. She was used to guys that looked like that flaunting their looks proudly, but he didn't seem the type. He looked out at the world with a blank seriousness. It was a look she was well acquainted with from the many times she'd seen it staring back at her in the mirror.

She shook her head and realized how silly she was being. She turned away and headed deeper into the trees. She found an oak with thick branches growing close to the ground and used them to climb to the top. She settled down on one of the upper branches and leaned her back against the thick trunk. The familiar position brought her back to the many times she'd taken refuge in the tall pine trees back home when the other kids were teasing her. She closed her eyes.

Soon the Beavers were calling for her, and she had to climb down again. The Beavers were walking toward the dock the boy had been sitting at, but he was gone now.

"Do you want to go for a swim dearie while Ern and I haul in these fish?" Martha asked, giving one of the lines an experimental tug. Mimie glanced at the dark water uneasily.

The lodge had partially been constructed on a long sand bar near the shore. The dam at the end of the sandbar created a nice, slow-moving pond, but the rest of the river raced along at full speed. For someone who didn't know how to swim, the swift current was certain death.

"No thanks." Mimie sat down on the edge of the dock.

"Ok, suit yourself." Ern tugged on a thick rope tied to one of the support beams. The line was ripped out of his paws, and the whole platform shook violently. Ern and Martha exchanged gleeful looks and lunged at the rope.

"Want some help?" Mimie asked.

"Yes! Ern caught a firefish," Martha said in a strained voice.

"What is that?" Mimie wondered. Ern let go of the rope.

"You've never heard of a firefish?" he asked in a disbelieving tone. Martha groaned, the rope was slipping out of her hands. "Oh, sorry dear." Ern grabbed the rope again and handed some to Mimie.

The fish put up a good fight and almost dragged them into the river a few times. After a final heave they pulled the heavy fish out of the water and onto the dock. Mimie looked at the fish they had caught in wonder. It was easily the most beautiful thing she had ever seen. Its scales were a deep shade of dark blue, almost like flattened sapphires. It had light blue eyes and flecks of red that glistened on its fins and tail.

The fish stared at them fiercely. Mimie leaned in closer for a better look. Martha grabbed her wrist and threw her away from the fish just as it opened its mouth and spat a huge wall of flickering blue flames at her. Ern grabbed a knife from the side of the dock and ran toward the fish.

"Stop!" Mimie yelled. "What are you doing?"

"Those scales are worth a fortune on the market." Ern tapped his paw against the dock impatiently.

"No. This isn't right, we have to let it go," Mimie said stubbornly. She wasn't sure why she felt so strongly about this, but she wasn't giving in. Martha crossed her arms.

"Fine, throw it back," she grumbled. The fish was too heavy for Mimie to lift on her own, so she rolled it back to the water instead. It landed with an impressive splash and was gone in seconds. She heard shuffling behind her and turned to see Ern and Martha staring at the ground.

"Sorry."

"It's alright dear, there's more to life than precious scales that could have made us very wealthy."

Ern shook his head and walked back to the lodge.

"Wait," Martha exclaimed, looking down. "Some of the scales got knocked off."

They waited a few seconds to make sure the firefish wasn't planning to come back and set the dock on fire, then dove at the blue scales. Each one was a little bigger than Mimie's thumb. They collected a small handful and seemed satisfied with their bounty, they set off toward the lodge as cheerfully as before.

Martha left the scales in the water basin, then pulled out three Aspen sticks.

"I'm sure you must be starving," Martha said and handed her one of the sticks.

"Thanks," Mimie muttered. Martha sat down at the table next to Ern and motioned Mimie to sit beside her. They watched her expectantly. Mimie chewed on the end of the stick in what she hoped was a convincing manner, trying not to get splinters in her tongue.

"How do you like it?"

Mimie wasn't sure what to say and tried to find a place to discreetly spit the pulp out of her mouth. She settled on hiding it between the folds of her shirt.

It wasn't long before the sun began to sink, casting the lodge in eerie shadows. Martha hurried over to the small window by the door and tugged the curtains shut.

"Time for bed," she declared.

The only light that came in was the ghostly glow that streamed from the smoke escape. Mimie walked to her bed and sat down. She knew she was too on edge to sleep, but she curled up on her side and closed her eyes regardless. She listened to the sounds of the night, crickets, the Beavers soft breathing.

A few hours later she was still awake. She grew bored counting the cracks in the floor and counted the sticks making up the walls instead. She was at 200 when a strange noise outside caught her attention. The crickets fell silent. She sat up and stared at the door, apprehension prickling the back of her neck. The bridge creaked as if something heavy was standing right outside the door. She barely dared to breathe.

The small strip of light coming from the window disappeared, and she knew something trying to peer inside. She forced her frozen muscles to unlock and crawled toward Ern and Martha's nest. As she got closer she glanced toward the window. All the color drained from her face, and she fought back a scream. Peering in through the small opening between the curtain and the wall was the pale face of a man. His skin was stretched tight over his skull, and a mop of greasy black hair hung to his shoulders. He was so close to the window Mimie could see his breath on the glass. Ern snored loudly in his sleep next to her, and the man's sunken dark eyes flicked toward her face. A disgusting smile spread across his white lips. He disappeared from the window.

Seconds later heavy fists slammed against the door so hard it sent tremors through the lodge. Martha jumped to her feet in alarm and almost fell into Mimie's lap.

"What's going on?" Ern hissed in fear.

"Slave catchers." Martha ran toward a rug in the middle of the floor. Mimie and Ern stumbled after her. Martha threw the rug to the side and tugged furiously on a silver ring embedded in the floor underneath it. A square piece of wood paneling pulled loose which exposed a hole that led directly to the river.

"Ern you first, swim for the opposite bank," Martha ordered. He nodded without question and dove through the hole. "You're next," she said.

Mimie shook her head and backed away from the dark water. "I can't swim!"

"Now is not the best time to tell me that! This is the only way out Mimie; you have to jump."

CRUNCH! CRUNCH!! CRUNCH!!! The door was caving in; heavy blows from the outside were splintering it. Dread filled Mimie's stomach at the thought of being captured. She had no idea what they would do with her and didn't want to find out.

Martha didn't wait for any further protests; she shoved Mimie as hard as she could, and sent her sprawling through the dark opening into the freezing water below. With a gasp Mimie surfaced and latched onto the branches of a small tree that hung in the water next to her. She used them to pull herself up onto a nearby sandbar, and lay there panting in the darkness. Looking around, she saw the dam was close by and stumbled toward it in the meager moonlight.

She tested it with her foot to see if it would hold her weight. The dam was made from thick logs and sticks expertly crafted together with mud and various plants to keep it in place. The logs were slippery though, and she teetered back and forth trying to keep her balance. She was making good progress and was just thinking about a safe place to dry off and spend the night when she heard a loud CRACK! A stick snapped under her, and she fell hard onto her side. A sharp pain shot through her hip, and she had to clutch her hand over her mouth to keep from crying out. She inspected the damage but didn't see any blood. She tried to pull herself to her feet but fell again as the structure jerked beneath her. Water leaked through the logs, and she knew she had to get out of there fast.

She stood up, but the structure couldn't hold her weight. The entire thing gave way. There wasn't time to scream as the rushing water and debris swept her out of the shallow channel and into the deeper portions of the river. Mimie grabbed onto a thick log to keep herself afloat. It was wrenched from her arms as something slammed into her side. Water crashed over her head before she could suck in a breath. Thrashing blindly, she managed to catch hold of another log and choked in a breath. The bark bit into her skin as the current fought to tear it from her grasp.

From the corner of her eye she caught sight of a figure running beside the river and waved her arm to get his attention.

"Help!" She lost sight of him as the log rolled. It slipped out of her grasp. A piece of debris smashed into the side of her head, stunning her. Her vision flickered and she drifted downward. Her chest screamed for air, but her arms weren't working the way they were supposed to. She was dimly aware she was on the bottom of the river, but couldn't feel it as her body dragged across the rocks. Black spots danced in front of her eyes.

A cold wave washed across her face as a dark shadow swam toward her. Strong hands firmly grabbed her arm and pulled her back to the surface. The stranger worked his way toward the shore, swimming at an angle to escape the current. He pulled her onto the beach and sank to his knees on the sand next to her. Mimie alternately coughed, and gasped for air. She collapsed onto her side, shivering.

"Can you walk?" her rescuer asked, wiping the water out of his eyes. She didn't respond, his voice sounded like it was coming to her through a tunnel. "Come on then." He scooped her into his arms. She hung there limply, a splitting headache drowning out almost everything else.

The warmth of his skin was almost painful against her frozen limbs, and she realized with a twinge of embarrassment that she was resting against the bare skin of his chest. He carried her up the steep bank with little effort and set her down on something soft. Grass? Mimie shivered without his added warmth and curled into a ball. "Hang on a sec, ok?" he muttered and turned to leave.

"Where are you going?" Mimie choked out.

"I'll be right back."

"S-s-slave catchers," Mimie said through chattering teeth. "Th-they broke down the door." He stared at her with a mixture of shock and horror.

"Are the beaver's ok? Where are they?"

"I d-don't know." Mimie tried to sit up, but a splitting pain raced through her left side causing her to double over and clutch at her ribs.

"Lay back," he told her. "I won't be gone long, I promise." He stood up without another word and disappeared into the surrounding trees. Mimie closed her eyes and waited for him to come back. Every shadow made her flinch, as she imagined the sunken faces of slave catchers watching her from just out of sight. Feeling vulnerable brought back memories of Zance. Her heart pounded in her ears as she fought back the memories, and the terror that came with them.

When her rescuer finally returned, the irrational terror dissipated. He was carrying a bundle of cloth, a quiver with silver arrows, a bow, and his sword. With a jolt she realized she recognized him. He was the same person she'd seen sitting on the docks earlier, Koren.

"Did you find them?" It made her cringe to hear how pathetic her voice sounded.

"No." Mimie felt the worry and tension coming off him in waves. "I'll check on them in the morning. The lodge is too far away to go there right now. Here," he said, handing her one of his shirts. "You can wear this for now until we find you some dry clothes. There's this too if you want it." He handed her a cloak and turned his back so she could change.

She took it gratefully and used it to cover herself while she pulled off her shirt, threw the soaked material aside, and pulled on the warm, dry one. It wasn't a perfect solution, but she did feel better, especially when she wrapped the cloak around her shoulders.

"Ok, I'm done."

Koren gathered the materials to make a fire. When he had what he needed, he used two stones to get a blaze going. Mimie curled up on her side and rested her head on her arm. Why was he helping her when he should've been out looking for Ern and Martha? He didn't even know her.

He filled his bladder bag with some water from the river and then threw in one of the hot stones from the fire. When it was cool, he took it out and replaced it with another one. Soon steam was rising from the bag. He fished out some leaves from his pack and sprinkled them inside to flavor the water.

"Are you hurt?" Koren wondered.

"No," Mimie said automatically. Why was she lying to him? "Well… my head stings a little," she confessed.

"Mind if I take a look?" He phrased it as a question but didn't look like he was going to take no for an answer. He helped her sit up, and lightly felt for any bruising. She flinched as his fingers brushed along the back of her head. "There's a fair sized knot there."

He looked into her eyes for a second with an analytical stare, trying to figure out if she had a concussion. His eyebrows pulled together briefly in concern, then he grabbed the bladder bag and poured the hot liquid into a small wooden cup.

"Drink that, it will help bring down the swelling." He handed her the cup. She sipped at it and smiled as the warmth spread through her. "Did one of the slave catchers attack you?"

"No," Mimie replied, confused by his question. She followed his gaze to the purplish bruises on her wrists. Her cheeks warmed and she looked away, biting her lip. Koren seemed confused by her reaction, but didn't press her further.

"Let me know if you need anything else." He moved toward the other side of the fire. Mimie finished her tea and noticed the warmth was making her feel drowsy. She curled up on her side and wrapped the cloak more tightly around her shoulders. She closed her eyes and allowed herself to fall into a light sleep.

CHAPTER 5: KOREN

⟵⟵⟶⟶

Mimie awoke the next morning feeling disoriented. She listened as the river splashed against the rocky bank, and heard the songs of birds twittering overhead. She wasn't used to sleeping outside, but the freedom of it felt incredible. The one downside was sleeping without a pillow. Her neck protested as she sat up and stretched. She glanced around the tiny clearing, and tangled her fingers in the thick grass. It was shaded by sycamores ringing the perimeter. A huge willow tree stood near the river, its vines dropping down into the water.

Koren was sitting next to the fire on a large gray rock with his back turned to her, poking the burning logs with a stick. He turned a stick over, and the log on top of it fell and sprayed a shower of hot embers at him. He let out a shout and fell backward off his rock. Mimie giggled, then quickly covered her mouth and fell quiet as he looked at her with a surprised and slightly embarrassed smile.

"Morning," he greeted, with one leg still draped over the rock. "How are you feeling?"

"Like I almost drowned," Mimie yawned. Her eyes lingered on his face, but she forced herself to look away, hoping he wouldn't see the blush in her cheeks.

"You're Mimie right? The Beavers said you were going to be staying with them for a little while." Mimie's blush deepened at the thought of him lugging her unconscious body into the beaver's dam and threw the hood of his cloak over her head to hide her face.

"I'm so embarrassed you saw me like that."

"Don't worry about it, you hardly even drooled on me." Mimie groaned and pulled the hood down further over her face. "I'm kidding, relax. It wasn't a big deal, come out of there you look like a turtle," he scolded, pushing the hood off her head.

Her breath caught as his hand brushed her cheek. She tried to think of something to say, but his vivid green eyes made it difficult to think clearly. She shook her head to break the trance. Someone like him could never be interested in someone like her. She wasn't even sure they were the same species! It was best to bury those feelings and chuck the shovel in the river.

***

Koren looked at the girl in front of him in bewilderment, why had she turned away from him like that? Maybe he shouldn't have told her she resembled a turtle, he hadn't meant to hurt her feelings. He sighed; he'd never been very good at first impressions. Still, he wished she would look at him. Her eyes were an intriguing shade of blue, though he had no name for their exact color. Her copper brown hair fell around her face, and she brushed one side behind her ear. She glanced back at him shyly and smiled. She had a beautiful smile.

He wished he'd asked the Beavers where she had come from yesterday when he'd carried her in, but he hadn't thought about it at the time.

"You aren't from around here, are you?" he finally laughed.

"No, I came from the other side of the wall." Koren felt heat rush to his face and bile rise in his throat. She was a human, he'd helped her, and she was a human! Surprised alarm flashed across her face as he backed away from her. Rationally, his mind told him she was harmless, but that didn't matter. He suddenly wanted to be as far away from her as possible.

"Why are you here?"

"I don't have to tell you anything, Koren," she growled angrily, crossing her arms. She stood up and turned her back on him. "I'll leave your shirt with the Beavers."

He stared at her in shock as she stormily grabbed her shirt from the branch it was drying on.

"Here's your cloak." She pulled it roughly from her shoulders and threw it at him.

With it gone, he noticed a peculiar blue mark on her arm. It was a thin crescent moon with a broken star next to it. He recognized it with a slow trickle of horror as the Key Guardian tattoo. He stared at it for a few seconds and felt his hostility melt into embarrassment.

"Sorry, I didn't realize who you were." He wondered how he could escape without making himself look like more of an idiot than he already had. He saw her wipe her eyes with the back of her hand and realized he'd made her cry. What on earth was wrong with him? She got up and walked toward the river without looking at him, which made him feel even worse. He stared at the ground, and then glanced her way again when he heard her trip over something.

"Are you ok?" He walked toward her and offered his hand to help her up.

"I'm fine," she replied, and ignored the gesture. Her callousness toward him shouldn't have amused him as much as it did. She rose unsteadily to her feet and tried to step out from under the willow tree, but another root rose out of the ground and caught her foot just as she was about to take a step. She lost her balance and fell hard onto her side, cringing visibly. Koren glared at the tree with narrowed eyes.

"Knock it off Olive, you've had your fun!"

"Koren, you're talking to a tree," Mimie told him, glancing at her palms with a grimace. "I'm a bit of a klutz, don't worry about it."

"No, he did it on purpose, and he needs to apologize."

"Koren... it's a tree." He ignored her and walked up to it, wondering how she would respond to what he was about to do next. She was probably going to scream and run away. Maybe that would be for the best, but he wasn't sure that that was what he wanted. Something that roughly resembled a face formed in the bark and stared at him with a mischievous smile. Koren raised an eyebrow.

The tree glanced down at the ground and pulled its root back into the soil. A rustling sound filled the air.

"He says sorry," Koren told Mimie.

"Oh," she said, looking pale. Well, at least she wasn't screaming.

"Have your scouts seen any new trouble?" He might as well make sure the way was clear before he took Mimie back to the beavers. Olive hesitated, and then a faint hiss of leaves filled the air.

"What! The slavers are moving toward Silver Rocks! Has anyone told Luna yet? ...Ok, good, who is the closest Guardian?" More rustling. Koren thought a moment. "Alright, tell her I'm on my way." There was a pause, and Olive gave him a grave look. He heard what the leaves said, but he didn't want to believe it.

"Why didn't anyone tell me!" he shouted. His head was spinning.

"What?" Mimie asked.

"The slave catchers took Martha last night." He was still in shock; the words sounded strange to him. Out of place.

"She didn't make it out of the lodge?"

Koren shook his head numbly. He knew the captives were often killed well before they reached their intended market. Martha was running out of time. The idea of what she was probably going through made him feel sick to his stomach.

"Tell Angora to stop all the migrating parties she can before they get to Silver Rocks, and tell Mo to sink any slave catcher supply ship he sees on the river." The tree nodded and its face melted back into the bark. Koren threw his stuff into his pack, his thoughts tumbling over one another chaotically.

***

Mimie watched Koren uncertainly, trying to think of something to say.

"You aren't thinking about fighting them, are you?" Mimie thought of the slave catcher's soulless black eyes and shuddered.

Koren didn't answer right away; he was too busy fashioning his quiver to his back. Mimie changed into her shirt and returned the loaned one back to him. He stuffed it in his bag.

"It's my job to protect everyone; I'll do what I have to." He kicked dirt over the embers of the fire, and looked over his campsite to make sure he hadn't forgotten anything. Seeming satisfied, he walked past her, picked up his cloak and put it on. "Come on, I'll take you back to Ern," he said and headed into the trees.

Mimie struggled to keep up with the quick pace he set. After they had been going for a while, Koren called out, "How is it someone as small as you can make so much noise?"

"I'm not doing it on purpose."

He grunted skeptically. "How long are you staying with the beavers?"

"I don't know yet, I'm still figuring things out." Koren cleared a fallen log as tall as her hip and waited for her on the other side. Mimie stared at the decaying wood. She hopped up and slid one leg over, straddling its massive girth. A line of tiny ants pooled on either side of her as they struggled to find the scent trail she had disrupted. Mimie was careful to avoid them as she slid her leg over the log and dropped to the ground.

Koren pushed an aspen branch aside to clear the path. As Mimie passed him he released the branch and it whistled as it snapped backwards.

"Who are Mo and Angora?" she wondered.

"They're other Forest Guardians. It was just me for a while, but with all the problems that have been going on, I decided it was time to rope in some help."

"Understandable." Koren weighed her response against what he wanted to say next. After a few seconds, he turned away again without saying anything. Mimie blushed and looked at the ground. Why was she so bad at this?

After a while, the trees thinned, and they stood on the bank of an immense, cold looking stream. Mimie wrinkled her nose.

"I'm pretty sure you'll be able to touch the bottom," Koren told her with a good-natured smirk. Mimie ignored him.

He sat down on the loose gravel near the stream bank and pulled off his shoes. Mimie sank to the ground next to him and did the same. Her shirt pooled in her lap as she leaned forward to untie her shoe laces. They were still damp from her excursion in the river last night. She rolled up her pant legs until they were above her knees and grimaced at her white legs. She snuck a glance at Koren. There was a fresh scratch across his calf that had barely started to scab over. She felt a stab of guilt as she realized he'd probably gotten it from pulling her out of the river last night. His almond skin held very few freckles, even on his forearms which saw the most sunlight.

"Ready?" He stood up and offered a hand to Mimie. She allowed him to tug her to her feet and walked toward the stream. Mimie waded out into the muddy grass and winced as the icy water touched her feet. She clutched her shoes more tightly to her chest and took another step. She was rewarded with a loud squish as mud oozed between her toes.

"This is disgusting." The water rushed passed her ankles, making it hard to keep her balance. Once she was out a little further out the mud became rockier and the course edges dug into the bottoms of her feet. The babble of the stream calmed her nerves. She paused for a moment, listening to it with her eyes closed. Something crawling on her leg brought her back to reality. She looked down and found dozens of black spots perched on her skin. She leaned down and splashed them off with water from the stream, relieved when they turned out to be gnats instead of leeches.

Koren was already on the other side waiting for her. Teetering on the uneven ground, she hurried toward him and tried not to splash him as she climbed onto the bank. She sat down next to him and waited for her feet to dry so she could put her shoes back on. Her bangs were hanging in her face, but she didn't want to touch them with her wet fingers. She picked the grass off her shins and noticed a small cut on the bottom of her foot. There were several rocks embedded in it, wincing, she pulled them out. The cut was bleeding. She wished she had something to put over it so the blood wouldn't get in her shoe.

Koren's lip curled at the sight of it. This surprised her, he seemed like the type of person who wasn't fazed by anything, let alone a little blood.

He pulled out a strip of cloth from his pocket. "Here, tie this around it."

"Thanks," Mimie said, and gently wrapped the soft fabric around her foot. "Why do the slave catchers want to attack Silver Rocks?"

"There's a large herd of unicorns there that they've been after for years. They're hoping if they bring in more people they can win through brute force." Koren's shoulders sagged, as if his words carried more weight than he was telling her. "The beavers lodge is just over the boulders up ahead; we should be there soon." She could tell that he was trying to change the subject, so she let it go.

Koren followed a deer path up a slope that wound through the moss covered rocks. Grass lined the edges of the path and the thick canopy overhead created dappled streams of light. Mimie soaked in the beauty of it, taking her time to listen to the chorus of cheerful birds in the treetops and investigate strange plants she didn't recognize.

"It's even prettier in the fall and winter," Koren told her. She was surprised he hadn't snapped at her to hurry up yet.

"Are those your favorite seasons?"

"You could say that, but the other ones are beautiful too."

"I've never been a huge fan of snow. It always gets in my shoes and makes my socks all wet and gross."

"All the seasons have their drawbacks I suppose. It's funny; I lost someone close to me in a snowstorm once. A reasonable person would hate the snow after that."

"A blood-soaked rose is still a rose. It's a little saddening to look at but no less beautiful than it was before."

Koren grimaced.

"What I mean is, losing someone in a snowstorm doesn't make the snow any less beautiful. It still hugs the bare branches of the trees, and glitters with the refracting light of trillions of little crystalline structures catching the sun's rays."

"There's also the cozy feeling of snuggling up next to a fire and drinking warm tea," Koren added.

"Exactly. I hate the cold but I can still admire the beauty and mystique of the snow."

Koren led her to the top of the slope where the ground turned into steep rocks. He climbed nimbly onto the first rock and offered his hand to Mimie. She ignored it and struggled up to the top of the rock.

"Stubborn woman."

Mimie laughed and took the lead. "I'm not trying to be difficult, I'm just used to doing everything on my own."

She edged around a sharp corner and headed for a sandy pathway between two huge rocks. The path led to a small ledge with spiny, shrubby bushes evenly spaced throughout. They ranged in color from charcoal black to smoky gray.

Koren held his arm out in warning. "Don't touch the plants, they'll drag you underground." They seemed harmless enough to Mimie.

"Yeah right," she scoffed.

"I'm serious, be careful," Koren said as he edged into the clump of weeds. The plants were growing close together, and she had no idea how she was supposed to get to the other side without touching one. Koren was already halfway across, so Mimie hurried to catch up with him. Something scratched her left arm. Before she could react one of the plants wrapped itself around her wrist.

Mimie screamed and tried to pull free, but the plant was stronger than she expected. All the branches were reaching for her now, and Mimie desperately worked to claw the thin branch off her arm. Another one wrapped around her ankle. It pulled so hard it knocked her off her feet. Koren calmly walked over to her with a smug smile.

"Do you believe me now?"

The branches were swarming her now, cutting off her airway. Koren pulled out his sword and severed the plant from its base. Mimie choked in a breath and ripped the branches away from her throat. She untwisted the vines from the rest of her body and threw them away from her.

"Thanks," she panted.

She stared at the plants warily as she continued on, careful not to let any of them touch her. Once they reached the far end of the field, they scrambled up another small ledge.

"What are those devil things?" Mimie glanced back and glared at them, her heart still pounding in her ears.

"Clingers," Koren replied. "Sorry to take you through there, this is the fastest way to the lodge."

Mimie leaned against a stone wall and saw the top far above her. "We have to climb this, don't we?"

"We can wait a second. I don't want you to pass out halfway up."

"I'm not going to pass out," Mimie grumbled. "Let's go."

She glanced at the crumbling wall, not sure she trusted it to hold her weight. There was a unique joy she got when she was climbing something, but that was predicated on the fact that the thing she was climbing didn't crumble and kill her. She touched her fingers to the rough surface and dug them into a large groove. She tested her weight and scaled the wall quickly, slipping into the comfortable rhythm with ease. She tried not to look down. A fear of heights, and a fear of falling seemed odd in someone who liked to climb things as much as she did, but in reality it made her hold on that much tighter.

She unclenched her jaw in relief when her hands brushed a small dip in the rock at the top of the ledge. After using it to hoist herself up she wiped her sweaty palms against her pants. She peeked over the edge to check on Koren, and felt an odd tingling in her toes as she watched him hang precariously dozens of feet above the ground. He didn't seem overly concerned about the height, but that didn't stop Mimie from feeling nervous. Once he was within reach she grabbed his shirt and helped him up. His eyes crinkled in amusement at her obvious concern. He stood up and brushed off his hands. Rustling to their left rose the hair on the back of Mimie's neck. Koren rushed toward the sound, panic in his eyes. Mimie raced after him, afraid of what she would find. She froze in horror when the forest came into view. Her legs shook as a mournful wind whispered through a sea of charred black leaves in front of her.

Koren cursed under his breath.

All the plants in front of them had been smashed flat in a long scar that stretched as far as Mimie could see in both directions. The trees were charcoal black like a fire had recently gone through, but the plants were still intact, and there was no trace of smoke in the air.

"What happened?"

Before Koren could answer a twig snapped close by.

"Look out!" He yanked her out of the way as a volley of arrows sped toward them. A sharp pain stung her palms as she threw her hands out to break her fall. Koren collapsed next to her with an arrow lodged in his leg. She fought the urge to scream.

Their attacker emerged from the trees with a smirk. "I was hoping I'd run into you, forest scum."

Koren's teeth locked together with an audible snap, as he quickly pulled his bow from his back. The slave catcher pulled out a knife and ran toward him. Mimie shrank back. Koren notched an arrow, pulled the string back and released. The slave catcher dropped like a stone. Koren set the bow aside and turned his attention to his leg. He grabbed the arrow and started to pull it out.

"Don't you dare!" She'd seen people die by pulling out an arrow before they saw a healer.

"It's fine. I don't think it's that deep." He picked up one of the stray arrows. It was a pointed stick with a few straggly feathers attached. "These aren't meant to kill. The end looks pretty smooth, I should be able to pull it right out." Mimie wasn't convinced.

"If it hit a blood vessel you could bleed to death when you pull it out."

"There are healing supplies in my bag, don't worry I'll be fine." He gritted his teeth and pulled out the shaft, throwing it away from him. Mimie searched around in his bag for some cloth and handed it to him. He pulled up his pant leg to get a better look at the wound and cleaned it off with some water from a canteen he carried. There wasn't much blood, but the wound still looked painful.

"Keep pressure on it, it might not be bleeding now, but that doesn't mean it won't start later." He rolled his eyes and pressed the cloth over it. Mimie scanned the trees, feeling exposed out in the open with no cover nearby. "Why did you step in front of me?"

Koren shrugged. "That was a crappy shot, it was just bad luck that it hit either of us." They heard gruff voices in the distance.

Mimie's shoulders tensed.

"We should go." Koren tied a strip of cloth around his leg and stood up. He climbed down the final rock ledge onto the trampled grass below, and limped toward a deer path. Mimie found a stick lying on the ground and handed it to him.

The leaves above them made a faint, melodic rustling sound as the wind wafted through them, almost like they were singing.

"What are they saying?" Mimie's eyebrows pulled together as she touched the blackened bark of a nearby tree.

"Love comes softly to our sisters sleeping in the skies, time moves slowly for a soul that never dies. Strangers come and give rise to the hate that lies buried deep in flesh and bone. They tell their stories, but they are never home. They keep saying that over and over again. I don't know what it means."

"It sounds sad."

Koren nodded in agreement.

"Can I ask you a question?" The words escaped before she could stop them.

"Sure."

"What happened to the trees? Why are some of them black like that?" Mimie crossed her arms as she waited for his reply.

"The Slavers have this orb thing they stab into the bark of a tree and it separates the spirit from its physical form. The person can then use the sphere to reanimate a corpse and create this zombie thing that will do whatever the slaver wants. The rest of the tree then dies and petrifies this lovely charcoal color."

"That's barbaric!" Mimie pictured someone doing that to Naowa, and cringed.

Something moved in the bushes. They waited tensely for the

unseen enemy to appear, but nothing happened. Mimie and Koren exchanged uneasy glances, and kept going.

They headed toward the river. As the rumble grew louder, Mimie knew they were getting closer to their journeys' end. Would she ever see Koren again after this? Maybe he'd come by the lodge sometime before she had to leave. The thought made her feel sad. Gradually the trees vanished, and opened into a vast clearing.

"Keep an eye out for Ern," Koren instructed. "I want to make sure he's ok."

The lodge wasn't in good shape, most of the logs on the bridge had fallen in, and the splintered walls were barely holding together.

Koren clenched his jaw, surveying the damage. Mimie considered knocking to see if Ern was inside, but the bridge looked on the verge of being swept away. Besides there wasn't enough of the door left to knock on anyway. Koren picked up a piece of the splintered wood and touched a carving in the side.

"Ern!" he called. "Are you here?"

They heard a scuffling noise under the bridge. "Koren? Is that you?" Koren tossed the piece of wood to the side and walked toward the bridge. He knelt down and helped Ern ease out from under it. Ern shook the sand from his fur and stretched. "Have you seen Martha? I've looked everywhere for her."

Koren shrugged, avoiding his gaze. He shot Mimie a pointed look warning her not to say anything. Ern's whiskers twitched in concern. "What happened to your leg?"

"Slave catchers, don't worry it's nothing," Koren insisted.

"At least let me look at it."

"There's no need, it's fine."

"Mimie, help me pin him down."

Koren rolled his eyes. "Nice try, but she's on my side."

"Actually, he should probably leave the bandage on." The mental image of her and Ern attempting to wrestle Koren to the ground almost made her laugh.

"I'll have Luna heal it when I get to Silver Rocks. In the meantime, I came by to return Mimie."

"No, she needs to go to Silver Rocks with you. There have been slave catchers going by here all day and you know how they are around fairies. She's not safe here. Besides, I think Luna might be able to tell her where she can find a teacher for her magic."

"What do you think, Mimie?" Koren asked her. Her stomach fluttered at the idea of spending more time with him. Still, she didn't want to force her company on him.

"I'll just climb up a tree and stay out of everyone's way."

"You're not safe there either. Slave catchers aren't the only dangerous thing in this forest."

"You'll need this," Ern said, ending the discussion. He grabbed her pack, and a light brown cloak off the bridge. "I was going to give it to you before, but..."

"Thanks." Mimie took the cloak and put it on.

"We better get going. Bye Ern, stay safe."

"You too!" He said, and pulled one of the loose boards off the bridge before it was swept away. He seemed to be salvaging what he could before the supports on the lodge gave way and it sank to the bottom of the river. She felt bad leaving him to work on the project alone, knowing he could probably use the help. She watched Koren in her peripheral vision as she followed him back toward the forest. Her ears felt hot. A silly response to this situation. It wasn't her fault Ern had insisted she stay with Koren, though she was privately pleased with the decision.

"Why didn't you tell Ern about Martha?" she wondered.

"If I told him, he would have gone after her, and I don't want him to get hurt." Even though he was limping, he still managed to set a brisk pace.

"Are you sure you want to push yourself like this? You have to be in a lot of pain, unless your species somehow doesn't feel pain?"

Koren smiled but didn't slow his pace. "Don't worry about me, I'll be fine." He paused for a second and then chuckled.

"What?" Mimie demanded.

"I'm surprised you haven't figured out what I am yet." She wasn't sure why that was funny but didn't say anything. "You'd call me folk, or Elvish."

"An Elf, I guess that makes since with the pointed ears and all."

"Yep. You though, you're a puzzle. Some sort of intermediate between a human and a fairy, not quite one or the other."

"So a freak of nature?"

"Basically," he laughed. Mimie looked at the ground; she knew he was teasing her, but the words still stung a little.

"Have you always lived with the Beavers?"

"No." His words were guarded. "They took me in when I was fourteen." Mimie resisted the urge to ask what had happened to the rest of his family.

"How was it, living with them." Mimie tried to picture it in her head but couldn't do it.

Koren chuckled once. "It took a while to convince them I was incapable of digesting wood. I guess it's a good thing I was born with good teeth. Otherwise, they would all be broken by now."

"Did they ever have children of their own?"

"Yeah, they have a daughter but she's mated now. How about you? Where are you from?" The green of his eyes matched the tree canopy overhead.

"I'm from a small town. I lived in a cabin there with my Grandma. She's a seamstress."

"Did she teach you anything? I have a hole in one of my pants that needs to be patched." He looked over the pair he was currently wearing and brushed the dust off the thread worn material.

"Unfortunately not. I proved to be a hopeless case and she abandoned the cause shortly after."

"I see, so if not sewing, what do you like to do?"

"I like drawing." Why hadn't she thought to grab her sketch

book? "You?"

"Archery and swimming. The swimming part because the beavers would have disowned me otherwise."

"I'm sure that's not true," Mimie laughed. Koren paused and searched the path behind them with narrowed eyes. "What is it?"

He abruptly pushed her into the tall grass by the side of the trail. Mimie threw out her hands to break her fall and bit her lip to stifle her protest. Her palms stung as they scraped against the course grass. She scooted to the left to make room for Koren as he ducked down next to her.

She heard the sharp clip-clop of trotting horses, and the jostling rumble of an approaching wagon. How had she missed it before? She caught sight of two black horses as they rounded the corner and swallowed hard when she saw the dark carriage they pulled. An eerie silence hung over it, raising the hair on the back of Mimie's neck. Koren worked his way deeper into the grass by slowly scooting backward on his stomach. Mimie tried to copy him with a lot less success. After a painfully long time, she got to a point where she was finally able to turn around. Koren waited for her there. He moved aside to give Mimie more room and winced visibly as his elbow snapped a stick. Mimie glared at him and held her breath.

There was a soft creak as the wheels came to a stop, and one of the horses stomped its foot impatiently at the delay. A few seconds later, the muffled thump of heavy boots hitting the ground cut through the silence that had fallen over the path. Koren grabbed Mimie's wrist and crouched lower to the ground. She squeezed her eyes closed, knowing that Koren would not be able to outrun the slave catcher if he discovered them. Loud footfalls approached where they were hiding.

Silence. Mimie could hear her heart beating in her ears.

The grass above her head abruptly parted. Mimie shrank back at the sight of the slave catcher. He had sunken features, coal black eyes, and cropped red hair. The sour stench of his breath triggered Mimie's gag reflex and made her eyes water. A broad, disgusting grin spread across his face as his dark eyes locked on Mimie's face.

"A fairy," he snarled. His accent made her skin crawl.

He reached for her, nails scratching against her skin. Koren kicked him away with his good leg. He reached for his bow, but the red head knocked it out of his hands and dragged him out of the brush. Another slaver emerged from the wagon to watch the brawl.

"Leave him alone!" Mimie yelled. She jumped on the red heads back and clawed at his face. He flipped her over his shoulder like she was nothing. She landed on the ground next to Koren with a hard thump.

"Little witch!" snarled the slave catcher, and pulled out a knife.

"No," snapped the observer. "Do you know how much she's worth?" The red head glared at her but put his knife away.

"Yes, I suppose you're right, and we can certainly get our money's worth, and more out of her on the way there." The animal look in his eyes made her cringe. Koren growled at them wordlessly and hid Mimie behind his back. "The elf is nothing to us, can I kill him?"

The observer nodded, uncaring. He turned back to the wagon and let out a piercing whistle. Six other dirty humans emerged from the back and stood stiffly by his side.

"Take the girl back to the wagon," he ordered. One of the newcomers pulled out a cruel looking blade. The red head grabbed Mimie's arm and tried to pry her away from Koren, but she held on to him for dear life.

"It's over, let go!" The man yelled and yanked on her arm. He flinched away from her as her skin started to glow and backed away. A powerful breeze whipped around her, getting stronger with every second.

"What's going on?" Koren yelled. "Are you doing this?"

"Hold on to me!" Mimie replied. Her vision flickered and the scene in front of her changed. In the vision she was standing at the base of a silver cliff, looking over a field of lush green grass. To her left was a beautiful pond. It had clear water, and lily pads covered with delicate white flowers. This was where she had to get them; this is where they would be safe.

***

Mimie went limp in Koren's arms, but the winds did not decrease. The pressure mounted; he was worried his eardrums were going to explode.

"Kill them!" the red head shouted. "They're getting away!"

The slave catcher's weapons were useless against them; the wind was so strong, anything thrown at them got stuck in it. The knives flashed around and around so fast they were nothing but a silver blur. When the pressure became almost unbearable, he and Mimie melted into a ball of light and shot upwards. They stayed airborne for a few seconds and then slammed into the ground. The impact sent Koren rolling across the grass. When he finally came to a stop, he felt dazed and disoriented.

Well, that was... intimate, he thought to himself. He opened his eyes and felt the sickening sensation that the ground was tilting upward. It took him a few seconds to recognize the feeling as motion sickness. He rubbed the back of his head and scanned his surroundings for Mimie. He found her laying on her stomach a few feet away.

"Are you ok?" Koren asked. She groaned softly, but otherwise gave no response. He crawled toward her. She her gentle features pulled into a slight smile.

"Let's not do that again," she muttered weakly. "Sorry, for the unorthodox form of transportation."

"Don't be, you saved my life."

"Hardly," she replied, closing her eyes and resting her cheek on the grass. Her long copper-brown hair spilled out across the ground like threads of silk. "When we were flying through the air, it was like we were a shooting star, so I made a wish." Her eyes scrunched up in the corners, and he saw the faint outline of dimples on her cheeks.

"I don't know if that counts, technically you were making a wish on yourself."

"Next time it snows I think I'm going to shrink myself down really small and ride a snowflake."

"Ok crazy." He looked over her shoulder and saw a unicorn

approaching from the base of the cliff. "Thank goodness," he muttered and waved his hand to get her attention.

CHAPTER 6: THE UNICORNS

←← ←← →→ →→

"Koren! What happened?" Luna exclaimed, lowering her horn and healing the arrow wound on his leg.

"It's a long story."

Even though Luna was a few thousand years old, the only thing that betrayed her age were a few white whiskers lining her muzzle, and her wise dark eyes. Her withers came to Koren's chin and her delicate head flowed smoothly into a muscular neck. Her milky white coat shimmered beautifully in the sunlight, as did her hooves, which were made from dark gold crystal. Her horn was made from the same material and sat squarely in the middle of her forehead, two inches above her eyes. It was thick on the bottom and tapered to a needle sharp point. Her main and tail were a light shade of silver.

"Can you walk? We need to get you two inside."

"I think so," Koren said pushing himself to his feet. "Do you want me to carry you?" he asked Mimie.

"No," she huffed and struggled to her hands and knees. Her face was flushed from the effort. He helped her up and swept her into his arms.

He followed Luna toward an obscure crack in the rock and edged his way into it. The light was dim, and Koren had to wait a few seconds before he was able to see anything. The passage was speckled with Moonstones, and the walls were perfectly smooth, like satin. The climb was over quickly, and before he knew it, Koren stepped into the bright sunlight at the top of the cliff. The ground was covered with thick, lush grass, and a single oak stood proudly in the center of the landscape. Huge silver boulders partially covered in moss were scattered here and there, and clumps of wildflowers swayed in the breeze. Koren shifted Mimie's weight, then followed Luna as she headed into the forest of silver boulders.

"It's just a little further," Luna told him. She weaved around a few more boulders, and then came to a halt in front of one that had become overrun by bright green vines. "The entrance is on the other side; vines cover it for privacy."

"Um, thank you," Koren muttered, and searched the outside until he spotted a shallow dip in the rock. He ducked inside and gingerly set Mimie down on a fluffy-looking grass pad. He settled down next to her with his back against the wall. She started shivering, so he took off his cloak and draped it over her. She grabbed the corner and tucked it under her cheek. He half smiled, and crawled onto his own pad, feeling drained from the long days journey. He curled up on his side with the intent to rest his eyes for a second, but was soon out cold.

***

Mimie sprinted through the darkness. A haunting laugh seemed to reverberate in the air around her, chilling her bones to ice. She was trapped; the laughter was closing in…

"Mimie wake up!" She jerked awake and saw a pair of green eyes hovering inches from her face.

"What?" Mimie rubbed her eyes drowsily.

"You were having a nightmare." Koren backed away from her. "You were thrashing around like a crazy person."

"What happened to your lip?"

"You decked me." He touched his finger to his lip to check for blood.

"Oh. Sorry about that."

"It's ok, it'll heal," he shrugged.

"I feel like all my limbs were ripped off and put back on backward." Mimie pushed off Koren's cloak and shifted onto her side.

"Well, shooting across the sky, and slamming into the ground doesn't exactly do wonders for your health."

"Yeah, yeah." She heard something outside the rock opening and saw Luna push her way through the vines.

"Sorry to interrupt. I came to see how you were doing," she said. Mimie watched her with wide eyes, unsure how to respond.

"We're ok. Thanks for checking in on us," Koren replied.

"You're welcome, it's nice to have you here Mimie. It's been a long time since we had a fairy with us." Mimie's frozen muscles thawed and she bobbed her head like an idiot. Koren shot her a look of concern.

"Mimie is the Key Guardian, she just came from the other side of the world yesterday."

Mimie cleared her throat. "I'm still getting used to the whole fairy thing."

"The magic you used earlier was pretty advanced for someone who just found out they were a fairy yesterday?"

"I don't know how I did that." Mimie massaged her head, the knot she'd received in the river were throbbing again. It made it hard to think.

"Magic is a rigorous discipline. It draws on the energy of the body and requires intense focus and study to control. It's dangerous to attempt something like that before you have been properly trained for it. The effort could have left you unconscious, or dead."

Mimie couldn't find in herself to regret her actions. The slave catchers were going to hurt Koren.

"There used to be a training program here, but when Zanties started kidnapping fairies they moved everyone to the main facility in a secluded jungle somewhere. Nowadays it's very rare to see any fairies outside of there."

"How would I find them?" This is why she was here. She tried to block out the pain from her headache.

"There was another program that was bigger than ours in the Dwarf Mountains. They have extensive maps in the central library that can tell you where to go. We'll talk more about it later, the humans will be arriving shortly, and the others are waiting for us." She turned to leave, Koren gathered his weapons and followed her out.

Not wanting to be left behind, Mimie climbed out the opening and shaded her eyes against the sunlight. She took in the sky, the grass, and the silvery rocks with a long sweeping glance. Luna weaved through the boulders and made her way toward a large tree in the center of the plateau. Mimie and Koren joined her there; it wasn't long before they were joined by other ivory figures. They came from every direction, one after another. Mimie counted four females in total, not including Luna, two yearlings, and a small spindly-legged foal hiding behind its mother's legs. The last three unicorns were muscular stallions. They pranced here and there, nipping the other horse's necks. Luna cleared her throat, and a hush settled over the herd. Luna flicked an ear in Mimie's direction.

"This is the Key Guardian. While she is here, she is under our full protection." Mimie shifted uncomfortably as all eyes turned toward her. "Looks like everyone is here except Oviet," Luna said with a subtle edge of contempt in her voice.

The words were just out of her mouth when Mimie heard a wild fluttering of feathers. A second later another unicorn swooped over the edge of the cliff and raced frantically toward Luna. She was noticeably different from the others. She had light gray wings and body, with a main and tail that were dark silver. Her eyes were wide and scared. Her delicate nostrils were flared and she was gasping for breath. It took a few seconds before she was able to choke out the words that turned Mimie's bones to ice.

"The humans are approaching the cliff!"

"How many?" Luna asked.

"I don't know, at least fifty," Oviet replied, "and more are on their way." Luna's face grew deathly serious as she turned to the stallions.

"We need every able body at the base of the cliff to fight off the

64

coming invasion. We'll meet you down there." The unicorns headed toward the tunnel.

Mimie watched them go. Eventually only Luna, Koren, the young foal, and Oviet remained under the tree.

Luna tossed her mane. "Keep me posted on how things are going, stay high, you'll be a target for archers." It took a second for Mimie to realize she was talking to Oviet because she never looked at her or acknowledged her in any way. Oviet spread her wings and disappeared without a word. Luna then turned her piercing gaze to Mimie. "Take Navi and hide, don't come out until me, or Koren comes to get you. Do you understand?"

"That's not fair! I want to help." Koren coughed to hide his laughter. Mimie glared at him.

"Absolutely not! I want you to go back to that rock and promise that no matter what happens you will stay hidden."

Mimie knew it was pointless to argue. "Fine," she grumbled.

She hated being treated like a child. She watched Koren climb nimbly onto Luna's back and wondered what she would do if he never came back. Her heart ached at the thought. He pulled out his sword and held on as Luna charged toward the tunnel. Mimie turned toward the distressed unicorn beside her.

"Come on. No use standing around here, let's go." Mimie headed back to the hollow rock. She paused when the unicorn's velvet muzzle brush her fingertips. She patted the little unicorn's neck reassuringly and continued on.

When they reached the rock, the unicorn trotted inside and curled into a ball in the far corner. Mimie leaned against the wall and stared off into space. She hated feeling so useless.

**

"She's not going to stay in that rock," Koren told Luna as they trotted away.

"I know," Luna replied, "but one can hope." Koren looked back. By now Mimie was so far away he couldn't see her anymore.

Luna trotted down the tunnel. She paused before emerging onto the open field and Koren slid off her back. He got his bow ready and notched an arrow.

Luna stepped into the sunlight and joined the ranks of the unicorns who had already gathered at the bottom. Koren positioned himself near the tunnel entrance.

A human holding a chain led a group of slavers out of the forest at the far end of the clearing. Koren tightened his grip on the bow. The stallion next him tossed his mane with flared nostrils. The strong muscles in his legs flexed as he shifted his weight from hoof to hoof. The sounds quieted as Koren locked his focus on the humans ahead. His shoulders tensed. The humans' wild hair hung in tatters and they eyed the unicorns like starving dogs eyeing a scrap of meat. They shoved past one another, quarreling for spots near the front.

The slaver holding the chain spun it above his head with a shout. The others surged forward, streaming from the trees in waves. Koren shot several arrows in quick succession, then stepped back and planted himself in front of the tunnel entrance.

The ground beneath his feet shook as the unicorns charged. Their legs blurred as they bore down on the humans. A slave catcher slipped past them and ran toward Koren. An arrow dropped him to his knees. Koren shot another human to his left. His movements were automatic, clinical even, aiming where a single arrow could inflict the most damage. They came at him from every angle but none could get close. The stench of blood burned his nose. When he was nearly out of arrows he pulled out his sword. A stallion hung back to guard the entrance while Koren fought his way toward Luna. The humans were no match for her quick, powerful horn. Together they worked their way toward the forest so they could cut off the reinforcements.

Once he was under the cover of the trees, he examined every shadow for signs of danger. He spotted a wagon ahead and jogged toward it. He took out the driver with his bow and severed the ties holding the horses to the wagon.

Half a second later, Koren ducked as an arrow flew over his head. He rolled to the side to avoid another assault from the human holding a crossbow. Luna kicked the weapon out of his hand and Koren smashed his bow into the side of his head. The sting of a chain lashed across his forearm and wrapped around the wrist holding the bow. The bow fell from his hand as he lost his balance. He clawed off the cold metal and drew his blade. The chain wielding slaver wound up for another strike. Koren ducked and veered left, testing the human's defenses. A grating screech filled the air as the man blocked the blow from Koren's sword with heavy armor strapped to his arm. They circled one another. The slaver wore a sneer as his black eyes probed Koren's defenses. The chain whipped out and caught him behind the ankle. A heavy weight slammed into his chest as he fell backward. Grimy hands locked around his throat and choked off his airway. Koren tucked his chin and elbowed the slaver in the face. He grabbed the human's arm and rolled to the side, using the leverage to dislocate his shoulder. The human screamed and struggled to escape Koren's grip.

Koren watched Luna finish off the last human and return to his side. She glanced down at the hapless slaver with a raised eyebrow, probably wondering why Koren hadn't killed him yet. Koren shifted his grip and applied pressure to the slaver's dislocated arm.

"Where are you keeping your prisoners?"

"Why should I tell you, forest scum?"

Luna stepped on a pressure point in his shin.

"Ok, ok, they're north of here, in a clearing just off the road!" Koren released him and got to his feet.

"Go back to the others. I'll join you as soon as I can." He gathered his weapons and ran beside the slave catcher's path as it wound deeper into the woods. The shadows reached out to hide him from any scouts that may have been looking his way.

He stopped short when the trees abruptly ended, and crouched down behind a bush. He peeked through the branches and saw a clearing with eight large cages sitting in the center of it. A guard was circling the perimeter with a pair of keys jingling at his side. Koren waited until the guard was a few feet away, then pulled an arrow from his quiver and notched his bow. He shot the unsuspecting guard in the chest, stood, and stole his keys.

He ran toward the closest cage and covered his nose, the smell was unbelievable. Dozens of furry faces turned toward him. A few climbed on top of each other to get a better view of him through the bars. He put his finger to his lips to quiet their delighted yowls, afraid it would draw nearby slave catchers to investigate.

Koren shoved the key into the lock and turned. The lock made a soft click then fell to the ground. He opened the door and stepped aside as one by one the creatures made a dash for the forest. He moved on to the next cage, and the next one, until only one remained. He thrust the key into the last lock and turned, but nothing happened. The lock was rusted shut. He growled in frustration as he met Martha's panicked gaze.

"What's going on here!" a human voice yelled.

He hadn't counted on the next group of reinforcements passing by so soon. There was no way he could take all of them on by himself, especially when he only had three arrows left. He desperately tried to turn the key, but it refused to budge. Something streaked from the forest, snarling viciously and launched itself at one of the humans.

Koren kicked at the lock, hoping to break off some of the rust that was caked on it, and then tried the key again. After an agonizing minute of focused effort, the lock clicked and fell to the ground. Koren swung the door open and stepped back as the animals swarmed out. Martha paused before making her way into the trees.

"Be careful." She put her paw on his arm and then made her way toward the trees. A pack of wolves grappled with the slave catchers. The humans retreated to the safety of the wagon and urged their horses into a run. The snarling pack regrouped and loped over to where Koren was standing in the middle of the clearing. The alpha eyed him with bright yellow eyes. His jet black fur was still standing on end from the fight.

"I heard talk of an attack on Silver Rocks. Is it true?" The wolf's lips pulled back over his teeth as he spoke.

"Yes."

A grizzly stepped out from under the shade of a gnarled oak tree.

"If there's a fight going on, I want in." He lumbered over to join them.

"Anyone else?" Koren aimed his question at the surrounding trees.

Another bear stepped forward, as well as a small forest dragon. Koren smiled at the volunteers gratefully and led the way back toward Silver Rocks. The unexpected reinforcements added new confidence to his stride.

"Wait for me!" cried a small voice at his feet. A squirrel weaved back and forth between his legs. "I want to fight too!" He saw its thick, bushy tail and couldn't help but find it cute. "This is my preferred form, but I can be bigger if you'd like."

It stepped away from them and morphed smoothly into a black unicorn.

"A shape shifter," Koren exclaimed in surprise. "Perfect."

"You can ride on my back if you'd like. I can get you to Silver Rocks faster." Koren accepted the offer without hesitation and swung onto his back. The unicorn broke into a smooth canter and raced up the trail, the others followed closely on his heels.

A little while later Koren held up his hand and brought them to a halt. He peered into the clearing and found the silver cliffs looming in front of them. The unicorns were badly outnumbered and were corned against the cliff side. One of the stallions was restrained in chains. There wasn't a moment to lose. With a savage cry he urged the black unicorn into a run and charged into the throng of humans. The other animals were close behind him.

***

Mimie stared moodily at the entrance to the hollow rock and stretched to relieve her back from the soreness caused by leaning against the hard wall. Mimie looked at Navi and found her curled up in the grass, fast asleep. A shrill scream ripped through the silence and Mimie was on her feet in seconds. She ran to the opening and struggled to see in the bright light. A commotion caught her eye. One of the young unicorns was trying to fight off a large group of slave catchers, all armed with ropes and swords. Mimie could hardly bare to watch as one of the humans slashed at her side and made her scream again.

"Now see what you've done, ruined her lovely coat," one of them laughed.

Mimie couldn't let this go any further. She picked up a piece of crumbling silver rock and threw it at the back of the laughing man's head. It shattered on impact, and the man crumpled to the ground. The other men fell silent and looked warily in her direction. Mimie threw a second rock and hit a different slave catcher in the face. The distraction gave the unicorn just enough time to escape. When the slavers saw her galloping away, they took off after her and forgot about Mimie. She headed back toward the hollow rock.

A few seconds later a strong hand grabbed her arm. The attack was so sudden she didn't have time to scream before the man pulled her against his chest and clamped a hand over her mouth. She bit down on his finger and didn't let go until she tasted blood. As he yelled in pain, she jammed her elbow into his gut. The man released her and Mimie sprinted blindly away from him.

She weaved quickly around the huge rocks, but the man was gaining, she couldn't shake him. After emerging in a large grassy field she knew she was trapped. The cliff edge stood ominously in front of her. Slowly, she turned around and faced the man lurking in front of her. His right eye was swollen shut and blood trickled from his forehead where the rock had hit him. Mimie took a step backward and felt the cliff edge against her heal.

"We can do this the easy way, or the hard way, fairy," the slave catcher growled. "Either you come quietly, or I push you off this cliff."

"The cliff, please," Mimie replied. The man sprang at her so fast she didn't have time to react. In a quick swipe, he grabbed Mimie's arm and yanked her away from the edge.

"Too bad sweetheart." He took out a rope from his grime covered jacket and used it to tie her arms down tightly at her sides. When he was finished, he shoved a piece of cloth in her mouth and pulled a bag over her head. He tried to drag her behind him, but she refused to cooperate, so he threw her over one shoulder. The position hurt her ribs but there was nothing she could do about it.

After an hour, Mimie felt herself slip off the man's shoulder and fall to the ground. There was a jingle of keys, and then a slight creak. The slave catcher picked her up and roughly shoved her into an enclosed space. He slammed a door shut behind her, and she heard muffled footsteps walking away. When she was sure he was gone she wiggled out of the bag and used her shoulder to pull the gag out of her mouth. The smell of feathers alerted her she was not alone. Hesitantly, she glanced over one shoulder and saw a gray flying unicorn with a dark silver mane and tail. Her golden horn caught the sunlight with a dazzling sparkle.

"Oviet?" Mimie asked in surprise. Oviet avoided her gaze, her dark eyes sad. Mimie peered through the barred window, but nothing seemed familiar. The silver cliffs were nowhere to be seen and the dark forest around her was filled with nothing but lonely, chirping crickets.

"Where are we?" Mimie asked quietly.

"What does it matter?" Oviet glared at the wall.

"Someone will come looking for us. I know they will." Mimie tried to inject as much enthusiasm into her tone as possible.

"No one's coming," Oviet assured her.

"What about your family, surely they-"

"I'm a half-breed. Luna doesn't think creatures like me should be born, let alone allowed to live." Her scowl deepened.

"And your parents?" Mimie asked.

"My Dam was Luna's daughter. She died giving birth to me. The stallion that sired me disappeared shortly after I was born. Luna took me in as an act of charity."

"Well Koren's not like that. As soon as he sees that we're gone, he'll come after us."

"Even if you're right, he won't get here in time." She motioned toward the barred window. Mimie's heart shuddered in fear. The man she'd injured was walking toward them holding a cruel blade at his side. He was flanked by two other slavers. All three were looking directly at her. She swallowed.

"Koren, where are you?" Mimie breathed

***

Koren tried not to look around; the scene was too gruesome. He grabbed a dead slaver by the arm and dragged him toward the growing pile in the middle of the field. The grass was slick with blood. It was on his hands on his shoes and he wanted nothing more than to wash it off. The stench of it turned his stomach. He dumped the body on the pile and paused to catch his breath. Sweat ran into his eyes as he leaned over and rested his elbows against his knees. He grabbed a wooden shovel and thrust the point into the soft earth. The shape shifter morphed into the form of an elf and helped him. When the hole was deep enough Koren kicked the bodies into it.

He bent down and grabbed a hand full of dirt. He clenched it tightly in his fist as he raised his hand above the bodies. He began the ritualistic words that would lead these human's souls to their fate in the afterlife. The phrase was meant to be spoken by loved ones so he clipped the words to fit a stranger's burial.

"In peace may your soul rest among the stars. Rejoin the ones you have lost and become one with the earth that once gave you life." He dropped the handful of dirt over the bodies to close the ritual.

He ignored the raw ache in his palms as he picked up the shovel and threw dirt over the fallen slavers. He didn't stop until they were completely covered. He used the handle of the shovel for support as he stared at the yellow prairie that spread out beyond the forest.

Soft hoof falls approached him and stopped a short distance away. Luna tossed her silver mane. "You are kinder than I am. I would have thrown those bodies to the wolves." He ignored her comment.

"I'm going to go check on Mimie." He stabbed the shovel into the ground and motioned for the shape shifter to follow. The elf morphed into a small sparrow and flew onto his shoulder. Koren stopped by the pond to clean himself off and then headed toward the concealed tunnel. He walked with measured steps, the sound echoing back to him off the stone walls. He'd retrieved most of his arrows, but he knew he'd still have to make more. He reached back and felt one of the feathers. He wasn't sure he was ready to face Mimie yet. Though he'd washed his hands well, he was sure she'd still be able to spot the blood on them. She'd see the tarnish on his soul, see the blood debt weighing on his shoulders.

He reached the hollowed-out rock much too soon. It was quiet inside, he pushed the vines aside and stepped through the small opening.

"Mimie, are you here?"

Navi got to her feet and shakily walked toward him.

"I've been alone for hours," she moaned and shoved her head under his arm.

"Hours," Koren breathed, letting the word wash over him.

In a daze he stumbled back outside and leaned against the rock. He heard a thunder of hooves as two unicorns raced toward him.

"Koren!" the mare gasped. "We've been looking everywhere for you." She paused a moment to catch her breath. "Your friend, she's been captured by a slave catcher. They were attacking me and one must have seen her. I came back to check on her, but she was gone. Blaze and I searched everywhere. Oviet is missing too. I'm sorry."

Koren turned to the bird on his shoulder. "Can I ask you for a favor?"

"Of course," he twittered.

"I think she's probably in the forest somewhere. Will you help me find her?" The sparrow jumped off his shoulder and morphed into a huge eagle. He lowered his wing so Koren could climb on his back. Once Koren was securely in place the eagle spread its wings and soared into the sky.

"How are you going to find her? The slave catchers could be anywhere by now," the eagle reminded him. Koren ignored the bird and scanned the trees for any sign of a wagon.

***

The man with the sword held it loosely at his side. He brushed his greasy brown hair over his head with his claw-like fingers. His menacing black eyes were fixed on Mimie's face. The bruising around his eyes and nose was more pronounced now. His right eye was almost swollen shut.

The slaver next to him grabbed his arm in restraint. "Are you sure you want to do this, Bruce? Those two are worth a fortune! We could retire, find ourselves some ladies. Think about it."

"They're not worth the trouble Spider Fingers," Bruce replied. "Do what you want with the unicorn, but I'm killing the slippery little witch. What do you think Stone?" Bruce asked the man to his right.

"Do what you want," he replied in a bored monotone. Bruce took his disinterest as a yes and unclipped the keys from around his waist. Spider Fingers stopped him.

"Not here," he hissed. "It's almost sunset and the silver worms are probably out looking for them."

Bruce hesitated. "Fine." His lip curled in irritation and he stalked to the front of the wagon. The other two followed him. He cracked his whip, and the two black horses sprang forward into a brisk trot.

"Should we scream? If someone's in the area maybe they might hear and send for help." She struggled to stay upright as the wagon jolted back and forth.

"Or the slavers will decide you're not worth the trouble and kill you that much sooner." Mimie fell silent, a feeling of hopelessness washing over her.

Bruce urged the horses into a run. Mimie and Oviet were thrown into each other at every turn, and the jostling bumps sent them sprawling across the floor. The animals continued their reckless pace until Bruce pulled them to a skidding halt and announced,

"This is plenty far enough."

Mimie waited for the others to contradict him and felt her stomach contract in fear when they didn't. She heard a loud thump, and then three pairs of heavy boots landed on the ground and walked into sight. Bruce already had the keys in hand and he wasted no time unlocking the door. As soon as the latch was free Mimie kicked it, and the door swung open, hitting Bruce in the face and knocking him over backward. Several curse words slurred together as he wiped the blood from a fresh cut on his nose. Mimie fell out the open door and landed on top of him, cutting off what he was about to say next.

The other two grabbed her by her shoulders and pulled her off of him. Bruce was so angry his pale face had turned a dark shade of purple, but that could also have been a new bruise forming, she wasn't sure.

"Take her into the trees," he snapped.

Mimie searched the leafy canopy for any sign of Koren. She found nothing to suggest there was anyone around to help her. Rough hands against her back shoved her forward. Thick roots crossed her path and she struggled not to trip over them. Cold sweat trickled down her back as she tried to think through her panic. The slavers jerked the rope binding her arms and brought her to a jarring halt. She glanced over her shoulder and caught sight of a flash of silver as Bruce pulled out his knife.

"Aren't you forgetting something?" Mimie exclaimed, trying to stall for time.

"No." Bruce tested the point of the knife with his finger.

"You can't kill a fairy without first granting her last request." Mimie tried to appear confident as she said the words.

Bruce smirked in mocking amusement. "Sure princess, what would you like?"

"I want you to untie me," Mimie replied.

"And why would I do that?"

"Because... if you don't, you'll be cursed," Mimie explained.

"That's stupid," Bruce growled. "You're lying."

"Well, I tried to warn you." Mimie's shoulders trembled and her voice shook a little as she continued. "I've already caused you so much suffering. I would feel awful if you denied me my last request, and as a result died horrible, tragic deaths."

"That is complete nonsense," Bruce snapped.

"Is it?" Mimie put as much innocence and sincerity into her tone as possible. "Don't blame me when your eyes fall out and your hair catches on fire."

Bruce shifted his weight back and forth as he worried the handle of his knife between his fingers. "Alright, alright. Stone untie her so she'll shut up." He handed Stone his knife and watched with a scowl as he cut the rope binding Mimie's arms to her sides.

"Happy now?" he spat.

"Definitely— OH MY GOSH WHAT IS THAT??!" Mimie yelled, and pointed at something behind them. All three of the slave catchers whipped around and Mimie bolted into the trees.

"Hey!" Bruce yelled, "Get back here!" Out of nowhere she heard the twang of an arrow and saw Bruce drop like a downed bird. Koren was standing directly behind him with his bow still raised. Mimie saw Spider Fingers turn and run, but another silver arrow sent him tumbling into the underbrush. Stone fixed his gaze on Koren and raised his palms in surrender.

"Get out of here," Koren snapped. Stone nodded and backed away into the trees. When he was gone Koren lowered his bow, but his posture remained tense. "You can't seem to stay out of trouble, can you?" Mimie avoided his angry glare.

"Thank you for coming to look for me."

"What happened? Why did you leave the rock hollow?"

"One of the unicorns was in trouble. I wasn't going to stand by and watch the humans abduct her. So I threw rocks at them. In hindsight, I realize that wasn't the best way to handle the situation."

"You were the one that messed up this guys face?" His shocked tone irritated her.

"I had no intention of coming quietly."

She heard footsteps behind her and turned to see Oviet walking toward them with a mouse running up and down her back.

"You and Oviet go ahead, I'll catch up in a second," Koren muttered and headed toward the bodies of the two slavers.

"What are you doing?" Mimie asked.

"Getting my arrows back of course." Mimie shuddered and watched Oviet's long, silver tail disappear into the shadow beneath a tree. The hair on her arms prickled uncomfortably.

"Koren," she called. Her shoulders grew tense as she waited for his reply. "Koren? Where are you?" To her horror, she saw Stone emerge with a knife pressed to his throat.

"You better do exactly as I say fairy," he threatened in a low voice.

"I don't make deals with murderers," Mimie snapped, trying to sound braver than she felt. Koren used Stone's moment of distraction to lock Stone's arm against his chest. With both hands still on Stone's wrist, he ducked under his arm and used the full force of his body to drive the blade into his side. He pushed Stone away from him and stepped back, looking like he was ready to break his neck if he tried anything else. Stone gasped in pain and crawled into the trees.

"Let's go," Koren said and turned to leave.

"That was incredible, where did you learn how to do that?" Mimie exclaimed.

"My older brother Quinten taught me, he was good with weapons."

"Was?"

Koren kicked a clump of leaves and stepped over a tree root. "He died."

"Oh. I'm sorry."

"It was a long time ago," he shrugged.

Mimie let the subject drop. Oviet and the shape shifter were waiting for them by the wagon.

"What took you so long?" asked Oviet. Koren picked a leaf out of Mimie's hair, by the set of his lips she could tell he wasn't going to answer. The mouse scurried down Oviet's legs and climbed up to Koren's shoulder. A desire to pet its fluffy head distracted Mimie. Instead, she hid her trembling fingers behind her back and silently willed them to stop shaking.

"You can ride on my back," Oviet offered. "It'll be faster than walking."

"You mean fly back?" A thrill of excitement passed through Mimie as she imagined herself high above the trees.

"How are you getting back, Koren?"

The shape shifter jumped from his shoulder and morphed into a black dragon. Mimie rolled her eyes and attempted to hop onto Oviet's back. She lifted her wings so Mimie wouldn't rip out any of her feathers.

Koren took a half step in her direction. "Would you like some help?"

"No, I got it." Mimie tangled her fingers into Oviet's mane and tried to heave herself onto her back by kicking out her legs. She slid back to the ground with a loud huff.

"Please let me help you," Koren laughed.

"Yes. Please," Oviet added, wincing as Mimie pulled on her mane.

Koren took her silence as an invitation to step in. He cuffed his hands and she used them to steady her left leg as she swung her right over Oviet's back. Mimie avoided eye contact as her ears warmed in embarrassment.

"Thanks."

"No problem," Koren walked toward the dragon and climbed onto his shoulders with sure, nimble movements. Once he was in place the dragon spread its wings and raked enormous claws into the ground as it pushed off into the air. Oviet watched it disappear over the trees in grudging awe.

"Hold on tight," she warned and launched herself into a full gallop. Mimie felt her hair streaming out behind her and clung to Oviet's neck. Oviet spread her wings, with a few strong thrusts they were rising on the air currents. Mimie felt her stomach drop but she quickly got used to the feeling and watched the treetops rushing by below her. She couldn't believe it; they were actually flying!

"This is incredible!" she exclaimed. Koren was lucky he got to live in a world where such amazing things were possible. She turned her face toward the setting sun and soaked in every minute of the experience.

CHAPTER 7: GOODBYES

↞ ↞ ↠ ↠

Koren was waiting for them when they got back. Oviet landed at the base of the cliff and Mimie jumped off her back. The shape shifter morphed into a bird and twittered idly on Koren's shoulder.

"Don't be put out," Koren laughed when he noticed Oviet glaring at the bird. "His wings were twice as long as yours."

Oviet mumbled something under her breath and walked away. She didn't get far before Luna's sharp voice stopped her in her tracks.

"Oviet, go find a way to make yourself useful!" Oviet flinched, and turned to face her with lowered eyes.

"What would you like me to do?" she asked.

"I don't know, look around and find something!"

"Alright." Oviet looked at the ground, and her tail drooped as she turned away.

Koren took the opportunity to distract Luna, and spare Oviet a lecture that was sure to be on its way.

"Have you seen Angora," asked Koren. "I need to talk to her about something."

"She's scouting the forest for any surviving humans."

Mimie watched the exchange from afar. After seeing the way Luna had treated Oviet, Mimie was afraid to interrupt. As she approached, she kept Koren between her and Luna in case she needed to use him as a shield. She mustered her courage and peeked out from behind his back.

"Luna?"

"Yes dear child?" The fondness in her tone surprised Mimie, especially when it had been so sharp only moments before.

"You told me earlier that the dwarfs could help me, do you know where I might find them?"

"Yes, they are northwest of here, across the plains, and the red canyon."

"Thank you." She would leave in the morning at dawn. That was not a goodbye she was looking forward to. If Koren wasn't too busy, maybe he'd help her gather more supplies. It was a good excuse to spend a little more time with him.

"Koren!" Martha's shrill yell made him jump. He looked at her sheepishly and led her to a shaded rock.

"I was so worried about you! What took you so long to find me?"

"There was a lot going on. I came to get you as soon as I could."

"I could have died, and look at the state of my fur! It's disgusting!" she exclaimed.

"There's a pond over there you can use to clean off," he told her. She sniffled once and walked toward it.

"Sorry about that, she's been in a terrible mood all morning," Ern said, hobbling toward him from the trees. "Mimie will need someone to accompany her. Have you found anyone yet?"

"No, but I'm looking into it." Koren said.

"I think we both know who the obvious choice is." Koren stared as a plant near his feet. Mimie watched the exchange in confusion.

"I'll talk it over with Mo, see what he thinks about it."

"How are things going with Angora?" Ern sat down and pulled his large tail into his lap. Koren shot Mimie an uncomfortable look.

"I ended things with her a while ago." Ern wanted more of an explanation, but that was all Koren was willing to say. Mimie settled down with her back against the wall.

"How are you feeling dear?" Ern wondered, eyeing her with concern.

"I'm ok. Koren, would you mind helping me gather some supplies before I go?"

"Sure, let's go now. The light isn't going to last much longer." He pointed across the unicorns' field of lush green grass toward the yellowish prairie beyond. "You'll be going through there. You know how to use the position of the sun and stars to make sure you're heading northwest, right?"

"Sort of," Mimie shrugged.

"Do you know how to hunt?"

"I can fish, and set traps." She hated the way he was looking at her; it was similar to the concerned look Gram had given her before she left.

"What about water and fire?"

"I asked you to help me gather supplies, not interrogate me." Mimie felt sorry for her harsh tone, but didn't apologize for it. She glanced over at Martha, who was floating on her back in the pond muttering to herself. "What is she saying?" Mimie asked Koren.

"You probably don't want to know." His expression was troubled.

Martha did a quick once over to make sure she hadn't missed a spot, and then walked back to them. She was still muttering something under her breath, but it sounded like nonsense to Mimie. Koren's head shot up at one phrase in particular.

"Martha!" he snapped, throwing a meaningful look in Mimie's direction.

"She doesn't know what it means," Martha replied defensively.

"You put soap in my mouth for talking like that!" Koren didn't like double standards.

"Did I?" she laughed.

"So tell me about the howler that got into the forest a few weeks ago," Ern said, trying to defuse the argument before it got started. "I meant to ask you about it last time you came to visit, but I forgot."

"What's a howler?" Mimie asked.

"It's a creature of the night. It lives in caves during the day and comes out at dusk to hunt. They're usually only found in the mountains, but occasionally one will find a cave in the forest and decide to stay," Ern said. Mimie shifted her weight and pulled a twig out from under her leg.

"What does it look like?"

"Imagine a skeletal, furless wolf, with rusty red skin and huge bat ears. Then give it a hunched back, large bony spikes protruding from every vertebra, a stubby rat like tail and huge claws. Couple that with a hypnotic howl that lures anyone within hearing distance to their death, and you've got a howler."

"How did you manage to get rid of it?"

Koren half smiled "Well, the first time I heard the howl I was far enough away that I wasn't affected, but I couldn't let something that dangerous stay in the forest. So I found a pair of ear plugs and tracked it back to its cave."

Mimie wrapped her arms around her knees. "Were there a lot of bones inside?"

"The howler hadn't been there for very long. I found a deer carcass, that's about it. I came back that night around midnight and tried to bring it down while it was hunting, but my sword couldn't cut through its skin. They'll die if exposed to direct sunlight so I provoked the howler into chasing me. When the sun came up, it was too far away from its cave to make it back in time. I didn't want to kill it, but if I tried to force it to move somewhere else I had no guarantees that the howler wouldn't just come back." Koren glanced at the sun and sprang to his feet. "Oh, I almost forgot. I'm supposed to be meeting someone right now." His eyes were apologetic.

"Go, go I don't want you to be late," Martha said. He jogged toward the tree line.

"Good to see he hasn't changed a bit, always rushing off somewhere. Ern and I used call him our little bird. We'd turn to each other and say, 'where has our little bird gone off to today?' We try not to be too hard on him. He was just a tiny little thing when we found him, all cut up and freezing in the snow. Well, tiny for a fourteen year old. It was a miracle we happened across him at all, really."

"What was he doing out there in the first place? Where was his family?"

"He didn't tell us much, other than he'd just escaped from a human town where he was being used as a slave. He goes back there sometimes, almost like he's looking for someone. I asked him about it one time, but he never gave me a straight answer."

"Here," Ern offered, giving Mimie his travel bag. "You'll probably be needing this more than I will."

"Thanks," Mimie replied. It was filled to the brim with sticks and there was a water canteen shoved near the bottom. The canteen was made from wood with a cork stopper. Mimie pulled it out and showed it to Ern. "Where on earth did you get this?" she wondered.

"I swiped it from a lizard that won't be needing it anymore." Mimie decided not to ask. She glanced back into the bag.

"You guys should probably keep these. You'll get more use out of them than I will." Mimie said and dumped them out next to Martha. "Although, I suppose I could use them for firewood," she mused.

"These are from pristine saplings!" Ern snatched them into his lap. "It would be an insult to nature to use them for something as petty as firewood."

"You're right, shame on me," Mimie laughed. There was a plant growing nearby with yellow spotted leaves and green shriveled looking beans; she considered the plant's possibilities.

"Is that safe to eat?" she wondered.

"I think so. You'd have to ask Koren, he knows more about that than I do," Ern replied. Mimie walked over to the bush and picked an armful of the beans, then threw them into her bag. Ern and Martha led her to other plants and helped her fill her sack to the top with enough food to comfortably last her four days. They also helped her roughly decipher what was eatable and what would most likely kill her.

They spent the rest of the evening lying in the soft grass together. Mimie yawned and curled up next to Martha, watching the stars twinkle in and out of the cloud cover. The night was calm and almost silent, except for a few bugs chirping in the distance. Her thoughts turned toward Koren, and she wondered if he would get back in time for her to say goodbye. He was still a mystery, a puzzle that she hated leaving unsolved. She closed her eyes and sighed. It was going to be a lonely journey to the Dwarf Mountains.

***

Koren wandered through the trees back toward the cliff side. After hours of thinking it over and talking to Mo about it, he'd finally come to a decision. He'd gone through a long list of candidates, but no one seemed good enough. There was only one person he trusted to go with Mimie, and that was himself. Mo had said he would find another Guardian to replace him while he was gone. Angora wouldn't be happy about it, but he didn't care how she felt anymore.

"You're not leaving without saying goodbye, are you?"

He clenched his teeth and turned around. Angora always had a knack for showing up when he least wanted to see her. No, that wasn't fair, she was a loyal friend and a fierce fighter. He shouldn't let his annoyance at her taint her good qualities. However few there were.

"You're not going to change my mind, so don't even try," Koren warned.

"Fine," she pouted and played with her long tightly braided hair. She was used to getting her way, but her usual tricks didn't work on him anymore. Underneath the beauty she was extremely shallow and self-absorbed.

She was still mad at him for breaking up with her, but he refused to let her manipulate him into feeling sorry about it.

"I wish you would stay." She blinked her long eyelashes. "We need you here."

"No you don't. Mo said he would find a replacement for me."

"I don't want a replacement. I want you." She stepped in front of him and blocked his path. The statement made his skin crawl.

"Well, you'll have to get over it because my decision is final," he said, pushing past her.

"You're wasting your time with her, you know. If you want a girl to follow around, there's plenty right here." Koren gritted his teeth and tried to control his rising anger.

"There's nothing going on between me and Mimie, and even if there was, it wouldn't be any of your business," he snapped. "She has a long way to go and she needs someone to look out for her."

"Demoted to a babysitter, what a waste."

"Go away Angora." Somehow she always brought out the worst in him, that's why he'd ended their relationship.

"Fine, but don't come crawling back when you get sick of her!"

"I won't!" Koren said coldly. They glared at each other for a few seconds, then she backed away and disappeared. Koren sat down with his legs crossed and pinched the bridge of his nose.

What was he thinking? Would Mimie even want him to come? He realized he'd never actually asked her. He found that he was excited about the prospect of getting to know her better and was almost jittery as he settled down by the cliff side.

He laid down on his back, set his quiver aside and held his bow in one hand while feeling the familiar twang of the string with the other. It was a beautiful night, and for the first time in a long time he dozed off feeling untroubled.

He woke still feeling a little drowsy and stretched. The sun was hot against his face and he was filmed in sweat from sleeping so long past dawn. He slung his quiver and bow over his shoulder and headed toward the far side of the cliff where the battle had taken place.

"Morning," Koren called to Martha who was laying on her back in the pond nibbling on a stick.

"Morning," she replied.

"Where's Mimie?" he wondered, noticing she wasn't there.

"She's gone," he heard Ern reply. "She left early this morning; she told me to say goodbye to you for her."

"She was alone?" Koren exclaimed. "Is she insane? Why did she go by herself?"

"I guess you forgot to tell her that you wanted to go with her," Ern replied. "If you leave now, you can probably catch up to her."

"She could be miles out by now. I don't have time to track her down on foot. I have to go find Luna!" Koren exclaimed. He gave Ern a tight hug. "I love you guys."

"What about me?" asked Martha indignantly, climbing out of the pond.

"Sorry," Koren laughed and wrapped his arms around her. "Be safe, ok," he told them. "Ask Angora to walk you home." They nodded, waving goodbye as he raced toward the tunnel that led to the top of the cliff. He headed toward Luna, who was standing under the central tree, and stopped in front of her, gasping for breath.

"What is it?" she asked in alarm.

"Oviet…where's Oviet?" Koren choked out.

"I don't know, I told her to stay out from under hoof and I haven't seen her since," Luna told him. "Why?"

"I need her," Koren said. He didn't feel like explaining the details.

"I'll summon her." Luna hated Oviet, but she tried harder to be civil when he was around, at least that was something. She saw one of the stallions passing by, "Bone, go fetch Oviet," she called. He nodded once and galloped toward the southern end of the plateau.

"Thank you," Koren said quietly, finally managing to catch his breath. He felt better when Oviet landed in front of him.

"Yes," she asked, a slight hint of irritation in her voice. "Bone said it was urgent."

"I need you to help me look for Mimie, she left early this morning and I don't have time to track her on foot. Is that ok Luna?" he added, suddenly remembering she was there.

"She will be more useful to you, than with us." The harsh words made Oviet flinch.

"We have to leave now, Mimie could be in danger."

"Ok, well you better get on then!" Oviet exclaimed as she suddenly realized what he was offering her. She was willing to do anything that would get her away from Luna. He swung nimbly onto her back and held on as Oviet took off into the sky.

CHAPTER 8: A DANGEROUS JOURNEY

↞ ↞ ↠ ↠

It was still dark when Mimie opened her eyes, but she knew dawn couldn't be far off. A chill breeze blew her hair back, and she wrapped her cloak tighter around her shoulders. She scanned the cliff face and then turned her gaze to the yellow plains that stretched endlessly before her. She walked up to the beavers who were sleeping nearby and gently shook Martha's shoulder.

"Are you leaving already dearie?" Martha yawned.

"Yeah," she replied, pulling both of them into a tight hug. "Thanks for everything."

"No problem! Have a safe journey and stay out of trouble!" Martha told her.

"I'll do my best, say bye to Koren for me." Mimie slung her pack over one shoulder and took a deep breath, leaving was harder than she thought.

Luna said to head northeast, or was it northwest? She looked up and tried to find the North Star, but clouds obscured most of the sky. She started walking and decided to correct herself based on the position of the sun when it appeared on the horizon. The sun rose in the east, right, or was it the west? This was going to be harder than she thought.

After an hour, she noticed the stars fading out of view and the first small line of pink blossoming across the horizon.

"Well, no turning back now," she thought and picked up her pace.

It was around noon when Mimie sat down for her first rest. The day had been lonely and monotonous. A small bird landed beside her and pecked at the ground by her feet.

"Can you talk?" Mimie asked it. It chirped and cocked its head sideways in response. "I guess not. Hey do you have rabies? If not I'd really like to eat you." She held her hand out to see if the bird would come to her, but it flew away. Wanting to satisfy her hunger, she pulled a few shriveled green beans from her bag. They tasted horrible, but she choked them down and set off again.

After a while she looked up and saw a huge purple mountain in front of her. She felt a renewed sense of confidence and hurried toward it. She found it odd that the purple mountain was floating in the sky, but strange things happened here all the time, so Mimie didn't think much of it. She walked until the sun went down and she couldn't see where she was going anymore. She sat down, set her bag beside her, and wrapped her cloak around her shoulders.

"I should probably start a fire," Mimie muttered to herself. She pulled all the grass out of a small area and lined it with rocks. She placed two sticks and the grass she had uprooted in the middle of the circle of stones, and used two smaller rocks to make a spark. It quickly ate through all the grass, and Mimie had to scramble to find more twigs to keep it from going out. Once she was satisfied that the fire was not going to burn out anytime soon, she curled up on her side with her back to the flames and tried to doze off. She would sleep in tomorrow, and then continue walking after she put the fire out.

After a while, she heard something scuffling around in the bushes. She opened her eyes and tried to see past the small ring of light the fire cast around her, but it seemed as if the whole world had fallen into complete darkness. She caught a glimpse of something small and white weaving through the grass and strained to see it better. She wouldn't have cared except for the nagging concern the creature might be something that could eat her. Whatever it was, there were a lot of them. She saw a twitching nose emerge from the grass, followed by a pair of beady black eyes. To her relief, Mimie realized it was only a bunny.

"Hey there little guy." She reached out to pet it and laughed at the smile tugging at its lips. Her hand froze as the smile turned into a snarl that exposed a mouth full of needle-sharp fangs. She pulled her hand back as a milky film washed over the rabbit's black eyes, turning them a luminous white. All around her, she saw dozens of other glowing white eyes dancing back and forth at the edge of the firelight. She backed away from the creature, but stopped when the heat of the fire and the musky smell of smoke overwhelmed her. The snarls were closing in, and Mimie shuddered as she realized the last thing she might ever see were those revolting fangs.

With the fear came a familiar numbness creeping up her arms but she wasn't sure that would be enough to save her. The demon rabbits attacked, swarming over Mimie in a wave of teeth and fur. A surge of intense heat exploded out of her. With an ear-splitting crack the rabbits were blasted into the air. For a moment it seemed as if the whole world had been turned inside out. The sudden violence of it all surprised her and it took what seemed like a long time for her mind to start working coherently again. The fire had been extinguished by the blast but she was worried it may have caught the surrounding grass on fire.

She opened her eyes and saw white balls of fur falling from the sky around her. A large shadow blocked out the moonlight.

"Oviet?" she mumbled. What was she doing way out here?

"Mimie?" she heard a familiar voice call; it was Koren. He was here too, why? As soon as Oviet touched the ground Koren slid off her back and ran toward where Mimie was laying on the ground.

"Hi," Mimie laughed and started coughing.

"Come on, we need to get you away from here, can you stand up?" Koren asked urgently.

"Why?" Mimie asked. She watched the rabbits fall from the sky with a bemused expression.

"Because you don't know how to follow simple instructions and now you're in the heart of southern Parabit territory."

"I was following the floating purple mountain," Mimie explained.

"There aren't any mountains around here, least of all purple floating ones."

"You don't know," she argued weakly, trying to get to her feet. Koren helped her and draped her arm across his shoulders. It felt good to let him be in charge. "How did you find me?" Mimie asked.

"Well, first I looked along the path you should have taken, and when I couldn't find you there, I spent all day looking everywhere else. I saw your campfire and a bright flash of light. You didn't honestly think I was going to let you leave without saying goodbye?" he laughed, leading her toward Oviet. Mimie's heart fell.

"Oh," she mumbled. He was just here to say goodbye. "Well, goodbye then," she said and pulled her arm away. "Sorry you had to come all the way out here." Koren stopped and turned to face her. When he knew he had her full attention, he said,

"Mimie I didn't come to say goodbye. I want to go with you."

"Really?" she asked, afraid to believe it.

"Someone has to make sure you don't get lost," he laughed.

"Thanks." She swayed a little as she struggled to keep her balance.

"Are you ok? You don't look so good." Koren's forehead creased with concern. Mimie almost threw up as the ground swayed toward her. Koren caught her and scooped her into his arms. The movement was swift, for a second she wasn't sure if it had happened at all. He walked with her in his arms like her weight was nothing. She felt like she was floating, that she was tiny in comparison to the impressive form that had swooped out of the sky to save her.

Sometime later, Mimie opened her eyes and blinked to clear away her blurred vision. Her legs were stiff, and her back was sore from lying in the same position for too long. These were barely noticeable in comparison to her throbbing headache, which tuned out everything else. She thought that was what had woken her, but then something brushed across her ankle. Suddenly she remembered the Parabits and came to the conclusion that one was about to bite her toes off. She lashed out blindly and realized too late that she'd just decked Koren in the face, again.

"Aw!" he snapped. "What was that for?" Mimie forced herself to focus and saw him backing away from her, rubbing his jaw. She realized her mistake and apologized.

"Sorry, I thought you were going to bite my toes." He stared at her in disbelief, then abruptly started laughing. "Wait," she muttered and then let it go, realizing he wasn't listening anymore. She rubbed her eyes. "Where are we?"

"We're a day out from Red Rock Canyon," Koren answered, poking something in the fire.

"How long have I been out?" She massaged the kinks in her neck.

"All night, and most of the morning. Your snoring was driving me crazy."

"I do not snore. You're such a liar," Mimie laughed.

"Wow, that's an excellent way to talk to the guy who just saved your life, again," he countered.

"I had it under control," Mimie insisted.

"Sure," Koren snorted. She vaguely noticed his cloak was wrapped around her and pushed it off. "You used magic again," he accused, still poking at something.

"I can't control that, when I get mad or scared it just comes out. Where's Oviet?" Mimie was surprised when she couldn't find her nearby.

"She's sleeping, she needed to rest."

"What are you making? It smells good." She eased into a sitting position and massaged her temples.

"If you're nice to me I might share."

"What is it?"

"Parabit," he answered with a sheepish expression.

"The ones I killed?" Mimie's lip curled in disgust.

"I didn't want to waste the meat," Koren explained. "So you don't want any?"

"No, I want some. I'm starving!" He stabbed a smoking bundle with his stick and handed it to her.

"Careful, it's hot," he warned as she reached out to take it. She snapped off the end of his stick and carefully unwound the grass from the meat. She tore into it and winced as it burned her mouth, but didn't slow down. Koren grabbed a few more rabbits from his pile and got to work skinning and gutting them. The knife scraped against something metallic, and Koren dropped the rabbit in disgust.

"What was that?"

Koren turned to her and held up a human finger bone with a golden ring attached to it. His arm was stretched far away from his face as though he were afraid it carried a disease.

"Some of the other parabits had bones in them too, but I didn't realize they were from a human." He threw the bone aside and continued to cut up his rabbit. Mimie finished her food feeling slightly sick, and laid back down. A flash of light caught her eye, and she saw the gold ring lying in the grass close by. She reached over and grabbed it, figuring it had come loose when Koren had flung the bone away from him. She held it up to her face and examined it. She tried to be sneaky about it, not wanting Koren to catch her.

"What are you looking at?" Koren wondered, trying to see through the tall grass hiding her from view. Mimie shoved it into her pocket.

"I'm not looking at anything," she replied innocently. Koren raised an eyebrow but didn't press her. He probably felt guilty for feeding her something that had recently eaten someone. Koren finished cooking the meat and then kicked dirt over the fire. He put the spare meat into the food pouch and settled down next to Mimie. She took the bag from him and noticed it was only half as full as it had been the day before.

"Hey, what happened to all my food?" she demanded.

"Who helped you collect those beans that were in there?" Koren wondered.

"Ern and Martha. Why?"

"You had one in there that was poisonous, and several more that were strong hallucinogenics."

"I guess that explains the floating purple mountain I was

following."

"Yeah, everything that's left should be safe. Let's pack up." He grabbed a stick and walked toward where Oviet lay curled up in the grass. He poked her in the shoulder, and then jumped back. Oviet opened her eyes and yawned.

"That was anticlimactic," Mimie laughed.

"Is it morning already?" Oviet shook out her coat to get the lingering grass off. She was so happy to be away from Luna she didn't care what time she had to wake up. She stretched out her wings, ruffled up her feathers, and tucked them back into her sides.

She was stunning, even without the sleek white coat of the other unicorns. Mimie tore her eyes away, picked up Koren's cloak, shook the grass off of it, and handed it to him. She helped him put out the fire, and then Koren pulled a black cube from his pocket.

"What's that?" she asked.

"It's a space cube, a friend made it for me," he explained, putting it on the ground and expanding it.

"That's handy," Mimie muttered as he tossed the food pouch into it. He slid the lid back on and shrunk it down to the size of a pebble. He put the black cube back in his pocket and grinned.

"Cool right?"

"Yeah, I wish I had one. I guess that explains how you're able to carry around so much."

"You could probably learn how to make one for yourself eventually, it's pretty basic space fairy magic." He gave her a leg up onto Oviet's back. Mimie clenched her legs against Oviet's sides as she spread her wings and broke into a gallop. Oviet wasn't used to the extra weight and struggled to become airborne. Mimie closed her eyes, hoping they weren't about to fall to their deaths. Koren squeezed her hand reassuringly and fished out a handful of beans from his pocket to snack on.

Slowly, Mimie relaxed as she became accustomed to the weird feeling of flying. She watched the ground go by in a blur and noticed a large herd of strange looking animals to their left. They had massive shaggy bodies, round heads, short legs, and a petite horn in the middle of their foreheads that sloped downward.

"What are those?" Mimie asked.

"Mushrooms." Mimie scowled at his sarcasm. The creatures let out a few thunderous bellows but otherwise ignored them. "They're called Karakadon. They have a brain the size of a bird's, and three stomachs. You can't hunt them because their meat is poisonous, making them more or less useless."

"We should land so I can pet one," Mimie insisted.

"No way," Koren replied. "They might trample you."

"Please? They look so fuzzy!"

"No," he laughed.

"Let her have her fun," Oviet scolded, drifting toward the ground. "Besides, I could use a drink anyway, and they're right by the river."

"Fine, but be quick. We still have a lot of ground to cover today."

Mimie slipped off Oviet's back and cautiously approached the Karakadon. She kept low in the grass so she didn't startle them; a lioness stalking her prey. Except she was feeble and small, and if this went badly, she had nothing to save her except an overprotective elf and a unicorn. The herd seemed to pay her no mind, and she was able to creep close enough that she was almost standing among them. A little calf stopped digging at the ground and studied her curiously. A small nub of a horn was just poking out of its forehead, and it still hadn't lost all of its babyish roundness. The shaggy creature trotted up to Mimie and thrust its muzzle into her shoulder.

"Hi," Mimie laughed and scratched it behind its long unkempt ears. A bigger Karakadon raised its head and grunted softly. The calf pivoted on its slender hocks and headed back toward its mother. She sniffed at him, snorted, and then went back to grazing. Mimie decided not to push her luck and walked toward Oviet with an enormous grin on her face.

"You're such a child." Koren sat up from the grass he was laying in. "Was it worth the delay?"

"Definitely, that was the most awesome thing ever."

"I'm glad," Oviet said around a mouthful of grass.

"Alright, we better get going," Koren urged and helped Mimie onto Oviet's back. Once she was settled he swung on behind her and held on as Oviet worked her way into a run. She spread her wings wide and used the winds to ascend upwards. They flew for the rest of the day and finally landed a half hour before sunset in a field with large rocks scattered everywhere. Koren hopped off Oviet's back and found a flattened rock, which he used to dig a shallow trench in the ground.

"What are you doing?" Mimie asked, yawning.

"Making the ground a little more comfortable," Koren explained. He pulled out a knife and cut stalks of grass. When he had enough, he gathered it up and threw it in the hole. Mimie decided to copy him and grabbed a rock to dig one for herself. The ground was a lot harder than he made it look, and she couldn't seem to get through it. "Here, take my hole," Koren offered, seeing that she was having trouble. Mimie was too tired to argue and gratefully collapsed onto the spongy grass he had laid down. He pulled out the space cube and tossed her a sleeping sack.

"Why do you have two of these?" Mimie wondered seeing him pull one out for himself. He shrugged.

She remembered how drained she felt from using magic and frowned. "I wish I could fight without magic; it would make life so much easier."

"I guess." Koren cut stalks of grass for his hole.

"You and Oviet can protect yourselves. If I didn't have this stupid magic bursting out of me... I just wish I could be more useful."

"Would it make you feel better if I taught you how to fight?"

"Maybe," Mimie muttered, closing her eyes.

"And magic is definitely not stupid. It's actually kind of intimidating." Oviet groaned loudly in annoyance and turned her back on them. "We should probably go to sleep before she murders us," Koren whispered.

They fell silent, and Mimie curled up in her cloak. Even though she was exhausted, sleep evaded her. She listened as Koren's breathing became more regular and knew he had fallen asleep. She rolled onto her back and glanced up at the stars with a half smiled. She wasn't alone anymore, and she thought that maybe her life had finally changed for the better. Koren mumbled something in his sleep and shifted onto his side.

"I'm sorry..." She made out and listened more carefully to hear the rest of it. "I didn't mean too." He was unquestionably feeling guilty about something, but what? He repeated the same phrases over and over and finally fell quiet. Mimie was almost asleep when she heard him call out for someone. The name wasn't familiar to her, but it still set her on edge for some reason. Emily. He was calling out for someone named Emily.

Mimie curled onto her side and threw her cloak over her head to block out the sunlight that was shining into her eyes. Oviet was already awake and was off in the distance by the river. Koren was still asleep so she quietly grabbed the food pouch and fished out a few nuts to nibble on. The nuts were more to curb her appetite than satisfy it. What she really wanted was some bread and bird eggs. Koren shifted but didn't get up.

"How did you sleep?" he muttered with his face tucked into his arm.

"Good, that pad was super comfy. Thank you."

"Good," he muttered. His voice was deeper than usual. Mimie tried to run her fingers through her hair and found it to be a tangled mess. She put down the food pouch and made her way toward the river. When she reached the pebble-strewn bank, she knelt down and cupped her hands to get a drink. She then flipped her hair upside down and submerged it into the cold, clear water until all of it was soaked. She rung it out and shook her head back and forth to dry it a little.

"What are you doing?" Koren laughed. Mimie jumped in surprise at his sudden appearance and rushed to compose herself.

"What? You've never seen a girl dry her hair before?"

"Not like that," he countered, still chuckling in amusement. Mimie flipped her hair right side up and laughed when she saw the side of Koren's hair sticking up at a funny angle.

"I can tell what side of your face you spent the most time on last night."

"Oh, this?" Koren replied, running his hand through his hair. "Yeah, it's pretty bad."

I would use the word adorable, Mimie thought to herself, but she didn't share this out loud. She scooted over to give him access to the deeper water by the bank and watched as he splashed water on his face, then used it to return order to his hair.

"We should probably get going," Oviet suggested.

"Ok," Mimie said, and walked back to the campsite to grab their supplies. She threw them into the space cube and shrank it down to pocket size. Koren dragged his feet and hopped onto Oviet's back. He offered Mimie his hand, pulling her into place in front of him. Oviet took off into the air. As Mimie felt the familiar lurch in her stomach, she laughed nervously and gripped Oviet's mane for support.

"You ok there?" Koren wondered.

"I don't know if I'll ever be able to get used to this," Mimie said, watching the world rush by below her.

It wasn't long before the grass turned into red patches of bare rock and then fell away into a canyon. Oviet swooped down into the shadow of the deep red walls, and as she sped around the tight corners Mimie finally realized how fast they were going. She had a morbid vision of them crashing into one of the walls and resembling a bug smashed flat by someone's shoe. The great rivers that had carved out the canyon were gone now, the river beds far below them held nothing but parched red dirt.

It seemed like it would be easy to get lost in this sea of plateaus, but Oviet appeared to know where she was going, and Koren always let her know when she took a wrong turn. Mimie felt something pressing into her leg and put her hand in her pocket to dislodge it. She froze when her fist closed around something cold and hard. The ring. She held it close to her face and studied it. It was big enough to fit around her thumb and was light silver in color. She tilted it back and forth, experimenting with the way the light reflected off its shiny surface.

"What are you looking at?" Koren asked, peering over her shoulder. Mimie handed it to him and blushed as panic twisted his features. "Where did you get this?" he demanded.

"It was on that bone you pulled out of the Parabit. I put it in my pocket and I must have forgotten it was there…" Mimie trailed off at the expression on Koren's face.

"Do you realize what this is!" Koren groaned. When Mimie didn't answer, he yelled, "It's a tracking device!"

"Why are you still holding it!" Oviet yelled at Koren. "Get rid of it!"

"Right." Koren tossed it down to the riverbed below in disgust.

"Why was a tracking device ring, stuck on a human finger bone, inside a carnivorous rabbit?" Mimie asked tentatively.

"The better question is why you would put that same ring in your pocket!" Koren snapped. "Orient makes traitors wear them so he can track them. It has an enchantment on it so once you put the ring on, you can't take it off again, or you'll die."

"That would have been a nice thing to tell me before I picked it up."

"Well, I thought you'd be grossed out enough that it was on a dead person not to touch it."

"What can I say, I have a natural curiosity."

Koren's reply was cut short by a sickly familiar whooshing sound. An arrow with a rope attached to the end flew across Oviet's path, creating a perfect trip wire. It hit Oviet squarely in the chest and sent her flailing wildly into the cliff wall. Mimie pulled up her leg so it wouldn't get crushed from the impact, but in doing so she lost her balance and slipped sideways. Something swiped at the tip of her fingers, Mimie assumed it was Koren, but he wasn't quick enough. All of a sudden there was nothing but air between her and the ground. She might have screamed, but there wasn't enough air in her lungs. The free fall lasted only seconds before she fell hard onto the riverbed below.

Men in dull blue uniforms emerged from the crevices in the wall beside her and worked their way down into the riverbed. These were the soldiers that had killed her family. They were coming closer. The dusting of red over their uniforms held a disturbing resemblance to blood. The soft crunch of gravel close behind her told her she wasn't moving fast enough as she fled on hands and knees. She could taste the rich mineral flavor of the dust and hated the dry, gritty feeling it left behind. Her movements became more panicked as they closed in on her. Every muscle tensed as a pair of hands locked onto her arm. A small scream escaped her as they jerked her to her feet, but the sound choked off as her throat closed in fear.

A Zantie lumbered toward her. He was wearing an official looking symbol on his uniform that the other Zanties didn't have. He saw the ice forming on the ground at Mimie's feet and raised his eyebrows in surprise.

"A fairy!" he exclaimed. "I want Orient informed immediately!" One of the Zanties nodded and walked back toward the cliff side.

"What about the others, sir?" a Zantie close beside the commander asked. "Would you like us to shoot them down?"

"No, the fact that they're still around implies they care whether this one lives or dies," he said, with a sharp nod in Mimie's direction. "I'd rather they be taken alive so I can question them." One of the Zanties holding her took out a knife and pressed it against her throat. The sharp edge dig painfully into her skin.

"Alright you two, if you don't want to see your little friend bleed out in front of you, I suggest you land," the commander yelled up at them.

Mimie opened her eyes and saw Oviet disappear over the landmass. Her heart fell. The Zantie leader frowned and searched the skies, waiting for them to reappear. He didn't have to wait long; Oviet swooped down to the canyon floor and landed twenty yards away from the Zanties. Koren slid off her back and raised his hands above his head in surrender.

"Good choice, but when I tell you to do something, I expect it done immediately."

The Zantie holding the knife to Mimie's throat tightened his grip on her and slashed the blade across her left arm, just above her Guardian's mark. She screamed in pain and fought to shove the

Zantie off of her, but he was too strong. Her vision blurred with tears, and her arm throbbed painfully. Blood flowed from the open wound, down her sleeve, and dripped from her fingertips. The commander leered at Koren, waiting for his response. Koren narrowed his eyes but remained silent. If the commander scared him, he hid it well. Mimie was feeling light headed from pain and loss of blood. She swayed unsteadily and the Zantie allowed her to crumple to the ground.

"Search them, make sure they aren't hiding any weapons," the commander barked. "I want them questioned and a full report filed in two hours." He headed back toward the tunnels. As soon as he was gone Koren dropped to Mimie's side and looked her over in concern.

"Alright, you heard the boss. Move it!" one of the Zanties snarled. Mimie saw Koren glare at him, but he bit back his retort. He scooped her into his arms and followed the Zanties as they led them toward the red cliffs. Mimie hid her face against Koren's chest and clung to his shirt like it was a lifeline.

"Don't worry, I won't let anything happen to you," Koren promised in a voice so quiet only she could hear it.

The blood was still flowing down her arm. She applied pressure to it with her hand, and that seemed to help, but the blood drying on her fingers made them feel sticky. She desperately wanted to wash it off but pushed the discomfort to the back of her mind. They had bigger problems at the moment.

They were taken to the top of the plateau through a natural opening in the rock and stopped in front of a holding cell. Mimie heard the scraping of a key in an old lock and the squeak of the door as it opened. Koren walked inside, and Oviet followed after him, the soft clip-clop sound of her hooves echoing through the chamber. The Zantie slammed the door behind them and locked them in. Mimie waited to hear him gloat about what the Zanties were going to do to them, but he said nothing. He turned away indifferently and disappeared into the tunnel that led to the top of the plateau. His indifference was almost more frightening than anything he could have said to them.

When he was gone, Mimie realized she was holding her breath and exhaled loudly.

"Set her down. I can heal her arm," Oviet muttered around something in her mouth. Mimie felt herself being lowered to the ground and had to make a conscious effort to force herself to let go of Koren's shirt.

"Sorry I got blood on you."

"Don't worry about it." He stepped back to give Oviet more room. It was intimidating to have Oviet's horn so close to her face, but when the point touched the wound the relief was instantaneous.

"Thank you," Mimie said gratefully. "I don't suppose there's anything you can do for my shirt?" Oviet snorted in amusement and dropped what she was holding in Koren's palm.

"Sorry, you'll need a wash bucket and an old-fashioned needle and thread for that," she replied. Koren put the small object he was holding on the ground and Mimie recognized it as the space cube. He expanded it and pulled out two of his knives from among the weapons he had stashed in there.

"That's brilliant!" Mimie whispered. Koren smiled and hid the knives in his belt.

"It was Oviet's idea." He returned the cube to his pocket. Mimie listened to the sound of approaching footsteps and hid behind Oviet as two Zanties appeared and unlocked the door.

"Fairy!" One of them snarled. "Let's go, we have a schedule to keep." Mimie didn't move. The Zantie pulled out a thick wooden club, and walked toward her threateningly. The other Zantie stood in front of the bars with his hand on the handle of his sword. Mimie looked back and forth between Koren and Oviet, waiting for them to do something, but they averted their eyes. The Zantie ignored them and let down his guard. That must have been what Koren was waiting for. With a flash of silver, his knife lodged itself in the neck of the Zantie in front of her, and the chest of the Zantie by the bars. The club dropped to the floor with a loud clatter and the Zantie's hand fumbled around his throat. Mimie backed against the wall and shuttered as the Zantie collapsed at her feet. She edged around the body, feeling sick.

"Let's go. We don't have much time," Koren muttered. "Stay close."

"No problem," Mimie replied, shaking. He pulled out the space cube, expanded it again, and removed the rest of his weapons. He strapped the sword to his waist and swung the arrow quiver over his shoulder. He held his bow in his right hand and shrunk the cube down once more.

"Ok, we have two options," Koren muttered. "We could go to the top of the plateau and take off from there, or we could fight our way back out into the canyon."

"There might be more guards on the top, but we can also get out of range of their archers faster," Oviet suggested.

"That's true," Koren reasoned. "Ok, let's go then. We have to do this fast, if they catch us again, they'll kill us on the spot."

"That's comforting," Mimie replied.

"Sorry, I'm just being realistic." He removed his knives from the dead Zanties and handed one to Mimie. She held it away from her in disgust.

"What am I going to do with this!"

"It's a weapon, when someone tries to grab you, you stab them with it." Koren pulled an arrow from his quiver. He hugged close to the wall and inched forward, holding his bow ready in case a Zantie turned up. They saw light up ahead, but it was flickering with how many people were walking across the opening. As they got closer Mimie clutched the knife handle and held it close to her side, knuckles white. She stayed close to Oviet and felt her muzzle brushing against the back of her shoulder. She heard the crunch of the Zanties footsteps on the loose rock outside the tunnel and tried to keep her breathing in check. Her heart was racing, her pulse pounding in her ears.

"The prisoners have escaped!" She heard a Zantie yell and let out a squeak. Koren released his arrow and quickly pulled another from his quiver. Oviet pushed past her and opened her wings threateningly. Mimie had to run to keep up with her as she shoved her way through the Zanties and out the tunnel opening. Koren took out Zantie after Zantie with his bow, and Oviet kept them at bay with her slashing horn.

The entire southern end of the plateau was covered with long white tents. At the head of the plateau there was a huge dam holding back a wall of water; if Oviet had gone another hundred feet, they would have run straight into it. The water drifted to the left and disappeared along its new course carrying sinister looking boats that were loaded with armory materials.

Mimie held the knife out at an awkward angle in front of her, using it more as a shield than a weapon as she clung to Oviet's flank. She felt a sharp tug on her left arm as one of the Zanties ripped her from Oviet's side. The jarring motion knocked the knife out of her hand and it clattered to the ground beside her. Oviet tattooed the Zantie with a solid kick to the chest. As he stumbled backward, his fingers caught the tear in the fabric of Mimie's shirt, doubling its size and exposing her Guardian's mark. She rushed to cover it with her hand, but it was too late, a Zantie had already seen it.

"They cannot be allowed to escape! The girl is the Key Guardian!" the Zantie yelled. The commander rushed wild-eyed from his tent.

"A Key Guardian? Impossible! Orient killed them all years ago!"

"Get on my back!" Oviet yelled. Normally that was something Mimie had trouble with, but she swung on smoothly from all the adrenaline racing through her system. Koren jumped on behind her and clenched his legs against hers as Oviet broke into a gallop. Mimie tangled her fingers into Oviet's mane and hung on for dear life. Oviet knocked aside any Zantie that tried to get in their way, and charged toward the edge of the plateau. She gathered her feet under her as she approached the edge and used her strong back legs to propel them into the air.

"Shoot them down!" shrieked the Commander.

"Oviet head east!" Koren yelled. Something flashed on the edge of Mimie's vision. They weren't arrows; they looked more like small darts. Mimie snatched one out of the air as it whizzed past her arm and studied it. A clear liquid floated around inside a little flask with a needle attached to it. "NEUROTOXIN, FLAMMABLE!" was written on the side in dark ink under a small warning symbol. She looked toward the river the Zanties had redirected and saw a steam-powered ship with crates full of weapons and dynamite passing close by the stone barrier.

"Oviet! Turn around, fly over the dam," Mimie yelled.

"Are you crazy?" Koren yelled back, "no way!"

"Trust me!" Mimie said firmly. "Oviet turn around!" She grunted from the effort of whipping herself around and sped toward the dam without question. Mimie waited until a ship passed close by the stone barrier and handed the dart to Koren, trusting his aim more than her own. He realized her intentions and a wicked grin spread across his face as he threw the dart into the ship's smoke stack.

Oviet flapped wildly to get them out of range, soaring high above the river. The ship was the size of a large pebble below them when a thunderous bang split the air and a bright flash of light temporarily disrupted her vision. The sounds around her were muffled as she covered her face to protect herself from the scalding heat and the debris cascading in all directions. A small piece of metal grazed her arm, but she otherwise escaped unscathed. Mimie peered down to survey the damage and kept a careful grip on Oviet's mane to ensure she wouldn't fall.

Cracks fanned out from the damaged portion of the stone structure, spewing streams of water onto the parched riverbed. The cracks grew larger until the entire structure gave way. The liquid wall crashed into the canyon with enough power to sweep away the crumbled portions of the dam as though they were driftwood. The remaining ships were sucked into the riptide and smashed to pieces.

The Zantie camp was in chaos. From the high vantage point, they resembled a swarm of ants surging from an ant hole. Mimie couldn't revel in the victory long, Koren rubbed at an angry red welt on his arm. He'd been hit by one of the darts.

"It's just a little sting, nothing to worry about," he assured her, but didn't meet her gaze.

"That was a neurotoxin they hit you with. You are most definitely not ok."

"The dwarfs have medicines that can treat the toxin if we get there soon enough," Koren said. His movements were becoming jerky and random as he lost control over his limbs.

"Here, climb in front of me," Mimie said, carefully edging behind him. She could support him better that way.

"Don't you dare let me fall off," he threatened. The words were barely understandable without the use of his tongue, which had become paralyzed.

"I won't," Mimie assured him. "I hope you know where we are going," Mimie said to Oviet.

"I do," she replied. "I think we can get out of this canyon by nightfall."

"How much time do we have until the toxin shuts down his lungs?"

"He probably won't make it until morning at the rate it's spreading."

"We better hurry then." Oviet picked up her pace and cautiously stayed out of range of the darts in case the other base camps tried to ambush them. Mimie searched the place where the blue of the sky met the red of the canyon and willed anything to appear there to show that they were nearing the canyon's end. When the sky turned the same blood red as the canyon, she finally saw something.

"Oviet, are those…mountains?"

An enormous stone arch stood proudly in front of them as they neared the end of the canyon. It made Oviet look like a speck of dust as she soared through it. Beyond the red rock, the ground crumbled away into a quiet valley shrouded in mist. The valley rose up at the far end and swelled into massive peaks.

Oviet drifted toward the valley floor, her legs shaking as they touched down on the thick grass. Her wings drooped at her sides, and her back was slick with sweat. Oviet trudged to the side of a small pond and sank to the ground under the protection of the scruffy trees. Mimie stepped off her back and pulled Koren off as well. He grunted, but she couldn't understand anything he was saying.

The cover of darkness and the mist concealing the red canyon from view did nothing to placate Mimie's nerves. Anything could be lurking out there. She wrapped Koren's cloak securely around him, and Oviet curled her wing across his back to help keep him warm. Mimie took a long drink from the pond and cleaned the blood off her arm. She felt the spot where the knife had slashed open her skin, but a small line of raised skin was the only trace of it she could find. She splashed some of the water on her face, hoping the cold sting would help make her more alert. She wiped her eyes on her arm and crawled toward Koren. She placed her fingers on the side of his neck, and could barely feel a pulse. She desperately wanted to save him, even if she had to drag him up the mountain herself.

The mist was thicker now. Mimie couldn't see more than a hundred feet in any direction.

Something fell on her back from the tree above her and knocked her to the ground. She screamed and threw it off in alarm. When she turned to face the creature, she found to her intense relief that it was a dwarf.

CHAPTER 9: ORIENT'S MANOR

A young servant girl hurried up the spiral staircase of the west tower. Torches lit her path, and the menacing light did nothing to help her panicked mood. In her small hand, she clutched a thin letter stamped "urgent", which was addressed to Orient. This was the first time she had ever been to this side of the castle. Orient hardly left his study, and almost no one had ever seen him face to face. The girl was not looking forward to the encounter. Orient was expecting her, and he did not like to be left waiting. The girl reached the top of the stairs and stood facing a wide oak door. She took a few deep breaths to stop her loud panting. She approached the door and knocked softly. She trembled as she took a small half step back.

"Enter," growled a deep voice from within.

The girl carefully pulled the door open as wide as she dared and slipped inside. She winced as the hinges squeaked shut behind her. A large leather-backed chair faced away from her toward a warm fireplace. Flickering shadows danced dimly across the walls. Keeping her eyes on the floor, she approached the side of the chair and held the letter out to Orient. He snatched it from her hand and snapped, "Did you decide to stop in the kitchens on your way up here, useless girl!" The servant whimpered and took a step back, avoiding his piercing brown eyes. He examined the letter with a grunt and then shoved it back at her. "Read it," he commanded. The girl was so flustered she nearly dropped the letter, but after a few seconds she managed to get it open and read:

Orient,

With the greatest respect, I regret to inform you that I have found another Guardian. She looks to be about eighteen and is traveling with an elf and a flying unicorn. She is headed for the black mountains, which I'm sure you know is too vast and dangerous for us to post troops inside. I have called for a perimeter to be made on the far side of the mountains, but we have no guarantee of recapturing the Guardian. We believe she might be a hazard to your leadership. How would you like us to proceed? I hope you are well.

Sincerely,

Commander Bruce Warmpue

The girl dared to snatch a glance at Orient's face. He didn't look angry, as she feared, he merely thoughtful. He was stroking his short, dark beard while he stared at the fire. "I can't believe I missed something so obvious," he chuckled to himself, "of course the wench's daughter survived."

He turned his head and addressed the servant girl cowering next to him. "Have someone write a letter back that says, I want her brought to me alive and unharmed, I don't care what you do with her friends. Use any force required. Tell the good commander he is fired and my son Richard will be taking over the Zantie armies from now on. Go and fetch him for me, I have a task for him."

"Yes sir," the girl said with a bow and hurried toward the door, but she stopped with her hand on the door handle. "There is one more thing…"

"What is it?" asked Orient with a scowl.

"Nickolas has run away again." The girl braced herself against his anger and cringed into the door.

"How did he get out of his room!" Orient shouted. "I locked him in and placed five guards outside the door!"

"He tied his sheets and clothes together to make a rope and climbed out his window," the servant girl replied.

"That darn window, of course," Orient growled. "It appears that the boy cannot be reasoned with. I am sick of wasting valuable resources tracking him down. Send the guards after him, I want him hung for treason. He's too much like his mother, soft." He stopped talking and turned around in his chair to face the girl. "Are you still here!" he shouted. Startled, the girl ran out the door.

It broke her heart to transfer this message. Nickolas was a good man, he had come to see her before he left. She hoped against hope he would finally get away like he had been aspiring to do since he was a child. She would buy him time by sending the guards in the wrong direction, but that was the best she could do. She took the stairs slowly— anything to let him get further away.

***

Orient fumed in his high back chair. He hoped another servant would come through his door so he could have the pleasure of tossing them out his window. To calm himself he stroked the locket sitting on his chest. Fourteen years he'd been trying to figure out the locket's secrets. The answers were inside this new Guardian, he could feel it. She would open the locket for him, and after that he would be unstoppable. Nothing would ever stand in his way again. Even if he couldn't catch her, he had no doubt that she would eventually come to him. It was only a matter of time. He laughed a long, cruel laugh and sank deeper into his chair.

CHAPTER 10: THE DWARFS

⟨⟨⟨ ⟨⟨ ⟩⟩ ⟩⟩

The dwarf standing in front of her was a small, wild-looking man with tangled black hair that obscured most of his face. His weathered features and clothes seemed better suited to a rough stone carving than a small man. She knew it was rude to stare, but she couldn't help it.

"We have to go, now. Come with me, you'll be safe in the mountains," he said in a gruff voice.

"What were you doing up in that tree?"

"I patrol this area regularly, that tree is one of my rest stations. You must come now! The Zanties know you're here and they're closing in on your position."

"Right, sorry. Just a second," she said. Oviet had fallen into a light sleep but sprang to her feet as Mimie shook her awake.

"What, what's wrong?" she demanded through her disoriented stupor. "Where did he come from?"

"He fell out of a tree, but that's not important, kneel down so we can get Koren on your back." Oviet sank back to the ground uneasily. Mimie walked over to Koren and struggled to get her arms around his waist. She dragged him onto Oviet's back and the dwarf helped position him so that he was leaning against Mimie's chest. There wasn't much room left, but the dwarf squished on behind

Mimie and held onto Oviet's tail with one hand to help him keep his balance.

Oviet pinned her ears and ground her teeth as the dwarf shifted around. She wasn't pleased with the arrangement, but she kept her thoughts to herself. As she broke into a gallop Mimie struggled to hang on to Koren. She wasn't very good at keeping her balance when it was just her, let alone when she was holding another person, who was not only unconscious, but also weighed twice as much as she did. It was easier to hold onto him once they were in the air, but also more nerve racking. He was dead if she dropped him.

"I'm Bernin by the way," the dwarf said, pulling her from her worries.

"Mimie," she replied. "Where are you taking us?"

"I'm escorting you to Kirmikberg. There is a healing facility there and several other resources you may find useful."

"Thank you for helping us, I don't know what we would have done without you."

"No problem, helping wayward strangers escape the Zanties is my job," he replied. Oviet headed up the steep slope of the mountain range and flew around the rock outcroppings. The moonlight bathed the bare rocks in an ivory glow, which was just bright enough for them to see where they were going. They flew over deep valleys where the ground dropped off to hundreds of feet below them. The mountain air smelled of crisp pine trees, reminding her of home. Koren's condition was getting worse. He was pale, and his skin was cold to the touch. He didn't have much longer. She wasn't sure he'd make it to midnight let alone the morning. Oviet set her teeth in determination and forced herself to fly through her fatigue. She sensed Koren's worsening condition and pushed herself faster than Mimie had seen her fly at full strength. She tore through the air at reckless speeds, her chest heaving. This was a race against the clock, and the clock was winning.

"The mountain pass is on the right, between those two crumbling mountains," Bernin yelled. Oviet surged between the two eroded peaks. She turned into a narrow pass and did her best to stay clear of the shear walls. The pass led them to a large valley. Mimie looked down and saw fields of agriculture along with herds of strange looking animals in wooden pens. At the far end of the valley, there were two statues of dwarves, both hundreds of feet tall, carved into the rock. Their large battle-axes crossed one another to guard the entrance to a small opening in the mountain. There was just enough room for Oviet to land. Exhaustion made her clumsy and she nearly lost her footing as she landed.

"I'll run ahead and tell the healers you're coming," Bernin said and jumped off Oviet's back. "Follow the moonstones! The rest of the tunnels have traps in them to keep intruders out," he yelled as he sprinted down the passageway.

"Lovely," Mimie muttered. She shook a mental image of Oviet falling into a spike pit from her mind. Oviet coughed on the thick foam in her mouth and lowered her head to the floor, heat radiating from her body in dense waves.

"I need a minute," she gasped, trying to catch her breath. Mimie was feeling lightheaded herself, no doubt from all the blood she had lost earlier.

When she had recovered slightly, Oviet followed the trail of moonstones embedded in the ceiling. She started off at a slow walk but picked up the pace as she caught her breath.

It wasn't long before they saw light in the distance and were soon standing on the edge of a huge cliff. Mimie looked out into an enormous chamber lit by thousands of moonstones. It was roughly circular in shape with a massive column of stone rising through the center. Other caves dotted the walls, which were all connected by a stone outcropping or a ladder. Each cave was precisely aligned in a grid system so that the least amount of distance had to be crossed from one cave to another. Rope bridges crossed the open space and connected to the center pillar. A stone walkway had been carved in the central column and it spiraled from floor to ceiling.

Two female dwarfs hurried across the bridge in front of them carrying a stretcher. It swayed beneath them, but they didn't seem phased by it. Their clothes were dark tan and their granite colored hair was pulled back tightly into buns. Oviet got down onto her knees so Mimie could slide Koren off her back onto the stretcher. The dwarfs helped and then swiftly headed back across the bridge.

"Are we allowed to go with them?" Mimie asked.

"I'm not walking across those rickety planks of death. No way," Oviet replied, pinning her ears.

"You have wings! If you fall off just fly to the other side," Mimie countered. She wasn't overly excited about crossing the bridge either, but it was better than waiting here on the ledge.

"No," Oviet responded firmly.

"Fine, you can do what you want, but I'm going." Mimie stepped out onto the bridge and took care not to look down. She heard a grumpy murmur behind her and a creak as Oviet stepped out onto the wooden boards. Mimie glanced behind her and chuckled at how Oviet's legs were splayed out.

"This is stupid," she declared. "I'm just going to fly across. I have no interest in falling off this thing." She backed off the bridge and waited. Mimie hurried across to the center column to get out of her way and watched anxiously as she flew over. There was only a small amount of room for her to spread her wings, but she traveled across without much difficulty. She landed on a ledge next to a cave on the opposite side of the chamber. There was a large triangle carved into the entrance above it and two healers stationed outside. Mimie climbed up the spiral walkway until she reached the bridge leading to the cave. She crossed it quickly, anxious to be back with Koren. Oviet couldn't fit through the low entrance, but she promised to wait outside.

Mimie walked into the small passage and found herself in a rectangular room. Moonstones lining the ceiling and walls cast the room in a silvery light. A doorway covered with a sheet stood on her right, from which healers came and went, but Mimie had no idea what was inside. The two longer walls were lined with beds so small they looked as though they were made for children; the legs were also shortened and the frames nearly touched the floor. Koren was next to the back wall on one of the few large beds. She hurried over to where two healers were bending over him in concern and leaned against the wall.

"Excuse me," one of the healers said to Mimie. "We need you to bring his organ functions back to normal, it's the only way we can neutralize the toxin."

"What?" Mimie said in confusion. "I'm not doing anything to his organs. Is he going to be ok?"

"We don't know yet. The patient's metabolism has slowed to almost nothing. We won't know how much damage was suffered until his metabolism returns to normal and the antidote is allowed to spread through his system."

"So what do you suggest?" Mimie muttered, fearing she already knew the answer.

"Stop influencing him."

"I can't," Mimie told her. "I don't even know what I'm doing." She closed her eyes and tried to find the source of the magic. It was hard to find and even harder to stop. Koren twitched as the toxin spread through him like a flame licking across a piece of paper. The veins in his neck bulged, his eyes flew open and his breathing increased until his chest was heaving. He tried to say something, but all that came out was a strangled moan.

"What's happening to him? Do something!" Mimie yelled. A healer approached with a needle and stabbed it into his neck. Koren relaxed and sank back into unconsciousness as the medicine washed over him.

"After sustained neurosuppression, the nerves in the body become hypersensitive and can cause painful sensations throughout the body, all we can do now is wait. Elves are severely allergic to neurotoxins; permanent brain damage can occur in only a few hours. I don't know what kind of condition he'll be in when he wakes up again, but hopefully you slowed his immune response and metabolism down enough to prevent any significant harm."

The healers left them alone and pulled a curtain around Koren's bed to give them some privacy. Mimie hesitantly put her hand on his arm. The warmth of his skin felt good on her cold palm. She pulled on the threads coming from the rip in her sleeve and tried to ignore the stiffness the blood created in the fabric. Her anxiety battled with her exhaustion as she pulled a chair beside Koren's bed and sank into it. She tried to keep her gaze fixed on the opposite wall, but her eyes always seemed to wander back to his face. She willed his eyes to open, for him to say something sarcastic. At least then she'd know he was all right and that her friend was still in there somewhere. She nodded off into a light sleep, her chin resting on her palm. As soon as Koren showed signs of stirring she jerked awake.

"Welcome back to the living," Mimie yawned. Koren half opened his eyes, and his mouth twitched into a smile.

"Have I been out for a while?" he asked in a low voice. He rubbed the place on his arm where the dart had hit him. "My arm still burns." He looked around in confusion. "Where am I?" He tried to sit up, but his arms wouldn't support him.

"I forget what name they called the mountain, but you're in a dwarf infirmary."

"Ah, I see," he croaked. "Thanks for staying with me."

"No problem."

"Can I have something to drink? I'm so thirsty," he coughed. Mimie told one of the healers and she returned a few minutes later with two cups of mint tea.

"Thank you," Koren said and drained the cup in a few gulps. Mimie gave him hers and he quickly emptied that one as well. He wiped his mouth on his arm and watched as another healer approached him with a long strip of cloth and a bowl. She sat down next to him and dipped the end of the material in the water.

"This might hurt a little," she warned, and dabbed the cloth on the angry red skin around the place where the dart had hit him. Koren winced and looked away from her.

"You should examine her as well," Koren told the healer. "She fell back in the canyon and might have some injuries she's not owning up to."

"I'm all right," Mimie assured him.

"She's a bad liar," Koren said. He winced as the healer wrapped the cloth around his arm.

"Rest. You have been through a lot," the healer told him and turned her attention to Mimie. "What did you land on?" she asked.

"My side, the ground was soft though. I have a few bruises, that's all."

"You should get some rest; you look like the walking dead," Koren told her.

"Use this bed here, I'll see to it that no one disturbs you," the healer added. Mimie looked back and forth between them and felt her stubbornness crumble. She kicked off her shoes and climbed into the bed next to Koren's. Her ankles hung off the end of it so she curled up on her side, fatigue weighing on her. Now that she knew Koren was ok it was easy to close her eyes and sank deep into the comfortable warmth.

After what felt like a few minutes later, Mimie felt a poke in her side.

"Go away," she groaned and rolled tighter into her blanket.

"Come on Mimie, if I have to get out of bed so do you." Mimie glared at him, but couldn't hold the expression for long. He was wearing a hilarious floor length, peach nightdress.

"They took my clothes," Koren grumbled. "I wouldn't look so smug, they took yours too." Mimie threw off her blanket and found that she was wearing a nightdress as well. "The healers said they wanted to wash them. As soon as they bring them back we can head off to the library," Koren said, walking back to his bed and sitting down.

"I can't believe I slept through that." Mimie shook her head and shuddered. "If we just have to sit here why did you wake me up?" she demanded and pulled the blanket over her head.

"I was bored," he explained. Mimie muttered something unintelligible.

Someone walked through the curtain, and Mimie shook off the blanket. She was relieved to see one of the healers walk out holding their freshly washed clothes. Koren took the pile from her and sifted through them, handing Mimie hers. He started to pull off the nightgown but noticed Mimie was still standing there.

"Don't look," he snapped and pulled the curtain closed that separated their two beds. Mimie laughed and pulled off her own nightdress.

"I wasn't!" she yelled through the curtain.

"Liar!" he yelled back, and she just laughed. She pulled the nightdress over her head and put on her regular clothes. Mimie checked her upper arm and found that they had even stitched the shirt back together for her. She was amazed at how kind and generous they were.

The healers looked Koren over and diagnosed him with a clean bill of health. Mimie was relieved to be out of there, she hated the sterile smell and the oppressive feeling of sickness that hung over the place. Plus, they had needles in there; she hated needles. Oviet was snoring loudly by the entrance but jerked awake at the sound of their footsteps.

"Hey guys," she yawned. "Good to see the color back in your face Koren. Bernin left a get well present here for you." She nudged two moonstones lying on the ground with her hoof.

"That was kind of him," Mimie said and reached down to pick up the stones. She tucked them into her pocket and searched for a cave that might be a library.

"The healers said it was a few levels up," Oviet told her, guessing from her expression what she was looking for.

Mimie headed for the rope ladders that led to the upper ledges. Oviet carefully flew up there and waited for them to join her. Mimie wrapped her fingers around the wooden rungs and started climbing. The ladder swung unsteadily back and forth; Mimie peeked over her shoulder and gulped. The cave floor was a hundred feet down. Her fingers clammed with sweat and an odd weakness entered her arms.

"You doing ok?" Koren called from below her, he seemed unaffected by the height.

"Fine," she grunted, trying to pull herself together. She kept climbing and used Oviet's leg to steady herself as she climbed onto the ledge. "I hope they don't let children climb around on those death traps," she grumbled.

A dwarf emerged from the cave entrance holding a book. He nearly dropped it in surprise when he noticed them standing there.

"Are you the librarian?" Koren asked.

"No, that's Rowghen."

"Is he in right now?"

"Yes, but he's in a bad temper. I mean he's never been the friendliest of sorts, but it's been appalling lately. I think a few screws have come loose in his old age."

"Thanks for the heads up." Mimie didn't do well with abrasive people so this was not an encounter she was looking forward to. She let Koren lead the way and followed him into the passageway. It wasn't long until they emerged inside a vast chamber filled ceiling to floor with books. The complete silence in the room seemed to press in on her. "Hello?" she called. The sound echoed off the walls as she waited for a reply.

"What do you want?" a gruff voice behind a bookshelf snapped.

"Are you Rowghen?" Mimie asked.

"Who else would I be dim-witted tinkler?" The small man appeared from behind the shelf and glared at them. "Get that half breed abomination out of here before it dirties my floor." Oviet pinned her ears and pawed at the stone angrily.

"Don't," Mimie muttered as Oviet took a threatening step forward.

"I hope you have a good reason for interrupting my valuable study time," the dwarf growled, picking a book off the ground and gently placing it back on a shelf.

"You should show more respect toward the Key Guardian," Koren said. The dwarf froze and looked at them like he was seeing them for the first time. "Guardian you say, interesting, interesting. Quick, come with me," he hissed. "I have been waiting for you." He put a finger to his lips and led them deeper into the library. Mimie and Koren exchanged raised eyebrows and followed him. He walked through a maze of shelves and suddenly stopped in the middle of a walkway and pulled a book from the bottom of a small stack.

"Why are we hiding?" Oviet asked the dwarf irritably.

"Shush half breed, they'll hear you!" snapped the dwarf.

"Who?" Koren asked, looking around as if he expected someone to emerge from behind a bookshelf.

"The shadows," Rowghen whispered with wide eyes. "They're always watching, always."

"If you say so," Koren said to humor him. Rowghen flipped the dusty book open to a place with a tattered piece of fabric marking the page, revealing a map. He pointed to the center of a mountain range and said,

"You are here. This is where the fairies are." He pointed across the page to a blank spot in the corner labeled Death Valley. This mountain used to be an essential teaching facility, but all the fairies have gone now, even the ones that were supposed to take new arrivals to Death Valley. You'll have to make the journey on your own." Koren peered over the book and traced the course of the river with his finger.

"If we follow the river it should take us right there. That sounds easy enough."

"Why is Death Valley blank?" Mimie wondered.

"No one that goes there to map it ever comes back. The shadows take them away." Mimie glanced at the hand drawn scribbles on the page and tried to make sense of them. The dwarf shut the book and replaced it gently on the shelf. "I trust you lot are capable of finding the exit on your own? I'd rather you not linger, it's loud enough in here without your extra jibber jabber." Mimie looked at Koren, who shrugged. The dwarf was a nut case, should they really trust his instructions? She'd have to; finding the fairies was the only way she could become powerful enough to defeat Orient. They walked back out onto the ledge and hesitated before crossing.

"Would you like to go first?" Mimie offered.

Oviet spread her wings and glided to the exit platform. Mimie and Koren crossed a bridge to the center column, walked down the winding path and across another bridge. Mimie was happy when she was standing on solid rock again. She was ready to leave this world of perpetual night and see the sun again. They followed the moonstones and climbed onto Oviet's back when they saw sunlight streaming in up ahead.

Mimie allowed the fresh air to fill her lungs and held on tightly as Oviet leaped into the sky.

CHAPTER 11: THE GRASSY HILLS

⇐–⇐–⇒–⇒

That night they made camp in a small valley and left early the next morning. It was hard for Mimie to imagine life in the rocky slopes. She'd yet to see anything bigger than a bird and even those were few and far between. It was a relief when the jagged cliffs fell away and the tops of pine trees spread out beneath them. The change was so complete it made her feel disoriented.

"Oviet! Do we want to be out in the open like this with Zanties so close by?" Koren yelled over the wind.

"Probably not," she replied. "This forest doesn't seem to be too large, we should continue the rest of the way on foot, at least until we find a way around the Zanties." They searched for a clearing. Oviet spotted a small gap in the trees and swooped lower. She didn't realize until it was too late that a smaller tree occupied the space they were trying to land in. The other trees reached out to snare them, and soon they were hopelessly tangled in a clump of branches twenty feet off the ground.

"Great. Now what?" Oviet growled as she tried to pull her legs free of the thick branches. Mimie examined their situation and decided they were going to have to cut some of the branches. When she voiced this idea out loud, Koren stared at her in disbelief.

"Or we could just ask them nicely to move."

"I suppose that would be the more diplomatic approach," she consented. He climbed down to the ground and tapped on the tree's trunk. An angry rustling filled the air, and the branches groaned in protest under Oviet's weight. Koren said something in a firm tone she couldn't hear, and the branches started to shift. Mimie gripped Oviet's mane for dear life and hoped that the tree wouldn't dump them on the ground. The tree released them roughly, and then returned to its original shape.

"Come on. Let's go before she changes her mind about smashing us," Koren muttered and led the way through the thick trees.

They stopped around dusk and made camp in a circle of thick bushes.

"Do we have any food left? I'm starving," Mimie muttered.

"No, we finished it off yesterday. You could look for some mushrooms and pine nuts, I bet there's a lot of them around here."

"Are there any animals we could hunt?"

"Yeah, but we don't have a way to cook them. We can't risk building a fire, the Zanties might see it."

"Fine, but I hate mushrooms," she grumbled. She grabbed one of the moonstones and gathered together some cones that were lying on the ground, then picked mushrooms off rotting logs. The smell of pine was stronger here than she remembered it being back home. It hung thick in the air like burning incense. She returned when her arms were full and dropped her load in front of Koren. He inspected the mushrooms to make sure she hadn't grabbed any poisonous ones and looked through the cones with a frown.

"The squirrels have gotten to these. We'd be better off with unopened ones that are still on the tree, but there might still be a few seeds left, if we're lucky."

Oviet looked up from the grass she was grazing on, "Too bad you guys can't eat grass. There's plenty of that around."

Mimie pulled the cones back toward her to extract what few seeds were left. Koren helped her, finishing two cones by the time she had finished with one. After what seemed like an absurdly long time, she tossed the last cone aside and stretched out her sore back. Koren ate a few of the mushrooms and looked at the seeds, but made no motion to reach for any.

"Do you want some?" Mimie asked.

"You have them."

"Are you sure?"

"Yeah, you need the protein more than I do. I know you don't like them, but you should eat some of the mushrooms too. They'll boost your immune system."

"Blah," Mimie muttered as he handed her one. She nibbled at it and gagged. "It tastes like that log it was growing on," she complained. Koren pulled out the sleeping sacks from the space cube and handed Mimie hers. He pulled his a little ways away and curled up on it. Mimie unwound hers from the crumpled ball it was in and laid the wrinkled fabric down on some pine needles. She crawled inside and munched on the pine seeds. She squinted through the tree canopy and stared at what little she could see of the stars. She turned her head to look at Koren, his eyes were closed, but she didn't think he was asleep yet.

The hair on the back of her neck prickled uncomfortably. She scanned the trees around her, but it was too dark to see much.

"Koren?"

"Go to sleep," he mumbled quietly.

"I think something's watching us."

"You're imagining it." Mimie fell silent and strained to hear in the near total darkness. It was too quiet; the crickets had stopped chirping. Something moved in the bushes to her right. She was able to make out a shadowed figure.

Something flashed in the starlight and hit the form in the chest. Mimie looked over to see Koren wide-awake holding a knife and reaching for his bow. Oviet lifted her head, but Mimie cautioned her to stay down. The figure crumpled and all was silent again.

"That was a scout." Koren put away his weapons. "There could be more of them out there. We should take the night in shifts."

"I'll start," Mimie volunteered. She was too on edge to sleep anyway. Koren nodded and disappeared back into his sleeping sack.

Mimie set the moonstones down on either side of her for light and grabbed a clump of pine needles. She pulled them off the central stalk one by one and broke the dry leaves into smaller sections. Her movements were automatic, secondary; her mind was somewhere else.

She stood up and paced back and forth as she wondered what Gram and Zarin were doing. She wasn't sure what the time difference was, but she imagined that they were only a few hours behind. Maybe the sun had just set. Gram would be finishing dinner with a friend. Zarin was probably in his room tinkering around with something he'd made in the blacksmith's shop that day. How long had it been now? A week? She was losing track of the days. Koren and Oviet already felt like family, and she felt more at home with them than she ever had back at the village. Oviet was like a sister to her. Koren was the best friend she was in love with. It didn't matter that he would probably never return her feelings. She continued to hope he might see something in her worth loving; even if she couldn't find that part herself.

She lifted up her sleeve and glanced at the yellowing bruise on her wrist. She was damaged goods. He deserved better, shame welled up in her throat like bile.

Suddenly the moonstones seemed too bright. She stuffed them in her pocket. The crickets were too loud, much too loud, like they were screaming in her ear. Why couldn't they just be quiet for a second? Her breathing increased until she was hyperventilating. The tips of her fingers tingled, and she shook violently. An intense bolt of fear made her want to run, but she couldn't move. She was either going to faint or die, she wasn't sure which.

Koren heard her strangled gasps and sat up.

"Mimie?" he called in alarm. Please don't let him see me like this, Mimie quietly begged any deity that would listen. He knelt beside her.

"What's happening to me?" she choked out.

"You're having a panic attack. What you feel is scary, but it's not dangerous. It will pass in a few minutes." He took a deep breath and slowly let it out. She tried to copy him and gradually calmed down.

"Is this the first time it's happened to you?"

"Yeah," she avoided his gaze. "I'm not going crazy am I?"

"No."

"You seem like you have a lot of experience with this." Mimie wiped the sweat from her forehead and pushed her bangs out of her eyes.

"I had a few while I was living with the beavers. The first time it happened they rushed me to a healer, but I was fine again before we got there. It was embarrassing."

"What triggered them?"

"I've lost a lot of people that I cared about deeply, I would think about something happening to the beavers and this irrational grief would wash over me." Mimie pulled her sleeve back and showed him the bruise on her wrist. She watched him match his fingers to the pattern with a frown.

"Did someone hurt you?"

"I keep telling myself that if I bury the memories deep enough they'll go away, but it hasn't worked so well." She wiped a tear out from the corner of her eye and hid her face in her hair. Koren leaned his back against a tree and pulled her into a tight hug.

"Before I met the beavers I spent a few years as a slave in a human village. My original owner died, and I was left to her daughter. She stabbed me in the leg one time with a fork because I didn't finish the dishes fast enough."

He touched the healing cut on Mimie's lip with the tip of his finger. She held her back rigid, reminding herself that Koren was her friend and she trusted him. He let his hand fall.

"Did he rape you?" The question sent a surge of heat through Mimie's cheeks. She pulled out of his arms and felt the breathlessness returning.

Koren's green eyes were fierce. "He's lucky there's a wall between us or I'd kill him now, tonight."

Mimie felt a smile twitch in the corner of her mouth. "Go back to sleep. It doesn't make any sense for both of us to stay up."

"You sure you're alright?"

"Yeah."

"Goodnight then." He walked back to his sleeping sack. Mimie continued her watch for a few more hours, and then woke Oviet. Relieved of her duties, Mimie gratefully collapsed onto the soft material of her sleeping sack.

Koren shook her awake the next morning a little before dawn. Mimie ate a small handful of pine nuts for breakfast and helped him pack up camp.

Mimie took in the dark green pine needles as they made their way through the forest and watched the tops of the trees sway in the light breeze. The clouds were painted red and orange as the sun rose, and the stars slowly winked out of view. The birds swooped from one branch to another, twittering as they went about their morning routine. The forest felt alive with energy, everywhere she turned something moved, ran, or scurried.

Mimie walked behind Koren and watched the breeze tousle his hair. His arm swayed gently at his side and she noticed the way his relaxed fingers curled ever so slightly into his palm. She imagined how warm his fingers would feel against hers if she allowed them to touch. Feeling guilty, she moved to stand beside him where she could better behave herself.

There was a break in the trees ahead. Koren slowed down and peeked out between two bushes. Mimie caught glimpses of the river and an odd shimmering in the air.

"The Zanties set up an energy field, we'll have to go around it."

"Why don't we just fly over?" Oviet said.

"I don't know how far up it goes, and if we underestimate it'll fry us." Koren turned around and headed back into the trees. Mimie glanced around and the glint of metal caught her eye. She walked closer to investigate and found a hole dug in the ground with metal bars covering it.

"I'd leave that alone if I were you. It's an old prison shaft used by the Zanties. There must have been a base here at one time."

"I think it's worth poking around inside, we might be able to use it

127

to get under the energy barrier."

"I doubt that, unless they somehow tunneled through the river," Oviet laughed.

A flash of insight lit up Koren's face. He examined the structure more carefully. "I think I've seen something like this before. The human I was enslaved to lived in a military town. The Zanties kept holding cells underground for the prisoners. When the prisons were full, the Zanties flooded them as a quick way to kill everyone. There was a passageway that led to the river so the Zantie who flooded the tunnel could escape. If this one is built the same we could use it to get under the energy field."

Mimie helped Koren heave the heavy metal bars away from the opening. She paused in front of the dark tunnel and held the moonstones in front of her for light. Thick wooden beams supported the ceiling and walls to prevent cave-ins. The metal torches mounted to the beams had long since burned out.

Oviet shuddered. "I don't like this."

Mimie handed Koren one of the moonstones and held the other out in front of her for light. The tunnel was cool and had a thick earthy scent. Mangled tree roots poked out from the walls here and there, holding a sickening resemblance to dismembered limbs. Mimie rubbed at her arms to get rid of the goosebumps and swallowed her unease. The musky air grew thicker as they worked their way down the steep path.

She saw a light flickering ahead of her in the darkness and stared at it curiously. "I wonder why that torch didn't burn out?"

Koren pulled out his bow and got an arrow ready. "Hide the moonstones."

Before Mimie could react the flickering light ahead disappeared and they heard a loud bell ring out.

"Crap," Koren hissed. He broke into a run and vanished in the darkness. Panic flooded through Mimie and she considered calling out to him. A moment later she heard a brief struggle and the muffled thump of a body hitting the ground. She held the moonstone out in front of her and inched forward. Her chest tightened when she caught sight of Koren standing over a man wearing a dull blue uniform. Koren motioned them to follow him and ducked into a side passageway. The path sloped upwards in a climb that left her feeling breathless. She heard shouting and saw an orange light growing brighter behind her.

They ran into a small chamber and splashed through a deep puddle to the far wall. Mimie held up the moonstones and discovered a large metal gate. Next to it was a thick wheel heavily rusted from the constant moisture in the room. Koren struggled to turn it. The gate groaned as it rose out of the water. Mimie ducked under it and found another gate a few paces behind it. Oviet dropped her head and joined her in the small space between the two gates as Koren lowered the door again.

"Tell me when it's a foot from the bottom," he called.

Once the door was back in the water, Mimie called out, "Ok!"

Koren squeezed through the gap. He wiped the moisture out of his eyes and walked toward the second wheel mounted on the wall next to them. Mimie heard loud voices as the Zanties swarmed into the chamber.

"Take a deep breath," Koren advised. Mimie reached up and felt her fingertips brush the slimy mud that made up the ceiling. We're all going to drown, she thought dully.

She took several deep breaths and let them out through her teeth. Koren opened the gate a few inches, allowing water to rush in. It climbed up her legs, and she felt panicky as it lapped at her waist and continued to rise. When the water level was up to her neck Koren cranked the wheel hard.

Mimie sucked in a deep breath and ducked under the second door into the cold gloom beyond. She kicked off the walls and used both hands to claw her way forward. Her clothes dragged at her, slowing her down. Every once and awhile her back would scrape against the muddy ceiling, reminding her that she had no air. This knowledge added to the fire mounting in her lungs. Panic gripped her in an arm of steel as the lonely darkness continued endlessly in front of her.

She was in agony, her chest felt like it was caving in. Weakly, she dug her fingers into the muddy wall just to keep moving, but she was fading fast. Finally, her desperate hands pulled her out the opening and into the river. She kicked in the direction she hoped was up, but the surface was still so far away. She watched the last of her air supply rise to the surface and drifted downward.

A cold wave brushed across her face as Koren latched onto her wrist and pulled her upward. A cool breeze stung her cheek and she gasped for air. She clung to Koren as they bobbed in the current. Once he caught his breath he swam toward the bank. She crawled on hands and knees onto the rough pebbles and hung her head in exhaustion.

"Thanks."

Koren coughed and wiped his mouth on his arm. "No problem."

Mimie glanced behind her and saw the energy barrier shimmering behind her. "We did it!"

"Let's go further downstream," Oviet suggested. "The Zanties are still looking for us."

"Good idea." Koren scooped Mimie off the ground.

"I can walk," she protested.

"I know," he said and set her up on Oviet's back, "but we can travel faster this way." He swung on behind her. Mimie held on as Oviet broke into a run. They worked their way through the tall grass along the river. Pebbles crunched quietly under hoof.

Mimie glanced behind her an hour later. The energy barrier was gone, taken down most likely so the Zanties could pursue them. Oviet noticed the change as well and worked her way deeper into the grass. She must have remembered the steam ships as clearly as Mimie did.

Her sudden clothes felt muggy against her skin in the heat; the unpleasant feeling negated any cooling effects the light breezes offered. Koren waved his hand back and forth to try and disperse the cloud of gnats that had settled around his face, but they refused to leave him alone. Mimie knew she was being paranoid by maintaining a constant visual on their surroundings, but she wanted advanced warning if their Zantie pursuers caught up with them. Her shoulders hurt from the tension she was carrying in them. She patted Oviet's neck and stroked her soft fur; it made her feel better.

They rested during the hottest portion of the day under a small tree. The meager shade wasn't much, but it offered the chance to escape the direct sunlight.

When they headed out again they walked to give Oviet a break. The itchy grass worked its way into Mimie's socks. She picked out the sharp agitators, but knew she was fighting a losing battle.

Oviet worked her way back toward the river as the sun set. The grass was greener there and the promise of food outweighed the danger of a Zantie ship seeing them.

Mimie and Koren set up camp while Oviet grazed. When they were finished, Mimie sat down and picked the grass out of her clothes. Koren settled down next to her and did the same.

He watched her from the corner of his eye. "Do you miss anyone back home?"

The question caught her off guard. "Gram," she offered.

"No boyfriend?"

Mimie laughed a little harder than was necessary. "That's very flattering of you to assume, but I've never had a boyfriend."

"Never? Well, you've kissed someone at least, right?"

"Nope. I'm sure that sounds crazy to someone of your vast experience and knowledge."

"A little. I had my first kiss when I was nine. In a graveyard ironically."

"That sounds very romantic." Mimie dug a difficult grass spine out of her sock.

"It was kind of wet actually, she was crying because her parents had just died." He changed the subject. "If you could have your perfect first kiss, what would it be like?"

Mimie blushed as she met his curious gaze and set the sock down next to her. "I don't know. Hugs are nice, can I just hug them instead."

"If you want to build a romantic relationship with a man you're going to have to kiss him, there's no way around it."

"I'm still trying to get used to the idea of being that close to someone's face and enjoying it."

"I bet it wouldn't be as bad as you think."

"If you say so." He seemed to take that as a challenge. He placed his palms on the sides of her face and leaned toward her. Her breath caught and her heart beat out an unsteady rhythm in her ears. His green eyes were guarded as he fixed them on hers, monitoring her reactions. He paused with his nose a hair width away from hers. She forgot how to breathe. He half smiled and moved his head so that his lips were less than an inch away from her ear.

"See, not hard or unpleasant at all," he whispered and pulled away from her. "Goodnight Mimie." He stood up and walked toward his sleeping sack.

"Night," she called back. Her legs felt like jelly as she made her way to her own sleeping sack and collapsed on top of it. Her heart was still beating out an irregular rhythm. What on earth was that? She would never understand that man. She smiled as she drifted off, enveloped by a strange euphoria that made her want to dance more than sleep.

Mimie stirred a little while later, disappointed to leave the dream she'd been having. She stared at the sky, in awe of its beauty, and wondered what had woken her. Koren and Oviet were still sound asleep, even the crickets were quiet, yet the night was filled with music. A soft hum echoed over the water. The surface created a perfect mirror image of the midnight sky while the moon bathed everything in a dream-like silvery glow. Mimie found herself inching closer for a better look without deciding too. She focused on glowing lights dancing under the surface and laughed. The humming grew louder as the water lights glittered faster. Their dance carried the lights further downstream, and Mimie eagerly followed them. She walked around Koren's sleeping sack, all the while getting closer to the water. Her peals of laughter harmonized with the music weaving through the air around her.

Mimie turned and faced the river; the waves were inches from her toes. The water stars gathered around her like they were calling

Mimie to join them. She closed her eyes and lifted one slender foot, then the other, into the chilly reach of the water. There Mimie paused; she leaned forward and found the stars were actually glowing yellow, eyes. At first she thought they belonged to a frog, but that wasn't quite right. Mimie took a half step forward, the eyes were enchanting. The humming was so loud she heard nothing else.

A webbed green hand grabbed her ankle. A scaly head with a long snout and pointed teeth rose out of the water, glittering eyes fixed on her face. Its sharp black claws dug into her leg as it dragged her further into the river. Mimie tried to kick the thing off, but it was strong and it wasn't alone. The hum turned into a blood curdling screech as more joined the first in trying to drag Mimie into the water. The reflection of the sky disappeared leaving the water as black as death. She screamed Koren's name as loud as she could, but the screeching was so loud he probably wouldn't be able to hear her. She clawed at the rocks on the bank in an effort to escape, but she knew it was no good. The gravel was so loose it gave her nothing to hold on too. Even if Koren had heard her screams, it was too late for him to do anything now; the monsters grip on her was too strong.

***

Koren jolted awake and clamped his hands over his ears; a piercing shriek was ringing off the river.

Oviet got to her feet and pinned her ears. "Go figure out what that is, and make it stop!" she yelled.

"Where's Mimie?" Koren demanded. "Oh no," he groaned and dove at the space cube. He shoved the lid off, and rummaged around inside until he found one of the containers of salt. He grabbed it and sprinted toward the place the shrieking was coming from. Up ahead the water was churning and his suspicions were confirmed. Mimie was fighting to escape the grip of several nymphs. He watched in horror as she disappeared under the water. He ran to the spot where she'd been dragged under and threw handfuls of salt into the water.

The surface seemed to boil and the shrieking grew so loud it brought Koren to his knees with his hands over his ears. The nymphs fled from the touch of the salt, giving Mimie a chance to escape. She crawled toward Koren and he grabbed her arm, firmly pulling her out of the water. One determined nymph was still clinging to her leg.

Mimie tried to shake it off, but it refused to let go. Koren grabbed a pinch of salt and held it up in warning. The nymph hissed at him and bared its pointed teeth. Koren flicked salt at it, and angry red blisters formed on its papery skin. The creature screamed, and jumped back into the water.

Mimie sat down on the gravel with her head between her knees and tried to catch her breath. She looked shaken, but had no obvious injuries. He offered her his hand and helped her to her feet. She followed him back to the campsite in a daze. His ears were still ringing from the loud shrieks and the beginnings of a headache knotted his brow into a hard line. Oviet had fallen back asleep.

Mimie collapsed onto her sleeping sack. Koren listened as her breathing became more regular and used the steady rhythm to help him fall asleep.

***

Mimie opened her eyes and watched the blurred pencil sketches on the ceiling of her bedroom suddenly come sharply into focus. She jerked upright and blinked a few times. Her room was exactly as she had left it. She swung her legs out of bed and lifted up her pillow. The familiar weight made her feel sad. She grabbed her sketchbook and headed outside. The empty hallway that led from her bedroom to the front door seemed longer than usual. She listened for Gram in the kitchen, but the cabin was silent. As she passed the high-topped counter Gram often used for chopping vegetables, she dragged her fingers across the smooth surface. Rubbing her fingertips together she felt a chalky film of dust. The door squeaked as she opened it, and swung stiffly on its hinges. She peered outside and found the grass growing wild against the front porch. The other cabins were nowhere in sight. Unpleasant stirrings of loneliness pricked at her belly.

"Hello, is anyone here?" The only sound was her echo repeating the question back to her.

She froze when she heard singing coming from the trees. There was something magical about it, something secret and mysterious. The song grew fainter, and Mimie rushed to follow it. Everything flew past her in streaks of light and color as she sprinted through the tall grass toward the trees.

It was a lady she was following. The lady danced from tree to tree and melted into the shafts of sunlight. The woman was happy; she smiled at Mimie, then giggled and danced away. Mimie broke through the trees and looked around, everything was silent. A flowing creek ran parallel to her path. The water was still and small glittering bugs skimmed across the surface. Bees hovered over the flowers that grew near the water's edge.

The lady's back was turned toward Mimie and a breeze played with her hair. Mimie sat down under a huge tree and leaned her back against its trunk, enjoying the sunshine. Her notebook lay open on her lap. The world paused as she pulled out a pencil and touched it to the paper. She sketched a few lines, then scribbled them out.

After a while she closed her notebook, the world seemed to shift and the bees were once again humming and the skimmers were doing their little circle dance upon the water. As Mimie watched the lady singing and dancing in the forest right next to the water, the woman turned her head and looked back at her. For a moment she looked right into Mimie's eyes. Mimie's mind filled with questions. Did she know me? Had we met before? She was beautiful, there was no doubt but where and when had they met before?

"I guess I will never know," Mimie sighed. She leaned back against the tree and enjoyed watching the lady sing and dance with the bees.

With a jolt, Mimie recognized the lady's melody and realized it was the one Gram used to hum to her when she was little.

The music stopped abruptly, and Mimie blinked in confusion. The woman was nowhere to be seen, and the flowers wilted in her absence. Voices whispered to her as a man stepped from the shadow of a tree. He mouthed one word to her, run.

"Dad?" Mimie asked. The whispers grew louder. He tried to take Mimie's hand, but his fingers past through her palm, unfelt. "Where's Mom?" Mimie demanded. The man backed away from her. The forest was filled with strange noises. Eyes stared at her without blinking from the treetops. A scream filled her ears, but it took her a few seconds before she realized it was her own.

"Mimie, wake up," Koren said, gently shaking her. Mimie blinked a few times and tried to rid herself of the unsettled feeling she had in her stomach. It was still dark outside; she threw the blanket over her head with a grown.

"I'm not getting up. It's too early."

"Sorry, you had a nightmare. I was worried about you."

"I'm fine." Lack of sleep made her feel irritable.

"I thought you might want some breakfast, but you can go back to sleep. I'll just eat the rest of it."

"Breakfast?" Mimie perked up a bit. She wiggled out of her sleeping sack and wandered over to where Koren was waiting by a small fire. He handed her a flat rock with eggs, and some cattail shoots. She was touched that he would go through the trouble of preparing this for her. It must have taken forever to find the eggs and even longer to find the shoots amongst the tangled grasses. How early did he have to wake up to do this for her? "Thank you." The words seemed inadequate.

When she was finished she set the rock aside and stretched.

Koren nudged it toward the fire with his foot. "Are you up for some training this morning?"

"Training?"

Koren handed her a stick. "Wait a second," she protested. "You didn't tell me this was what you had in mind!"

Now that she was armed, Mimie knew she was free game so she backed out of Koren's reach. He jabbed at her experimentally, but she knocked it aside.

"Is that all you got?" Mimie challenged. Koren smiled and dived at her. She veered to the left and smacked him on the back. Koren lifted his arm and Mimie went for his exposed left side, but it was a trick. He cracked his stick down on top of hers and sent it flying from her hand. It narrowly missed Oviet, who was sleeping nearby. Mimie raised her hands in defeat and tried to hide a mischievous smile. When Koren lowered his stick triumphantly. Mimie raced past him, dived over Oviet, and grabbed her stick; all in a smooth tuck-and-roll. Koren was right behind her.

136

"Resorting to cheating now are we?" he laughed.

"No, that was called the fake and run," Mimie replied.

Koren grunted as he blocked her next blow. He swung at her, but she danced out of his reach. He crossed his arms and teased, "You're not even trying."

"Yes, I am. Did you not see that awesome flip I just did?" He took advantage of her distracted indignation and whacked her arm, then moved out of her reach at the last second.

"Aww! That hurt you distracting creep."

He jumped at her, and Mimie realized she had left her right side exposed. She jumped back and aimed a counter-swing at his stick to break its momentum. Both sticks shattered on impact and wood chips flew in all directions. Koren examined the small stump in his left hand with an amused smile.

"I guess we'll have to call this a draw," he decided and threw what was left of his stick into the fire. Mimie did the same. "Your reactions are good, but it takes time to get the actual techniques down. Your stance, for one, is terrible, and your grip is all wrong."

"I think you might be wasting your time with this," Mimie grumbled. "I don't know if I want to learn how to more efficiently hurt someone."

"You'll have to at some point if you want to survive in this world."

"Well, since we're all awake now, I guess we might as well get an early start," Oviet said grumpily, glaring at the shattered sticks. Mimie nodded in agreement. She rolled up her sleeping sack and tossed it into the space cube. She did the same with Koren's and the rest of their stuff she found lying around. By the time she finished the first rays of morning were just barely glowing on the horizon.

She hoped Koren would stop being paranoid and let them fly, she had no interest in spending hours picking weeds out of her clothes again.

"Ready to head out?" Koren asked.

Oviet's feathers were still ruffled from sleep. "Not really."

Koren ignored her listless mood and led the way into the tall grass. Mimie's shoulders drooped, it didn't look as though they would be flying today. Oviet glanced longingly at the sky and shook a clump of weeds from her back foot.

"Remind me why we're walking again?" she growled.

"We can't risk the Zanties seeing you."

"Fine," she grumbled, "but if I have to walk so do you, don't expect me to carry you."

"I think we should be able to fly too," Mimie said to Oviet.

"In that case," she replied. "Mimie, you can ride on my back, but Koren, you have to walk."

"Feeling spiteful much?" he laughed.

"And," added Oviet, "next time we fly you have to ride in a harness so every time we pass a big hill, it smacks you in the face."

Mimie kept her eyes on her feet to watch for potholes in the uneven terrain. She gasped and jumped back in surprise when she saw movement out of the corner of her eye. A green and brown snake coiled up near her feet. The snake raised its head in a strike position and rattled its tail at her. She backed away from it and knocked into Koren. His face had gone ghostly pale, and his hands were trembling like he was staring down a hungry bear instead of a rattle snake.

"Let's get out of here," Oviet snorted. She pranced as though she were standing in a spider's web. Mimie swung onto her back. "You coming?" Oviet asked when Koren didn't get on right away.

"No harness?" he teased, his voice strained.

"Get on bonehead before we leave you," Mimie laughed. He kept a careful eye on the snake and quickly jumped on behind her. Oviet spread her wings and took to the skies.

Looking back the way they had come, Mimie could still see the huge black shadow on the horizon where the mountains were. Ahead, the river extended far into the distance. It wound through the grass like a snake with liquid scales that shimmered in time with the way the wind blew the grass. The long road ahead betrayed the vast distance they still had to travel. The grassy hills met the sky in a choppy line at the horizon. The sky was dark blue and filled with fluffy white clouds.

"Fly lower," Koren scolded. "You're getting too high." Oviet snorted and rolled her eyes at him. Once they had passed the tall grass she touched down again on a stretch of bare ground. Koren hopped off and wiped his palms against his pants, Mimie had never seen him so visibly shaken.

"I'm the one that almost stepped on the snake, and you look worse than I do," Mimie said in concern. Koren laughed weakly and struggled to compose himself. He set his shoulders and pressed forward, searching the ground with an intensity that unsettled her. She added irrational fear of snakes to the list of things she knew about him.

They continued walking for the rest of the day and stopped when a touch of pink entered the clouds. Koren left to hunt and Mimie gathered together sticks to make a fire. Her woodpile was small, but it was enough to cook any meat he brought back. She arranged the kindling on a patch of bare earth and used two firestones to get a spark. She carefully blew the glowing embers into a flame.

Koren returned a short time later holding a small ram. He dropped the carcass by the fire and skinned it quickly with his knife. Mimie fixed her gaze on the fire and fed it small sticks to keep it going. It crackled and sent glowing red embers into the air. Koren snagged one of the sticks from her pile and sharpened the end with his knife. He cut off slabs of meat and skewered the stick through them. When he was finished, he rubbed salt into the meat and mounted it on a spit to cook.

"Will you watch that?" Koren asked as he gathered all the unused animal scraps together.

"Sure." Mimie watched him carry the scraps off and disappear. The meat was sizzling on one side, so she turned it over to let the other side cook. The smell wafting from it made her mouth water. By the time Koren returned it was almost finished. He grabbed one of the canteens and used the water to clean the blood off his hands. Mimie picked up one of his knives and cut a slit in one of the thicker pieces of meat. It was still a little pink inside.

"I'll take over." Koren turned the meat again and threw another handful of sticks on the fire. Five minutes later he removed the meat and set it off to the side to cool.

Mimie glanced up at the stars. It was hard to see them through the cloud cover, but they twinkled faithfully in and out of view. The full moon was bright ivory and illuminated the clouds around it with a broad circle of light. Koren pulled her out of her reverie by handing her some of the meat. She tore off a large chunk and chewed it thoughtfully. A full belly made her sleepy and she drifted toward her sleeping sack. The warmth of the fire felt good against her side. She closed her eyes and fell asleep.

Thick fog permeated the air when she woke the next morning. Dew drops collected in a thin film where the skin on her arm had been exposed the night before. She brushed the moisture away and combed her fingers through her hair.

A chill morning breeze left a trail of goose bumps on her arms. The clouds had darkened from the night before and a light drizzle peppered her cheek. Koren rubbed his eyes and retreated deeper into his sleeping sack to avoid the rain.

Mimie stared apprehensively at the flashing black clouds on the horizon far in front of them. "I have a bad feeling about today."

Koren shrugged off her concerns. "The Zanties won't be able to track us in the storm. This could be our chance to give them the slip." The fabric of the sleeping sack made his voice sound muffled.

Mimie looked at Oviet to gage her opinion on the matter. She shrugged and went back to grazing. Mimie grudgingly climbed to her feet and shoved her sleeping sack into the space cube. Mental images of getting struck by lightning set her on edge.

Her nerves tightened into a hard knot as she climbed onto Oviet's back. She waited for Koren to hop on behind her and clenched her legs against Oviet's sides as she burst into a run. The opposing winds lifted Oviet into the sky as she opened her wings.

A clap of thunder made Mimie wince. The rain picked up. It soaked through her shirt, and the wet fabric clung to her skin. A flash of lightening lit up the sky; Mimie peered over Oviet's shoulder and gulped when she saw the ground far below.

Oviet continued flying for another hour, all the while plunging deeper into the storm. The rain came down in sheets. It penetrated the waterproof coating on Oviet's flight feathers and made it hard for her to stay airborne. They were buffeted by the wind as they drifted lower and lower. Oviet's soaked wings threw off her balance as she touched down on the slick grass. Her legs slid out from under her and she fell sideways.

Mimie hit the ground hard enough to knock the breath out of her. An icy wind swept over her drenched clothes, chilling her to the bone. She shivered and lifted her face away from the mud. The fog made it impossible to get her bearings. She pushed herself unsteadily to her feet and crossed her arms in an effort to conserve warmth.

The squelch noise of mud sucking at boots rang out from somewhere in front of her. Cold dread sank into her stomach. They weren't alone.

CHAPTER 12: THE STRANGER

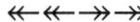

Mimie squinted and picked out the outline of a man in a midnight blue cloak. She scooted backward as he continued his advance. Her hands closed on a rock and she raised it threateningly.

"Stay away from me!"

He saw her alarm and backed away. "It's ok, I'm not here to hurt you. Put down the rock."

Mimie narrowed her eyes in disbelief. "What do you want?"

"I thought you guys might want some shelter. You'll catch your death if you stay out here." Oviet's legs shook as she tried to stand. Koren braced his shoulder against her side to help steady her.

"That's very kind of you. Thank you," Koren said.

Mimie still felt uneasy, she hung back with Oviet as Koren followed the hooded stranger.

"I'm Nickolas by the way," the man called over his shoulder.

He seemed to know the terrain well and walked purposefully toward a rock outcropping. As they neared it Mimie discovered a tent and a warm looking fire. Nickolas threw back his hood and sat down next to it, holding out his hands to warm them. Water dripped from his shaggy brown hair onto his dark blue cloak. His eyes were the same color as the fire.

Oviet shook out her coat sending muddy droplets of water flying everywhere. Her legs were blackened from the mud and it was caked on both her sodden wings. Mimie pushed her back out into the rain and used the downpour to try and wash some of the mud off.

When she was finished she noticed Koren staring at a seal emblazoned on Nickolas's cloak. Koren's eyes narrowed. Nickolas covered it self-consciously.

"So, I hear there are Zanties in the area," Koren said. Nickolas pursed his lips and shrugged.

"Tea?" he offered, holding up a kettle.

"No thanks."

While Nickolas poured a cup for himself Koren discreetly reached behind him and tugged Mimie's cloak further up on her shoulder to make sure her Guardian's mark wasn't visible.

The man seemed friendly enough. Mimie didn't understand what was causing Koren to feel so uneasy but she humored him and pulled the material of her cloak tighter around her shoulders. Oviet ruffled her feathers and groomed them into place using her teeth and upper lip.

"That symbol on your cloak. I think I've seen it somewhere before."

Nickolas shifted uncomfortably. "It's nothing I'm proud of, believe me." Mimie watched the exchange feeling tense. Koren knew something about Nickolas that she didn't. "If I had anything else to wear I'd leave this cursed thing behind in the mud. You can drop the pretenses. I know you know what the symbol means."

Mimie stared at Koren, her eyes demanding an explanation.

"That's Orient's family crest. Nickolas is his son."

Mimie threw a horrified glance at Nickolas and waited for him to deny it. He didn't. Oviet pinned her ears and glared at him.

"It's open plains for the next two miles. If staying here makes you uncomfortable, you are welcome to go your separate way and freeze."

"This has to be a trap," Koren whispered to Mimie from the side of his mouth.

"I cut ties with my father a long time ago. I'm not a threat to you." Nickolas threw a log on the fire and stirred the embers with a stick. The smell of the smoke mixed with the smell of rain soaked mud and dampened feathers. Mimie shook her head, she didn't know what to believe.

"What are you doing out here?" she wondered.

"I'm trying to reach dragon valley. I heard there was a rebel group gathering there. I have information about the castle and my father's army."

Mimie wasn't sure she believed him but relaxed her tense posture when Koren did. She sneezed and felt her nose starting to run. Nickolas offered her a handkerchief without meeting her gaze.

"Thanks," she mumbled and blew her nose. The scratchy beginnings of a sore throat alerted her she was getting a cold.

Koren pulled out the space cube. He tossed a sleeping sack on a dry section of rock and fished out some tea leaves. In an uncharacteristic act of good faith he barrowed Nickolas's kettle and filled it with water. There were no large stones around to heat up the water so he didn't have much of a choice. To his credit he cleaned it thoroughly. Mimie doubted Nickolas had poisoned the last batch of tea but it was good the be careful just in case. She shivered and wrapped her arms more tightly around her knees. Koren set the kettle on the coals and waited for the water to heat up. After the tea was ready he poured some into a cup and handed it to her.

"I threw some medicine herbs in there, they should help your cold."

"Thanks." Mimie sneezed into her arm.

The mint tea soothed her throat and helped thaw her frozen limbs. Her stomach growled, reminding her she hadn't eaten breakfast that morning. Using the wall for support she pushed herself to her feet. The rain had let up somewhat meaning she could search for something to eat.

Koren held out his arm to bar her path. "What are you doing?"

"I'm hungry. I was going to go down to the river and look for some cattail shoots."

"You sit down. I'll get them for you," he offered.

Nickolas stood up. "I need to get more water, I'll come with you."

Mimie glanced back and forth between the two of them, trying to decide if it was safe to leave them alone together. Koren grabbed his bow and left. Nickolas followed him. Oviet settled down next to Mimie and draped a wing over her shoulder. Mimie stroked her soft feathers and tried not to imagine Koren and Nickolas killing one another.

She watched the rain drip down from the lip of the outcropping and splash against the grass below. The rain had left the air smelling fresh and clean. If a damp chill hadn't settled into her clothes she might have found the weather extremely enjoyable. She took off her shoes and tried to warm her frozen toes by moving them closer to the fire. They were just starting to thaw when she heard a commotion come from the direction of the river. She put her frigid socks back on and stuffed her feet into her shoes.

Oviet didn't seem overly concerned. She yawned and rested her head against her leg.

Mimie used the loud voices to guide her toward the river. She worried a strand of hair between her finger tips and realized it was caked with mud. She ran her hands through the rest of her hair. If felt like a family of pack rats had moved in and had a mud fight. There was no other way, she had to wash it. First she had to check on Koren and Nickolas though. She worked her way through the tall cattails and headed toward the commotion, growling in exasperation.

Nickolas's face was covered in mud and a huge crab was dangling from his ear. Koren was laughing so hard at Nickolas's attempt to get it off, he could barely stay on his feet. Mimie rushed to Nickolas, pried the crab's pinchers apart and pulled it off his ear. Before it could pinch her, she tossed it back into the river.

"Koren! What's the matter with you?" Mimie demanded, glaring at him. Something flew past her head and she ducked instinctively. A huge mud ball landed square in Koren's face, cutting off his laughter. He used both hands to wipe the sludge away from his eyes, then flicked it off his hands with a look of disgust. Now it was Nickolas's turn to laugh. Mimie suppressed a chuckle and then quickly composed herself. "Nickolas, knock it off!"

Koren advanced on him threateningly. Nickolas held his ground and crossed his arms; both of them looked ridiculous with mud crusting on their faces. Mimie pushed between them.

"That's enough!"

Nickolas muttered something under his breath and stormed away. Koren watched him go with a look of disdain on his face.

"How did this start?"

"Nickolas suggested we go to a human town for supplies. I told him there were plenty of resources here, but he didn't believe me. So I decided to show him how rich the mud is. I thought there might be some worms, but the crab was a bonus." Mimie rolled her eyes. "I wish you hadn't thrown the crab back. I was going to cook it up for dinner tonight."

"You're impossible." Mimie covered her mouth, and bent over as a round of coughing shook her frame. She wiped her mouth on her arm. Her head ached, and it felt like her brain had liquefied and collected in her sinuses. Koren handed her the shoots he'd collected and turned to leave. "Where are you going?"

"Hunting." He pulled his bow from his back and disappeared into the cattails.

Mimie leaned down and splashed water on her face. She flipped her hair upside down and submerged it in the water, careful to avoid the sandy bottom. Once it was wet, she crushed up some roots with a rock to make a creamy paste, and rubbed it into her hair. She washed it out in the stream and used a stick to pull the tangles out. Feeling refreshed, she turned to head back to camp, munching on the shoots.

When she reached the rock outcropping she found Oviet trying to roll a small log into the center of their campsite. Mimie watched her efforts in amazement.

"Where did you get that?"

"I tripped over it." Oviet grunted as she shoved harder against it. "I'm collecting wood for the fire tonight." With a final grunt, she shoved it onto the woodpile and paused to catch her breath.

"I need to grow more fur. It's freezing out here." Mimie sat down and drank the rest of her tea. She leaned her back against the rock wall and closed her eyes. Footsteps alerted her to Koren's return. He was carrying two pheasants, one in each hand. He dropped them by the fire and sat down on his sleeping sack. After a moment his eyes widened in alarm and he jumped to his feet.

"What?" Mimie asked.

Koren lifted up his sleeping sack and shook it. A snake fell out. She heard Nickolas laughing a short distance away as he left to go gather more wood. Koren's face flushed red in anger. Before he could take it out on the snake Mimie stepped protectively in front of it.

"I need some air." Koren growled. He showed his hands in his pockets and left. Oviet suppressed silent laughter.

Mimie glared at her. "This is not funny!" Oviet made a greater effort to hide her amusement and grazed on the green grass nearby. "Alright, you've had your fun," Mimie said and scooped the snake off the ground. Compared to the large rattlesnake she had almost stepped on this snake was pathetically tiny. It wrapped around Mimie's arm as she carried it far away from Koren's things. When she had gone a sufficient distance away she carefully slipped the snake off her arm and set it gently in the grass. It slithered away and disappeared from sight.

Koren returned a little while later looking slightly more calm, but still angry. He sat down and plucked the pheasants a little more violently than necessary. Mimie threw more wood on the fire for him and collected the thick grass he liked to wrap meat in for cooking. He cut the meat into sections with his knife and seasoned it with herbs he'd found around the river. He wrapped it in the grass and waited until the fire burned down a little bit before placing the grass bundles on rocks directly on the embers.

Koren seemed oddly smug, but Mimie was too tired to figure out why. When Nickolas came back Koren pulled the meat off the fire and let it cool before handing it to him. Mimie pulled off a chunk of her pheasant meat and tore into it hungrily.

Something small and furry ran across her lap, making Mimie jump in surprise. Nickolas was sitting on her other side and the rat jumped at his face. Nickolas hit it away from him, but in the process dropped the meat he was holding. Another rat raced toward it and dragged it away.

"Hey!" Nickolas yelled, and started to get up. Mimie stopped him.

"You're not going to get it back now," she laughed. The rat stopped and took a few nibbles of the meat, then scurried toward the tall grass with its prize. After a few steps, it suddenly fell over and began twitching violently. Nickolas's face turned pale white, then bright red. He turned a fiery gaze toward Koren.

"You just tried to poison me!" Koren looked disappointed, but calmly denied it. Nickolas kicked the stump away that he was sitting on and glared at Koren wordlessly. Mimie was mortified that Koren would do such a thing and winced at Nickolas's harsh tone. "Alright, if you want to kill me, fine, but do it face to face like a real man. Not like a coward!"

"A coward?" Koren roared. He ran at Nickolas and tackled him to the ground. "Cowardice is your father's men invading elvish kingdoms, and killing women and children." Nickolas landed a punch to Koren's jaw and locked his arm against the ground with his legs. Koren tried to shove him off, but Nickolas held on tight.

"You're right, my father is a coward, but you aren't the only one his greed for power has hurt. He kidnapped my mother, forced himself on her in every way possible, and then murdered her." Nickolas pulled up his shirt exposing thick scars on his chest and back. "He did this to me when I was thirteen because I refused to kill someone. I know you hate that monster, but at least you didn't have to live under his roof. I escaped, and now I'm trying to do some good in the world. I'm sorry if you are so full of hate that you can't see that." He shoved Koren away from him. Koren rubbed his jaw and tried to think of something to say.

"I'm sorry," he muttered after a long silence, "and I wasn't trying to kill you," he admitted. "I just wanted you to think that, but to be fair the food probably would have given you terrible indigestion."

"That was still uncalled for," Nickolas replied heatedly.

"I know, I'm sorry."

Nickolas pinched the bridge of his nose.

"Can we put this behind us?"

"Yeah," Koren said looking at the ground. Nickolas relaxed out of his tense stance and headed toward his tent. Mimie finished her food in silence. She threw the remains into the fire and pulled her sleeping sack from the space cube. She wiped her nose on her arm and curled up in its warmth. Koren made her another cup of tea and put out the fire.

"I'm a first class idiot, aren't I?" he muttered. Mimie sipped at the tea and weighed her response carefully.

"A little bit, yeah," she teased. He shoved her shoulder playfully.

"Night," he said and disappeared behind the space cube. Mimie smiled. It had been a rocky night, but at least now things were finally looking up.

The next morning Koren agreed to stop in the human town to get more supplies. Nickolas needed a horse, and they needed more food. It didn't take them long to pack up in the morning. Nickolas's tent folded into a compact bundle at his side and the space cube held everything else. Oviet couldn't carry three people so they had to walk there, a fact that she wasn't overly excited about.

The hills leveled out as they made their way west of the river. Scraggy woodlands rose out of the grass, and the sparse canopy shielded them from the view of any passing Zanties.

"I hate to be negative Koren, but how are we going to buy anything? We don't have any money." Koren thought a moment and then looked at Nickolas, who shrugged.

"Hmmm…" Koren muttered and eyed Oviet speculatively.

"Please don't look at me like that," she said.

"If we cut off a few of your tail hairs that should be more than enough to barter for a horse," he said and approached her tail. She spun around, blocking him. "Stop moving!" he complained. Oviet snorted and pointed her horn at his face.

"You are not touching my tail!"

"Your main would work as well..." he replied, and reached toward it. Oviet snapped at his fingers.

"Don't even think about it!"

"Fine then. Everyone hop on, it looks like Oviet has decided to carry the three of us to Dragon Valley after all," he said. Oviet flicked her tail angrily in his face and laid her ears flat against her head.

"Fine, but do it quickly before I experience an involuntary spasm and kick you in the face."

Koren grabbed a small bundle of hair and cut it off with his knife. Oviet scowled. Koren tied a knot in the hair at one end to keep it together and carefully wound the silvery strands around his palm.

"I'm not going with you," Oviet grumbled. "It will be too hard to disguise me. I'll wait for you out here."

"We'll be back by dark," Koren assured her

"If not I'll know I need to come looking for you."

Nickolas turned his cloak inside out so the symbol on it wouldn't be recognized. Mimie took in the immense block wall that loomed in the distance.

"Hoods up," Koren muttered. "We don't want anyone to recognize us."

Mimie pulled her hood over her head and patted Oviet's neck. It felt wrong leaving her behind, even if it wouldn't be for long.

It was another mile before they reached the town. The wall surrounding the outside was made from large stones plastered together with mud. Grass and vines grew in patches between the stones as if the plains were trying to tear it down. The front gate was in the same condition. The old wood was peeling and the rusted hinges supporting the heavy door sagged under its weight.

"This place looks abandoned," Mimie told Nickolas.

"The Zanties have no doubt picked it to the bone, but I'm sure we can still find what we need."

"Zanties?" Mimie asked, feeling uneasy.

"Don't worry, we'll be in and out. No one will even notice we were here."

Koren was tense, but he didn't say anything. Mimie made sure her hood covered her face and followed Nickolas as he walked toward the gate. He knocked twice on the dark wood and took a step back. A small slit opened in the door at eye level, and piercing gray eyes studied them from the other side.

"State your business."

"We have items to trade in the marketplace," Nickolas said firmly. The man narrowed his eyes.

"It's not often we get such mysterious visitors," the guard muttered. "Please, come inside." The gate made a terrible grinding noise as he pulled it open and he stepped aside to let them pass. They quickly filed past him and headed straight for an alleyway to their left. Mimie turned and saw the guard studying them; she took a step closer to Koren and tilted her chin downward so the cloak would obscure more of her face.

"This place gives me the creeps," she complained. Koren squeezed her hand reassuringly. The set of his shoulders told her he felt the same way.

The alley opened up into a vast courtyard lined on both sides with run down houses. Silence hung in the air as thick as the dust collecting on the streets. The place seemed to be mostly deserted except for a young couple rushing their two small children inside one of the buildings.

"Excuse me!" Mimie called and walked over to them. The women threw a panicked look at her husband and froze. He whispered something to her, and she continued rushing the children into the building. The man sized Mimie up. She shrank back under his piercing glare and asked in a small voice, "Do you know where we can find a stable?"

"There's one over there," he replied and pointed to a narrow street. Mimie started to thank him, but the man had already disappeared. Mimie frowned and walked back to Koren and Nickolas.

"What was his problem?" Koren muttered.

"I don't know, but the sooner we get out of here, the better," Mimie replied. They stayed close to the walls and briskly walked the direction the man had indicated. Every few feet they would pass a door, or a grimy window that was tightly sealed and had a thick black curtain covering it.

When they emerged from the road the first thing they noticed were the remains of old stores. Cobwebs were visibly covering the doors, and the windows were boarded up. Nestled into the far corner was a wooden barn, which seemed to be in considerably better shape than the rest of the buildings.

"There," Mimie pointed and they headed toward it. Koren and Nickolas followed more slowly, keeping an eye out for danger. When Mimie reached the stable she peered into one of the dusty windows, but couldn't see any signs of life. She walked to the door and knocked three times on the aged wood. She waited a few seconds, and then knocked again. The door opened with a loud squeak and a shower of dust rained down on the small balding man standing in the doorway. He glared at them.

"What do you want?" he demanded, brushing the dust from his clothes.

"We need a horse," Koren replied.

"Really," the man snapped, "and how do you intend to pay for said horse." Koren gritted his teeth at the man's rude tone and reached for his sword handle. Nickolas put a cautioning hand on his shoulder.

"We have a valuable item in our possession. We would like to trade it for one of your stock," he explained curtly. Distrust was evident on the man's face as he studied them, but he stepped aside to let them pass.

"Alright then. My name is Albert, the horses are this way."

The light was dim and it took a minute for Mimie's eyes to adjust. The air was thick with the smell of musty straw and the beams holding up the ceiling creaked ominously overhead. Albert led them to a long row of stalls lining one side of the barn and introduced them to his horses. Most of the stalls were empty except the last five. There was a big chestnut gelding that snorted fiercely as they walked by. Next was a young buckskin mare, then an old gray stallion. He seemed thin and frail, but his eyes still held a fiery glow that promised a horse that had been fantastic in its prime. She moved over to the next stall and saw that it contained a small bay mare. She had a slender body and a refined dished head.

"She's pretty," Mimie muttered and reached inside to pat the sweet horse's nose.

"Her name is Fire Lilly," Albert said. "Careful, she bites." Koren dragged Mimie away as they moved on to the final stall. Mimie squinted into the gloom, and movement in the black shadows caught her eye.

The massive creature stomped its hoof once, then walked a few steps closer to them. He was a huge black stallion with a golden horn set squarely in the middle of his forehead and a white star on his chest. He ruffled his long silky feathers and tucked them more firmly against his back. Mimie felt her jaw drop.

"I got him as a colt from some traders a while back," the man explained, looking at the horse fondly. "His name is Octavious."

Horrible coughing from behind a haystack caused Mimie to flinch.

"That doesn't sound good," she muttered, watching the man hurry toward the sound. Mimie followed him and saw a frail woman with a bulging belly lying on a tattered sheet. Albert hovered over her and offered her a ladle of water.

"Here," Koren offered, and unwound Oviet's hair from around his palm. "If you're in the trade business, I'm guessing you know what this is, and how hard it is to come by." Albert stared at the hair in amazement.

"How did you get that?" His eyes reflected its pure silver light in awe. "I've never seen hair that pristine. The only silver unicorns in this area have been untouchable for decades." Mimie exchanged a glance with Koren, unsure how to answer.

"How we got it isn't important. We want to trade it for Octavious," Koren told him.

"No, no," Albert muttered. "I couldn't part with him, and besides, he's not tame. No one has even ridden him before. Take the chestnut; he will be a good strong horse for you."

"Silver unicorn hair can cure any human illness, as I'm sure you well know. Your wife and the child she is carrying are dying. Is Octavious worth more to you than their lives?" Albert bit his lip and walked back to Octavious. Koren followed him. "Black hybrids don't have any healing powers. What use is he to you cooped up in here? Take the trade. Save your wife and child."

"Ok, ok. This is practically robbery though, I hope you know. If I wasn't in such a desperate situation..." He unlocked Octavious's stall and glumly stepped aside to let them pass. Octavious threw his head up and retreated into the far corner of his stall as they approached.

"Careful," Albert warned. "He hates strangers." Nickolas ignored him and took a small step in the flying unicorn's direction. The horse's nostrils flared, and he pinned his ears back. Nickolas cooed softly to him as he slowly made his way forward. The horse pricked its ears, then swiveled them back again. Nickolas held out his palm toward the horse and waited until Octavious sniffed at his fingers to move any closer. To Mimie's surprise, Octavious stepped forward and pressed his nose against Nickolas's shoulder. He laughed and patted the horse's neck affectionately. Mimie watched as Albert handed Nickolas Octavious's halter and lead rope. Nickolas expertly slid the bridle over Octavious's head and coaxed him out of the stall. He led the way toward the exit, but Mimie stopped him.

"Can I take him?" she begged. Nickolas half smiled and handed the lead rope to Mimie. She fell behind the others as she admired the large creature's impressive form. She patted his soft neck and pulled a stray piece of straw from his mane. Once they reached the exit, Octavious flicked his tail back and forth in agitation.

Mimie hung back as Koren and Nickolas pushed their way outside and let Albert say goodbye.

"It's been fun you devil. Be good now," Albert muttered with tears in his eyes. Mimie opened the front door, and the bright sunlight turned the world blindingly white.

A strong hand clamped over her mouth and Octavious's lead rope was ripped out of her hand. He reared up in alarm and let out a shrill nay. Mimie bit down on her attacker's fingers and jabbed her elbow into their ribs. She knocked the breath out of them, but that wasn't enough to break their grip. She waited for her eyes to adjust and caught sight of dull blue fabric. Her heart fell; the Zanties had found them.

Koren and Nickolas seemed dazed. Koren had a bruise forming above his eyebrow and Nickolas had a split lip. The Zanties held onto them tightly and patted them down, looking for weapons. Mimie spotted the gate guard standing behind them, smirking. She glared at him but doubted he saw it.

The Zantie holding Mimie ripped back her hood to expose her face. He studied her intently for a moment and chuckled darkly.

"Well, well, well, a fairy, an elf, and a traitor traveling with a flying unicorn. I've heard tell that the Guardian is hiding out in these parts. You wouldn't happen to know anything about that would you?" he hissed the last part against Mimie's ear. She shuddered and shook her head weakly. "So if I lift up your left sleeve, I won't find the mark of the moon and the star?"

Mimie closed her eyes and tried to stop her body from shaking, a weak attempt at appearing braver than she felt. The Zantie knew she wasn't going to answer and didn't seem to require her to.

"Come with me," he growled and pulled her toward the alleyway in between the houses. She knew the Zanties wanted her alive, but she wasn't sure what they were going to do with her friends.

Occasionally, she saw a few shadowed people watching from their doorways. None tried to help her though a few seemed like they wanted to. The alley opened up into a larger courtyard. It might have been a marketplace at one time, but now the stands were deserted. Her captor marched her toward another Zantie standing guard and shoved her toward him.

"Watch her. I'll be right back," he said, then turned and walked away. The other Zantie, a brunette, looked at her in surprise, but quickly recovered and grabbed her arm. Mimie glared at him and muttered,

"I will sneeze on you." Pathetically it was the most threatening thing she could come up with. The Zantie raised an eyebrow but otherwise ignored her comment. A few minutes dragged by, then

Mimie felt the Zantie holding her jerk to attention. She glanced up and recognized the man walking toward her through the unsettling resemblance to his brother. Nickolas had a twin.

"Is this her?" He demanded in a low voice. "I want to see the mark for myself."

Mimie pressed her lips together and tensed as her original captor approached her and forcibly pushed her left sleeve to her shoulder. Her mark was unmistakable; fear curled into her stomach as she wondered what they would do next.

"Take her to the holding cell. A wagon will be here at sunset to pick her up."

"Yes sir," the brunette replied and pulled her toward the far end of the courtyard. Mimie turned and saw Nickolas's brother follow the other Zantie in the direction Koren and Nickolas were being held. The air suddenly felt thicker. She tried to tell herself they would be okay, but she didn't quite believe it. Angrily, she turned back to her captor.

"Do the Zanties plunder and destroy all the villages they occupy or did this one do something special?"

"Watch your mouth," the Zantie growled and pulled her under a dark brick doorway.

Mimie tried to keep track of the dimly lit corridors they passed through, but it was hard when they were all identical. Finally, the Zantie stopped in front of a wooden door with a single barred window toward the top. A torch that had almost burned out, hung on the sidewall next to it. The Zantie pulled a pair of keys out of a concealed pocket, opened the door, and firmly pushed Mimie inside. As he closed the door the thick wood quivered against its stone frame. The scrape of the heavy lock sinking into place echoed through the small room.

***

Nickolas gritted his teeth in pain as the Zantie holding him pressed a knife against his back. Koren was struggling beside him, and Octavious was snorting irritably from behind. Nickolas wondered why he didn't try to fly away. Maybe he'd been taken at such a young age that he had never learned how.

The Zanties led them down an alley, turned sharply to the right, and dragged them under a low archway into a small chamber. The Zantie restraining Nickolas shoved him toward the wall to the right of the entrance and tied him to the water pipe that ran horizontally across the wall. The knots were tight; he could already feel the blood loss to his hands creating tingling sensations in his fingertips. Their weapons were thrown into a pile in the alleyway and one of the Zanties stayed behind to guard the doorway.

Nickolas threw himself forward to test the strength of the ropes and felt tingles of pain work their way from his wrists to his shoulders. There was no other way, he realized. The rope had to be cut.

"Ripping your arms off isn't going to help anyone," Koren snapped. Nickolas ignored him and watched the Zantie guarding them carefully. He was sitting down outside the archway looking bored. Nickolas leaned closer to Koren and whispered,

"There's a knife in the side pocket of my boot. The Zanties forgot to check there."

"What do you want me to do about it?" Koren asked.

"Pull it out obviously."

"How do you expect me to do that, I can't exactly use my hands." Nickolas grimaced at the thought of what he knew would have to be done. "No, no way," Koren said, realizing what he had in mind.

"Would you do it for Mimie?" Nickolas asked. Koren glared at him.

"Fine, give me your leg," he said in defeat. Nickolas checked to make sure the Zantie wasn't paying attention then lifted his right foot toward Koren. Koren used his knee to support it and grabbed Nickolas's pant leg between his teeth to pull it out of the way.

"This is so weird," Nickolas groaned.

"Would you like to switch places?" Koren searched for the side pouch that held the knife. He tried to get the handle between his teeth, but it was too far down in the shoe. He loosened the laces, and, with a look of disgust, stuck part of his face into the boot to get a grip on the handle. With a precise tug, he pulled the knife free and held it in his mouth. "Your boot smells like something died in there," he complained. "What now?"

Nickolas turned around and wiggled his fingers at him. Koren shoved his foot away and strained to reach his hands. Nickolas managed to grab the handle and twisted it into position. The blade rested against the rope, ready to sever it at a moments notice.

A few minutes later he heard the echo of footsteps signaling the approach of someone from the alley. A cloaked figure swept into the room like a shadow and paused facing him. An icy chill traveled up Nickolas's spine as his brother's cold eyes bore into his.

"What's wrong with you?" Richard demanded. "How could you betray us like this?" Nickolas felt suppressed anger rise in his throat like bile. In all the years living in the castle he had never stood up to his brother, he'd been too afraid to, but that had to end, now.

"A better question is why I didn't do it sooner!" Richard recoiled like Nickolas had physically slapped him. His eyes hardened.

"I might have pardoned you and let you come home Nickolas, but now you leave me no choice." He pulled a dagger from his belt, but Nickolas was faster. He cut through his restraints and hurled the knife at Richard. It struck him in the chest, and he crumpled to the floor, shocked.

There was a moment of stunned silence. Nickolas stared at his brother's body in horror and felt tremors work their way up his arms.

"Look out!" Koren kicked him to the side. A blade spun past Nickolas's elbow, narrowly missing him. The projectile hit the wall and clattered to the floor by his feet. He picked it up. Before the Zantie could reach for another weapon, Nickolas sent the knife spinning back at him. The Zantie tried to sidestep the attack, but wasn't fast enough. He dropped to the ground as the blade buried itself in his side.

Nickolas walked over to where the Zantie had fallen, picked him up by the collar of his uniform and slammed him against the wall by the archway.

"Where is the Guardian?"

"What Guardian?" the Zantie replied with a sneer. Nickolas grabbed the handle of the knife and gave it a sharp twist. His captive screamed.

"She's locked in prison a few buildings from here!" His voice was strained and his eyes rolled with pain. Nickolas let him fall to the ground and turned back toward Koren. He picked up the knife Richard had dropped and used it to cut Koren free. Koren pulled the ropes off his wrists, and gingerly felt his side. When he pulled his hand away, Nickolas saw that his fingers were stained red with blood. Koren paled and swept the side of his cloak out of the way to examine the damage. His side was soaked in blood, and more was pouring from a deep gash just below his ribcage.

"There's healing supplies in the space cube," Koren muttered. "They put it with the weapons."

Nickolas nodded and ran into the alleyway. He leafed through the weapons pile and quickly picked out the small black cube. Koren was leaning heavily against the wall when he returned. Nickolas set the cube on the ground and expanded it, rummaging around inside for the med pack. He tore it open and pulled out a thick pad of cloth. Koren took it from him and gently pulled the blood-soaked clothing away from his skin so he could press the fabric directly against the wound.

"How did that happen?" Nickolas asked.

"When the Zantie threw the knife at you, it rebounded off the wall and sliced open my side."

"In that case we need to clean the wound out immediately. Zantie blades are notorious for causing blood infections." He searched in the space cube until he found a canteen and unscrewed the top quickly. Koren took it from him, removed the cloth he had placed over the long gash, and rinsed it out. "Do you have an antiseptic in here?" Nickolas asked.

"No," Koren replied. "Don't worry about me, I'll find some later. Right now we need to find Mimie and get her out of here." He replaced the cloth and tied a longer strip around his waist to hold it in place. He pushed off the wall and threw the canteen back in the space cube. He then walked over to the weapon pile and grabbed what he could easily conceal, putting the rest of his weapons into the space cube. Nickolas didn't feel the need for stealth and replaced his where they would be clearly visible. Koren shrank the space cube down and put it in his pocket.

"I think I know how we can get Mimie out of here, but you're not going to like it…" Nickolas muttered.

"How?" Koren wondered.

Nickolas walked over to his brother's body and switched out Richard's cloak for his own. Koren watched him in surprise and then caught on to what he was implying. He helped Nickolas drag the body over to the horizontal bar, and tied it in place.

"You'll have to scowl more if you want to fool the Zanties," Koren said.

Nickolas rearranged his features into the annoyed look of contempt he had often seen on his brothers' face. It wasn't hard to reproduce given all the years he had spent mocking that expression behind his brother's back.

"Creepy," Koren muttered.

"How do you feel about impersonating a Zantie?"

"They would see through that in a second, especially considering how much blood is on the uniform."

"Ok, then what are we supposed to do with the body…" Nickolas paused a moment as an odd idea struck him. "How big does that space cube get?"

"We are not putting a body in the space cube, that's disgusting," Koren replied, crossing his arms. "Orient wants Mimie to open the key. Take me along as your captive to force her to cooperate and say I killed the Zantie when he was untying me."

Koren picked up a length of rope and tied a quick slipknot to bind his wrists. Nickolas untied Octavious's halter from the bar.

He led the way into the alleyway and made a sharp right, leading them down the long corridor to the courtyard it opened up into. Several Zanties leaning against a building close to them snapped to attention when they saw him. Nickolas gave them a curt nod. Koren

160

was putting on a good show of being a dejected captive. Nickolas gave the rope a sharp tug and walked over to the Zanties.

"Where is the Guardian being held? I want to personally oversee her transport."

"She's in a holding cell over there," the Zantie replied, pointing to a gap between the buildings that led into another courtyard. Nickolas almost thanked him, but bit his tongue before the words could come out. Instead he glared at the Zantie.

"Why are you just standing here, go find something useful to do," he snapped. He turned away and held his face in a hard mask in case anyone else spotted them. He walked between the buildings into a deserted market and quickly spotted the rundown jailhouse by the number of guards standing outside the entrance. He pulled Richard's hood lower over his face and marched up to the closest Zantie.

"Take me to the Guardian," Nickolas growled.

The Zantie promptly moved aside and let them pass. Nickolas shoved past him and handed Octavious's lead rope to a guard standing nearby.

"This animal better be in pristine condition by the time I get back, or I will hold you personally responsible."

The Zantie swallowed hard as he led them into the jail and walked down the corridor at a brisk pace. Nickolas noticed the strain this was putting on Koren.

"Slow down you're not running a marathon!" The Zantie muttered an apology and slowed his pace. Koren discreetly threw Nickolas a grateful look.

At first Nickolas could hardly see where they were going, but after his eyes adjusted to the dim light, it made walking on the crumbling stone floor much easier. They turned sharply around a corner and Nickolas found himself in the darkest hallway yet. A single torch was the only source of light, and it had burned down to almost nothing. Its flickering shadows illuminated a door in the middle of the hallway. The Zantie standing guard outside the door snapped out of his daze at their approach. He lifted his arm in a stiff salute and stepped quickly away from the door.

"Is it sunset already?" the guard yawned.

"Do you have a problem with me taking the guardian early?" Nickolas asked coldly. The guard realized his mistake and rushed to apologize for his slip. Nickolas cut him off and yelled, "Get out of my sight!" The Zantie ran down the hallway. Nickolas struggled not to smile. He pulled the key off the hook by the side of the door and shoved it into the heavy lock. It clicked and he swung open the cell door.

Something leaped at him like a feral cat and scratched at his arm as he tried to block her escape. He was surprised at Mimie's strength and how difficult her thrashing made it to hold onto her. Her eyes locked on his face and she froze.

"Nickolas?"

He groaned aloud in exasperation and dropped the charade. He pulled out his sword and rounded on the Zantie in the hallway. Koren slipped out of the rope and removed a knife from inside his cloak.

The Zantie paused in surprise, but he recovered quickly and pulled out his sword. He lunged at Koren and slammed him hard against the wall. Koren gasped in pain and dropped his knife, eyes unfocused. Nickolas pulled the Zantie off him and threw the guard to the ground. The Zantie was on his feet again in seconds, glaring furiously at the three of them. He lashed out at Nickolas. Mimie came in from his left and slammed a torch into the side of the Zanties head. Nickolas dodged the embers that flew at him.

"Sorry for blowing your cover," Mimie muttered in a dejected tone.

"It's ok. How did you know it was me?"

"The cut on your lip." Koren pushed off the wall and joined them, looking even paler than before. "What happened?" Mimie demanded, looking him over.

"Unfavorable run in with a Zantie guard," he replied vaguely.

"We need to make it look like I am transporting you two outside the settlement to the wagon," Nickolas said, reclaiming their attention. "If the Zanties figure out our deception before we get out of the city, we might not get out at all." He cut the rope lying on the ground in half and sheathed his sword. He tied loose knots over Koren and Mimie's wrists and led them in the direction he hoped was the way out.

Koren's condition, though severe, was to their advantage. It made him look less like a threat. The Zanties barely took note of them as Nickolas paused and gave his eyes a second to adjust.

"Bring my horse," he barked at the Zantie holding Octavious, "and the rest of you, make sure a wagon is ready for our departure."

Nickolas tried to appear confident as he led them through the buildings, but in truth he only semi-knew where he was going.

Eventually, they reached the gate that led outside the settlement and found the gate guard eyeing them greedily.

"Your Highness sir, I was wondering about the reward you promised me?"

Nickolas stopped. He turned toward the little man and allowed the anger, and disgust he felt to show plainly on his face. The man squeaked and backed away. Nickolas pulled a knife from his belt. "Did you still want that reward?"

The guard's eyes opened wide and he shook his head rapidly from side to side.

"Good choice."

Nickolas opened the gate himself. Koren and Mimie stumbled after him. The wagon hadn't arrived yet, which would make things easier. Nickolas turned his knife on the Zantie holding Octavious. He was dead before the surprise could register on his face. Octavious jerked back in alarm and let out a surprised nay.

"Hurry," Nickolas urged. "Koren climb on Octavious's back. You're in no condition to run."

Koren nodded and accepted help from Mimie as he struggled onto the large flying unicorns back. Octavious pinned his ears.

Nickolas broke into a run, pulling Octavious with him. He headed for the sparse woodlands in front of them where Oviet was waiting. They broke through the trees just as loud shouts rang out behind them. Galloping hooves signaled Oviet's arrival and she slid to a stop in front of them.

"It's nearly sunset! What took you guys so long?"

"We'll explain later." Nickolas helped transfer Koren to Oviet's back. Mimie hopped on behind him and helped keep him steady.

Nickolas tied the other side of Octavious's lead rope to his halter to make a pair of makeshift reins, and used them to follow Oviet as she headed deeper into the woodland. She flew across the river and waited for him on the other side. Octavious threw up his head in protest as Nickolas tried to urge him into the water. Sounds of pursuit from behind them made Octavious more anxious and he pranced back and forth along the edge of the water. Oviet's nickered encouragement helped him overcome his fear and he worked his way into the water. He swam the distance quickly and trotted up the opposite bank. Octavious paused to ruffle his feathers and shake the water from his coat. The shouts coming from somewhere behind them were getting louder. Nickolas weighed their options carefully in his head.

"We need to split up. I'll get the Zantie's attention and lead them away from you. It's too conspicuous for us to travel together, you go on, I'll be ok on my own."

"Are you sure?" Mimie said.

"Yeah, good luck with the fairies."

"Safe travels." Koren muttered.

Oviet touched noses briefly with Octavious and nickered a goodbye. She turned and swooped smoothly into the air, staying low so the Zanties wouldn't see her. Nickolas watched them get smaller and smaller until they disappeared into the skyline.

***

"You and Octavious seem to have bonded pretty quickly," Mimie said.

"Well, it's not often I come across others like me."

Mimie placed her hand on Koren's arm "How are you feeling?"

He removed his hand from his side and stared down at the blood with an empty expression. It was like he was in a trance.

Oviet landed in a field sheltered on all sides by looming hills. Mimie slipped off her back and tried to help Koren, but when the full extent of his weight bore down on her, she couldn't support him. They both fell to the ground.

"Aww," he groaned.

"Sorry." Mimie lifted herself off of him and supported her weight on her hands. He glanced up at her and half smiled, amused. His gaze was so intense she got lost in the color of his eyes. It took a few seconds before her mind caught up with her actions, and she pulled away.

"Let me see the wound, I'll do what I can," Oviet said.

"Ok." Koren's eyes flicked back to Mimie's and searched her face for a few seconds. "Don't look, ok?"

"Why not?" she demanded.

"Just trust me," he said.

He pulled up his shirt, exposing the wound so Oviet could see it. He cringed as he pulled away the makeshift bandage. Oviet bent down over him, and he closed his eyes in relief as the wound healed. He rested his head heavily against the grass. Mimie's eyes drifted and her stomach turned when she saw the angry red line across his side.

"I wish I could have worked on this sooner," Oviet muttered. "It's probably infected now. Total bed rest, understand?" Her tone was stern.

Koren rolled his eyes. "Yes Amma."

Mimie took the space cube from him and expanded it. She pulled Koren's sleeping sack out and laid it next to him. He quickly shuffled onto it while Oviet's head was turned.

"I saw that," she growled and trotted off into a tall clump of grass. Mimie picked up the blood soaked bandages and buried them in a hole a little ways away so the blood wouldn't attract predators. She got some clean cloth and a shirt from the space cube. She helped Koren change and dug another hole for the bloody shirt. Koren reached for her canteen and wet a cloth so he could wash the remaining blood off his skin.

"Do you think it's safe to start a fire?" Mimie asked.

"Probably not," he replied.

Sunset was upon them, Mimie shivered as the warm air receded with the sun. She sat down on her sleeping sack and wrapped her cloak more tightly around her shoulders. Koren scooted closer and curled up against her leg. Mimie stared at him in bewilderment. Hesitantly, she put her hand on his back and felt the warmth of his skin soaking through his shirt. Lightly she traced a pattern across his back with her finger. The moment felt surreal; like a happy bubble that could burst at any second.

Koren's breathing eventually became more regular until she knew he had fallen asleep.

CHAPTER 13: NOWHERE LAND

⇐ ⇐ ⇒ ⇒

Mimie opened her eyes and saw the moon directly overhead. At first she wasn't sure what had woken her, but jumped into a sitting position when she heard a low grown beside her. The night had a sharp edge to it but she hardly noticed because Koren's body was radiating heat. She placed her palm on his forehead and was instantly worried; his skin was scorching hot.

"Your hand is freezing," he muttered weakly. She tried to pull away, but he grabbed her wrist and replaced her palm on his forehead. "No. It feels nice."

"Why didn't you wake me up when you felt the fever coming on?" she demanded.

"You looked so peaceful," he told her with a half-smile. He was shaking even though he was burning up, so she draped her sleeping sack over him and then replaced her palm on his forehead. Dark circles were forming under his eyes from fighting the fever all night.

"It feels good to have you close like this. It takes the edge off the pain."

"Good," Mimie muttered.

"There's something I have to tell you," he said, meeting her gaze once more.

"What?" Mimie asked. He smiled weakly.

"I've always thought you were beautiful."

Mimie looked at the red patches of skin on her arms. She thought about her too round face and her hair that was currently tangled beyond help.

"I'm not," Mimie replied softly and turned away. Her shoulders curled inward.

"You can believe what you want, but it doesn't change the truth." He fell quiet and his green eyes reflected the starlight as he stared up at the heavens. He scooted closer until his head was resting in her lap. Mimie froze, not sure how to respond. The sleeping sack had fallen off so she pulled it over him again so he wouldn't get cold.

"I hate this," he grumbled against her leg. "I feel like my brain is melting."

"I'm sure you'll feel better by the morning," Mimie replied, and replaced her palm on his forehead. Her mind spun as she tried to isolate which emotions she was feeling. Was it really so hard to believe that he could fall for her? Of course it was, especially when his behavior could easily be explained by the simple fact that he was sick and just wanted the comfort of another person— nothing more.

His breathing became more even. She gently moved away from him, curling up in her cloak to keep warm. She tried to keep her feelings in check, but couldn't stop the odd flutter in her chest. She remembered falling asleep, however briefly, snuggled against his chest and felt guilty knowing the interaction had meant more to her than it had to him, as if she'd deceived him in some way.

I don't make the calls when time stands still

This is a dangerous game I play with myself

I steal a moment

I make it mine

To hold forever in empty arms

When the sand runs out.

She fell asleep with the lines repeating themselves over and over in her head.

She woke up again a few hours after sunrise and opened her eyes in confusion. How had she managed to sleep so long past dawn?

"How is he?" Oviet asked from the clump of grass she was laying in.

"I don't know, you tell me," Mimie replied and scooted away from him. Oviet got to her feet, walked over to Koren, and nudged him with her nose.

"Five more minutes," he groaned and pushed her away.

"He's fine," Oviet laughed and walked away. Koren sat up groggily and rubbed his eyes.

"Thanks for staying up with me last night."

"No problem," Mimie replied, not meeting his gaze. The flush from the fever was gone, and the coloring in his face had almost returned to normal. She started to stand up, but he stopped her.

"I'll pack up camp." There wasn't much to do and he had it finished in minutes. "Let's get out of here, we've already lost enough daylight."

"Sounds good to me," Oviet said, pushing herself to her feet and stretching out her wings. They climbed onto her back, and she took off into the air. Mimie grimaced at the lurch in her stomach and suddenly remembered how hungry she was. Her stomach growled loudly to voice the complaint.

They landed in the middle of the day to give Oviet a rest. Mimie took the opportunity to refill their water canteens and look for sprouting plants to eat. She got lucky and found a clump of blackberry bushes. Most of them weren't ripe, but she collected the ones that were in a pouch to share with Koren. Koren pulled out his bow and walked over to the river. He notched an arrow and aimed for a large fish swimming in shallow water. Mimie watched carefully and was amazed when the arrowed went straight through the fish's eye.

"Holy cow, where did you learn how to do that?"

"My brother taught me, the trick is to aim deeper and closer than the fish appears because of the way the light bends when it goes through the water." He retrieved the fish, gutted it and made a quick fire to cook it. While he was busy doing that Mimie found a soap root and settled down on the stream bank to wash her hair. When she was finished she combed through the tangled strands with her fingers and returned just as Koren was putting out the fire. They waited a minute to let the fish cool and then picked pieces off it with their fingers. Ordinarily, Mimie hated the taste of fish, but with how hungry she was it didn't bother her. They ate the blackberries and sprouts she'd found, then headed off again.

After a few hours the grass faded into fine white sand. The river had disappeared with it and they had to switch to using the sun to navigate. Mimie glanced at the ground in wonder.

"Amazing..."

"We'll see how you feel when we land and the local wildlife tries to eat you," Koren replied.

"What are you talking about, there's nothing around for miles."

"Are you familiar with the concept of sand liquidation?"

"Not really," Mimie replied.

"The animals here have a large organ in their body that stores enormous amounts of air. They blow it out through skin pores and the air liquefies the sand around them so they can swim through it."

"That's fascinating. What else do you know about them?"

"If you take a walk on the open sand, something will try to eat you. I learned that lesson the hard way."

"What were you doing way out here?" Mimie wondered.

"Just exploring, meeting new people. That was before I decided to become a forest Guardian. We won't be able to fly over all of this before nightfall, but there are rock patches that pop up every once and a while. We'll be safe on those."

"So how do they breathe in the sand? Do they have gills like fish?"

"Not that I've seen, they come up to the surface to breathe like whales." Koren smiled at her intense interest in the subject. "If you watch closely maybe you'll spot one and then you can see for yourself." Mimie peered over the side and watched the sand carefully.

She didn't see anything. As the temperature increased she grew bored of her vigil. She took the water canteen from Koren and sipped at it, being careful not to drink too much so they could conserve it.

"This is miserable," Oviet complained. Mimie yawned and felt her eyelids drooping.

She was relieved when Oviet landed late in the afternoon for the night. The hard rock they landed on housed several palm trees with patches of moisture collecting at their roots. Some of these patches had fresh grass growing on them. Oviet busied herself grazing while Koren pulled a length of rope from the space cube and tied a rock to the end of it.

"What are you doing?" Mimie wondered.

"Sand fishing," he replied. "I'm going to need your help, though." He led her toward the edge of the rock and demonstrated what he wanted her to do. He swung the rope that held the rock over his head and then let it fly out onto the open sand. It landed with a soft thud and then he dragged it back and handed it to Mimie. She took it from him and watched as he got his bow ready. He nodded to her and she stepped away from him so she wouldn't accidently hit him with the rock. She threw the rock but it didn't go nearly as far as his had. She dragged it back and tried again.

After the sixth throw her arm was getting tired, but her efforts were rewarded when she saw something in the sand following the rock as she dragged it back. The sand seemed to boil around whatever was swimming through it and it glided along as easily as a fish swimming through a stream. Koren aimed his bow carefully and waited until the sand creature was close enough to the surface that the plates on its back were visible. He let the arrow loose, aiming for the joint between the armor. The arrow sank deep into the creatures back and it let out an eerie scream. Koren lunged at it before it could dive back into the sand and quickly hauled it up onto the rock.

The creature resembled a giant worm as thick as Mimie's leg. It was reddish-orange in color with thick brown plates on its back and several legs that came to a sharp bony point. The two legs in the front were the longest and it lashed out at Koren with one, trying to stab him with it. The plates were thicker on its head and it didn't have any eyes. Its mouth was full of tiny needle-sharp teeth, and it had wicked looking tusks on the sides of its jaw. All in all, it was one of the creepiest looking things she had ever seen.

Koren pulled out his sword and ended the struggle quickly by stabbing the creature in the neck. It rolled onto its back and the legs twitched as lingering nerve activity continued in the body.

"I am not eating that," Mimie declared, feeling sick.

"Just try it," Koren urged. "This is the only thing we're going to find out here that's edible."

He pulled out a knife and cut the legs and head off, throwing them out onto the sand. He dug his fingers into the joint where the harder body plates met the softer belly plates, prying them apart. There was a loud crack, and the pinkish-white meat within was exposed. It was similar looking to the freshwater crabmeat back home. Once the shell was open, he cut the outer layer of muscle. He peeled it away from the innards, coming away with a long, roughly rectangular sheet of meat. He cut it into six strips and gave three to Mimie. She took them and grimaced as she watched him eat his raw.

"That is beyond nasty," she told him.

"Stop complaining and just eat it," he snapped. She pouted, and turned away from him.

"Fine," she muttered and took a tentative bite out of it. The meat was slimy and had a rubbery texture. She choked it down and gagged, then washed her mouth out with a little bit of water to get rid of the lingering salty taste. After eating that she would never complain about the taste of fish again.

"Guys..." Oviet called, "I think we may have a problem." Koren and Mimie joined her on the other side of the rock island. Mimie shaded her eyes and saw a sand cloud approaching them in the distance.

"It still looks pretty far away," she muttered. "Can we find a way around it?"

"It's moving too fast, we wouldn't have enough time," Koren replied.

"So what do we do?"

"You and I can stay in our sleeping sacks. I'll tie my cloak around Oviet's head to keep the sand out of her eyes." Mimie stared in apprehension as the pale cloud inched its way up the horizon line. Koren pulled out the space cube, removed their sleeping sacks and then shrank it down again.

"How much time do we have left?" Mimie asked.

He studied the sand cloud and replied, "Five minutes, maybe less."

He walked over to Oviet and draped his cloak over her head and around her horn until her head was completely covered.

"It is a good thing I'm not claustrophobic," she grumbled.

"Don't step on us, okay?" Koren told her and grabbed the sleeping sacks. He gave one to Mimie.

"Try to move around a lot so the sand doesn't bury you. Otherwise, you could suffocate."

"That's encouraging," Mimie said apprehensively.

"I'll hit you with my elbow every once and a while to make sure you're okay."

"Alright." Mimie spread out her sleeping sack and crawled inside. She pulled her knees to her chest and tucked the lip of the sack under her. She felt Koren doing the same beside her. Something nudged her side

"Can you feel that?"

"Yeah," Mimie replied, she elbowed what she thought was his arm and asked, "Can you?"

"Yep." She could barely hear him over the wind. A whooshing sound covered the roar as the sand rushed over them, and it suddenly became hard to breathe. Koren nudged her again. She elbowed him back and wondered what she would do without him. She wriggled around when the load on top of her became heavy and tried to find ways to entertain herself. It was hot in the confined space and sweat dripped into her eyes. She wiped it away with her arm, but it made little difference.

When she was sure the storm was over she struggled free of the sand that had piled on top of her and tore her sleeping sack away from her head. The breeze felt glorious on her feverous skin.

"Everyone still alive?" Oviet called.

"Yep," Mimie replied watching Koren struggle free of his sleeping sack.

"In that case, could someone please take this thing off my face?"

"Sorry," Mimie replied and rushed to her aid. When Oviet was free, she shook out her mane and coat then ruffled up her feathers to try and groom the sand out of them.

"Any idea how long it's going to take us to get out of here?" she wondered. Koren shrugged and replied,

"Hopefully, it will only take another day and a half."

The sun was almost gone leaving the sky a bloody looking red. They retired to sleep but Mimie had the nagging fear another sandstorm would hit them in the middle of the night, so she didn't sleep very soundly. The skies were clear the next morning when she woke up. They packed up quickly and once they were on Oviet's back, she took to the sky.

Mimie watched the ground rushing by beneath them and, to her surprise, saw a strange looking thirty-foot animal jump out of the sand and then dive back into it and disappear.

"WOW!!" Mimie yelled, almost falling off Oviet's back "Did you see that?" Koren grabbed her arm and pulled her back with an amused smile. The creature was a shimmering blue color with scales made of stone. It had a green plate on its head and was blind like the worm. The body was streamlined with a long head, large fins, and a powerful looking tale.

"I believe that was a whale," Koren told her.

"Awe, do you think it would let me pet it?" Koren smacked his palm against his forehead. "Is that a no?" Mimie laughed.

"What is it with you and wanting to pet strange things?" Oviet asked. Mimie shrugged. She kept her eyes on the sand hoping to catch sight of more sand creatures, but no such luck. The air was hot and dry, and soon Mimie found she was uncomfortably thirsty.

"Koren?" she croaked after a while.

"Yeah?" he replied.

"Do we have any water?"

"Not much," he muttered, handing the canteen to her. She took a sip of it and gagged. It was hot and had an aftertaste of wood.

"We are going to shrivel up and die," she groaned

"No, we aren't. A day with no water isn't going to kill us."

"A day with no water in this heat might," Oviet contended.

"Not helping," Koren replied.

They stopped on another rock island at noon. Mimie hopped off and sat in the shade beneath one of the palm trees. The sand was damp here as well and she gathered it together to make a sand sculpture. She patted it together in the rough shape of a mountain and then dug tunnels through it.

"You should make a model of Koren's head," Oviet laughed. Mimie smiled and flattened her mountain. She shaped out Koren's face and laughed. Koren glanced over her shoulder and tilted his head sideways.

"That looks kind of scary," he remarked, "like a cross between a pig and a bat."

"The sand is drying out, ok?" Mimie laughed. They left shortly after that and flew the rest of the day until pure exhaustion finally forced Oviet to give up. She drifted toward a rock island, and when she reached it, her legs gave way. Mimie and Koren were thrown from her back. Mimie rolled a few times across the sandy rock, but she was too tired to move.

Bright sunlight blinded her even though her eyes were closed. She ignored it and was drifting off again when something tickled her neck. Mimie opened her eyes, blinking while she waited for the blurriness to clear from her vision. She looked down, surprised to see a small green lizard curled up on her arm. The lizard twitched in its sleep and flicked its tail across Mimie's neck. After a minute or two the lizard lazily opened its eyes and yawned. It froze as Mimie's face came into view. The lizard hissed at her and then ran to the top of one of the palm trees.

"Good morning to you too," Mimie laughed and got to her feet. She yawned and walked a few steps backward as she was stretching. She tripped over something behind her.

"Ouch," Koren muttered, still half asleep. "Mimie get off."

Mimie smiled and carefully got to her feet. "Sorry," she apologized and brushed the sand off her front. Her stomach growled, but she cringed at the thought of having to eat more worm meat. Her hunger could wait, she decided. Koren pushed himself to his feet and shaded his eyes against the sun. "What are you looking at?" Mimie asked. She followed his finger and was surprised to see a green smudge on the horizon. "Are those trees?" she asked hopefully. Oviet perked up immediately and jumped to her feet.

"Really?" she asked, checking for herself. "Let's go then!" she exclaimed. Mimie smiled, and she and Koren quickly hopped on her back before she flew off without them.

CHAPTER 14: KYRA

A short time later Oviet swooped toward the ground, and Mimie found herself in a tropical paradise. The air was more humid, and the scent of flowers blew toward her on the breeze.

"This is beautiful," Mimie muttered.

"Yep," Oviet agreed around a mouth full of grass. Mimie slid off her back and spun around in slow circles, taking a second to appreciate the sights, sounds and smells. All those made more drastic by the sand she could still see stretching out behind her.

"I want to take a look around," Mimie told them. Koren opened his mouth to object, but changed his mind when he saw how much she was enjoying herself. Mimie passed through a curtain of leaves and entered a clearing covered by a canopy of branches. Wildflowers ranging in every color imaginable, covered the jungle floor. A chorus of colorful birds sat in the trees and gracefully swooped through the air, while a creek filled with crystal clear water bubbled down a small waterfall. Bright green frogs croaked idly on lush, moss-covered rocks in the middle of the water and tall reeds grew along the bank casting long, irregular shadows over the ground.

Just to Mimie's right grew huge pink and red flowers that smelled sweeter than anything she had ever encountered. Gently, she stroked one of the petals and found it velvety soft. At her touch, a rainbow beetle sprang out of the flower and flew at her face. Surprised, Mimie stumbled back a few steps and bumped into Koren. He reached out an arm to help her regain her balance and chuckled at her apologetic expression. Mimie brushed her fingers across the flowers they passed and laughed when the beetles jumped out and startled Oviet.

"Mimie, stop it!" she snapped.

Koren pulled her to the other side of him and laughed, "Stop being a nuisance."

"Ok," Mimie sighed. The small trail they were following wound through comfortable looking thick green grass. She considered falling over into it, but then thought of all the beetles that were sure to be living in it and changed her mind.

They walked for the next few hours in silence, looking for a break in the branches that would be big enough for Oviet to fly out. As they pushed further into the jungle the trees grew larger and the canopy overhead became thicker and more impenetrable.

"Maybe this wasn't the best idea," Oviet muttered.

Up ahead a light fog obscured the trail and made it hard to see where they were going.

"Do you want to turn back?" Koren asked.

"Yeah, that's probably the best option," Oviet sighed. "Wait, I think I see a break in the canopy up ahead." Mimie saw it too, a small beam of light shining down through the fog. They walked toward it, but when they got close enough to see the size of the gap, Mimie noticed there were too many young trees growing under it for Oviet to be able to spread her wings.

"Darn, I was hoping we wouldn't have to backtrack," Oviet grumbled.

"Let's head back to the trail." Koren searched the surrounding trees and frowned.

"What?" Mimie asked.

"Did we come from there, or over here?" he wondered pointing in two different directions.

"I don't know, I can't see anything through this fog," Oviet replied.

"What should we do?" Mimie wondered, stepping closer to Koren.

"The fog thins out a little up ahead, let's walk over there and see if that helps any."

Untamed branches reached out and snagged on Mimie's clothes while dead leaves crunched loudly underfoot. A numbing cackle sounded in the distance. Mimie grabbed Koren's arm and hung on for dear life.

"What was that?" Oviet asked quietly.

"I don't know," Koren muttered and drew his sword. "Keep moving." Mimie had the uneasy feeling something was watching them. The trees seemed to be closing in on them from all sides, and it wasn't hard to imagine shadows hiding in the gnarled roots. The strange cackling sounds continued, coming from every direction.

Mimie spotted a black bird with bright yellow eyes hopping up and down on the upper level of a branch. It cackled, and she realized the bird was what had put them all on edge. Mimie loosened her grip on Koren's arm.

"Those are scavenger birds," Oviet observed. "Why are they following us?"

"They're not," Koren replied in a tight voice. "They know a predator is close by, they are waiting for it to attack."

The birds were going crazy, three more had joined the first, and they were flapping from branch to branch.

A flash of movement caught Mimie's eye, and she spun around. A large black cat with glowing green eyes and a scorpion tail stalked toward her through the fog. She knew what was going to happen half a second before she saw its strange tail whip up into the air. There was no time to scream, no time to think, as a huge spike flew directly at her chest. Mimie fell backward; she was too stunned to feel the pain. When she recovered enough for the profound ache to register, she found that her entire body was paralyzed.

***

"Mimie!" Koren screamed, he threw himself between her and the beast, but it was too late. He glared at the snarling animal while Oviet moved into position beside him. She lowered her head and pawed at the ground threateningly. The Scorpion Cat roared and paced back and forth in front of them, snarling. Koren saw the cat's tail whip up and dodged the spike as it flew at his face. Before the Scorpion Cat could launch another attack, Oviet reared onto her hind legs and galloped toward its left side. While it was distracted, Koren ran toward it from the other side and, in a fluid swing, cut off its tail.

The Scorpion Cat yowled in pain and rage. It rounded on Koren and raked its claws across his forearm. Koren lost his balance and fell sideways. Oviet charged toward the cat and kicked it aside with a well-aimed blow to the ribs. Koren struggled to his feet, pulled a knife out of his belt and threw it at the cat's heart. It moved at the last second, and the blade sunk into its side instead. The cat screamed and charged at Koren. Oviet tried to kick it again, but it sidestepped out of her reach and lunged at Koren.

The impact knocked the breath out of him and he landed hard on his back, his sword fell his hand. He tried to push the cat off his chest, but it was too heavy. He felt its breath on his neck and screamed as it sank its teeth into his shoulder.

Half a second later it yelped and released him. Koren shoved it off and saw it fall to the side. He struggled up onto his uninjured arm and was surprised to see two silver arrows lodged deep in the cat's rib cage.

"What the..." he said, and noticed two female warrior elves standing on the path in front of him, their bows still raised. They were partially obscured by the fog, but quickly became more distinct as they swiftly walked closer. Koren was uncomfortably aware of the pulsing warmth seeping down his side and arm. He was in no condition to fight if they had hostile intentions. Oviet trotted over to him and examined the bite marks on his shoulder. She healed the punctures quickly. The claw wounds were ragged and filled with debris from his fight with the scorpion cat. "This needs to be cleaned out before I can heal it, and the muscle put back in place."

"Ok, I'll get the water canteens," Koren muttered.

"Wait," one of the elves called. "An experienced healer should look at that." She pulled out a thin wooden whistle and blew it shrilly. He heard rustling in the distance and a few minutes later another elf burst from behind one of the bushes.

"What happened?" she demanded. Her thick brown hair was french braided around the crown of her head; she wore a white dress and had a twisted cord of gold string around her waist like a belt. Her sharp eyes took in the scene in front of her, and she didn't wait for an explanation. She walked over to Koren and knelt beside him, looking over his arm. Quickly, she removed supplies from her bag and handed him a small bottle.

"Take a few sips of this."

"What is it?"

"It's will dull your pain. You'll want it for when I pull your arm back together." Koren sipped at it and gagged, feeling the liquid burn all the way down his throat. A numb sleepiness overtook him almost immediately. She washed out his arm, which hurt, but the drug she gave him took the edge off the pain.

"You seem very familiar. Have you passed through here before?" Koren stiffened and didn't reply. Having someone recognize him was definitely not something he wanted. She pushed the muscle back into his arm and held everything in place as Oviet healed it.

"My friend over there needs help as well. She was struck with one of the scorpion cat's darts." The healer left him and examined Mimie.

"A lot of elves and fairies are deathly allergic to scorpion cat venom, but it seems she is one of the lucky few who is not. Aside from the puncture wound she only seems to be experiencing temporary paralysis." She motioned Oviet over and had her heal the wound as soon as she pulled out the spike. "Cynthia, Avia, get them back to the village."

"Yes Evangeline," they replied. Cynthia helped Koren to his feet and draped his arm over her shoulder. She led him forward, and Koren followed numbly after her.

***

Mimie felt Avia scoop her off the ground. Mimie wasn't sure where they were going, or how long it was going to take to get there. The thickness in her head, and the elves rhythmic walking helped put Mimie into a stupor. After what seemed like no time at all Mimie heard a murmur of voices and assumed she had reached some sort of village. She was surprised to find that she could open her eyes and was glad the paralysis was wearing off.

Little houses were built in the treetops. The houses themselves were simple, but each one took advantage of every useable space. The branches of the trees made up the walls, and the leaves worked together to make a protected roof over the structures.

Avia's destination seemed to be an enormous tree in the center of the village. She passed through a curtain of leaves at its base, revealing a winding staircase inside. She carried Mimie up the stairs, and a few minutes later they emerged at the top of the tree. Evangeline was already there, and she had a pad on the floor set up for Mimie. Avia set her down on it and then disappeared back down the staircase.

Like the rest of the tree buildings, this one had been built to take advantage of every useable space. The walls and floor covered an irregular surface area, and in some places the branches came up right through the floor. From these branches hung thick curtains dividing the tree into smaller chambers. Each of these chambers consisted of four beds. She guessed that the whole tree could hold about 125 patients. Cynthia appeared with Koren in tow and laid him down on the pad one away from hers. She was recovering quickly and after a few minutes was able to move her head enough to look at him. He seemed restless and jumped at every sound.

"What's wrong?" Mimie wondered. She thought he would be happy to be around other elves again, but the tension in his shoulders said differently. Before he could answer, Evangeline stiffened and glanced toward the entrance. Mimie strained to hear what had made her jump to attention and could just make out the soft noise that signaled light footfalls climbing the stairs. A few seconds later their visitor slid gracefully into view; Evangeline curtsied respectfully and muttered,

"Your majesty."

Mimie's mouth opened in shock. The elf standing in front of her looked just like Koren, they had the same green eyes, blondish-brown hair, and similar facial structures.

How was that possible!

She waited for Koren to give her an explanation, but his expression was unreadable. Kyra's long hair was pulled up into a beautiful layer of curls, held in place by a twinkling golden crown. The dress she wore was made of white silk with gold flowers wound around it. She was beautiful, but the way Koren was responding to her made Mimie think the beauty was only skin deep.

"Kormont?" she asked hesitantly.

"It's Koren," he replied coldly. She seemed taken aback by his tone and crossed her arms.

"It's customary for a prince to be referred to by his full name. Anything else is simply bad manners."

"I'm not a prince. I left that life a long time ago," he replied. Kyra acted as though she hadn't heard him.

"It's so good to see you again after all this time," she said, a big smile lighting up her face. She pulled him into a hug and held onto him tightly.

"Kyra, get off." She let go and flashed him an apologetic smile.

"I'm having a celebration dinner in honor of my husband's birthday. You should join us," she said. Mimie couldn't help but notice the same invitation was not extended to her. "I know you're tired so I'll leave you to your rest. See you at sundown, Evangeline will show you where to go." She turned toward the stairs and disappeared.

Koren clenched his jaw and glared at the ceiling.

"What was that all about?" Mimie wondered.

"I don't want to talk about it," Koren replied, turning his back on her.

"If she's a danger to us, I deserve to know."

"She's not dangerous…well, sort of, I don't know. It's complicated."

"In what way?"

"When my family was driven out of their village by humans, they took refuge in a mountain valley. A terrible sickness killed off a large number of them until it was just Kyra, her bodyguards, Amelia, me and another elf named Emily," he said the last name quietly, almost reverently. "We were planning to leave the valley together, but when my sister Amelia got sick Kyra left her behind. I didn't even get to hug her goodbye. I told Kyra I wanted to stay, but one of the bigger elves picked me up and forced me to go with them. I kicked and screamed for them to let me go back, but Kyra had one of her thugs beat me until I blacked out. I was only nine.

The next morning I got sick too. I tried to hide it because I knew what would happen if anyone found out. I was right. Kyra abandoned me without a second glance and had her guards tie me to a tree when I tried to follow them.

I begged her. I screamed at her to come back until my throat was raw. If Luna hadn't come along and healed me, I would be dead right now. She has no remorse or accountability for her actions. She can't be trusted, and I think it's in our best interest to get out of here as soon as possible."

"Ok, we'll be polite and go to the banquet, then leave first thing tomorrow morning." Koren didn't look happy about it, but he grudgingly agreed. "Hopefully I get un-paralyzed in time to go with you." Mimie stiffly adjusted her weight and felt an almost unbearable pins and needle sensation spread through her. She scrunched up her nose and cringed, waiting for the feeling to go away. The paralysis faded slowly, and it wasn't until two hours later that it left altogether. She unsteadily pushed herself to her feet and stretched out limbs that were sore from being in the same position for too long.

"I'm glad to see that you have recovered," Evangeline said. "You may use the accommodations here to start getting ready if you wish."

"Thanks," Mimie said uncertainly.

"If you'll follow me, the ladies washrooms are back here." She led Mimie to the back of the tree where there were four rooms. Mimie glanced at Koren over her shoulder and saw him being led to the opposite end of the tree by another healer. Evangeline opened the door to the first room on the left and led Mimie inside.

"Call me when you are finished," Evangeline muttered and shut the door behind her.

The first thing Mimie noticed was the bathtub. Next to it was a large wooden table with a mirror on top and stool tucked under it. Mimie stared at the knobs on the tub and turned each of them experimentally until hot water came out. While the tub filled up, she pulled off her clothes and threw them into a pile by the side of the table. She stepped inside and closed her eyes as the roar and the warmth of the water enveloped her. When she was fully submerged, she turned the water off and closed her eyes again.

There were three unlabeled bottles on the ground next to her. She stared at them uncertainly and squeezed a tiny amount of each onto her hand to try and figure out what they were. The last one smelled the nicest so she rubbed it into her hair and let it sit. When her hair felt soft and silky, she rinsed out the cream and let the water drain from the tub. She reached for the white towel that was draped over the stool and shook out her wet hair. She toweled off her face and body, and then paused, realizing that she had absolutely nothing to wear.

"Evangeline?" Mimie called out uncertainly. "Are you there?"

"Yes, what do you need?"

"I wasn't expecting to be attending any banquets when I packed. Is there anything I could borrow for tonight?"

"Of course. I have a dress already picked out for you."

Mimie felt taken aback and opened the door a crack to grab it from her. Evangeline had also included fresh undergarments. Mimie put them on and then gently pulled the dress over her head. It was elegant and moved with Mimie as if it were made of liquid. It clung to all the right places and shimmered slightly when she moved. The dress was white with blue trim along the sleeves and neckline. A blue ribbon tied was around her waist and rested just above her hips. Mimie opened the door to let Evangeline in, and she dropped a pair of small white heels by her feet. Mimie slipped them on and found that they were a little too big, but didn't want to say anything for fear of sounding rude.

Evangeline led her to the stool and had her sit with her back to the mirror. She set a large bag on the table and pulled out a brush.

"So you and Koren are pretty close?" she said.

"Not in that way." Mimie blushed.

"I see," Evangeline muttered. Mimie fell silent, not sure what to say. Evangeline brushed all of Mimie's hair back and parted it off to the side. She grabbed curlers from the bag and rolled them into Mimie's hair. She then pulled out a bottle and sprayed its contents onto the curlers. Steam formed, and within minutes her hair had completely dried. Evangeline carefully unwound the curlers from her hair and broke up the curls a little bit. To finish things off, she pulled the front of Mimie's hair back, twisted it, and snapped a clip into place. She stepped back to admire her handiwork and nodded in satisfaction.

"Much better," she muttered and applied a thin layer of something sweet tasting to Mimie's lips to make them shiny. "You are ready," she declared.

"Thank you." Mimie pushed herself to her feet and glanced at her reflection in the mirror. The burns were barely visible on her arms, and her eyes seemed to glow a bright greenish gray. Beautiful ringlets framed her face and shimmered when she moved. "Wow," was all she could say. Evangeline smirked.

"Come on, Koren is waiting outside." She pulled Mimie to her feet and gently nudged her out the door.

"What about my clothes?" Mimie wondered, looking back and feeling distressed about the mess she had made.

"Don't worry about it. Go, have fun," Evangeline urged. She turned her around and pushed her out the door. Mimie struggled to keep her balance in the ridiculous shoes and felt her heart flutter when she saw Koren. He looked stunning. His blonde-brown hair was carefully messed up, and he was wearing a light green vest outlined in gold trim. Underneath was a black shirt with a high collar and sleeves that ended at her elbow. A black and gold belt wrapped around his waist and came together at a silver clasp. His pants were black with a single green and gold strip running down the side.

"You look beautiful," Koren complemented.

Mimie's cheeks turned red. "You look like a prince."

Koren shrugged. "Shall we go then?" he asked, holding out his arm. Mimie stared at it uncertainly, not wanting to show bad etiquette by grabbing it wrong. Koren helped her into the proper form and followed Evangeline as she walked toward the stairs. Koren and Mimie sauntered after her, neither of them wanting to go where they were headed. When they emerged at the bottom of the stairs, Koren held up the vines for Mimie. Evangeline was nowhere to be seen, but it wasn't hard to figure out where they were supposed to go. The massive tree lit by hundreds of candles.

"Want to make a run for it?" Koren asked suddenly.

"What?" Mimie laughed. She studied his expression, and her smile widened when she realized he was serious. "But I'm wearing this ridiculous dress, I would ruin it if I spent the night wondering the forest."

"I mean it, Mimie. I don't think we should go."

"Don't worry, I'll protect you," she laughed.

"It's not just me that I'm worried about," Koren muttered. Mimie tucked a lock of hair behind her ear.

"Koren...can I tell you something?" They climbed the stairs and stopped when they reached the lowest platform.

"Sure," he said with a guarded expression.

"I love you...rr shoes." Koren raised an eyebrow.

"What?" he laughed.

"I love your shoes, they're very nice," Mimie mumbled, feeling like an idiot.

"Um, ok." He inched along the wall trying not to bring attention to himself. Mimie smacked herself on the forehead with her palm and followed him. Suddenly a tall elf with black hair clasped him on the shoulder and exclaimed,

"Ah! Kormont you're here. Kyra and I were getting worried that you'd gotten lost or something."

"It's Koren," he corrected, pulling out of the elf's grip.

"Oh sorry, I'm Visailios. Kyra and I are so happy to have you here." He gave Koren a broad smile and then seemed to notice Mimie. "Who's this?" he asked, winking at Koren.

"This is Mimie." She curtsied and gave him a shy smile.

"Nice to meet you Mimie. Come sit with us, our table is this way."

He led them across the room to a short table made of polished wood. A white tablecloth was spread over the top of it and small candles were floating in water filled silver bowls, which cast a flickering shadow over the people sitting there. The table held five chairs, two of which were already occupied by Kyra and a very young elf Mimie assumed was her son. He was sitting in the last chair furthest to the right, and Kyra was seated in the chair next to him. Visailios took the seat next to Kyra, and Koren took the seat next to him, which only left the last chair on the left. Mimie sat down and noticed the little elf was staring at her. Mimie gave him a warm smile and he giggled. She chuckled as the small elf inched out of his chair and slowly approached her. "Teodor, don't make a nuisance of yourself," Visailios laughed.

"He's okay," Mimie replied, and watched as the small elf shyly approached her. He had Koren and Kyra's bright green eyes, and his father's black hair.

"My lady." He bowed. Mimie guessed he was about four or five. He reached out his arms for her, and she pulled the small child onto her lap.

"Hi Teodor," she greeted. "What a little gentleman you are." He smiled at the praise and then held his arms out for Koren. Mimie handed him over and Koren set his nephew on his lap. He grinned at the child and tousled his hair affectionately.

"Are you my Uncle?" he asked in a small voice.

"I sure am."

"How come I've never seen you before?" Koren stared into his wide green eyes and battled with what to say.

"I live far, far, away from here," he answered finally. This seemed to satisfy Teodor. He turned to look out at the crowd and then clapped his small hands joyfully.

"Yea! The feast is starting." He hopped off Koren's lap and ran back to his seat. Visailios ruffled his son's hair affectionately.

"He is adorable," Mimie whispered to Koren, "and he has your eyes."

"My father's eyes," Koren corrected.

"You two better go get some food before it's all gone," Visailios laughed. Mimie noticed a long table along the far wall loaded with food. She followed Koren over to it, and nearly gaged when she saw her options. Mimie pointed to a blue slice of meat and whispered,

"Is that cooked all the way?"

Koren laughed. "Don't worry it's just the seasoning. Do you want me to find you something?"

"You're the best," Mimie told him. "Just so you know: if it's still alive, I don't want it." Her lip curled in disgust as she eyed the soup to her left. The broth was green and it had thousands of little white worms swimming in it. Koren smiled, bemused. Mimie walked back to her seat and watched as he tried various food items and put them on a plate.

"Do you want anything to drink?" Mimie jumped, it wasn't the question that surprised her. It was the speaker. Kyra was waiting for an answer.

"Um, sure," Mimie muttered. "Water please." Kyra disappeared in the crowd and Mimie wondered why she was being so nice to her, maybe she was turning over a new leaf. Kyra came back a few minutes later and placed a glass in front of her. The water was crystal clear and so cold it had condensation dripping down the side. Kyra smiled at her, but Mimie thought she saw something dark concealed behind her eyes. She left before Mimie could thank her; so maybe she was just trying to look good in front of her husband.

Koren came back a few minutes later with two plates and set one down in front of her.

"Thank you," Mimie said. There was colorful, sweet smelling fruit, muffins, regular colored meat, and steamed veggies. Mimie spotted movement on Koren's plate and wrinkled her nose in disgust. "Is that a worm?" she asked. Koren grinned and pulled a small white worm out of his salad.

"Hummm…it appears so," Koren mused. "I could have sworn I picked them all out."

"Can I hold it?" Mimie asked.

"Sure, but I thought you said you don't like worms," Koren laughed.

"I do like worms; I just don't like to eat them." Koren placed the worm on Mimie's palm.

"I think I will call you Silvia," Mimie said and stroked the worm with her pinkie finger.

"You shouldn't play with your food Mimie," Koren laughed.

"You are so ugly, Silvia," Mimie crooned. "Yes you are."

"Way to make her feel good about herself, how do you even know it's a girl?" Koren wondered,

"That is irrelevant," Mimie laughed. She made sure no one was watching and then faced the wall behind her.

"What are you doing?" Koren asked, chuckling at her attempt to be sneaky.

"Liberating Silvia," Mimie replied. She parted the branches and gently placed the worm on a leaf. The leaf dipped down and the worm fell off. Mimie tried to catch her, but she wasn't fast enough. She turned back to Koren with an anguished look on her face. Koren was struggling not to laugh. "Koren?"

"Yes?"

"I think I killed her."

Koren clutched his side and laughed so hard he drew curious stares from the crowd sitting near them. Mimie scowled and ate the rest of her food in silence.

"Would it help if I got you another one?"

"No," she snapped. Koren chuckled quietly and ate the rest of his salad.

A little while later Mimie noticed elves moving tables out of the middle of the floor. On a raised platform in front of the dance floor, a few elves began a melodic trill on a cue from the royal family. The music was like nothing Mimie had ever heard before.

"What kind of instruments are those?" Mimie whispered quietly to Koren. "I recognize the strings and the tambourine, but what is that shell looking thing some of them are playing?"

"That's an Ocarina," he told her. Mimie listened to the haunting woodsy tone and tapped her foot in tune with the melody. Couples made their way onto the floor and began dancing. Mimie sipped at her water, watching them. Her heartbeat increased as Koren held out his hand. She held her breath, knowing what he was about to ask, but still not quite believing it.

"Would you like to dance?"

"With you?" Mimie asked, choking on the water she'd just swallowed. "I mean, sure that would be fun." She drank the rest of the water and set the empty glass down on the table. She took a few calming breaths before following him and fought the urge to curl inwards and hide. Instead, she focused on the way the soft curls brushed against her cheeks when she walked, the swish of the fabric from her dress, and the quiet confidence that came from feeling beautiful.

Why was she so concerned with convincing herself that she was unlovable? Indeed, love was a mystery, an unexplainable attachment to one person over another, but the first step to letting someone love her was learning to love herself. She'd spent more time belittling her appearance than the bullies back home. Why had she allowed that to happen? When had she taken cruel lies and made them truth? She spent so much time shutting everyone out it was like she had developed armor around her heart. She had thought the armor made her strong, but what if she was wrong? What if the real strength came from knowing her value was not something that could be determined by other people? She suddenly felt powerful, not because magic was crackling in the air around her, but because she had given herself permission to be loved.

Koren stopped in a pocket of space and raised one of her hands in the air. She walked around him, and he let her fingers slip from his grasp as he dipped into a bow. Mimie followed his lead and curtsied.

He reclaimed her hand and spun her back into him. She followed him into a complex series of spins and hops. The candles placed in the leafy branches glowed like stars, and the sweet smells of the jungle wafted around them. After a few songs the tempo slowed, giving Mimie a chance to catch her breath. Koren led her into a slower song. He spun her around a few times then cuddled her against his chest and held her there.

"That was fun," he muttered, also sounding breathless. "It's been a long time. I'm surprised I remembered the steps to that."

"It was fun. I'm glad we stayed."

"You really do look beautiful tonight," he complimented. "Thank you for dancing with me." Mimie rested her cheek on his shoulder and smiled.

"You're welcome," she told him. Mimie sighed; she wanted to tell him so badly it hurt. Koren, I love you. Why was it so hard to get the words out? "Koren, I—" Kyra tapped on his shoulder and Mimie stopped midsentence. She stepped back and put her hand on the back of her neck self-consciously.

"What do you want Kyra?" Koren asked in irritation.

"There is a nice young elf on the far left platform who has requested to dance with you. She is the daughter of my high councilor. It's not good for the kingdom to see you spending so much time with a commoner." Mimie glared at her, but Kyra never acknowledged her presence.

"I will spend time with whomever I want to, Kyra," Koren snapped. "If it causes the 'kingdom' so much distress to see us together, then we'll leave." He turned away from her, and Kyra grabbed his arm angrily. "Don't touch me," he growled and ripped his arm from her grasp. They passed Visailios on the way out, and Koren waved a stiff goodbye.

"Are you guys leaving?" he asked in disappointment.

"Yeah, happy birthday, it was nice meeting you," Mimie called as Koren pulled her toward the stairs. He was still fuming when they reached the base and headed back toward the healers tree.

"I can't believe how rude she was to you," Koren growled. "I am so sorry to have put you through that."

"It's ok. I know how she is. I'm glad I went, it gave me a chance to dress up and eat a nice dinner." Nausea washed over her and she stumbled into Koren.

"Are you ok?"

"I think I may be seeing that dinner again soon," Mimie muttered, clutching her stomach against the growing pain. Koren helped her up the stairs to the healing tree and set her down on one of the pads.

"Evangeline," he called. "Are you here?" She pushed aside the curtain that obscured another patient she was working on and hurried over to them. She didn't need to ask what happened, the flushed undertone to Mimie's skin said it all.

"Here let's get you into something more comfortable," Evangeline suggested and rushed to get her a nightgown. Mimie guessed that her real worry was that Mimie would throw up on the dress. Evangeline handed her the sleeping gown and led her to the closest washroom. Mimie pulled the door shut and struggled out of her dress. She threw it to the side, and pulled on the nightdress. She ached all over and heat seemed to be radiating off of her. Her heart was beating faster than normal, but she hardly noticed. She slumped to the floor and rested her cheek on the cold wood. She closed her eyes. It was like she had swallowed a flame and a soap taste hovered in the back of her throat. She heard a knock on the door.

"Go away," Mimie commanded in a hoarse whisper.

"Are you dressed?" Koren asked while opening the door. Mimie smiled in spite of herself when she saw him stumble over her shoes because he had his hand over his eyes.

"You can look, I'm dressed," Mimie muttered. Koren caught sight of her on the floor and sank down next to her.

"Evangeline!" he yelled. Evangeline peered through the open door and froze when she saw Mimie curled up on the floor. She pushed Koren to the side and placed the back of her hand on Mimie's forehead.

"She has a fever, and her eyes are dilated," Evangeline reported.

"She was fine an hour ago," Koren exclaimed. "What's going on?

Is it food poisoning?" Evangeline examined his panicked expression and weighed her next words carefully.

"Mimie," Evangeline said. Mimie opened her eyes and struggled to focus on her. "What was the last thing you ate or drank?"

"A glass of water," Koren answered for her.

"Who gave you the glass of water?" Evangeline asked.

"Kyra," Mimie croaked. Koren and Evangeline exchanged a look.

"She wouldn't dare," Koren growled, and then his expression darkened. "I'll kill her," he promised. He started to get to his feet, but Mimie grabbed his arm.

"Don't leave," she moaned. "Oh no, I think I'm going to…" She crawled toward the washtub and threw up. Koren held her hair out of her face and rubbed her back comfortingly. "Get out of here," Mimie coughed, horrified that he had to see her like this.

"No," he said firmly. "I've had days where I've puked my guts out too." Her stomach heaved again, cutting off her response, and then she hung limply over the side of the tub. She dry heaved a few more times, but there was nothing left to throw up.

Evangeline gave her some water to rinse her mouth out with, and then Koren scooped her off the floor.

"Is there anything you can give her, like an antidote maybe?" Koren asked Evangeline.

"No, it will pass in a few hours." She went back to her other patients.

***

Koren sank onto one of the pads and leaned against the wall. Mimie whined pitifully and he pulled her closer. How could Kyra do this to her? What did she possibly have to gain by hurting Mimie?

He remembered the way Mimie's eyes had lit up while she listened to the music in the dining hall and pulled out the space cube. Buried at the very bottom, still wrapped in Emily's handkerchief, Koren knew he would find his Ocarina. It had been a long time since he'd played it. There were too many sad memories attached for him to find pleasure in the music.

That wasn't the case now. He wanted to play again, not for himself, but for Mimie. He knew it would make her feel better, and wanted her to know that part of him. After expanding the space cube, he rummaged around inside until he found what he was looking for. He pulled the Ocarina out and let the soft fabric fall away from the glossy white and red surface. Mimie saw what he was holding and smiled in spite of the pain she was in.

"Still full of surprises I see," she croaked. "It's beautiful."

He raised the mouthpiece to his lips and felt an unexpected joy wash through him as the first quivering note broke the silence. The feeling surprised him so much he almost stopped playing. The song drifted into a lullaby as the notes weaved through one another. Mimie's eyelids drooped, fighting sleep. A small smile pulled at the corners of her lips. Her breathing became more even and her grip on his shirt loosened. Koren continued playing and waited until she was in a deep sleep before gently setting her on the pad next to him. He set the instrument aside and quietly walked into one of the dressing rooms where Evangeline had left him some nightclothes. He changed into them quickly.

When he returned to Mimie, he found her curled up on her side. He easily scooped her into his arms again and was amazed at how perfectly she fit there. He rested his head on top of hers and breathed in the sweet smell of her hair. The familiar guilt pulled at his stomach. He'd almost forgotten about her— Emily. For a long time he'd felt there was a hole in his heart that no one could fill. He wanted to move on, but the part of him clinging to the hope she was still alive prevented that.

He didn't want to feel alone anymore, and Mimie had healed his heart in ways she would never know. All he wanted was to be close to her, to keep her safe. He imagined growing old with her, her head resting on his lap while he whispered how much he loved her into her ear. He smiled as he dosed off and cradled Mimie close.

He was almost asleep when he heard a strange sound. All his senses were suddenly on high alert. He heard the noise again; it was the creak of a stair. The sound was soft, almost undetectable, which meant whoever was climbing the stairs did not want to be heard.

Koren gently laid Mimie down on the mat and dove toward his

sword, which he had foolishly leaned against the wall several feet away. He heard the footsteps grow quiet. He glanced toward the stairs and met Kyra's cold gaze. Fear filled his chest as he recognized the look on her face. It was the same one she had given him the night she had left him to die.

CHAPTER 15: ALONE

"Kyra," Koren growled.

Two burly elves appeared behind her with ugly sneers on their faces. She moved aside to let them pass. Koren lunged for his sword and dodged the elves as they charged toward him. One managed to trip him, and Koren tumbled to the floor. He grabbed at Koren's legs trying to get a good grip on them, before he had the chance Koren yanked his legs out of the elf's grasp. Koren flipped over onto his stomach and crawled toward his sword. He was inches from the handle when a crushing weight slammed into him and knocked him onto his side. The elf tried to pin him down, but Koren punched him square in the nose and broke it. He kicked the elf away from him and grabbed the handle of his sword. The elf's lip was bleeding, but he pushed himself to his feet and pulled out his own sword.

"Drop it!" Koren saw Kyra kneeling by Mimie's head with a knife to her throat. His face went blank with shock.

"You wouldn't," he gasped.

"Put down the sword," she commanded in an icy voice. Koren let it fall from his hand.

"Why are you doing this?"

"I made an arrangement with the king of Lethia. Complete control over his military in return for a prince to marry his daughter."

"I'm not going to marry anyone," Koren replied.

"You don't have a choice. I can't send Teodor, he's too young."

"I'll escape," Koren promised.

"You think so?" Kyra laughed. "I had a feeling you would say that."

"Why did you poison Mimie? She's never done anything to you," Koren demanded.

"Yes, well, I couldn't exactly have her telling everyone about my plans. You involved her when you brought her here, so the only one you have to blame is yourself." Koren glared at her.

"I will never forgive you for this."

"You might think differently when I tell you Emily is alive and I know where you can find her."

"You're lying."

"No, I'm not. As soon as I take control over the Lethian army, I won't need you anymore, and you'll be free to go. Do this for me, and I will tell you where Emily is." Koren continued to glare at the ground and said nothing. She's lying, she always lies, he said to himself furiously. "Well, I'll let you think about it on the way to Lethia."

"I won't do it Kyra, I'm not going to be your pawn," Koren growled. "There's nothing you can promise me that will change that."

"Why must you always be so difficult? I didn't want to do this, but you leave me no choice." She nodded to the Blonde. He pulled a small vial from his pocket and walked toward Koren. "Drink it or she dies," Kyra threatened. Koren stared at the vial warily.

"What's it going to do to me?"

"Wipe your memory. Don't worry it only lasts a few months." Koren didn't move. Kyra moved her knife closer to Mimie's neck. "I wonder how long it will take for her to bleed out?" She mused.

"She's the Guardian, do you want to kill Kolanna's only chance at stopping Orient?" Kyra paused, narrowing her eyes at him.

"That is true," she muttered, "but death is the kindest fate I have in store for her if you do not cooperate."

"Fine, I'll drink it," Koren snapped, "but you have to swear you won't hurt her."

"I swear she will leave here unharmed." Koren knew that was the only kind of guarantee he was going to get. The guard with the bleeding lip smirked and handed him the vial. Koren took it and stared at its contents warily. Thinking quickly, he knocked the space cube out of his pocket and nudged it toward the wall for Mimie to find.

He then closed his eyes and drained the contents of the vial. When it was gone he threw the empty container at the guard.

"There, now leave her alone," Koren growled. Kyra put her knife away and pulled out a note.

"What's that?" Koren demanded.

"Your goodbye letter. The princess has her own supply of memory drugs so in a few minutes you will forget Mimie ever existed. There will be no more of this Koren nonsense, your name is Kormont and from now on that is what you will be called."

"I hope your soul burns in eternal fire." Koren didn't know his body was capable of holding such hatred. Something slammed into the side of his head and he crumpled to the floor.

"Careful he's delicate," Kyra muttered. The guard grunted and roughly threw Koren over his shoulder. Kyra placed the small piece of paper on top of Koren's sword and walked toward the stairs calling, "Hurry up the wagon is waiting!"

With that the four of them disappeared.

***

Mimie yawned and stretched; the sickness that had overcome her last night had passed, and she was glad to be rid of it. Sunlight was streaming through the branches overhead, signaling they had way overslept.

"Koren wake up! We were supposed to leave hours ago." She glanced toward his pad and frowned when she saw he wasn't there. "Koren?" she called, no answer. She noticed he had left his sword,

199

and the space cube behind. Her heart sank into her stomach as she picked up the note. With trembling fingers she read:

Dear Mimie,

I can't go with you to Death Valley. I'm sorry I didn't tell you sooner; I guess I just didn't know how. I know you think there is something going on between us, but there isn't. I can't keep pretending. I'm sorry if I led you on. It kills me to leave you like this; you are a good friend of mine, but I love someone else, and I need to be with her right now. Ask someone else to look out for you, I can't do it anymore.

- Koren

Mimie read the note over and over in shock.

"Good morning, are you feeling any better?" Evangeline asked, emerging from the stairway. "Sorry, I didn't check in on you sooner, I was out collecting herbs all night."

Mimie didn't reply.

"Hey what's wrong?" she asked, looking at her for the first time. Mimie held the note out to her.

"It's from Koren." Evangeline skimmed over it, then read it again more carefully like she couldn't believe what she was seeing.

"This can't be right," she muttered in disbelief. "I wonder who the girl is he's talking about. Probably Emily. Kyra told me about her at dinner yesterday."

"What did she say?" Mimie asked, not sure if she actually wanted to know.

"Not much, just that he used to be in love with her and probably still is."

"Oh." Mimie curled into a ball on her mat. "Good for him."

"Forget about him, he's not worth feeling sorry over."

"I think you should leave now." Mimie struggled to keep her voice even.

Evangeline retreated toward the stairs. "Ok, but I can't let you travel to Death Valley alone. I'll go talk to Kyra, maybe she'll let one of the guards go with you."

Mimie frantically wiped at her eyes, but she couldn't get rid of the tears. The last thing she wanted right now was Kyra's help. This had to be a mistake, if she waited long enough Koren would walk back up those stairs and everything would be okay.

Mimie walked into the washroom to change, taking the space cube with her. She opened it and tried not to look at Koren's clothes as she pulled out her cloak, shirt and pants. She took off her nightclothes and pulled on the ones from the cube.

In the privacy of closed doors, she grabbed one of Koren shirts and clutched it close to her chest. She fought the urge to rip it in half and allowed herself to sink to her knees. She wasn't sure what to do with his things, but it felt wrong to leave them behind. She shrank the space cube and stuffed it into her pocket. She buckled Koren's sword to her hip and readjusted her balance to accommodate the unfamiliar weight.

She headed for the stairs and found Oviet waiting for her at the base of the tree.

"I heard about what happened," she muttered. "Are you ok?"

"Not really," Mimie told her.

"I'm so angry with him. I hope that cow Emily falls down a well."

"Don't say that. I wish him the best in life, even if I have no desire to ever see him again."

Oviet fell quiet and rubbed her cheek against Mimie's shoulder. Mimie patted her nose.

"Come on, let's go. Evangeline is asking Kyra if some of her guards can go with us, and she probably wants us to meet them by the royal's tree."

***

Koren had no idea who he was, where he was, or how he had gotten there. It was unbearably hot and he weakly tried to shove off the wool blanket that had been laid on top of him. Sweat soaked through his clothes. Thick rope wrapped around his wrists and ankles while a cloth tied tightly over his mouth prevented him from making any noise.

201

The floor rattled violently and he hit the back of his head against it. Based on the deep ache he felt, this had been going on for a while. Koren looked for some means of escape, but there was none. The rumbling stopped and the stillness felt wonderful against his head. It only lasted a fraction of a second. He heard the sound of pounding hooves, a cry of alarm from a voice he didn't recognize, a stunning impact, blackness, and pain. Yet when everything else seemed to pass away, a faint memory lingered, or more like the memory of a memory, a girl's face, her laughter, and then nothing.

***

Five, ten, then fifteen minutes dragged by and Evangeline still hadn't returned with Mimie's bodyguards. This place was a constant reminder of Koren's departure and she wanted to be rid of it. She tapped her foot for another minute and a half and then exclaimed, "Come on, we're leaving without the stupid guards."

"I can hear someone coming down the stairs, just wait a second," Oviet replied, blocking Mimie's exit. After a few seconds, Evangeline appeared at the base of the tree.

"Avia and Arqus are preparing for the journey, they will meet you here in a few minutes." She returned to the healer's tree.

"I know she is trying to help us, but I don't trust her," Oviet muttered.

"We'll be leaving soon, and then you won't have to worry about it," Mimie replied. She turned toward the stairway. "I'll be right back." She didn't wait for Oviet's response and pushed her way through the leaves.

Slowly, she made her way up to the first-floor platform. She walked through a doorway and found herself in the chamber she and Koren had been invited to last night. It seemed very empty now. Streams of light made their way through the vines, illuminating uneven patches on the floor. All the tables had been pushed aside, leaving the floor wide and open. She turned away from it, fighting tears. She had hoped coming here might give her some closure, but instead it only made the pain worse.

She walked back down the stairs and found Avia and Arqus waiting by Oviet. Avia had an intimidating seriousness about her that

Mimie had not noticed before. She had dark brown eyes and wore her thick black hair in a single braid thrown over one shoulder. Arqus had dark blue eyes and a good-natured smile. They were both dressed in traveling cloaks and had large saddle packs strapped to strange looking animals at their sides.

"Hello again," Avia greeted.

"Hi, what are those?" Mimie asked. The animals were taller than Oviet, with refined dragon-like heads. Black spikes lined the crest of their necks and their foreheads were covered in flakes of irregularly shaped colorful minerals. The trunk of the animals resembled that of a large cat. They had thick muscular legs, large paws, and a long tail with small black spikes covering the last three inches. Their wings were like those of a dragon's.

"They're called Ligons, the black one on the left is Drake, and the tawny one on the right is Kappa. We're ready to depart now if you wish."

"Yeah, that would be good," Mimie muttered. She watched them mount the Ligons and stared in amazement as they spread their giant wings. They were beautiful creatures, even if she worried they might eat her in her sleep. Mimie hoped onto Oviet's back and used her mane to pull herself upright. Oviet jumped into the air and followed after them. The village was difficult to see from the treetops, and all sign of it was gone in a few seconds.

"You know, it kind of annoys me that he didn't say goodbye to me either. I was his friend too, and I did carry his ungrateful butt across half of Kolanna."

"Yeah, the more I think about it, the more the whole thing seems fishy to me."

"You don't think he's in any kind of danger do you?" Oviet wondered.

"No, I'm sure he's okay, I guess it just feels weird to leave him behind without trying to find out what happened."

"He probably didn't want us to. Maybe it's best if we leave the past in the past and move on."

"How do you forget about someone who gave you so much to

remember?" Oviet fell quiet, unable to think of anything to say.

"What are they doing?" Oviet muttered irritably. Avia and Arqus were flying lower and lower until they suddenly disappeared into the trees. "I did not sign up to babysit my own bodyguards."

"They're probably getting a drink," Mimie suggested.

"Maybe," Oviet muttered. She pinned her ears and reluctantly swooped down to where she had seen the two Ligons disappear. The moment they entered the tree canopy they heard a horrible ear-piercing shriek. Mimie pressed her hands over her ears and felt Oviet lose control, slamming into a tree. They fell toward the ground but were intercepted by something soft and sticky, a spider's web.

***

Koren moaned and blinked as the world slid in and out of focus. The sound was muffled because of the gag still in his mouth. Everything hurt, he couldn't move, but he was sure numerous bones were broken. He was vaguely aware that he was lying on the roof of the wagon. Through the only barred window, he saw the wheels sticking up in the air. The wall was splintered on one side, leaving a gaping hole. As Koren looked through it, he could see another overturned wagon, and a horse lying limply in its harness surrounded by a pool of its own blood. He shuddered and turned his head the other direction so he wouldn't have to look.

His head was throbbing painfully; he must have hit it against something during the crash. He heard the rumble of another approaching wagon, and voices. He strained to make out what they were saying.

"Oh my," a female voice gasped. He heard footsteps.

"Both the drivers are dead," a male voice muttered gravely

"The horses too…"

"We better alert the authorities so they can clean up this mess."

"We can't just leave them here! The cats will get them!" the female voice exclaimed.

"Good riddance, along this old road, I bet you anything they were up to no good," the male voice growled.

"Thero!"

One of them walked past the shattered opening and into Koren's line of vision. The one named Thero was a tall, middle-aged elf with graying hair. He seemed to sense Koren was watching him and looked around uneasily. He caught sight of Koren and locked eyes with him for a second. Thero's were ice blue and they seemed to cut right into Koren's soul.

"Rio, come here!" Thero called over his shoulder. He cautiously approached Koren and seconds later a small, plump elf came running around the corner. She was about Thero's age, and Koren assumed she was his wife.

"Oh my goodness!" she exclaimed. She ducked through the hole in the side of the wagon and knelt down by Koren's head. Her hands fussed over him; scared to touch him without knowing how badly he was hurt. Thero pushed her aside and removed a knife from his belt. Koren tensed, but relaxed when he cut through the cloth wrapped tight over his mouth. He then severed the bonds around his wrists and ankles.

"You are going to be fine. How old are you?" Rio tried to distract his attention while Thero examined his injuries.

"I don't know," Koren muttered, his voice sounded strange.

Thero grabbed his right wrist and Koren felt a gut-wrenching, agonizing snap. A horrible scream ripped from his chest.

"Kill me," Koren begged. Nothing could be worth living through this pain. Thero pretended not to hear him. Koren felt him grab his upper arm and Rio braced her weight against him to hold him down. He struggled weakly against her hold. "Please, don't… Wait!"

He felt another crack and pain ripped through him so extreme he thought for sure he must be dying. He screamed even louder than before and felt tears running down his face. His breath came in ragged gasps, but after a few seconds his protests became more and more feeble until he finally lost consciousness.

Cold fingers pressed against the hollow of his neck. His eyes were so heavy he wasn't sure he could open them. Sweat dripped from his face, every breath was strained. There was a splint keeping his right arm straight, and another one on his left ankle. Thero grabbed Koren's arm and draped it over his shoulder. With Rio's help they gently eased him to his feet. He hobbled out the splintered wall toward their wagon. Even with the crude splint, Koren's left leg wouldn't support him, so they had to drag him there.

"Is there anything you can remember, anything at all?" Rio asked. Koren remembered the crash, the stunning impact, but that was all.

"There's nothing." His voice was as weak as the rest of him. He grunted as his leg gave out and tried to blink the sweat out of his eyes. Thero and Rio pulled him back to his feet.

When they reached the back of Thero's wagon, they helped him into it and he slumped against the floor. He was so dizzy; he hoped that if he closed his eyes the world would stop spinning, but it didn't. A moment later the wagon jerked forward. Rio scooted closer to him and took off her shawl. She waded it up and placed it under Koren's head.

"Thank you," he muttered.

"You're welcome honey," Rio told him and patted his hand. She was quiet for a little while and then Koren heard Thero say,

"Don't get your hopes up sweetheart. I'll do what I can for him, but he's in shock. He's probably not going to make it home."

"He'll make it," Rio said. She patted his hand again, the warmth felt good. He could see the girl's face again; hear her laughter, but it was so faint it disappeared when he tried to listen; everything disappeared.

***

"Lucky this web was here to break our fall," Mimie muttered. Oviet snorted. She looked down and saw the jungle floor 50ft bellow. The sight made her feel sick. She heard whimpering to her left and saw that Avia, Arqus, and their two Ligons were stuck as well. "Great."

The wind picked up a soft hum-like chant as it whispered ominously through the trees. Avia, Arqus, the Ligons, and even Oviet fell limp, their eyes filled with an unseen terror. The chant grew louder. The sound of it sent a shiver down Mimie's spine. Her vision flickered, and she caught flashes of a canvas ceiling. It was so quiet she could hear herself breathing. A flame licked by overhead, the smoke choking her. Panic filled her mind, she was going to burn to death.

Something sank its fangs deep into her right arm, breaking the trance. Mimie yelped in surprise, and found herself face to face with the biggest spider she had ever seen. She ripped her left arm out of the web and punched the spider in one of the many eyes that covered its head, knocking it off balance. It stumbled backward and lunged at her again, arms raised and fangs exposed. She suddenly felt as if she was facing revenge for all the tarantulas she had killed back home.

Using strength born from pure adrenaline, she ripped Koren's sword out of the web as the spider charged her. In a swing that was more luck than skill, she cut off the spider's head and watched as it fell from the web to the undergrowth below. The chant ended abruptly and the others were released from their trance.

"What happened?" Arqus asked groggily.

"I killed the spider."

"Oh yeah, that's right, I forgot fairies are immune to magical trances." Mimie didn't say anything; she didn't feel like explaining that she was only half immune. She shook her head to rid herself of the unsettling feeling the trance had brought on and looked down at her arm. The spider bite burned, but it wasn't anything life-threatening.

"Where there is one spider, there are bound to be more," Avia warned. Mimie had no intention of grappling with another one of the oversized monsters. She carefully cut Oviet's wings from the web so she could fly out. Avia and Arqus saw what she was doing and applied the same technique to free their Ligons. The procedure was risky. The web shuddered violently as Oviet pulled free and started to fall apart. By the time the Ligons had escaped, it was barely holding together.

Mimie put Koren's sword away and struggled toward the side of the web. The white threads stuck to her and tore as she tried to make her way across them. She felt the unbearable need to rip the sticky strands off of her, but didn't want to compromise the strength of the web.

She reached for the closest branch and felt the web stretching under her weight. Mimie grabbed it just as the threads snapped and suddenly found herself dangling precariously from the tree.

"Is everyone ok?" she called, heaving herself up onto the branch.

"Yeah." She heard Avia and Arqus call from an adjacent tree.

The tree was covered in tangled vines that she could use to get down, but they didn't look overly strong. She carefully grabbed a vine and used it to guide her decent onto the next branch. The going was slow, but she enjoyed it. There was a therapeutic effect she got from climbing things that she just couldn't get anywhere else. She would have liked to stay up there longer, but the threat of more spiders rendered that impossible. She walked over to Oviet and pulled the lingering bits of web off of her. Mimie felt dizzy and tired. She credited that to the spider bite and asked Oviet to heal it. Even after it was gone though, she still felt drained.

"Why did you guys try to land here?" Mimie asked around her newly formed headache.

Avia patted Drakes dragon-like head. "The Ligons needed water, they didn't get a chance to have any before we left. It was a mistake trying to land with the trees so close together. It won't happen again," Avia assured her. "There is a stream just over there. We'll be right back." They headed off into the trees and disappeared.

Mimie sat down with her back against a tree and massaged her forehead. The curls from the night before had tangled around her face and she tied them back with a cloth strip to keep them from tickling her nose. In this humidity they wouldn't last much longer, though. She wiped the sweat off her face with her arm and swatted at the gnats that seemed determined to fly in her ears.

After a short time Avia and Arqus returned and led them to an opening they had found in the tree canopy. It was a tight fit. Oviet brushed the tips of her wings against a few leaves on the way out, but they returned to open sky without incident.

***

Koren listened to the babbling trickle of a nearby stream. The sound was disconnected somewhat. Without looking, he knew that eventually it would lead to a sandy beach, where it flowed into the deep blue ocean. A child ran past him, laughing, and he saw that another was hot on his heels, mud obscuring his features. "Kormont you are so dead when I catch you!" the older one called. They collapsed in front of a large tree, gasping for breath. There was a hole at the bottom leading to an internal staircase. At the top was a large hut intertwined with the branches of a tree. A man emerged from the base looking stern. His eyes were a vivid shade of green, while his hair was shaggy blonde. He was wearing freshly polished military armor and a wreath of silver on his head that indicated his royalty.

"Stanton go wash that mud off your face right now," he commanded.

"Yes Appi," he replied, glaring at the other boy before walking away.

"Koren, it's dangerous out here. I don't want you boys playing without supervision."

"You never let us have fun anymore." Koren crossed his small arms and pouted.

"Someday you'll understand," his father said with a faraway expression. "Someday." He picked Koren up and tickled him affectionately, throwing him over his shoulder and looking around one last time, like he expected some unseen danger to emerge from the surrounding trees. "Hurry up, Stanton."

A woman emerged from the base of the tree. "I'll take him. You mustn't be so hard on them, they're only children after all." His mother smiled affectionately at him.

Her brown hair was twisted up into beautiful curls, with a silver wreath weaved through it. Her eyes were a blue-gray, and on her wrist was an elaborate bracelet made from gold and sparkling jewels. Her dress was made from fine blue silk. It flowed out behind her as she turned to head back inside.

"Thank you, Nadine. I have a patrol tonight, I'll be back late," he told her.

"Be careful, Cor," she said, resting her hand behind his neck and kissing him goodbye.

"I always am."

"Keep those generals of yours in check, we don't want to start something with the Zanties we can't finish."

"I'll be sure to do that," Cor said with a half-smile. He kissed Nadine one more time, tousled Koren's hair and disappeared into the fading light as the sun drifted below the trees.

Koren watched the scene unfold from above, like he was a ghost, like he didn't exist, a stranger to his own life. His mother stood stationary, her expression haunted. Koren reached out to her, but she didn't see him. His hand went right through her arm, unfelt. She turned away, leaving him standing alone as he stared after her retreating form.

Someone shook Koren's shoulder, sending tendrils of pain shooting through his broken arm. He gasped in pain and shock, recoiling from whoever had touched him. A girl with dark hair jerked her arm back in surprise and smiled at him apologetically. He glanced around the room to get his bearings, keeping the girl fixed in his peripheral vision. The walls were made of mud bricks, the ceiling from reinforced wooden planks. He was lying on a short bed that faced a doorway covered by a tan curtain. The only light came from a window above the bed. The girl who had shaken him looked at the floor uncertainly.

"What?" he said gruffly.

"I brought some water for you." She tried to hand him the glass, but he didn't move.

"I don't want it."

"Ok, I'll leave it here for you." She set it on his bedside table, then sat down on a stool next to his bed with her head resting on her palm.

"Can I help you with something?"

"I'm supposed to watch you and yell for my dad if you go into shock again," she explained. The intensity of her gaze and her close proximity made him feel uncomfortable. "If you're not going to drink the medicine you should probably go back to sleep."

"It has medicine in it?" Koren asked with a little more life. He struggled into a sitting position and grabbed it off the table. His throat was raw, but he choked it down, hoping to find some relief from the pain in his arm. The girl laughed.

"I figured that would make you drink it," she said with a satisfied smile. "My name is Kuria by the way." Koren could have introduced himself, but he chose not to reply; just hoped the girl was telling the truth about the medicine. He laid back down and closed his eyes. He knew he wasn't going to be able to go back to sleep.

The bulk of his injuries were on his right side, the side that had slammed into the wall when the wagons collided. The splintering wood had cut him to pieces. He saw blood stained bandages covering his chest, arms, and legs.

"You're not a criminal are you?" Kuria asked.

"No," he sighed.

"Well, I guess you wouldn't know even if you were. It must be so disorienting not knowing who you are."

"I'm freezing, can I have a blanket?" That was a lie; really he was self-conscious about that fact that he was only wearing briefs.

"Oh sorry, you looked like you were hot, so I pulled the blanket off you a little while ago." She picked it up off the floor and laid it on top off him again. He pulled the edge all the way up to his chin and felt a little better after that.

"You have lovely eyes," the girl told him. "I've never seen a shade of green quite like it." Koren closed his eyes and sighed.

He forced himself to stay awake while Kuria was there, but pretended to be asleep so he wouldn't have to talk to her. He didn't want to be ungrateful, but her presence made him feel uneasy. Thero came to check on him a few hours later and shooed her away.

"You look better. How do you feel?" he asked.

"Tired," Koren replied. Now that Kuria was gone, he could barely keep his eyes open, but he was reluctant to close them in case she came back. All he wanted now was to be left alone.

"I'll see to it that you have some peace and quiet."

"Thank you," Koren muttered. It was dark behind the curtains, so he knew it must be night outside. His arm was throbbing, but he closed his eyes and allowed himself to fall into a light sleep.

The next morning, Koren woke up to the smell of bacon and rolled over to find a small plate and a glass of water on his bedside table. Feeling restless from being in the same place for so long, he sat up and tested his balance. The room spun, and he collapsed back onto the bed. He closed his eyes and waited for the room to stop spinning. Hoping to dispel the feeling, he grabbed a piece of bacon and nibbled on the end. He was hungrier than he realized and finished the rest of the strand quickly. He savored the salty taste and washed the dryness out of his mouth with a bit of water.

"Oh good, you're awake," Rio said, walking through the curtain that divided his room from the rest of the house. "Let's take a look at how those cuts are healing." She set fresh bandages on the stool by the bed and had him lay flat on his back. "I'll be right back, don't move," she said sternly, and quickly walked out of the room. All the gauze was making him itchy so he absentmindedly picked at the edge of one of the bandages on his side. Rio came back a moment later with a rag and a bowl of water. She set those down on the bed next to him and gently peeled off the bandage he had been picking at. She wiped away the dried blood and saw that the cut was scabbing over on top of the stitches.

"Incredible," Rio muttered. "I guess we should have taken those out a while ago, I didn't expect it to heal that fast." She cut through the knots holding the stitches in place and tugged on one to test the how much the skin had adhered to it. It didn't come out easily and bled as she pulled it out. Koren winced and watched apprehensively as she reached for another one.

In total, he had 20 stitches, and it took over an hour to get all of them out. Some were more painful than others, but with the speed he was healing, he knew that he had no reason to complain. None of his cuts needed to be bandaged, so Rio took the strips of cloth out of his room. When she came back, she handed him the plate of bacon.

"Eat," she commanded. Koren was feeling hungry so he did as she asked without protest. "Has any of your memory come back?"

Koren coughed on the food he had just swallowed. "Um, no, sorry," he lied. Rio seemed disappointed but didn't question him about it further.

"Ok, let me know if you need anything," she said and pushed her way out the curtain. Even though Rio had taken him in, he still didn't trust her with his name, or his past. He cringed at the memory of the dark, stuffy wagon and didn't want to give her any information that might lead to his recapture.

He closed his eyes and sank into another memory. It enveloped him so completely it was like he'd entered a dream. He stood in a field of grass and blinked a few times to get used to the unnatural light There was a little boy standing a few feet in front of him. His blondish-brown hair was messy and tears ran down his dirty cheeks as heavy sobs shook his tiny frame. The boy trembled in front of a fire so bright it blocked out all other colors except the deep green of his eyes. The sound of clashing swords reached him on the wind and he saw figures moving beneath tall trees far in the distance. The glint of the metal armor flickered in the bright light cast by the fire.

"Appi!" the boy called out in his little voice, but the sound was carried away before it got very far. He took a step toward the fighting, and then another, until he was running straight for it.

"Kormont!" a voice called after him, "Kormont, no!" Koren saw Nadine run after the child, leaving her other children behind in an attempt to bring him back.

Smoke obscured the figures and the world shifted under him. He saw the boy get under foot of the fighting. His father mortally wounded trying to save him. It was his fault. Silent tears ran down his cheeks, it was his fault.

***

"Mimie, stop it!" Oviet snapped. This was the fifth time she had almost fallen off in the last hour.

"Sorry," she muttered, trying to regain her balance.

"I think we should stop for a little while. You need to lay down," Oviet told her.

"No, what I need is for us to keep flying." She wanted to put as much distance between her and Kyra's kingdom as possible.

"You are going to end up falling off and breaking your back on a

213

tree if you don't rest."

"We're not stopping," Mimie said stubbornly.

"You can't run away from your feelings Mimie. It doesn't matter how fast, or how far we travel, you are still going to feel them."

Mimie noticed Arqus drifting closer to the trees and groaned. "What now?"

Oviet followed him into the jungle canopy and trotted over to where Avia was standing next to Drake and Kappa.

"Sorry guys I have to pee!" Arqus called and disappeared behind a bush. Avia closed her eyes and shook her head.

"Sorry," she muttered. Mimie spotted some comfy looking ferns next to where Oviet was standing and climbed off her back. She curled up in them and felt herself drifting off. Only the idea of a giant bug crawling up her pant leg kept her awake.

Her thoughts turned to Koren, though she tried hard not to allow them to. Every time his name crossed her mind her fingertips went numb, as if her body was attempting to heal itself of the hurt he had caused her. Maybe that was why she felt so drained; his name crossed her mind a lot.

"Maybe we should make camp here for the night," Mimie suggested. "I don't know if I can go any further today." She had absolutely no energy.

Oviet looked at her in concern. "That spider could have been venomous, maybe we should take you back to Evangeline." A part of her wanted to say yes, hoping she would find Koren waiting for her when she got there, but she dismissed the thought immediately.

"I'm ok, just tired."

"The dark circles under your eyes make it look like you're recovering from a broken nose."

"That bad?" Mimie laughed. "I honestly don't know what's wrong with me. I don't feel sick, just drained."

"Maybe some food will help," Avia offered. She handed her the food pack and Mimie chewed on some dried meat without tasting it. "I'm going to go get some wood for a fire. I'll be back soon."

"Ok," Mimie muttered. She pushed herself stiffly to her feet and expanded the space cube. She pulled out the sleeping sack and used it as a pad against the poky grass.

Avia returned a little while later with an arm full of wood and quickly had a large fire going. There were some tea leaves left in the space cube, but Mimie didn't feel like going through the effort it would take to boil the water and make the tea.

When Oviet settled down for the night, Mimie pulled the sleeping sack toward her and crawled under her wing. Oviet wasn't the snuggly type, but she allowed it without protest. Mimie ran her hand across the soft gray feathers on the underside of Oviet's wing and listened as her breathing became more regular. Despite how tired she felt, the loud chatter of the jungle kept her awake. There was a bird screaming at the top of its lungs above them and crickets that were moving around in the grass below. Mimie covered her ears and gritted her teeth together. When the frustration was too much, she pushed out from under Oviet's wing, picked up a stick, and hurled it at the obnoxious creature. The bird let out a surprised squawk and moved on to a different tree in the distance. Mimie returned back to Oviet's side and closed her eyes, trying to rid herself of the sour mood that had penetrated her mind. When she eventually fell asleep, she was feeling grumpier than ever.

A while later Oviet stretched out her wings and yawned. It was time to get up. She pushed herself to her feet, packed up her sleeping sack and ate some dried fruit for breakfast. She made sure all canteens were full and all bladders were empty before they left, wanting to make up lost time from their early stop yesterday.

Once in the air Mimie silently watched the trees flash by in a carpet of green below. Oviet seemed to sense her mood and left her to her thoughts.

"Why is it so cold?" Mimie complained after a while.

"Look at how overcast it's gotten, there's probably a storm coming," Oviet muttered.

"Uggh," Mimie moaned. So much for making up lost ground.

***

Koren was thrown off balance as his subconscious immersed him in another memory. He watched a ragged crowd of people make their way down a hillside. The survivors from the human's attack were in poor shape, and his family was no exception.

At the front, he picked out his younger self and recognized his older twin brothers, Enzo, and Quinten, standing next to him. The teenagers were indistinguishable except for the fact that Quinten had green eyes while Enzo had grayish blue. His sister Amelia, a brunette elf with soft, caring features, was holding his younger self's hand. Kyra was trailing a little bit behind the others, her arms crossed sourly. His other sister Adelaide, who was barely more than a toddler, followed close behind Nadine.

The family was still in shock over the loss of Koren's father and his brother Stanton, who had been killed by wolves a few days earlier. They were standing closer than normal, and their eyes were glazed with pain. Nadine was showing the first signs of pregnancy, but the haunted look in her eyes showed no excitement.

"It stinks!"

"Hush Kyra," Nadine scolded. "There's probably a dead animal nearby."

"Do you want us to go look for it?" the twins offered. "We might be able to salvage some of the meat."

"I don't know boys…"

Amelia stopped short with a scream. She curled her body around Koren's and covered his eyes so he wouldn't see what had frightened her. Koren peaked through a space between her fingers and recoiled at the sight of a small girls body stuck in the branches of the tree. Her eyes stared at the ground as dried blood ran down her cheek and flies climbed in and out of her open mouth. Her skin was a haunting chalky white color while her clothes were old and travel worn.

"Her family probably didn't have time to bury her, and didn't want the scavengers to get her," Nadine said sadly. "What a terrible thing to not be able to bury your child."

"We can bury her now," Enzo offered.

"Thank you, if we're going to be staying in the clearing over there that's probably for the best."

"I can help him," offered one of the men from the group.

"I want to go home," Koren heard his younger-self whine and he clung tighter to Amelia. They were lost, they were alone, and they had no idea what fate awaited them in the valley beyond the trees. Koren closed his eyes and shuddered. He could almost smell the rotting body of the women and heard the branches break as they pulled her down.

A crack of thunder woke Koren with a start, and he bolted upright. The room lit up and then quickly fell into darkness once more. Rain pelted the ceiling. A light on the other side illuminated the curtain in front of him, and he saw a shadowed outline pacing back and forth in front of it.

"I just don't understand it, Rio. I have never seen anyone heal that fast. It's unnatural."

"I know," Rio replied. "Do you remember the old folk stories my Amma used to tell me?"

"Yes, but they were just that, stories."

"What if the story had some truth to it? It would definitely explain what's going on. I feel sad, I wish there were more we could do for him."

Koren tuned them out; he hated feeling pitied, although in their defense, they probably didn't know he could hear them. His head throbbed; intensifying the sounds around him. He groaned and threw the pillow over his head when he heard someone knock sharply on the door.

"I'll get it," Rio whispered. Her shadow fluttered over the curtain as she made her way toward the door. There was a quiet squeak as it opened, and the thunder abruptly sounded three times louder. "Can I help you?" Rio yelled over the storm.

"Can we come in?" a male voice shouted.

"The only room I have is taken by a wounded traveler!" A girl asked something, but her voice was too quiet to hear the words. "Speak up dearie!" Rio shouted.

"Might we use your barn then?" Koren had an odd feeling he had heard this voice before, though he couldn't place where.

"Oh, of course! Here, follow me and I'll show you the way! You guys are going to catch your death out here!" Rio's voice was cut off as she slammed the door closed. Koren threw the sheet off and tried to get up. He rolled off the bed and let out a muffled moan as he hit the floor. Thero must have heard him because he threw open the curtain and shouted,

"What the devil are you doing!"

"I, I have to...." Koren gasped. Thero ignored him and walked to where he was struggling across the floor. He tried to help him to his feet, but Koren pushed him away.

"I have to go outside."

"Why!" Thero demanded, shaking his head in disbelief. "Kuria help me, the boys lost it!"

"I have not!" Koren shouted. "There's someone outside and I, she..." but no one was listening.

"He's going to hurt himself!" Kuria exclaimed. "We have to knock him out. At least until this storm is over!"

Maybe he was going crazy, but it felt imperative he find out who the girl at the door was. Thero pulled something from the pocket of his cloak and injected it into his arm. He went limp and felt Kuria and Thero dragging him away from the doorway.

Koren used the last of his energy to lift his head as he saw someone passing by his window.

"Emily?" he called out, but whoever it was didn't hear him.

The memories washed over him again as he sank down through the layers of time. He emerged in a dark field. A small structure stood nearby crudely constructed from leaves and sticks. Nadine was inside lying on a grass pad with a pregnant belly bulging from the middle of her thin frame. His younger self was curled in a ball nearby. Quinn woke them as he approached from the shadows.

"Sorry Amma," he said, discouraged. "Rations have been cut again. We don't have enough hunters to feed everyone." He handed her and Koren a small portion of meat, then headed toward another shelter nearby where another family was waiting. Nadine broke her meager portion in half and offered it to Koren, but he shook his little head furiously. He put his hand on her belly and offered her his entire ration.

"You keep it," Nadine said, gently pulling him close to her. Koren shook his head stubbornly, broke his portion in half and placed it her hands. Tears appeared in Nadine's eyes as she stared at it, and she affectionately ruffled her son's hair. He was too weak to argue about it anymore and curled back into a ball. She sat still for a moment, sucking on the dried meat, then grimaced in pain, and clutched at her bulging stomach. Koren opened his eyes and sat up in concern, watching her fearfully.

"Sweetheart, go find Amelia," she choked out. "Tell her the baby's coming." Koren nodded wordlessly and stumbled off into the night calling shrilly for Quinn, Enzo, and Amelia. Amelia appeared within seconds. She grabbed a damp cloth and laid it on her mother's head. Nadine labored for hours, her screams filling the night, and then it was over. Amelia cleaned off the baby and cradled it in her arms.

"It's a girl," she said.

"Why isn't she crying?" Nadine asked. "Is she ok? Let me see her!" Amelia handed her over. Nadine cooed to the baby softly, but she didn't move.

"Freya," Koren said softly. "We should name her Freya."

"Ok sweetheart," Nadine said, her voice breaking with pain. "That's a perfect name." Amelia held her arms out for the baby, but Nadine waved her away. "No, I want to hold her tonight," she muttered. "We can... bury her tomorrow." Nadine stroked the babies face and softly hummed a lullaby. "I want her to know how loved she was as she transitions into the next world."

The memory faded as the sedative dragged Koren down into darkness.

***

"This is horrible, we just got back into the air!" Oviet complained, glaring at the sky. "Why is the world so against progress!" A crack of thunder interrupted them. Mimie shivered as the wind picked up.

"I don't want to find out what it's like to be struck by lightning. We better play it safe and land before the storm hits." Another thunderclap exploded overhead and Oviet swayed violently to the left.

Mimie glanced toward the ground and noticed a road winding through the trees. It was bound to lead somewhere, and if they were lucky they might even find a house they could use to wait out the storm.

"Maybe we should follow that road!" Mimie shouted over the wind.

"But it's heading perpendicular to the river, we'll be going the wrong direction!" Oviet protested.

"Just trust me!"

"It's not you I don't trust, it's your lousy sense of direction," Oviet mumbled to herself. Mimie ignored her.

"Avia, Arqus! Follow Oviet!"

Oviet wheeled around and glided toward the road. The two Ligons landed seconds later and splattered mud all over them. The rain picked up, and the misty haze it created made it hard to see.

Oviet trudged down the road, which had flooded with two inches of water. Every step she took plunged her hooves deep into the slick mud. Mimie pushed her soaked hair out of her face and shivered as water saturated through her clothes. It was so dark they had to rely on the occasional flash of lightening to light their way.

Mimie shielded her eyes against the rain and caught sight of a small hut off the road up ahead. It was the only building they had seen so far. The path leading up to it was less muddy than the road, so Oviet was able to trot up to the huts front door. Mimie jumped off Oviet's back and landed in a large puddle of mud. She pulled herself free of it and walked toward the door.

"Wait, we don't know these people, it might be dangerous!" Arqus yelled. He dismounted his Ligon and ran to catch up to Mimie. Mimie ignored him and knocked loudly on the thick wooden door. It was quiet for a second, and Mimie glanced at the warm light pouring out of the window. She heard footsteps, and Arqus pushed protectively in front of her. The door swung open and a friendly middle-aged elf peered out at them through the rain.

"Can I help you!" she yelled.

"Can we come in?" Arqus asked. Mimie crossed her fingers behind her back.

"The only room I have is taken by a wounded traveler!" she shouted back. Mimie's spirits plummeted; she searched the yard and noticed a dark shape looming up next to the house. She pointed at it.

"Can we use your barn?"

"Speak up dearie!" the elf shouted.

"Might we use your barn then!" Mimie screamed.

"Oh, of course! Here, follow me and I'll show you the way! You guys are going to catch your death out here!" The elf grabbed a lantern from the side of the door, and then slammed it shut behind her. "I'm Rio by the way!" she introduced herself. Mimie shook her hand.

"I'm Mimie!"

Rio led them toward the dark building, stumbling as her boots sank into the mud. Mimie helped her pull the door open and stepped out of the rain.

"It's not much," Rio said, pushing her wet hair out of her eyes, "but at least it's better than being out in that storm."

"It's perfect. Thank you," Mimie said. The air smelled of fresh straw and chickens. The Ligons claws clicked against the wooden boards as they entered.

"You're welcome dear. What were you doing out in that storm in the first place?"

"Just traveling..." Rio seemed to sense her desire for privacy and didn't ask any more questions.

"The hay loft is up there," she pointed to a stairway, "and there's plenty of fruit in here, so feel free to help yourselves." She started to walk away but seemed to remember something and turned back.

"Oh, and one more thing, please make sure your Ligons don't eat my chickens."

"Don't worry, they won't get anywhere near them," Avia assured her. Rio nodded and walked back out into the rain. As soon as she was gone Oviet tested the wooden stairs, and hurried toward the hayloft, her stomach growling audibly.

"Night," Mimie muttered to Avia and Arqus. The Ligons' snake like eyes followed her as she started up the stairs.

"Mimie wait..." Avia muttered, and took a step toward her. "Look, I know that Koren's absence hasn't been easy for you, and I just wanted to say that I'm sorry." Mimie froze with her foot on the bottom stair and reluctantly turned to face her.

"It's ok. It's not your fault he left."

"I know, but I feel like I should have warned you about him," she explained.

"What do you mean?" Mimie demanded.

"Well, when I first came to Talanthia I heard stories about him. I was told that he ran away from his responsibilities when his people needed him most. Kyra barely managed to keep everyone together and built our great kingdom out of nothing, with no one to help her. Kyra says she isn't bitter about it, but that doesn't change the fact that he abandoned his own people. Elves like that can't be trusted." Mimie bristled, but held herself in check.

"You can believe what you want," she growled. She took the stairs with more force than necessary, and when she reached the top, she turned the corner so sharply it clipped her shoulder. "Aw!" she hissed and kicked the wall in frustration. Her foot went right through the soft wood and got stuck. Mimie froze, feeling embarrassment and shame wash over her in equal measures. She glanced around to make sure no one was looking, and tried to inconspicuously pull her foot out. As it came free she lost her balance and fell sideways, nearly falling down the stairs. Mimie pushed herself to her feet and rubbed her palms, which had gotten scraped up in her fall, and stumbled toward Oviet.

"Mimie, they have alfalfa!" Oviet exclaimed around a mouthful of hay. Mimie smiled in spite of herself and patted Oviet's shoulder.

"Are you going to be up for a while?" Mimie expanded the space cube and leafed through it until she found a pair of dry clothes.

Oviet narrowed her eyes. "Yeah, why?"

"Will you make sure the Ligons don't eat the chickens?" Mimie pulled on the dry clothes and hung her wet ones from the rafters. Oviet watched her for a moment, chewing loudly before she finally grumbled her consent.

"Thanks." Mimie buried herself in the hay to keep out the damp chill and closed her eyes. She shifted a few times to rid herself of the pokey stems, but there was no escape from them. She itched her arm and wiped her runny nose on her arm. A loud clap of thunder shook the barn and dust rained down on her from the rafters.

It was going to be a long night.

CHAPTER 16: IRONY

⟨⟨ ⟨⟨ ⟩⟩ ⟩⟩

Mimie woke up a few hours before dawn and couldn't fall back asleep. One or two sharp pieces of straw were pressing painfully into her back, and no matter which way she shifted she couldn't get rid of them. Finally, she gave up and pushed herself to her feet. Oviet was fast asleep nearby, and Mimie tiptoed toward the stairs to avoid waking her up. She pulled her fingers through her hair in a futile attempt to bring order to it and made her way toward the barn door. She quietly pulled it open and stepped outside. The rain had finally stopped, and the world seemed cleaner. The fresh air was just the thing Mimie needed to sort through her thoughts.

The moon and stars were partially obscured by the wispy remains of the storm clouds, but they were clearing away quickly. Mimie wondered what Koren was doing. The tears came silently, and she almost didn't notice them except for the chilled streaks they were leaving on her cheeks. She glanced toward the hut and then at the wild greenery that threatened to swallow it. She wandered toward the road, trying to avoid the mud and not quite succeeding.

Her destination was a log that sat under a tree beside the pathway. She sat down on the damp wood and glanced in both directions, waiting for something, but not sure what. She heard a noise behind her and whipped around. She scanned the dark trees and saw a small, plump figure approaching from the hut.

"You're up early," Rio stated.

"Yep." She scooted over, and Rio sat down next to her. "I felt like watching the sunrise this morning."

"It's Mimie, right?" Rio asked.

"Yeah," she muttered.

"Are you ok, you look upset about something?"

Mimie stared at the stars. "A good friend of mine left a few nights ago."

"What was his name?" Rio shifted her weight on the log, looking for a more comfortable position.

"Koren." Mimie felt her heart cringe and took a deep breath. "I don't want to talk about it."

"I apologize for being nosy, it's been a long time since I spoke with a fairy. I wish you the best of luck on your travels. I have to go take care of the chickens."

"It was nice talking to you," Mimie said. Rio patted her on the shoulder and stood up. Mimie hoped the Ligons hadn't destroyed anything. Rio was half way to the barn when the door burst open and Oviet, followed by the others, rushed outside.

"Thank you for letting us stay!" Oviet yelled breathlessly as they rushed past her. Mimie realized the procession was headed straight for her and wondered if she was in trouble for not telling them where she went. "Hurry, get on," Oviet hissed when Mimie was within hearing distance. Mimie scrabbled onto to Oviet's back and no sooner had she pulled herself up, then they were in the air.

"What's going on?" Mimie asked, struggling to hang on.

"The Ligons plucked all the feathers off several of the chickens," Oviet explained.

"You were supposed to watch them!"

"I know, I know, but I was never very good at babysitting. Besides, they're Avia and Arqus's responsibility. They should have been watching them!" She yelled the last part so that Arqus could hear her.

"I told you I was sorry," he shouted back, "and technically she said not to let them eat the chickens, which they didn't." Mimie rolled her eyes and glanced behind her at the small hut.

"Are you sure we got everything?" Mimie asked.

"Yeah, why?" Oviet replied.

"I don't know. I have this weird feeling that we forgot something important."

***

A commotion outside made Koren jerk upright and look around in confusion. Dawn was not far off, and as he watched he saw five figures run past the window headed for the road. He was sure one of them looked like a flying unicorn. He rubbed his eyes in disbelief and scooted closer to the window to see what was going on. Before he could get a look at the riders, the Ligons, and the flying unicorn were in the air.

He carefully limped toward the doorway and pushed the curtain aside. There was no one in sight so he headed for the front door.

"Where do you think you're going?" Thero demanded.

"Crap," Koren muttered under his breath and froze with his hand on the door handle. "I need some fresh air," he explained.

"Well, be careful of the mud, and don't forget these," he said, walking over and handing him a pair of wooden crutches.

"Thanks," Koren replied. He braced the supports under his arms and stepped outside. Holding the crutches was a challenge with his broken arm, but he managed and shuffled out onto the front porch. He heard Rio scream and hurried over to the barn to see what was wrong. He pushed the door open and saw feathers everywhere. He stood with his mouth open and watched as Rio chased half a dozen featherless chickens around the barn. She rounded them up one by one and locked them in an empty horse stall. Koren heard the door open and turned in time to see Kuria drop the empty pail she was holding.

"What's going on?" she giggled. "Amma you're covered in feathers."

"Quiet, help me clean up this mess," Rio snapped. "Those darn

Ligons plucked my chickens. They're going to be a nervous wreck for weeks and I won't get a single egg out of them." Rio took a deep breath to calm herself down and brushed the feathers off the front of her apron. Kuria grabbed two brooms that were leaning against a wall and handed one to Koren. Together they attempted to sweep the feathers into a pile.

"A fairy, though, in our barn," Rio said with a smile. "I wish I could have talked with her more this morning, she seemed like she was having a rough time."

"How so?" Koren wondered.

"She was upset about losing a friend. I think Koren was his name."

"Koren? That's my name."

"I guess that explains how you're healing so quickly."

"What do you mean?"

"Life fairies form a Saiamuria, or healing bond with anyone they would give their lives to protect. A lot of people believe a bond like that only happens in folk stories, but I know better, and here's the proof."

"I have to go after her."

"No one's going anywhere," a cold voice sneered. Koren searched the room and glared at a Lethian warrior standing in the doorway. Her black hair was pulled back into a tight braid, and she was covered in thick leather armor with a black sword hanging from her hip.

"It's rude to eavesdrop," Kuria growled. Rio placed a cautioning hand on her shoulder.

"Quiet," she hissed.

"We've received an anonymous tip that you're harboring the prince," the warrior told them, looking pointedly at Koren. Rio's hands clenched into fists and she replied coolly,

"You were misinformed."

"Hand him over to us, or I will kill everyone here. Starting with her." The Lethian threatened glaring at Kuria and taking a step in her direction. Koren blocked her advance and stood in front of Kuria with his arms crossed. The Lethian drew her sword. "Get out of my way."

"No."

"Stubborn as ever I see," said a second elf standing in the doorway. "He's definitely the one we've been looking for." She was blonde, but otherwise looked the exact same as the other warrior.

"He's not going anywhere with you," Rio snapped.

"He belongs in Lethia with Princess Morguay. We've come to escort him back there."

"I'm not going," Koren replied. "You do not get to tell me where I do, and don't belong."

The black haired warrior swung her sword at him. He blocked the blow with the end of his crutch, but the sword cut it in half.

"Run!" he told Rio and dodged another blow. Rio dragged Kuria out a side door and they disappeared from sight.

"Put that away!" the Blonde hissed. "We need him alive, remember? Just grab him!" He ducked into one of the stalls and worked his way toward where the horses were kept. He picked up one of the chickens at his feet and threw it at them. They dodged it.

He reached the door to the stable, but it was locked. He turned around and saw both warriors closing in on him. There was nowhere left to run, and he was unarmed. The Blonde grabbed his injured arm and twisted it behind him, pain shot through him and he fell to the ground. He tried to crawl away, but the Blonde knocked him over onto his stomach and pinned his arms to his sides with her knees. The pressure on his arm was excruciating but he refused to let anything more than a grunt escape him as he tried to throw her off. She pulled a cloth out of her pocket and covered his nose and mouth with it. Before he knew what was happening, he felt like he was falling through the floor into darkness.

***

The forest beneath Mimie flew by in an uneven green blur.

228

"Are we almost there yet?" she asked for the second time.

"We're not any closer than when you asked me a minute ago," Oviet snapped. "You will know exactly when we get to Death Valley because everything will be black." Mimie fell silent and stared moodily at the ground. The air was warm and extremely humid; beads of sweat formed on Mimie's face and her legs stuck to Oviet's sides. "I can't keep this up much longer," Oviet gasped. "I can't breathe when the air is this humid."

"Let's take a break," Mimie offered. The road looped around and ran beside the river. It was free of trees, so Oviet decided to land there. As soon as she touched the ground Mimie slid off her back and stretched. She wiped her forehead with her sleeve and wondered into the shade. She was too tired to stand, so she sat down on a rock and yawned. Avia and Arqus landed beside them and headed into the trees. Oviet followed them; Mimie figured she should probably do the same. They were headed toward the river, but she already felt wet and muggy enough, so she decided to stay on the bank. Oviet didn't wait for the others; she walked into the river and submerged herself all the way up to her neck.

"I hope that river doesn't have crocodiles in it," Mimie laughed.

The others waded in as well, but the calm serenity only lasted until Arqus decided to send a huge wave of water at Oviet's face. After that, it was an all-out war. The others were so absorbed in what they were doing they didn't hear something moving around in the trees by the road. Mimie picked up Koren's sword and could just make out a plump figure on horseback approaching them. The figure climbed down from his or her saddle and ran toward her.

"Mimie, is that you?" a familiar voice asked breathlessly. "I got here as fast as I could."

"Rio?" Mimie asked in shock. "What are you doing here?"

Rio threw back her hood and massaged at a stitch in her side.

"Koren's in trouble." Mimie took a step back in shock. "The tall elf with the blondish-brown hair, you know him right?"

"Yes, what happened?"

"He was kidnaped by Lethians. They're going to force him to

marry Princess Morguay."

Mimie felt her knees go weak. "Why would they do that?"

"Someone made a deal with them. Lethians are savages, they always have been. In the disorder since Orient took over they have been getting more powerful, and now it seems like they are trying to unite Koren's kingdom with their own."

"Koren doesn't have a kingdom, his sister does."

"Is his sister a nice person?" Rio asked.

"No."

"Then she probably offered him up to them in hopes of securing a military alliance. I used to serve the princesses and saw the horror they were capable of first hand. You have to get him out of there."

"Which way is Lethia?" She knew Koren would never leave without saying good bye. She should have known he was in trouble. What kind of friend was she?

"This road will take you there. Just keep heading straight and you'll find the outer villages."

"Ok," Mimie growled and went to find Oviet.

"Good luck," Rio called and led her horse out of sight. Oviet was still in the river, oblivious to what had happened.

"Oviet, I need to talk to you," Mimie called. Oviet climbed out of the water and shook droplets from her coat.

"What's up?" she asked.

"Koren's in trouble. Kyra sold him out for a military alliance. I just talked to Rio and she said she saw Lethians kidnap him."

"Should we tell Avia and Arqus?"

"I don't know, but Kyra wouldn't want us to stop whatever she has planned. We don't have time for a fight if they're working with her." The idea of one of the Ligons coming after her made her shudder.

"The guards were appointed by Evangeline. I doubt they were in on Kyra's plan." Avia noticed their tense posture and walked over in alarm.

"What's wrong?"

"The Lethians kidnaped Koren, and we think Kyra covered it up." The words came out harsher than she intended. She glared at Avia daring her to contradict what she had said.

Avia crossed her arms. "Kyra would never do something like that, and even if you're right, you can't go to Lethia, you'll be slaughtered."

"Are you going to try and stop me?" Mimie demanded.

"No, but I think you're making a mistake."

"I am not going to leave him there, so you can either help me, or go home. It's your choice."

"I'm not going on a suicide mission. If you do this you do it alone," Avia told her and turned away. "I'm sorry. I will return to Talanthia and inform Visailios of what has happened. Goodbye Guardian, safe travels."

"Bye." Mimie led the way toward the road. She hopped on Oviet's back and held on as she leaped into the sky.

"Which way am I going?" Oviet asked.

"Follow the road," Mimie replied, "and stay low. I don't want them to see us coming."

***

Koren felt someone shoving something in his mouth and coughed. The liquid burned all the way down his throat and made him feel sick to his stomach. He was dimly aware that he was in another wagon and wondered how long he had been there. Footsteps walked away from him, but he couldn't see anyone. Someone shut the door to the wagon, locked it, and then walked around to the driver's seat. The wagon jerked forward.

"What was that?" he coughed.

"Something to help you relax." Koren glanced through the barred window and saw the blonde-haired elf that had attacked him at Rio's barn. "We'll be in Lethia in ten minutes."

Koren ignored her and rolled onto his side, why was this

happening to him? A little while later the wagon stopped, and the door flew open. Koren squinted against the blinding sunlight and felt someone roughly drag him out of the cart. They untied him and set him on his feet. He blinked a few times and tried to get his bearings, but it was hard when his vision was sliding in and out of focus.

"Where is he?" a high-pitched voice demanded. "Where's Kormont?" Koren looked to his left and saw an elf pushing through the crowd surrounding him. The Princess had medium length curly blonde hair and she was wearing elaborate leather armor that didn't look like it would protect her in a fight. On her head was a gold ring of metal he assumed was a crown. She stopped in front of him and looked him up and down with a satisfied smile. "Get him cleaned up. I want the wedding to start as soon as possible."

"Wedding?" Koren asked in confusion.

"He's so cute," the princesses laughed and patted his arm. "Limara, get him ready, I want the ceremony to begin before dusk." The Blonde elf nodded and grabbed Koren's arm. She pulled him toward the closest building, which was made from large stone bricks, and pushed him inside. He limped along as best he could, but it was hard to walk when he felt so dizzy.

"What's wrong with me?" Koren demanded, stumbling into a wall.

"I drugged you," Limara told him, pushing him deeper into the building.

"Why?" Koren demanded.

"Stop asking questions," she snapped.

She led him down a long hallway to a small room. She dragged him inside and shut the door behind her. Inside was a small pool filled with bubbles. "Is that warm?" Koren asked.

"Yes," Limara replied, rolling her eyes.

"Why are you so grumpy?" he wondered while pulling off his shirt and cloak, which was difficult because of his impaired balance and injured arm.

"I'm not grumpy," she snapped and pulled a curtain closed to give him some privacy.

"Whatever you say," Koren replied, and took the rest of his clothes off. He kicked them to the side and jumped into the pool, letting himself sink all the way to the bottom. He stayed there for a few seconds and then swam back to the surface. It was deep enough that the water came to his shoulders, not including the three-inch film the bubbles formed on the top of the water.

Limara pulled back the curtain so she could keep an eye on him.

Koren scrubbed all the dirt off his arms. It felt good to be clean again. He stretched out his shoulders and let the hot water relax the tension that had settled there. He sank to the bottom of the pool again and closed his eyes. He came back up for air after a while, and shook the water out of his eyes.

"Don't do that," Limara scolded. "I'm not allowed to let you drown."

"How kind of you." Koren laughed and submerged again.

When he came up for air, she yelled, "I'm serious. You have enough drugs in your system you could lose consciousness, and then I would have to jump in and save you."

"That would be awkward. How about you just let me drown instead."

"You're ridiculous," Limara growled. She took out a knife from her belt and ran a sharpening stone over it. "Are you clean yet?"

Koren leaned against the side of the pool and pushed his bangs out of his eyes.

"No, I think I need to soak a while longer to get the rest off." He might as well enjoy his stay while it was pleasant. He closed his eyes and rested his head on his arm. The warmth made him feel sleepy, he started to slip off the edge. Limara grabbed his arm, jolting him back to reality. She dropped a towel on the ground next to him and left a stack of clothes on the table.

"Put those on when you're dry." She snapped the curtain shut again.

Koren climbed out of the pool and dried himself off. He shook out his hair and limped over to the stack of clothes. They were all made of leather, but were surprisingly comfortable. His shirt was covered in ornate designs and had decorative beading all over it. He pulled it on but struggled with all the knots. "You're taking forever," Limara complained.

"You should have thought of that before you drugged me. It's difficult to tie all these stupid knots when I can't see straight." He pulled on the pants and strapped them in place. Limara pushed the curtain aside and straightened his collar. His stomach twisted in discomfort as she appraised the way everything fit. "I'm sure the princess has plenty of suitors, why do I have to marry her?"

"Just do what she wants, and it won't be that bad."

"Easy for you to say." Koren glared at the ceiling.

"I could give you more drugs if you like." Koren nearly gagged at the memory.

"No thanks." He wanted to keep whatever dignity he had left.

"Come on, you don't want to be late to your own wedding."

She led him out of the stone building. Koren didn't pay much attention to where they were going. He avoided the gaze of the elves that passed him, his ears burning. Limara led him around the back of a large crowd to the base of a stone archway. It was covered in bright green vines and was beautiful, despite the unfortunate circumstances.

"I'll take it from here," a burly elf growled. He threw Koren onto a raised platform and chained thick shackles to his wrists. Koren jerked his arm out of the elf's grasp. The drugs were losing their potency, and he was able to balance on his uninjured leg without falling over. Countless elves were staring at him, making him feel self-conscious. The minister was chained next to him, looking glum.

"This is not how I pictured myself getting married," Koren muttered. The minister stared at him in pity, but said nothing. Koren stared over the crowd, searching for a friendly face. He strained his neck, hoping to spot Limara. He saw her talking to a girl serving fruit. The serving girl wasn't sneering at him like the other servants. She seemed oddly familiar, though he didn't know why. She glanced his way. A jolt of energy shot through him as their eyes met. Her hair shimmered with strands of gold and copper when it caught the sunlight, and she walked with an innate grace born only to fairies. He took a step in her direction without deciding to, but the chains stopped him.

He frowned when Limara snapped her fingers under the girl's nose and pointed to the king. The girl walked toward him and offered him some fruit, but he refused. She glanced back at Koren from time to time and smiled, making him feel better. At least there was one decent person in this place.

Music suddenly rang through the courtyard and dread sank into the pit of Koren's stomach. He tested the chains, but they wouldn't budge. He watched the princess and her father walk down the aisle. She was glowing with happiness and was walking faster than the tempo of the music. She had an ugly mole protruding from the side of her forehead that he hadn't noticed before. He stared at it in disgust. She was overweight, and every step she took sent ripples through the rest of her body. Koren tested the chains again, but they still didn't budge. He wondered if he could provoke one of the guards into killing him before he had to go through with this. Before he could act the princess stepped onto the platform and everything fell quiet. She faced the minister.

"The short version please." This couldn't be happening.

"We gather today to join these elves in holy union. By the power I hold, given to me by the great creator, I declare them joined as partners until separated by death."

Morguay squealed, she grabbed him and pushed her disgusting mouth against his. His face burned in humiliation as he struggled to pull free of her grasp. When she finally released him he frantically wiped his mouth off, feeling like he might be sick. The Princess didn't seem to notice and motioned to one of the guards. He unlocked Koren's shackles and pushed him toward her. Koren recoiled from her touch and sidestepped around her looking for an escape route. There was none.

***

Mimie jumped off Oviet's back onto the Lethian courtyard and found it deserted.

"Where is everyone?" Mimie wondered.

"I don't know, but I bet Koren is with them. How are you going to get him out of here?"

"I don't know yet," Mimie confessed. "I'm kind of making this up as I go along." Oviet rolled her eyes.

"Of course you are."

"Hey!" a girl in serving clothes yelled. "You aren't supposed to be here." She set down her platter of fruit and approached them angrily. Mimie and Oviet exchanged grins, they waited until the elf was within reach, and then Mimie pulled out Koren's sword and slammed the flat of the blade into the elf's head. She crumpled to the ground and Mimie dragged her out of sight. Mimie took the girls clothes and put them on. Then she threw her own clothes in the space cube.

"Stay in this area. I'll find a way to bring Koren back here."

"Good luck," Oviet whispered. "Don't forget your fruit platter."

Mimie walked to where the elf had set it down. She thought about spitting on the food but thought better of it. She wandered through the buildings and soon was completely lost.

"Hey!" a deep voice growled. "Why aren't you at the wedding?"

"I can't find it," Mimie confessed, hoping the huge elf wouldn't pummel her to death.

"It's around the corner and to the left. You can't miss it," he told her.

"Ok," Mimie replied, and walked in the direction he had indicated. It didn't take long to find the huge crowd of people. Row after row of benches were set up in a vast courtyard, most of which were occupied by sour looking warriors. The aisles between the seats were filled with elves making a feeble attempt at small talk. She weaved through the crowd and searched for Koren. She found him chained to a raised wooden platform under an impressive stone arch. He was staring into space, indifferent to what was going on around him. There were guards everywhere; if she was going to have any chance of rescuing him she was going to have to be crafty. He scanned the crowd as if he was looking for someone, and Mimie half dared to hope it was her.

"Stop standing around!" a blonde elf scolded, "and stop eyeing the prince. He's a person, not a circus animal.'"

"Sorry," Mimie said.

"He deserves better than this." She shook her head and frowned.

"What do you mean?" Mimie asked.

"You must be new here," the elf replied, rolling her eyes. "Look at him. He just wants to go home. I don't want to think about the shape he'll be in tomorrow. I might have to wipe his memory again." They wiped his memory? Mimie clenched her fists in anger.

"If you feel so strongly about this, why did you kidnap him in the first place?" It was nearly impossible to keep her tone neutral.

The elf narrowed her eyes. "I didn't have a choice. The queen wants to unite the kingdoms and the only way to do that is through this marriage." She fixed her gaze on Koren, her eyes filled with remorse. "He's looking at you."

Mimie blushed and snuck a peek at him through her eyelashes. He was definitely staring at her. She felt her knees go weak, and couldn't look away; she'd forgotten how great it felt to get lost in his gaze. The blonde elf snapped her fingers under Mimie's nose to get her attention and pointed toward the king.

"The ceremony is about to start, go see if the king wants anything to eat."

"Ok." Mimie walked toward him, pausing a few feet away. His guards glared at her but backed off at a warning glance from the king.

"Go sit down the ceremony will begin shortly." His tone was gruff.

Music filled the courtyard making Mimie jump. She saw Morguay coming around the corner of a building and shuddered. She shoved a small elf throwing rose petals out of the way and roughly joined arms with her father. She dragged him up the aisle, paying no attention to the tempo of the music. Once she reached the platform she climbed onto it and stood next to Koren. Horrified, he tugged at the chains holding him in place, but he couldn't get them off. After an impossibly short period of time Morguay turned toward Koren, wrapped her thick arms around him and kissed him.

Hot anger raced up her spine so intense the air crackled around her. Koren frantically wiped his mouth on his sleeve and a guard had unchained him. The crowd dispersed quickly, leaving Mimie a clear path to where the Blonde was waiting for Koren to climb down off the platform. Mimie watched from afar, not wanting to get close enough for them to realize she was following them.

The Princess headed toward a huge palace made of white brick, with a large gold dome on top. The stunning architecture boasted both strength and beauty. There were few windows, but ornate stonework gave the impression of high window arches. The palace doors were made of thick iron, and required the help of two guards to open. Limara lead them inside, and Mimie watched in frustration as they closed the doors behind them. The guards resumed their watch, a fearsome barrier between her and the inside of the building. Mimie felt the space cube in her pocket and played with it between her thumb and index finger as she tried to think of a plan.

An idea came to her, but it was so crazy she almost dismissed it. It was a long shot, but it was the only thing she could think of. She walked confidently toward the guards and stopped a few feet in front of them.

"A gift has just arrived in honor of Princess Morguay's wedding. The man claims it to be a cube that can expand to many times its size. It's filled with gold and other priceless treasures. He requests that it be brought to the princess straight away."

"Where is this cube?" one of the guards asked.

"It's on the other side of the palace. The man wishes to remain anonymous so I'll go to him and say that you have accepted his gift. I would give it to you myself, but as a servant he preferred I not handle the cube. Please wait until he has had adequate time to hide himself before following me."

"As you wish," the guard replied. "Give him my thanks for his generosity." Mimie nodded and walked far enough away she was out of sight of the guards. She set the space cube down on the hard cobblestone and expanded it. She quickly rearranged its contents so that both her and Koren's sleeping sacks formed a somewhat comfortable pad for her to sit on. She made sure no one was watching and then climbed into the space cube. Her heart pounded as she slid the lid over her head and was plunged into darkness. She squeezed her eyes shut, hoping she wasn't about to experience what it was like to be crushed. The pressure changed as the cube shrank, but the space inside it stayed the same. Mimie had enough air to last her another hour, but after that she would be in serious trouble.

The ground shook beneath her as footsteps approached. Her stomach dropped as she was lifted into the air with enough force to fuse her to the bottom of the cube. She felt the halting gait of the guard's footsteps and dug her fingers into the cloth of the sleeping sack as she tried not to imagine what it would feel like if the guard suddenly dropped her. It was hard to hear what was going on outside the cube. Voices were muffled and hard to understand, but from what she could pick out the guards had listened to her request and were taking her to the princess.

The air was growing thin by the time the guard finally stopped.

"This is for the princess, will you bring it into her chambers for me?"

"She has asked not to be disturbed, but I believe she is opening her gifts now. I will put it with the others." A silent moment passed and Mimie felt the cube being handed to someone new. The door closed and she grabbed the handle of Koren's sword, waiting. There was the sickening feeling of being lowered to the ground and some of the pressure eased as the cube expanded. The lid was pushed off as Morguay's greedy eyes peered inside. Greed quickly turned to shock as she spotted Mimie. Her piggy eyes were so wide they seemed ready to fall out of her head.

She didn't have time to scream before the butt of Koren's sword connected with her jaw, sending her tumbling backward. She was too dazed to move, but Mimie knew she would recover quickly. To buy time she searched through the space cube for a strip of cloth and some rope. At least with the princess bound and gagged it would prevent her from calling for help.

"Koren!" she called in a loud whisper. "Are you in here?" She found him in the next room sitting cross-legged on a large bed with a scarlet comforter. One wrist was shackled to a large iron sculpted bedpost. "I see you're already starting your honeymoon."

"This is not funny," Koren replied darkly, his cheeks turning red. "The key is on the dresser over there." Mimie grabbed it and unlocked his wrist. He slid off the bed and looked her up and down in confusion.

"Do I know you?"

"Not at the moment, but you'll recognize me when your memory comes back. Let's get you out of here."

"We don't have much time. Limara is standing outside the door, she checks in every once and a while to make sure Morguay is ok," Koren warned.

Mimie searched for anything that might be a concealed exit from the room. A large tapestry on the sidewall by the bed looked promising. When she moved it aside, Mimie found there was a door behind it. It was small, a way for servants to get in and out of the room. "How do you feel about tight spaces?" Mimie asked. She threw a pointed look at the space cube. Koren gulped once and didn't reply.

Mimie hurried down the dark passageway as quickly as she dared. It was dimly lit by torchlight, and the stale air smelled like dust and stagnate water. In her fist, she clutched the space cube and was acutely aware of the small person inside. She held her fist steady, so as not to jostle him, and searched for a way out. Somehow she ended up in the kitchen. The other servants too were busy preparing the feast in celebration of the wedding to notice her. One of the servants handed her an empty brown bag and told her to go get more potatoes.

Mimie searched for the place where the fresh food was brought in and slipped out between two wagons carrying crates of live chickens. She emerged in a vast marketplace and walked toward the smaller houses that crowded around the edges of the large courtyard.

Once in the shadows she set the cube down and watched it expand. Koren threw the lid off and gasped for air.

He stumbled out of the cube and sat down until he had caught his breath. Mimie pulled out the sword and handed it to him. "This is yours, you can use it a lot better than I can."

"I don't know if I can walk. My ankle's broken," he explained.

"I might be able to heal it enough that you can put weight on it. Once we make it to the outer villages, I have a friend waiting who can help us."

"Ok, it's worth a try," Koren muttered, lifting up his right pant leg. Mimie gently took off his shoe. His ankle was extremely bruised and swollen. She gently placed her palm on it and closed her eyes. She felt her fingers go numb and then pulled away to see if anything had happened. The bruising was significantly reduced; it was yellowish now instead of a blotchy purple color. She helped him to his feet, and let him use her shoulder for support as he gingerly set his foot down. "It's still tender, but I think I'll manage. Thank you," he told her. "You were the one at Rio's barn right? Mimie?"

"Yeah, that was me. Rio said what happened and I came as soon as I could." It was weird to think that Koren was a married man now.

"Spread out!" a Lethian guard yelled, running past the alley where they were hiding. "They can't have gotten far!"

Mimie ducked and pulled Koren down with her as she waited for the guards to pass. She glanced around the corner of the building and saw the tops of trees peeking out behind the buildings a ways away. It would be hard to get there, but that was their only chance. She motioned Koren to follow her and crept into the open. Every time a troop of guards went by they ducked behind a doorway and then snuck behind them. They ran into a problem when two groups of guards headed up the street from different directions. Koren tried the door handle and pushed his way inside the small dwelling. Mimie followed him and they sprinted through the main hallway. Koren bumped into a little girl holding a cup of water and she spilled it all over the floor. Koren put a finger to his lips and picked up the cup for her.

"Sorry," he whispered, and gave it back to her. "How do I get to the roof?"

She pointed to a door on their left.

"Thanks," Mimie called and wrenched it open. Sunlight streamed down from an opening at the top of the stairs and it blinded them as they emerged in a small garden on top of the roof. The guards were right behind them, Mimie screamed as one of them jumped forward and latched onto her ankle. "Get off me!" she yelled and tried to kick him in the face. He grabbed her other foot and dragged her toward him. She clung to the doorway with both hands, but she knew she couldn't hold on for long. Mimie's grip slipped and she tumbled down the stairs. The guard shoved her off him and seized her arm as she tried to run. He shoved her toward two other guards and yelled,

"Grab the prince!"

"Koren run!" Mimie screamed.

He raised his sword and challenged. "You want me? Come and get me."

Several guards pulled out swords of their own and charged toward him. Metal rang against metal followed by heavy thuds as Koren sent his opponents sprawling off the rooftop.

"Get her out of here," growled one of the guards holding Mimie's arm and rushed to join the fight. The other guard dragged her from the building. She heard the unmistakable sound of splintering wood and saw guards pouring onto the rooftop in front of Koren. Guards swarmed him and ripped the sword out of his hand. They dragged him back down the stairs and emerged from a doorway with him in hand.

"Take them back to the palace," one of the guards commanded. "The princess can deal with them there."

"That won't be necessary," a familiar voice called, pushing through the guards. "The Princess is right here."

"Where is she?" Morguay roared, her small eyes zeroed in on Mimie and she shoved the guard aside that was restraining her. Her face had turned various shades of blue and purple. She was even uglier now than she was before. Mimie wasn't sure how much of the color change was bruising and how much was from anger. She slapped Mimie with enough force to knock her to the ground and kicked her in the side. Mimie gritted her teeth to keep from crying out and glared back at her defiantly. "Where's Kormont?" The guard holding him shoved him toward Morguay and took a step back. Koren turned a shade of green at the sight of her and backed away. Morguay smiled and turned her piercing gaze back to Mimie. "You didn't really think you were going to escape did you?" she taunted.

Mimie glared at her wordlessly. Morguay narrowed her eyes and kicked her again, this time in the face. The force of the impact stunned her, and blood welled from her nose. It streamed down the side of her face, into her mouth and down her throat.

"Leave her alone!" Koren yelled. "I'm the one you want, remember?"

"You are no better than the Zanties," Mimie growled, spitting blood on her shoes.

"I was going to grant you a swift death, but now you'll beg for it long before it's granted to you. As for you Kormont," she snarled, turning back to him. "This is just a small taste of what's to come." She seized his broken wrist with both hands and twisted it sideways. Koren's knees buckled and he screamed in agony. Morguay released him and he fell onto his side clutching his wrist.

Mimie's tattoo glowed bright white and her skin flushed with the heat of the fury burning its way through her. She pulled the sword from the belt of the guard behind her and drove it through his chest. The other guards rushed at her, but a windstorm and a flash of light sent them sprawling backward into the surrounding houses. Mimie pulled a knife from the dead guard at her feet and hurled it at Morguay. The blade lodged itself in her throat and she fell to her knees, eyes bulging. Limara had been knocked out in the blast, and the other guards fled in fear at the dangerous look she gave them.

"Consider this a divorce," Mimie spat, glaring down at Morguay as her body fell still. "Come on, we have to go before the guards come back." Mimie helped Koren to his feet and pulled him toward the forest. Koren stared at her in shock and something else that was almost…fearful. The streets appeared empty, but she still felt on edge.

"Look out!" Koren exclaimed, pulling Mimie to the ground as an arrow whizzed past them.

"These people just don't give up," Mimie growled, allowing Koren to help her to her feet. The glow in her tattoo was fading, and she could feel that she'd overstretched herself again.

"Now what?"

Mimie heard guards running at them from all directions. They only had one option left. "Whistle," Mimie told him.

Koren didn't question her; he put his fingers to his lips and let out a piercing whistle. Mimie saw the elf notching another arrow in his bow; Koren stepped protectively in front of her. Oviet swooped passed the guard and knocked him off the roof with a solid kick. She landed in front of them and skidded to a halt.

"Mimie, what happened to your face?"

"Don't worry about it," Mimie replied. She waited for Koren to swing onto Oviet's back and then hopped on behind him. Oviet spread her wings and shot skyward. The Lethians were still after them, but Mimie knew they were safe for now as long as they stayed out of range of the arrows.

"There," Mimie panted. "Just like I planned." Oviet rolled her eyes and snorted.

"This is amazing!" Koren exclaimed, watching the trees fly by in streaks of color below them.

"What did they do to him in that nut house?" Oviet asked.

"They wiped his memory." Mimie pinched her nose to stop the stream of blood.

"Is it going to come back? He's kind of freaking me out..."

"Yes, it'll come back, and I'm not crazy. I can still understand everything you say," Koren snapped.

"Oh, sorry, well it's nice to have you back." Her wings created an audible whooshing sound as they caught an air current that carried them higher.

"Where are we going now?" he wondered.

"Somewhere safe. If it's all the same to you guys I'd rather not have the Lethians slit my throat in the middle of the night." Mimie saw the purple bruising on Koren's wrist and seethed in quiet anger.

"I could kill Kyra for doing this to you. She left us this so we wouldn't come looking for you." Mimie pulled the crumpled piece of paper out of her pocket and handed it to him. He smoothed it out and skimmed over it, frowning.

"Yeah, this isn't my handwriting." Mimie glanced at the position of the sun noting they had very little daylight left.

"Oviet…"

"I know. I'm looking for a cave."

"Why? A cave in this part of the jungle is bound to be crawling with various monsters," Koren pointed out.

"Exactly, which is why we will be safe from the Lethians, they wouldn't dare follow us into something so dangerous."

"Yes, that's very comforting," Koren replied, rolling his eyes.

"We'll just spread some salt on the ground, it will be perfectly safe. I think I see something up ahead."

The sun was just disappearing behind the trees as Oviet swooped down into the spacious entrance. She touched down on the cave floor, waited for Mimie and Koren to jump off her back, then stretched.

At Mimie's encouragement Koren lifted up the hem of his pants so Oviet could heal his ankle. He seemed suspicious at first but he patted her neck in gratitude when he was relieved from the pain. She healed his wrist as well then laid down in some grass.

Mimie pulled the space cube out of her pocket, expanded it, and pulled out the salt. She handed it to Koren and he poured it in a wide circle around them. Mimie then fished around for the sleeping sacks and threw them on the ground next to her. The floor of the cave was covered in thick patches of ferns so Mimie grabbed her sleeping sack and spread it out onto one of the denser clumps.

"Hey, I was going to eat those," Oviet complained.

"There are a million others in here, I think you will be ok."

It was getting darker by the second, and suddenly hundreds of moonstones flickered to life around them. Mimie grabbed her clothes from the space cube and headed toward one of the side chambers to change. She found one partially covered by vines and pushed inside. Green crystals glowed on the walls, and small fireflies fluttered to life as she disturbed their place on the ground. She ignored them and held onto one of the crystals as she threw off the gray servants dress and pulled on her own clothes. She kicked the dress aside and turned away from it.

Mimie had never thought of herself as dangerous, but in a moment of anger she had killed two people. She closed her eyes and tried to block out the guards shocked expression as she drove the sword through his chest, and the choking sounds Morguay made as she tried to pull the knife out of her throat. Darkness had burrowed its way into her heart and taken residence there. Mimie scowled at the wall; maybe if she had been able to think clearly, she wouldn't have done it. She pushed through the vines and watched Koren return to Oviet wearing his old clothes. He seemed ready to put the ordeal behind him, why couldn't she. The shadow of water dancing on the roof of the cave at the far end of the chamber captured Mimie's attention.

"I'm going swimming," Mimie announced loud enough for them to hear and headed off in the direction of the spring. She needed some time to clear her head.

"Mimie, I don't think it's safe for you to go off by yourself," Koren called.

"If it worries you so much, why don't you come with me?" He growled in defeat and followed her to the edge of the spring.

Water flowed from a small hole in the wall, down a five-foot drop, and into a deep pool that contained schools of brightly colored fish. Moonstones along the walls and under the water illuminated the pool a glowing, pearly white. The rocks were a rich blue-green color with moss covering almost every surface. When she reached the shelf above the pool, Mimie slipped her cloak over her head, tossed it to the side, and climbed down to the water. She dipped her toe in to check the temperature and found it pleasantly warm. She eased herself the rest of the way in.

Her nose was still tender, so she was careful not to touch it as she washed the blood off her face. She could have asked Oviet to heal it, but she wasn't sure she deserved to be healed. Koren sat down on the ledge above her.

"Are you ok?" Mimie met his concerned gaze, unsure how to answer. Her thoughts churned over one another incoherently.

"I think I should really be asking you that question."

He shrugged. "It's over now, I don't want to talk about it." Mimie fiddled with some moss. "We're not talking about me though. Is it what happened with Morguay and the guard back in Lethia?"

"Yep." Mimie couldn't face him when she felt so much shame over what she did. He tossed something to the side and climbing down next to her. He was just in his pants; he'd left everything else up on the ledge. Mimie felt heat rise to her face as she stared at his bare chest and forced herself to look away. He's in love with someone else, she forcefully reminded herself.

He jumped into the water next to her, soaking what little of her was still dry.

"Hey!" Mimie exclaimed, wiping the water from her eyes. The ripples he generated lapped at the walls, creating a sloshing sound that echoed off the stone.

"Come join me," Koren invited. He rolled onto his back and floated there effortlessly with his hands behind his head.

"I can't swim very well. I'd rather stay here where it's safe." Koren half smiled and swam toward her. He plucked her off the wall and pulled her out into deeper water. Mimie had no choice but to cling to him for dear life, or risk drowning.

"Relax. I'm not going to let anything happen to you." Mimie released her stranglehold and took deep breaths to calm herself. "Why did you want to go swimming if water scares you so much?"

"I don't swim, I soak, it's different."

"Ok, if you say so," Koren laughed. "You have some bruising under your eye." He reached toward her face and gently touched her cheek. Mimie looked down at his hand, and then into his eyes. Her skin tingled a bit where his fingers brushed against her face. He let his hand fall.

"I'm sorry you got hurt because of me." He fell quiet and stared at the water angrily. "I hate thinking about the way you found me in Morguay's chambers. Please don't tell anyone about that."

"I wouldn't," she promised. She knew all too well the shame that came from an experience like that. Mimie felt her hands shaking and hid them behind her back so Koren wouldn't notice. "When Morguay attacked you, all I could think about was making sure she could never hurt you again. I never stopped to consider whether it was the right thing to do or not."

"If the situation were reversed, I would have done the same thing," Koren replied. "Are you ok, you're shaking?" Mimie tried to get the tremors under control, but the more she fought them, the worse they got.

"Let's talk about something else, this subject is going to make me emotional."

"Ok." His eyes gentled and a smile pulled at the corners of his lips.

"What?"

"Has anyone ever told you how beautiful your eyes are?" Mimie blushed and looked away.

"You would be the first actually," she admitted.

"They change color with your moods I think. Right now they're going back and forth between gray and blue." Mimie had no idea her emotions were so visible. No one had ever paid enough attention to point it out to her before. Mimie moved to a spot where she could touch the bottom and watched the fish swim around. Koren rolled onto his back and floated there with his hands behind his head. Mimie wished she could hold herself in the water with the same ease.

"I wish I could do that."

"Do what?" he asked.

"Float like that? You're not even moving you're just, floating."

"Oh that," Koren laughed. "I feel like I learned it from somewhere, but I can't quite remember."

"Maybe the Beavers taught you."

"Beavers?"

"Yeah, you lived with them for a while. I met them, they're really nice."

"You seem to know a lot about me. Maybe more than I know

about myself at the moment." That appeared to trouble him.

"I doubt that, you don't like it when I ask about your past."

"You're a good friend Mimie. I'm glad I met you. I can teach you how to float on your back if you want. It's not hard."

"Thanks, but I'd rather not embarrass myself."

"Come on, just try it," he encouraged.

"Fine." She rolled onto her back and instantly started to sink. "See I told you I couldn't do it," she muttered and grabbed onto the rock on the side of the pool to support herself.

"Well then, there's your problem. Try again, and this time have a little more confidence in yourself," he instructed.

"No, it's too embarrassing." He swam toward her and pulled her away from the rock. "Hey," Mimie protested.

"Relax," he told her with an amused smile. His touch was so light if she closed her eyes she could almost believe she was flying. He was so close she felt the warmth coming off his skin. He pulled her closer until her arm was pressed against his chest. She could have stayed that way forever if he'd let her. I can't love him, she reminded herself. He loves Emily. This was stolen time. It was wrong of her to let him do this. As soon as his memory came back he would realize the mistake he was making, and resent her for letting him make that mistake. She pushed away from him. He looked at her in confusion but didn't say anything.

They grabbed the clothes they had removed before getting into the water and walked back toward where Oviet was curled in a clump of ferns. Koren carried his sleeping sack toward the far wall. Mimie felt too awkward to say goodnight and buried her face in her sleeping sack. Why couldn't things just be simple?

CHAPTER 17: EYE FOR AN EYE
⇐ ⇐ ⇒ ⇒

"Mimie! Wake up!" someone yelled. Mimie opened her eyes and saw Koren's blurry outline standing over her.

"What? What's wrong?" she wondered drowsily.

"It started raining last night after we fell asleep, the whole cave is flooding. Get up!" He helped her out of her sleeping sack and threw it into the space cube. He then shrank it down and shoved it in his pocket.

The water level was up to Mimie's ankles and rising quickly. In the darkness, she heard more than saw, water gushing over the sides of the cavern.

"I can fly us out of here, but we'll have to walk after that, I need to let my wings dry out. We have to keep going if we want to stay ahead of the Lethians."

"It's too late, they've already found us," Mimie said, trembling. She pointed toward the rim of the cavern where she saw blurry figures looking down on them.

"Let's go before they find a way in," Koren said. A flash of lightning illuminated the pale undertone of his skin. He picked Mimie up and slung her legs over Oviet's back, then hopped on behind her.

"Ready?" Oviet wondered. The rain was coming down harder than ever.

"Yeah, let's go," Koren said, squeezing Mimie's hand. Oviet

spread her wings and burst into the air. They were pummeled by a wall of water so thick Oviet could barely stay air born. It was impossible to tell where they were going and Mimie became increasingly afraid they were going to hit the wall. "Mimie look out!" Koren yelled. An elf with a crazed expression dove at her face. She screamed as he slammed into her and Koren, knocking them both off Oviet's back. Weightlessness sent Mimie's stomach lurching upward into her throat. She was so disoriented; she hardly felt the crushing impact when she hit the floor. She blinked a few times, too shocked to process what had just happened.

With a groan, she pushed herself onto her hands and knees and frowned, something red was swirling through the water around her. She followed it to an elf wearing red leather lying in a crumpled mess by a big rock. She recognized him as the elf that had knocked them to the ground. His face was hidden under his arm. She gently rolled him over and recoiled in horror. His glazed eyes stared blankly back at her while blood from a cut near his ear formed a wide pool of red around him. The cause of his death was probably a combination of blood loss and the sickening angle of his neck. She closed her eyes and backed away from the corpse. She had to find Koren, and he could be in similar condition.

"Koren? Where are you?" she called, no reply. She searched the flooded rock frantically, but he was nowhere in sight. Finally, she spotted something to her right and splashed toward it. She recognized Koren's traveling cloak and let her breath out in a sharp exhale. He was lying motionless on his side but he didn't seem to have any visible injuries. She shook his shoulder, but he didn't respond. The pounding torrents coming from the open sky above them let up a bit. A flash of lightning illuminated a covered passageway nearby. Mimie braced herself against Koren's weight and dragged him backward toward it. The floodwater sucked at her shoes causing each step to make a loud splashing noise. Koren stirred and brought his hand to the back of his neck with a groan.

"I think I hit my head," he muttered.

"You've got a thick skull, you'll be ok," Mimie replied, looking around for any sign of Oviet.

"Very funny," he snapped weakly.

"Do you hear that?" she wondered. Light footsteps were approaching them. Mimie's breath came out through her teeth as she recognized Limara.

"You should have known that it was pointless to run, you can't escape justice."

"How dare you talk to me about justice when you allowed the princess to commit atrocities to an innocent person."

"Whether you or I believe that Morguay was a good leader, or that her actions were right or wrong, doesn't matter. Her word was, and still is the law. You will face the punishment for the theft of her property, and for her murder."

"I am no one's property!" Koren snarled.

"I can see that no matter what I say, you're never going to stop hunting us. I have nothing else to say to you." She nodded at Koren, who put his fingers to his lips, and whistled. Seconds later Oviet came charging toward them with an angry fire in her eyes. Limara jumped out of her way to avoid her slashing horn giving Mimie a split second window to jump on her back. Koren was right behind her. Oviet snorted and galloped toward the far wall. Mimie tangled her fingers in her silver mane, every muscle tense. The rain was picking back up again; soon visibility would be as bad as before. Oviet spread her wings and soared toward the top of the cavern, careful to stay away from the edges.

Once they had left the cave, Oviet touched down in the nearby field and broke into a trot. She shook out her sopping wings and ruffled up her feathers. Mimie saw her ear swivel to the left and felt a disturbance in the air as something whizzed past them. Oviet jerked, and let out a shrill neigh. Her legs faltered and then collapsed. Mimie felt the strong hand of dread grip her stomach as she rolled to the side to avoid being crushed. She ducked as another arrow flew over her head. She dug her fingers into Oviet's gray fur and looked her over for injury. Koren let out an audible gasp. Mimie wanted to recoil, but instead she leaned around Oviet's shoulder to see what had caused horror to wash over his face.

An arrow had pierced deeply into her chest.

Oviet's eyes rolled wildly as she tried to get to her feet. Mimie squinted across the field and saw the Lethians sprinting toward them with a battle cry. Another arrow whizzed past her head from the assassin in the tree line. Koren pulled out his bow and returned fire. Mimie wrapped her arms around Oviet's neck and tried to pull her to her feet, but she didn't move. Koren locked his arms around Mimie's waist and dragged her backward.

"What are you doing?" Mimie shrieked, trying to throw him off. Oviet groaned low in her throat and kicked her legs in awkward, jerky movements. "We can still save her! Let me go!"

The Lethians charged toward them closing the distance faster than she could process. Mimie screamed wordlessly, trying to use shear will power to keep them back.

Koren dragged her into the cover of the canopy and ducked behind the thick trunk of a large tree. Arrows shot past them and embedded themselves in the trunks of nearby trees. Mimie watched in horrified silence as the Lethians swarmed over Oviet and raised their swords. Mimie covered her mouth, barely feeling it as Koren tightened the restraining grip of his arms.

Oviet screamed as the swords repeatedly plunged into her. The water around her ran red with her blood. The world blurred into an incomprehensible haze, Mimie couldn't think through it, she couldn't see. Koren was trying to say something to her. He gave her a rough shake, and his fierce gaze cut through her shock.

"We have to go back for her! We can't leave her!" Mimie cried.

"They will kill you! Do you understand?" He set his teeth. "We have to get across the river. That will buy us some time, don't fall behind."

He released his grip on her and edged into the thicker underbrush. When he was sure the Lethians wouldn't have a clear shot of them he broke into a run. Mimie stumbled after him and shoved her way through the thick vegetation. When the vegetation thinned somewhat Koren grabbed Mimie's wrist and sprinted across the wet mud. He helped her over a fallen log and urged her into a run again. Shouts behind them alerted Mimie the Lethians were catching up. When Koren finally came to a stop, Mimie dropped her head between her knees and gasped for air. She coughed once and massaged at a cramp in her side.

The river roared through a deep gulch in front of them. Mimie peeked over the edge. Storm water swelled into a swift moving torrent below. The only way across was a heavily rotted fallen tree two hands lengths thick that spanned the length of the divide. Koren edged around the gnarled roots and tested his weight. When the log held firm, he waived Mimie after him.

"This can't end well! You know that right?" she yelled after him.

"It's our best option. We have to make it work."

She climbed up the roots and started across. The trunk sagged under her and Koren's combined weight. Mimie carefully edged around a tree branch that was sticking awkwardly out to the side. She relied on the other branches to help keep her balance and felt her body tense as she stepped over a densely rotted portion of the wood. Mimie glanced at the rushing torrent beneath her feet and gulped.

The wet wood was slippery beneath her feet, and there was a stretch coming up without any branches to help her keep her balance. She heard rustling in the bushes behind her and hot pain shot up her leg as her calf was grazed by an arrow. She teetered back and forth as she struggled to regained her balance. She crossed the rest of the distance quickly and stopped when she reached the thin branches covering the arm's length gap between her and the river bank. Koren had jumped over the flimsy branches without much difficulty and was waiting for her on the edge of the gulch. The trunk jerked as a large piece of debris smashed into it and a look of alarm flashed across Koren's face.

"Mimie jump! NOW!" There was no room for negotiation. She closed her eyes and took a deep breath. To clear her vision, she pushed her rain-plastered hair to the side and tried to gather the courage to do what she knew she must. Suddenly there was a defined crack near the portion of the log she was standing on. She backed away and screamed as the log shifted under her. Koren was screaming something at her, but she couldn't hear him over the rain and her own panic. With mere seconds to act, she ran toward Koren and jumped.

The log snapped near the portion she was standing on and the tree was sucked into the river. She grabbed hold of the steep bank and landed with her legs in the water. Koren grabbed her arm and fought to break the river's hold on her. After a brief struggle, he pulled her to her feet and steadied her as she regained her balance.

"That was close," Mimie muttered breathlessly. Koren pulled her behind the safety of a nearby tree. Her heart was beating so fast she felt lightheaded. Limara approached the far bank and motioned for the warriors to stop. She watched the fallen tree disappear down the storm channel and scowled as she realized she'd have to wait until the floods died down to pursue them. An arrow embedded itself in the tree they were standing behind. Koren held Mimie tightly against his chest and waited. Eventually the Lethians turned and disappeared.

"We should keep moving," Koren muttered and led the way deeper into the trees. He held his sword ready at his side, but the immediate danger had passed. Mimie hung back, her feet dragging against the moss covered ground. An image flashed through her head of the Lethians swarming over Oviet.

Where was her magic when she needed it? Why hadn't she stood by her friend and blown the Lethians into oblivion when she had the chance? Her throat burned as sobs claw their way out of her chest. Her steps faltered and she fell to her knees gripping her sides. She hung her head to hide her face and made no attempt to wipe away the tears. Koren sat down beside her and wrapped an arm around her shoulders.

"We left her to die."

Koren lifted her chin and she saw his red eyes. "The arrow pierced her heart. There was nothing we could have done."

"I want to have a burial ceremony for her." Mimie wiped away her tears. She set her teeth in determination and started clearing away moss from the ground. Using a moonstone for light Mimie outlined a hole and dug out the wet earth with her fingertips. Koren didn't question her, and with his help the hole was soon an arm's length deep. Mimie sat back on her heels and smoothed out the walls, patting the earth until it was flat and symmetrical.

Koren found a large rock and used a stone to scratch Oviet's name into it.

Mimie filled the hole with moss and grabbed a handful of dirt. Koren did that same and held his fist over the grave. Her throat burned as the tears fought their way free. She began the words of the ritual Gram had once done for her parents. "I will miss you until the day I join you in the afterlife, in peace may your soul rest among the stars." Her voice choked off and she couldn't finish.

"Watch over us, and turn our hearts to good," Koren said the next line for her and rubbed her back. "Your soul has moved on, but you will live forever in the hearts of those that loved you. Go peacefully and rejoin the ones you have lost, become one with the earth that once gave you life." They dropped the handful of dirt over the grave to close the ritual.

"I don't know how she would feel about having an elven burial, but I think she identified more with us than with her own kind."

Mimie had always wondered why Gram used different words than what she heard at other burials in the village and guessed it was a cultural norm the Guardians shared with Kolanna over human customs. Either way, it felt appropriate. With Koren's help, she pushed the dirt back into the hole and rolled the large headstone into place. She brushed the dirt off her hands, picked a flower off one of the vines and placed it beside the headstone.

Koren dug around inside the space cube and pulled out his ocarina. He raised the instrument to his lips and breathed life into the music. The mournful notes weaved through one another in a continuously shifting pattern. The last note wavered as Koren lowered the instrument and replaced it back at the bottom of the cube.

"Thank you," Mimie whispered.

"We have to keep going," Koren reminded her. Mimie tore her eyes away from the headstone. She felt numb; like she'd sustained an internal injury so deep it had bypassed the nerves and she was bleeding to death without realizing it.

They walked for most of the day and stopped when the light faded. Koren led them to a secluded spot ringed on all sides by thick underbrush. He pulled out the space cube and rummaged through it until he found the food pouch. There was only a small amount of berries left. He divided them and offered her half. Mimie took them and ate the berries without tasting their overripe sweetness.

"I'm going hunting, those berries were barely a snack, let alone dinner. All the wood around here is soaked but bamboo holds out moisture really well. If we can track down the grove we walked through a little while ago, we can collect some and bring it back here." He motioned Mimie to follow him and retraced their steps to the grove he was looking for.

Mimie studied the dense stand of the green-segmented plants and wondered what sorts of things were hiding in there she couldn't see. The plants towered over their heads. Koren pulled out his sword.

"This isn't the safest way to do this, but it'll work." He hacked at the base of the stalk. They moved to the side as it fell toward the ground. Mimie hauled it out of the way as Koren moved to cut down another stalk. She was grateful for the distraction of the mundane task, it made her grief more bearable.

Koren brought down three stalks in total and arranged them lengthwise so they would be easier to carry back. They dropped the load in the clearing, and Koren showed her how to remove the leafy branches from the top of the bamboo with one of his knives. When that was finished he moved the stalks further apart and cut them into arm's length pieces with his sword. While he worked on that, Mimie cut several vent holes in the closed chambers so the bamboo didn't explode when it was thrown in the fire. When they were finished, they dragged the segments into a pile.

"That was a lot of work for fire wood," Mimie muttered, wiping the sweat from her forehead.

"Shall we go catch diner?" Koren grabbed his bow from the space cube. He led the way into the trees, stalking forward soundlessly. Mimie followed, trying to match the stealth of his footsteps. She listened for the rustling of branches, hoping to catch one of the annoying birds that had kept her awake a few nights before. Koren kept his bow low at his side with an arrow ready.

A fuzzy blur scurried down to the forest floor, and Koren let the arrow fly before it could disappear back into the canopy.

"Aww, that one was cute."

"They all taste the same in the end," Koren replied. He walked over to his arrow and removed it from the tree. He pulled the skewered animal off, and handed it to Mimie by the tail. She held it away in distaste. Koren caught three more, and then returned to camp. He left Mimie in charge of building the fire while he prepared the meat.

Mimie pulled some of the white fibers from the inside of the bamboo and used them as her fire starter. She then carved off large pieces of the woody material with a knife and gathered them into a pile. She used the fire rocks from the space cube to get a spark and carefully blew it into a blaze. Once firmly established, Mimie threw the larger bamboo logs onto it. They were lucky, only a light drizzle sprinkled down on them, nothing heavy enough to put out the fire.

Koren built a spit to roast the meat and set the food over the fire. They didn't have much to season the meat with, so Koren rubbed salt into it for flavoring. The warm aroma swirled around Mimie, coaxing her out of her numb stupor. Koren removed the meat from the fire and handed her one of the smoking bundles. After picking at it for a while she tossed the leftovers into the fire. She watched the flames with her arms wrapped around her knees. The heat was unpleasant in the warm humidity, but she hoped it might dry her clothes out a little.

The rain picked up again an hour later, soaking through her clothes and putting out the fire. Mimie pushed her hair out of her eyes.

There was no point pulling out the sleeping sacks when it was inevitable they would be rained on again, so they left them in the cube. The moss coving the floor of the jungle seemed to soak up the rain as fast as it could fall, so even though it was damp, it wasn't soaked. Mimie settled down on top of it and pulled a big leaf over her to keep the rain off. She listened to the soft pitter-patter of the droplets hitting her leaf and breathed in the musky smell of the rain-dampened moss.

***

Koren took the first watch. He tried to find a comfortable position against a tree, but the deep ache in his head and the damp surroundings made that difficult. The broad leaves overhead intercepted most of the rain before it reached him and he was able to stay relatively dry. He watched Mimie toss and turn under her leaf. He longed to reach out to her, to comfort her, but knew there was little he could do. Her posture the night before in the spring had made her feelings toward him very clear. The rejection still prickled at his pride. It was foolish to think she'd want him to stay with her after they found the fairies, he wondered where he'd go after that. The thought made him feel sad.

Water dripped from the leaves. He stared at it and felt a memory coming back to him.

Two figures were partially obscured in a thick rolling fog. He walked across the well-traveled spongy grass and realized he was in a grave plot. The two figures stared down at a pair of headstones perched over freshly dug earth.

"I'm sorry Emily," Koren heard his younger self say. "It's hard enough to lose one parent, let alone both of them."

"People die every day."

"I know, but that doesn't make it any easier." Her light brown eyes glistened with tears and he pulled her into a hug. She was extraordinarily beautiful, even now, as her shoulders shook with grief.

He remembered the first moment he laid eyes on her when her family had arrived in the valley as refugees. He'd felt drawn to her; she was so full of life in a place that had known nothing but death.

"What's going to happen to me now?"

"I'll take care of you," Koren replied, running his fingers through her soft dark hair. He knew they couldn't stay in the valley; the sickness was so deeply entrenched among them that someone died from it every day. The camp was dirty and overrun with rats and mosquitos. They didn't have time to look for anywhere else though because those who were still strong enough to move spent most of their time hunting, or digging graves.

Koren glanced at the other headstones and felt the familiar grief when his eyes rested on the rocks in the far left corner. He picked out Freya's grave, and then Adelaide's. She'd been one of the first claimed by the sickness. In front of that was Quinton, who'd died in a hunting accident. Enzo was next to him; he'd committed suicide by jumping off the cliff at the far end of the valley.

That was three weeks ago. Amelia had found him, she said his neck snapped in the fall and he probably hadn't felt any pain. She tried to put on a strong front for the rest of them, but sometimes Koren still heard her cry herself to sleep at night. Koren hated Enzo for doing this, he was one of the best hunters they had, and now there was less food to go around than ever. How could he have been so selfish?

"Koren?" Emily said quietly.

"Yeah?"

"I love you," she whispered. Koren turned to look at her in surprise and felt a warm feeling spread through him. Whatever happened, whoever else he lost, he would keep her safe. They would escape the valley together and start a new life. Nothing the world could throw their way would ever separate them.

"I love you too." He kissed her tear soaked lips. "Now and forever."

***

Mimie pushed the leaf off of her, glad her vigil was over. The morning air was tinted green as it filtered down through the trees. Water droplets sparkled on the leaves. The beauty of it irritated her. Birds chirped from somewhere up above and a butterfly landed on a mushroom growing on a fallen log to her left. She shooed the brightly colored creature away with a flick of her wrist.

The current in the river would be dying down soon; they needed to keep moving. Mimie woke Koren and tried to disguise their campsite as best she could. She skipped breakfast, feeling too on edge to eat.

Her pants were rubbing sores on the insides of her legs and wished she could change into dry ones. With the rain coming down in sheets every other hour; she knew it wasn't worth the effort though. Something pricked her skin, and she smacked at it reflexively. There was a small crunch and she discovered the smashed remains of a mosquito under her palm. She wiped the blood smear away and scratched at the itchy welt.

Koren was good at spotting fruit trees, and with his help the food pouch was soon filled with mangos, guavas, and figs. Mimie was better at climbing the trees, so when he pointed out a tree she would climb up to the fruit and throw it down to him. It was hard to find fruit that was ripe, but they managed to collect enough to last them until they reached Death Valley.

Koren had been distant throughout most of the day, and now he was the one that lagged in the back. She remembered the night they had danced in the light of thousands of candles, and he had played for her even though he hadn't played for anyone in years. So much had happened since then. Oviet was dead. Her stomach tensed against the resulting pain.

"Hey," Koren muttered. Mimie realized she'd fallen behind in her stupor of thought. She opened her mouth, and then closed it again, not sure how to vocalize what she was feeling.

"Hey," she answered finally.

"Can I ask you a question?" Koren wondered after a long minute of silence.

"Sure."

"Was there anyone in your village back home you had feelings for?" Mimie blinked in surprise.

"Not really. I had little crushes here and there, but they never turned into anything."

"So you've never been in love?"

"I don't know; I have limited experience with the subject."

"There was a girl I met a long time ago. We escaped from a human village and got lost in a snowstorm. I went to find help, but when I came back, she was gone. I tried to accept that I was never going to see her again, but part of me refused to give up hope that she was still alive. I'm tired of feeling like I died that day too. I want to move on, I just can't."

"If she loved you like you loved her, she would want you to be happy. She would know that we weren't meant to go through this life alone, and would be grateful to the person that brought you the happiness she wished she could. I know I'm not her, but that's how I would feel."

"Yeah, I guess that's true. As much as I want to be with her, I wouldn't blame her for trying to find happiness with someone else. I wouldn't like it, but I could accept it. You're a lot more selfless than I am I guess." Mimie was about to answer, but paused when she heard a loud yowl.

"Did you hear that?" she wondered. She heard the noise again and tried to pinpoint where it was coming from. "I'm going to check it out, it sounds like something's hurt."

"Mimie no, leave it alone," Koren groaned, following her into the trees. "You don't know what kind of animal it is."

Mimie heard the low rumble of the river and decided the sound was coming from that direction. She followed the yowling cries to the riverbank and saw a small cat with a distinct rosette pattern on its coat pacing back and forth. Its eyes were fixed on a tiny kitten that was stuck on a rock in the middle of the river. The tawny cat was lean and had a smaller than average tail with black stripes. It had a small face and large ears with a white spot on the back.

"That's a serval," Koren muttered, eyeing it carefully. They usually don't attack people, but we should still be careful."

The current had died down a lot since they'd crossed the river last, but it was still flowing too swiftly for the cat to safely cross it to retrieve its baby.

"How on earth did it get out there?" Mimie wondered.

"It probably got caught in the flood waters. If that's the case, who knows how long it's been there," Koren replied.

"There's a branch overhanging the river, I could climb onto it and grab the kitten." Koren still seemed uncertain, but there was nothing he could say that would change her mind. The kitten would die if they didn't do something.

"Saving random animals isn't going to bring Oviet back."

"Don't you think I know that!" He stepped back in surprise at her harsh tone. Mimie crossed her arms. "Every life is important and if I don't help I might as well grab that kitten and drown it myself." She turned away from him and tried to rearrange her features into something less frightening as she approached the serval.

The mother hissed at Mimie as she approached and stalked into a bush as she drew closer. Mimie climbed the tree by the river and felt her irritation subside somewhat as Koren followed closely behind her. She edged her way out onto the branch until she was over the kitten. It looked up at her with deep blue eyes and meowed pitifully. The branch was too high above the kitten to reach it the way she had hoped and she rethought her options carefully.

"Hold onto my legs," Mimie commanded, turning her body so that her stomach was resting on the branch.

"You're nuts," Koren replied, shaking his head. Mimie ignored him and inched further down the branch. The rough bark made it so she didn't slip forward, but she still needed Koren's help. "Fine," he growled when it was clear she wasn't going to listen to him and grabbed her legs to help stabilize her.

She inched forward and braced herself against Koren's arms. She was close enough that the spray from the fast-moving current dusted her cheeks. Her hair hung in her face, but she pushed it out of the way and reached for the kitten. It hissed at her and scratched her hand. Mimie pulled back and tried to ignore her building headache as blood rushed to her head. Her rib cage was also starting to hurt, but she wasn't going to give up. She inched down a little bit further and tried to grab the kitten by the scruff. It crouched down and backed toward the edge of the rock. Mimie made sure to move slowly, so that in its fear the serval didn't accidently fall into the water. After a few tries, Mimie felt her hand close around the scruff and pulled the kitten to its feet so that she could get a better grip on it. She inched backward until she was able to sit up again and tried to keep hold of the kitten as it squirmed and hissed at her. She waited for her headache to go away and, while keeping a careful grip on the animal, slid back down the tree. She set the kitten on the ground.

The mother emerged from the bush and watched Mimie with wary, amber eyes. Once the kitten was free, it walked on unstable legs toward its mother and rubbed its head against the bottom of her jaw, purring loudly. The serval licked the top of the kitten's head and led it away into the brush. Mimie felt her lips twitch into what was almost a smile. Seeing the kitten safe and happy eased her pain somewhat. She rubbed the scratches on her hand and tried to ignore the sharp sting they produced.

"Shall we keep going?" Mimie muttered, and led the way forward through the trees. Koren shook his head wordlessly and followed after her.

Mimie pulled a guava out of the food pouch and inspected it for blemishes. It seemed fine, so she cut off a bit of the yellowish green fruit with Koren's knife and plopped it in her mouth.

As the sun sank lower in the sky, a fog rolled in and Mimie was reminded of the night the scorpion cat had attacked them. The jungle seemed very dark around them, and the tangled roots of the trees looked as though they harbored unseen dangers. The canopy grew thicker, allowing in less light. Mimie spotted something odd, and stopped in front of a line of poles. Each one had red paint spattered on it and an animal skull mounted on top. She scooted closer to Koren and grabbed his arm.

"It looks like a warning," he muttered. "We must be getting close to Death Valley."

"Maybe, it looks more like a boundary." The poles stretched as far as she could see in either direction.

"A boundary against what?"

"I have no idea." She wasn't overly eager to find out.

"We should get some rest."

Koren turned away from the poles, which were setting both of them on edge, and walked further into the brush until they were out of sight. When they were a good distance away, they settled down to make camp. Koren expanded the space cube and pulled out the water canteens.

"I'm going to go refill these," he muttered.

"I'll come with you," Mimie offered. "I think there's a stream over there."

"It's better that we don't get it from a stream. Jungle water usually has parasites in it, so we'd need to boil it first. I'd rather get some from water vines or bamboo. He searched around the perimeter of a few trees until he found what he was looking for, a dark green vine as thick as her forearm. He cut a notch in it at eye level and then severed the vine near the base. He tasted the small trickle of water that flowed from it and nodded in satisfaction. He held the stream of water over the canteen and let it fill to the brim.

Mimie had lost her fear of the dark a long time ago, but now her nerves tightened as she glanced around the dark trees. Maybe she was imagining it, but out of the corner of her eye she thought she saw dark smoke gathering in the night. It always disappeared when she turned to look at it. Her heart pounded against her rib cage and fear slowly climbed up her throat. The more fear she felt, the more distinct the shadows became. They appeared closer and closer until Mimie whirled around and saw a smoky figure behind her with gleaming red eyes. The moment her gaze rested on it, it dissipated. She screamed and fell backward into Koren. He jumped, and drew his sword, looking around in confusion.

"What? What's wrong?" he demanded.

"Sorry, I let my imagination get the better of me. We're fine," Mimie panted. He helped her to her feet and grabbed the canteens he'd dropped.

"Let's go back." He led the way toward the clearing and settled down with his back against a tree.

Mimie sat down next to him and leaned her head on his shoulder. He stiffened in surprise, then invited her closer by wrapping an arm around her waist. Mimie wasn't sure where her unexpected bravery had come from. She breathed in the smell of him and tried to concentrate on that alone. A tear escaped from the corner of her eye and soaked into the already damp material of his shirt. Oviet was gone, how could she be gone. The tears turned to choking sobs and Koren tightened his grip on her. Mimie pressed her cheek against his chest and used the steady beat of his heart to lull her into an uneasy sleep.

It surprised her the next morning to find she was still curled around him. His cheek rested on top of her head, his breathing deep and slow. Her neck was starting to hurt but she didn't want to move for fear of waking Koren. When the discomfort turned painful she decided it was time to get up. Koren stretched and brushed the moss off his clothes.

Mimie used the moonstone for light as she expanded the space cube and searched for the food pack. She pulled out a mango and watched Koren strap on his weapons. She didn't want him to catch her staring and busied herself with peeling the mango. Neither of them commented about the night before, making Mimie wonder if she had done something wrong. She would never understand him.

They made their way back toward the boundary and paused between two of the poles.

"I'd feel more comfortable with this if I knew what was in there," Koren muttered. Mimie wasn't sure if she agreed. They left behind the cheerful calls of birds and were plunged into an eerie silence.

Not far passed the boundary Mimie felt her stomach clench, and froze. There was a dead tapir on the ground with its stomach ripped open. The kill looked fresh.

"Stay close," Koren advised, reaching for his sword. Mimie saw movement out of the corner of her eye.

"Did you see that?" She pointed to where she'd thought she'd seen a cloaked figure.

"Let's keep moving."

The underbrush was so thick it made traversing the wild landscape nearly impossible. Thick spider's webs hung in the trees above them. She cringed and kept moving.

They stopped in the afternoon to rehydrate and get their bearings. It was easy to get lost in the tangled underbrush. Koren reverted back to following the river to make sure they were heading in the right direction.

Mimie leaned against a tree and stared off into the gathering fog. She heard shuffling footsteps and froze. She glanced toward Koren, but he hadn't moved. She caught sight of a hooded figure hovering amidst the fog, watching her. The wind changed, carrying away the smell of wet soil, and exposing something more menacing, the smell of a rotting corpse. The figure took a slow step toward her. Koren had to have known he was there, but he never turned around.

"Koren?" Her voice was so hoarse he probably couldn't hear her.

"Koren?" Louder this time, but he still didn't respond. She could see the figure more clearly now; its eyes had a small ring of gold around a large, soulless black pupil. Its head was tilted slightly to the left, with blood stained lips turned up in a smile, something shiny and sharp in its right hand flashed silver in the dim light.

"Hello, fairy." Mimie grimaced as a slimy voice whispered to her from the back of her mind. Somehow the creature had penetrated her thoughts.

"Get out of my head," Mimie groaned, pressing both palms against her temples. "Koren!" she yelled again. He turned around and stared at her blankly. His eyes were so dilated she could only see a sliver of green around the edges of his pupil. It was like he was in some kind of trance. "You're doing this." Mimie suddenly realized. The corpse chuckled mincingly.

"Cleaver girl."

"Why?" Mimie demanded.

"You won't have to worry about it long..." Mimie tried to take a step toward Koren, but her movements were sluggish and slow. She was partially immune to the magical trance, but fear locked up her muscles further, making it harder to move.

The corpse extended a hand toward her neck. Mimie leaned away from it in disgust, but the tree behind her blocked her escape. The cold, bony fingers locked around her throat, cutting off her airway. Mimie tried to think through the haze clouding her mind. Finding her courage, she felt her muscles unlock and kicked the corpse away from her. She coughed and rubbed her throat, then walked over to Koren and pulled the sword from his hand. The corpse hissed and took a step back.

"Stay away from us," Mimie warned. The creature raised its knife, stiff legs dragging against the ground as it walked. It wasn't looking at her, though; its eyes were fixed on Koren. Mimie felt fierce anger course through her, she would not lose him too.

She swung the sword at the corpse and cut a large gash across its chest. A black, sticky looking liquid oozed from the wound. Her next strike decapitated the monster. The body turned to dust as it fell toward the ground, and whatever evil spirit was inside dissipated with a faint hiss.

Koren shook his head and rubbed his fingers against his forehead.

"What was that?" he asked, dazed.

"When it touched me I saw inside its thoughts," Mimie said with a shudder. "It called itself a shadow walker. The demons can't leave Death Valley, but if they conceal themselves inside a dead body, they can enter the forest. They have to eat the flesh of other animals to keep the body going, but it still degrades. If it falls apart before they get back to Death Valley, they disintegrate with it."

"So he wanted our corpses?"

"No, just yours. He wanted me alive, but I shoved him off before I saw why."

"How many of those things do you think are in here?" Koren shuddered.

"I don't know, but maybe they will think twice about attacking us after what I did to the last one."

"Don't look them in the eye, that's how it paralyzed me. I don't know if I'll ever forget those creepy yellow irises," he muttered.

Mimie wiped the black goop off Koren's sword on a tree and handed it back to him.

"Let's keep going," she muttered. They pushed on through the fog, setting a brisk pace. Sweat poured down Mimie's face in the humidity, and she continuously wiped it out of her eyes. She saw a few more figures watching them from the shadows of the trees, but none bothered them. Mimie felt the tension in her shoulders from the constant feeling of being watched, wearing on her.

"How much further do you think Death Valley is?" she wondered a few hours later. Sunset was upon them and the softened light made it hard to see.

"I don't know, but there might be a sign up ahead."

"A sign? Who in their right minds would come this far into shadow walker territory to put up a sign?" Mimie wondered incredulously.

"Maybe someone who was really dedicated to their job," Koren shrugged. "Let's see what it says."

The sign was constructed from a bamboo pole hammered into the ground with a wooden slate attached to it. Carved into the wood were the words: Death Valley 1 league; continue at your own peril.

"Maybe the fairies put it up," Mimie suggested. "If that's the case, you'd think they could have included a 'welcome' in that otherwise depressing statement."

"Regardless, this is good news, we should reach the valley in another 2 or 3 hours," Koren said. "We'll make camp up ahead and walk the rest of the way tomorrow."

"I am not sleeping with those creepy, disemboweling shadow walkers wandering around waiting to kill you," Mimie huffed.

"Demons don't like light. If we build a fire and spread salt around the perimeter of the camp site we should be fine," Koren assured her.

"Maybe," Mimie consented. They walked for another hour and made camp in a grove of trees. The combined canopies were exceptionally thick and locked out most of the moisture from the rain. Mimie expanded the space cube and pulled out the salt. She made a wide circle with it around the camp and then tossed it back into the cube. The vegetation near them was dry enough that they didn't have to go looking for bamboo.

Mimie volunteered for the first watch and sat down with her back to the fire. She scanned the dark trees but didn't see any signs of danger. Koren threw his cloak over his head to block out the light from the fire, and his breathing gradually became deeper as he fell asleep. Mimie supported her head on her palm and picked up a small rock. She threw it up and caught it in her palm again.

A pair of yellow eyes watched her from the shadows beyond the ring of salt. "You will not escape us."

Mimie dropped the rock and flinched as the voice entered her head. She ignored the comment. The shadow walker couldn't hurt them as long as they stayed inside the ring of salt and the fire didn't burn out. Even if the corpse did manage to put her in a trance again it wouldn't make a difference, she could fight it. If it got Koren, though, it could force him to break the salt circle, or stab himself.

A cold chill inched up her spine. She wouldn't let that happen, even if it meant staying up all night. The shadow walker disappeared from the tree it was lurking behind, but Mimie doubted it had gone far. She threw another log on the fire and picked up her rock again.

She turned her thoughts down easier avenues. There were four types of magic she'd have to master when she reached the fairies. She was good at life magic, but didn't know much about the other three. After studying the rock for a moment, she wondered if she could make it levitate. She focused on it, but nothing happened.

A nagging worry made her chew on the inside of her cheek nervously. If it rained hard enough, the salt circle would be washed away and the fire extinguished. It was unnerving to trust their lives to the mercy of the weather. She was tired, but sheer determination kept her awake through the passing hours. It was a relief when the sky lightened. She wanted to give them as much travel time as possible so she put out the fire and woke up Koren. He looked at the coming dawn in confusion.

"Have you been up all night?"

"Maybe," Mimie replied.

"This is going to be the hardest terrain we've crossed yet. It's going to be even harder traversing it sleep deprived."

"I'll be fine," Mimie assured him. "There was a shadow walker hanging around the camp last night. I was afraid if you sat watch it would possess you."

"I still wish you had gotten some sleep, even if was only a few hours. What are you going to do tonight when we have to camp in Death Valley? You can't stay up all night again."

"We'll deal with that when the time comes," Mimie replied.

They continued following the river. Koren stopped when they passed by a water vine and cut a notch in it near the top. He severed the thick stem near the base and used the resulting trickle to refill their water canteens. He replaced the cork stopper and handed one of the bottles to Mimie.

A few hours later they stopped in front of a curtain of moss and tangled branches. Mimie could feel the presence of something on the other side of it. Something evil.

Koren cut a path through the branches with his sword and ducked through the moss. Mimie followed him and froze. Wispy gray clouds rumbled over a charcoal landscape. After all the rich greens of the jungle, the sudden color change was hard to take in.

"Death Valley," Koren whispered.

CHAPTER 18: DEATH VALLEY

←– ←– →→ →→

Looking out on the soulless landscape Mimie couldn't help but think it might have been beautiful once. Clumps of delicate grass swayed in the breeze. Small trees lined the banks of the river, and large rocks rose out occasionally from among the sedges, all the way to the horizon far in the distance.

"I feel uncomfortable walking into demon territory without some sort of a guide," Mimie muttered, looking out into the blackened grass warily.

"The fairies get through here, so we know it's possible."

"Fairies are immune to magical trances, though, the demons can't hurt them, but they could make us stab each other if they wanted to," Mimie pointed out. "Or they could just eat our souls and leave our dead bodies to decorate their wasteland."

"That's very cheerful," Koren replied, glaring at her.

"I'm just being realistic."

"Well, at least we have a small defense against them, there isn't much salt left, but it should be enough to ward off an attack." He expanded the space cube and pulled out the salt container. He wanted to have it out, and ready in case some demons decided to pay them a visit.

"Ready?" he said.

"As I'll ever be." She paused where the fallen leaves turned from yellow to black.

"Ladies first," Koren offered, sweeping his arm in front of him.

"How very gentlemanly of you," Mimie said with a glare. She took a deep breath and stepped out onto the blackened earth. "It feels so empty," she shuddered.

Following the river seemed to be the most intuitive way to get to the waterfall, but Mimie had a feeling it was also where the highest concentration of demons would be. The river bent sharply in front of them as it cut across the land, forming a large 'C' shape. It would be easier to swim across and go up the other side so they wouldn't have to go as far out of their way.

Koren kept his eyes on the ground to reduce his chance of being put in a trance if a demon showed up. Mimie stayed closer to him than normal, close enough her hand occasionally brushed his. They walked for a while in silence, making her footsteps sound impossibly loud. She winced every time the dead plant material crunched underfoot. Several times she thought she saw a dark form out of the corner of her eye, but when she glanced that way, there was never anything there. The hairs on the back of her neck stood up, and she bit her lip nervously. As they neared the river, Mimie covered her nose with the collar of her shirt.

"What is that stench?" She tried not to gag. "It's putrid." They walked a little closer and Koren muttered,

"I think it's the water." Mimie's upper lip twitched in distaste as she noticed an oily film swirling under the surface and tendrils of yellowish looking steam rising into the air.

They weren't happy about it, but they took off their shoes, and cloaks, then stashed them in the space cube. Koren also put the salt back in the cube so it would stay dry.

Mimie found herself distracted by the way the muscles in Koren's shoulders moved beneath his shirt as he bent down to pick up the space cube. She could feel that her time with him was coming to an end. She regretted never telling him how she felt, but doubted it would make a difference. The tighter she tried to hold onto to him, the more she'd push him away.

Mimie took a hesitant step into the water and coughed on the yellowish smoke swirling around her. The water was deep enough that the bottom was beyond her reach, and she had to swim. The fumes coming off the water made her feel light headed and burned her lungs. Her skin prickled uncomfortably and her eyes watered. The prickling escalated to a burning sensation and her nose hurt from the harsh odor. Her awkward movements brought Koren to her side and he towed her to the opposite bank until she was able to touch the ground again. She coughed as she pulled herself out of the toxic liquid and felt a rash forming where her soaked clothes touched her skin.

There was a clump of charred bushes nearby where the air was clean of the burning fumes coming off the river. Mimie stumbled toward it and pushed her way inside to give her head a chance to clear. Koren joined her. He was close enough that she could have reached out and touched him if she'd wanted to, but she kept her hands carefully restrained at her sides.

She'd always considered jealousy to be a petty emotion, but that was before she knew how much pain it could cause someone. It bothered her that Emily was the one Koren dreamed about at night, that she was the one he loved. She knew it was selfish of her to feel that way. Koren deserved better than someone who resented his happiness just because he'd found it with someone other than her.

Mimie peaked through the branches at the sound of approaching footsteps and saw an elf appear along the riverbank looking disoriented. Mimie started to push her way out of the bushes but Koren held her back. Smoky shadows followed behind the elf, moving slowly, knowing that soon their prey would collapse from the vapors coming off the river. The elf stumbled toward the jungle in terror.

"We have to help him," Mimie hissed, prying Koren's hand off her arm.

The elf fell to his knees, wheezing and seemed frozen in panic. The demons swirled around him, red eyes gleaming, and appeared to savor his terror. One flew above the others and then turned and passed through the man's body. A scream of agony escaped his lips, igniting a frenzy among the demons.

One after another they passed through his body, growing stronger and more distinct with each pass. Their long snouts were distinctly canine, but they had the lumbering trunk of a bearlike creature. Mimie watched in frozen horror, crouching lower to the ground as if she could sink through it. Black blotches appeared on the elf's skin and grew larger with each demon that passed through him. When the demons had finally finished with him, it was as though he'd been turned into black stone. The agony and terror he had felt moments before his death were frozen on his face forever. The demons sniffed the air around them as if they could sense someone watching them. Mimie clamped a hand over her mouth to quiet her breathing, convinced they could somehow hear it.

"We need to get out of here," Koren whispered in her ear.

"I can feel the heat coming off your flesh day walkers," a slimy voice muttered in the back of her mind. "Come out come out where ever you are." Mimie held her breath, hoping they wouldn't be able to hear the frantic beating of her heart. A small breeze picked up, betraying their location by carrying their scent downwind to the demons. Relying on pure adrenaline Mimie yanked Koren backward, tumbling over him as they both fell out of the bush. The demons growled wordlessly. Mimie clutched her forehead as the sound ground painfully through her mind. A demon headed straight for her as though it intended to pass through her body. She wasn't sure what would happen if the demon touched her and braced herself against the pain if it passed through. A deep chill washed over her as the demon collided with her abdomen, but it turned away with a shriek at the touch of her skin.

"A fairy," the others hissed angrily. Koren used the demons momentary confusion to whip out the space cube and quickly pull out the salt. The demons were chattering excitedly to one another and abruptly tensed as though they were being physically restrained. They stumbled toward Mimie, snapping their jaws as though itching to sink their shadowed teeth into her. Koren backed away and pulled Mimie with him, he turned and sprinted across the hard ground. Mimie tried not to look behind her as she sprinted after him. The demons whined loudly as they struggled against the restraining force and their red eyes bore into her back as she ran.

Koren veered to the right and jumped over a ditch leading into a flattened plain. Little craters dotted the ground every few feet and would occasionally spew enormous quantities of the yellowish looking gas into the air. They were able to avoid them for the most part, but at the speed they were going Mimie became increasingly nervous that she would get her foot caught in one of the craters and break her leg. The deeper they plunged into the minefield the harder it was to see the river and make sure they were still heading in the right direction. Mimie risked a glance over her shoulder and saw the demons bearing down on them. She screamed and pushed her legs faster, but they were still gaining.

A crater erupted right in front of them, plunging her and Koren into a cloud of the toxic gas more potent than the little they had experienced in the river. Mimie coughed and tried to keep going, but her legs buckled and she fell onto her side. The momentum she had built up sent her rolling across the blackened dirt before she finally came to rest in front of a steaming crater.

"Are you alright?" Koren asked.

"Mostly." Mimie grabbed her arm. She'd twisted it in the fall.

"Run," he muttered. "The demons can't hurt you. You can still make it."

"I'm not leaving," Mimie told him. She refused to watch from afar while the demons consumed his soul.

He tried to push himself to his hands and knees, but the gas overcame him and he collapsed onto his side. Mimie poured the salt that had fallen from his hand into her palm and put herself between him and the demons. She dropped the salt into her pocket and kept her hand ready in case she needed to use it. As the demons stalked toward them, she crouched over Koren protectively. They would have to kill her before she allowed them to hurt him. The demons quickly surrounded her, pacing back and forth just out of her reach.

Mimie wasn't sure what they were waiting for, but if she could hold out against the gas long enough, maybe they would give up and leave in search of easier prey. It seemed like a long shot, but the only other option was to throw salt at them. She heard a snide edge to their thoughts as if they'd already won and were waiting for her to realize it too. A chill seeped into her bones as Koren lifted himself unsteadily to his feet. His eyes rolled and then turned as black as the surrounding landscape. The demons had possessed him.

His head jerked in her direction and he roughly pulled her to her feet. She tried to twist out of his grip, but he firmly scooped her over one shoulder and headed deeper into the crater field. His shoulder was pressing painfully into her ribs but she had a feeling her comfort wasn't among his first priorities.

She searched through the demon's minds trying to figure out what they planned to do with them, but their thoughts gave away nothing. She cursed the fact that Koren was so much stronger than her. Maybe she could fight her way out of his grasp, but even if she did break free, where would she go? She couldn't drag Koren with her while he was still possessed, but maybe there was a way to snap him out of it. Before she could act on any of her plans, Koren stopped in front of a crater making a soft gurgling noise. She sucked in a quick breath and held it as the gas erupted in her face. She tried to twist out of Koren's grip, but all she managed to do was use up her air supply. The last thing she remembered was the gas scorching down her throat as her burning lungs forced her to take a breath.

Mimie lifted her cheek away from a cold stone floor and coughed on the thick moldy air. It was pitch black, she sat up on her hands and knees and groped the air in front of her for some indication of where she was. Her fingers brushed against a scaly object. The slender body recoiled from her touch with a hiss. Surprised, she jerked backward.

"Koren?"

"Over here." Relief washed over her. Caution told her to be weary in case he was still possessed but she ignored it. Her need to be next to him was stronger than her fear.

She tried not to think about the intermittent slime her fingers slipped across as she searched for him in the darkness. Her hand found his arm. His skin was cold and a deep shudder passed through his body as something slid across the floor nearby. His breathing was shallow and irregular. Mimie curled around him and buried her face against his back.

"They're watching us."

A chill slid up her spine as she slowly glanced around. There were several places where the darkness seemed blacker than others. One of the shadows shifted under her gaze. Her grip tightened around Koren's arm. She heard a loud repeated clang as an unseen form dragged something across the bars in front of them, whistling as they did so. Chains rustled somewhere deeper in the cavern.

Koren pulled his arm from Mimie's grasp and wrapped it around her shoulders, putting himself between her and the noise.

"They left me alive for a reason you know, they want me to kill you. I saw it in their mind."

Mimie's throat burned as she pressed her face against his arm. She didn't know what to say. Silence fell over them. It was hard to tell how much time had passed in the darkness. What felt like hours, could have only been minutes. Counting the steady beats of Koren's heart was the only way to know for sure that time had passed at all.

"Everything is ready master." The words cut through Mimie like a knife. She wrapped her arms around Koren's waist, hoping if she squeezed him tight enough it would keep the demons from possessing him.

Torches flickered to life. The snakes recoiled from the light and fled toward small cracks in the cave walls. Koren's lip twitched in disgust as he watched them go, his face pale.

Mimie ignored them and focused her attention on a child standing beyond her cell near a stone alter. Her black eyes bore into Mimie's and a small smile played on the corner of her lips. Mimie swallowed hard. Her brown hair was twisted into a wild bun on top of her head, and her grungy clothes hung from her shoulders in tatters. Several of her teeth were missing, leaving wide gaps in her yellow stained sneer. There were deep scratches on her face, and arms in different stages of healing. They disfigured her face making her look more animal than person. She walked toward the cell door with a halting gait, one shoulder drooping lower than the other.

Mimie tried to focus on something else, anything else. There were red stains on the stone floor where the crusted rust from the bars had dripped down. She was mesmerized by the color and the stark resemblance it held to blood.

A key scraped against a lock, and the door opened with a loud squeal. The girl paused in the doorway, watching them. Her veins were tinged black and created a darkened matrix across her chalky skin. She ran her tongue across her cracked lips and glanced toward a shadow lurking in the back corner of their cell. It consolidated to the consistency of smoke and drifted toward them.

Mimie's heart hammered against her ribs as she put herself between Koren and the advancing smoke. It drifted around her, staying just beyond the touch of her skin. Koren stiffened as the demon struggled to take a hold of him. He clenched his jaw and a vein bulged in his forehead. His eyes rolled back as the demon's power overwhelmed him. Blackness flooded across his eyes. Mimie crawled backwards, distancing herself from him. His head snapped up and he grabbed her arm. Mimie was too stunned to fight as he wrenched her to her feet.

She slid across the slick floor as Koren dragged her toward the girl. Mimie grabbed the edges of the bars and braced her feet against the cell opening. The girl grabbed her arm and her sharp nails dug into Mimie's skin as she helped Koren force her through. A strong urine smell coming off the girl's clothes burned Mimie's nose and made her eyes water.

Mimie dug her heels in as they wrestled her toward a stone slab supported by an ornately carved base. The alter was ringed by low burning torches giving off incense. Koren shoved her toward the table and pressed his arm against her throat, cutting off her airway as the girl secured shackles to her wrists. Lights danced in front of Mimie's eyes as she fought the urge to pass out. Koren released the pressure and stepped back. Mimie closed her eyes and coughed on the sickly sweet smoke.

She tested the shackles on her wrists and felt them give a little. If she angled her hips toward her right hand, she could reach the salt in her pocket. The salt would offer her little protection, but it was better than nothing. Koren followed the girl to a series of clay bowls filled with paint. He knelt in front of her and removed his shirt. Mimie could do nothing but watch as the girl dipped two thin fingers into a bowl and traced them across Koren's skin. Inky black lines spread from her fingers across his chest and arms. Anger was the only thing keeping Mimie's head clear as she struggled to breathe. The girl added red lines to the black, finishing with one that circled his navel. If Mimie hadn't known his face better than her own, she wouldn't have recognized him. The girl drew lines across her arms and face. Once she was finished she returned to Mimie's side.

Mimie moved to the extreme edge of the stone slab. The girl pulled a knife from the folds of her shirt and tested the blade with her finger. Mimie watched the point warily. The girl clasped the knife against her hand and slid it downward to create a deep cut across her palm. Black blood flowed from the wound down her hand. She kept her fist clenched as she lowered the knife toward Mimie's arm. Mimie realized her intention and kicked her legs uselessly as Koren moved to restrain her. She screamed as the blade bit into her flesh. Koren's hold wavered, and she kicked him away from her. The girl withdrew the blade and touched her palm to the cut on Mimie's arm. Her blood burned Mimie's skin.

"Scream all you want little fairy, no one is coming to help you." Mimie cringed as a voice that could only belong to a demon entered her mind.

A dark laugh came from a corner of the chamber deep in shadow. Her heart shuddered, but she kept her expression fierce. A large paw stepped forward into the light; the muscular leg flowed into a wide chest and a thick neck. The demon pulled back his lips into a wicked snarl. There was nowhere to hide, nowhere to run. Its lumbering footsteps echoed ominously as it approached.

"It seems like you went through a lot of work just to eat me," Mimie challenged.

"I have no intention of eating you. The purpose you will serve is much more critical than providing mere sustenance." He stalked around the perimeter of the stone table, tail swishing from side to side. "Good job my pet," he praised, sliding his tail over the child's shoulders. She beamed at him.

The burning sensation in Mimie's arm intensified.

"We've been in this prison a long time," he growled, still circling. "When I break out of here, your kindred scum will be the first to die.

I cannot take their souls, but I will have the satisfaction of gorging myself on their blood and chewing their bones to dust."

Cold sweat trickled down the side of Mimie's face, her pulse pounded in her ears.

"I'm getting ahead of myself, first I need your magic. Brothers, come, our moment of triumph is at hand." Mimie glanced around the dark cave and glimpsed smoky forms consolidating in the shadows. They stared at her with unblinking red eyes.

Koren reached toward her and placed his palm on her tattoo. The other hand seized her throat, forcing her to lie back against the table. Her airway closed, though he was barely exerting any pressure. Tendrils of terror curled into her stomach.

"I'll let him live long enough to realize the part he played in your death. Then I'll tear out his throat. It'll be quick, merciful even."

Mimie glared at the demon with enough venom she hoped it physically burned him.

Koren muttered a chant in a quiet voice. A scream tore from her lips as pain ripped through her. Skin was being pulled away from muscle, muscle from bone. The demon's red eyes bored into hers. She could barely think. Her eyes rolled into the back of her head. Sweat soaked through her shirt and coated her palms. She twisted her wrists back and forth and felt them slip free of the shackles. She jerked her arm away from the girl and formed a fist around the salt in her pocket. She punched Koren, a knuckle cracked. He staggered back. With his grip broken the pain released her.

"No!" the demon roared, taking a step back. Mimie rolled off the table, hitting the floor with a loud thwack. She threw the hand full of salt in the demon's face. The salt burned the demon's skin, creating open soars. He howled in pain. Mimie sidestepped his snapping jaws and dug her fingers into the fur around his neck. She allowed what was left of her magic to race across her skin like a current of electricity. The demon wolf threw back his head, trying to shake her off.

The possessed girl backed away and fled to a small opening in a large pile of boulders. Her jerky gait distracted Mimie for a moment.

She returned her attention to the wolf and pushed harder, letting the magic scald through him. Holes of light burned through the wolf's skin. With an explosion of light, he was gone. His howls echoed off the walls and gradually disappeared into the silence that had fallen over the chamber. Demons scattered in fear. Seeing their leader vanquished had thrown the pack into chaos and several rivals fought viciously to establish their dominance. Their snarls faded as the fight moved to a bigger chamber.

Mimie wasn't aware she was on the ground until she noticed the base of one of the torches. She pressed her cheek against the cold stone to help ease her throbbing headache.

"Guardian, are you alright?"

Mimie glanced up in surprise and blinked a few times as she tried to process what she was seeing. A stranger knelt next to her wearing armor made from yellow energy. Her gray-flecked brown hair was pulled back in a ponytail and flowed from the base of her helmet. Under the armor she wore boots and a form fitting tunic.

"Where did you come from?" Mimie croaked, eyeing the woman's gleaming sword in suspicion.

"I'm from Iridescence, I came to help you. My name is Lilianna. We have to go you're not safe here."

"You're a fairy?"

"Yes." She draped Mimie's arm over her shoulder and pulled her to her feet. "I saw a vision that Malmothos would try to take your powers. I got here as soon as I could."

Mimie's wrists were bruised and the tops of her hands were raw. Blood oozed from the cut on her arm. Koren groaned and sat up, rubbing his jaw. She still barely recognized him with the red and black markings on his chest.

A low growl caught her attention. Mimie's head snapped up and she caught sight of an approaching demon. Lilianna stepped in front of her. The yellow light emitted by her sword reflected in the demon's red eyes as its lips pulled back in a snarl. Koren locked his arm around Mimie's waist to keep her from faltering. Lilianna charged the demon and dodged it's snapping teeth. She sank her sword into its side. The demon dissipated with a fait hiss.

"Come on, the exit's this way," Lilianna told them. "Stay close."

Mimie used Koren's shoulder for support as they stumbled after Lilianna. Mimie's chest felt tight and her mouth was uncomfortably dry. Koren glanced at Lilianna and bit his lip as he struggled with something he wanted to say.

"I'm sorry." The words came out strained as if he hated how painfully inadequate they were. The pain she saw in his eyes for the part he had almost played in her death were beyond words.

"I don't blame you," Mimie assured him. He grabbed a strip of cloth and wrapped it around the knife wound to stop the bleeding.

Lilianna led the way toward the darkest corner of the cave and started up a narrow pathway toward the ceiling. She held up her hand for them to pause as two snarling demons snapping at one another's throats crossed their path.

"This chaos will have consequences." It sounded like an accusation.

Mimie tensed as another demon lunged at them. Koren pulled her out of the way and Lilianna struck a fatal blow to it's flank. She jogged up the path leading toward the ceiling and held her sword ready at her side. The glow of her armor illuminated the path in front of them. When they finally reached the top Mimie saw daylight streaming in from somewhere ahead. The long, dark tunnel opened up into the middle of the crater field.

"This way," Lilianna instructed. She headed toward a hill on the far end of the crater field.

Mimie glanced behind her, but she couldn't see any signs of pursuit. "Why aren't they following us?"

"It'll take a day or two for a new leader to establish dominance over the pack. They can't act in a coordinated way until that happens. The weaker demons will keep their distance until the new alpha emerges." She didn't remove her armor and kept a watchful eye regardless.

Koren stopped for a second to look for a shirt in the space cube. As Mimie watched him pull it on a barely acknowledged thought surfaced before she could bury it again. Even now when she knew she didn't have a chance, she still hoped Koren would choose her over Emily. She couldn't bear the thought that the future she'd hoped to have with him was never going to happen. It felt like she was balancing on the edge of a knife, sooner or later she was going to fall one way or the other.

"We need to keep up a quick pace or we won't make it to higher ground before dark." Again Lilianna's words were directed at Mimie. Mimie clenched her teeth and bit back her retort.

At first Koren stayed by her side, but as the distance between them and Lilianna widened he moved to keep up with her. Mimie watched him go, a lump forming in her throat. She thought things would be different between them after what they'd gone through, that they would be closer. Had she done something wrong?

When they reached the steep hillside leading out of the crater field Mimie hung her head in defeat. There were parts so steep she had to crawl to avoid falling backward. Her broken knuckle throbbed, and her arm ached. Blood was beginning to seep through the bandage. She tried to keep weight off it by curling her wrist inward, but that did little to ease the pain. The loose gravel prevented her from bracing her weight and she slid one step back for every two forward. Lilianna and Koren had likely scaled the hillside and moved on by now. Her throat burned as her foot slipped and jarred her hand. The sun beat down on her face and sweat dripped into her eyes. Dust collected in her mouth in a thick, gritty paste.

After what she'd been through it was a miracle she could walk at all. Their lack of compassion infuriated her, and angry tears cut a path through the grime covering her cheeks.

She collapsed onto her side and cradled her hand, not sure she could go on. Koren would come back for her; he wouldn't leave her behind. Minutes passed, long enough for him to know she wasn't following, but he never came. She lifted herself onto her hands and knees, and found the strength to keep climbing.

When she finally stumbled to the top she found Koren and Lilianna resting in the shade of an overhang. Koren took a long drink from his canteen. Mimie fished hers out of the open space cube and took a small sip without looking at him. She swished the warm water around in her mouth to clear away the dust and spit it out on the ground.

"Are you ok? Your face is really red," Koren said in concern.

Mimie clenched her uninjured hand into a fist and bit her lip. With some effort, she rearranged her features into what she hoped was a more pleasant expression.

"I'm fine." The words came out closer to a growl than she would have liked. Lilianna stood up.

"Wait a second, Mimie still needs to rest. Drink more water," he urged.

Mimie uncorked the top and drank a little bit more. The water had an unpleasant aftertaste of plant sap from the vines they had gotten it from. Lilianna shifted her weight back and forth impatiently. Mimie contemplated throwing the water canteen at her head. Maybe a concussion would teach her to have more patience.

Mimie pushed herself to her feet and followed after them as Lilianna worked her way along the top of the ridge. Mimie checked the position of the sun; they only had a few more hours of daylight. They stopped in a sheltered valley below the ridge and set up camp.

Koren expanded the space cube and pulled out their sleeping sacks. Mimie spread hers across the rocky ground and curled up on it. She shifted back and forth as she tried to find a comfortable position. One of the rocks was pressing painfully into her hip so she fished it out and tossed it away from her. The other lumps and bumps the remaining rocks presented were annoying, but bearable.

Lilianna surprised her by setting a small black cube on the ground.

"I know you two must be starving," she muttered once it was fully expanded. Her space cube was twice the size of Koren's. Lilianna leaned over the side and pulled out some jerky. Mimie didn't have much of an appetite. She took one of the smaller pieces Lilianna offered her and chewed without tasting it. She worried briefly about who would watch the camp but she was too tired to articulate her concerns out loud.

The next morning Mimie opened her eyes and registered a dull pain in her side. She stretched and crawled out of her sleeping sack.

The hard ground made her miss the soft moss that covered the jungle floor. It was better to wake up damp with ants crawling on her than wondering if the rocks had left permanent impressions on her spine.

Koren was the last one to sit watch, he'd used the time to take a wet rag and scrub the markings off his chest and arms. She saw the stained material sitting next to him as he pulled his shirt back on. He pushed himself to his feet and walked over to Lilianna's space cube. He rummaged around inside and came away holding some bread and cheese for breakfast. Mimie made due with some dried fruit, her appetite still not fully returned.

They would reach the waterfall by noon. She didn't want to spend what little time her and Koren had left angry with him, but she couldn't help it. She stared at the ground miserably.

Lilianna was cheerful as they set off. Mimie hated her for it. Koren stayed up with Lilianna again, striking up a casual conversation with her about fairy culture. Mimie could have kept up with them if she'd wanted to, but she couldn't face Koren.

This was supposed to be exciting! She had finally reached the end of her journey. Everything she'd worked toward was within her grasp. It wasn't enough to fill the hole that was burrowing its way inside her heart. If Koren noticed her mood, he didn't comment on it. Would he miss her at all when they parted ways? She knew he didn't share her feelings, but they were still friends, right?

It had been two hours and he still hadn't looked at her. The only time she got any response from him was when she stepped in a hole and twisted her ankle. She was pretty sure it was sprained but she didn't want to make a big deal out of it. She gingerly sat up and pulled the rocks out of the cuts on her palms.

"Let me see." Koren examined her palms and brushed away the debris. She hardly felt the pain. Her nerves were more concerned with other things, like the exact texture of his fingertips and the warmth of his hand against her wrist. He pulled her to her feet and quickly noticed her pronounced limp. "Only you could fall in a pothole on otherwise flat and level ground." Mimie let out an uneasy laugh, and then the moment was over. They kept walking and he went back to the conversation he was having with Lilianna. It was amazing how much his touch affected her when she knew each moment with him might be her last.

After a few more hours of walking, they stopped to take a break. Mimie pulled out her canteen and sat down in the shade of a big rock. The black landscape didn't bother her anymore; it matched her mood.

"We're making good time," Lilianna told them, oblivious to Mimie's sour attitude. For all she knew Mimie always acted like this. Mimie took a sip from the water canteen and swished it around in her dry mouth. "So how long have you and Mimie known each other?" she wondered.

"Not too long," Koren answered. "A few months."

"Oh, ok." She changed the subject. Mimie tuned her out, and it wasn't long before they were moving again.

Soon the roar of a waterfall caught her attention. "Is that…what I think it is?"

"Yes, it won't be long now," Lilianna replied.

As they got closer, Mimie saw the first signs of life. The rocks were returning back to dusty brown, and cautious wildflowers added small pinpricks of blue and purple to the landscape. After another hour, they were standing on the edge of the most enormous waterfall Mimie had ever seen. The sky seemed to wrap around to embrace her and the edge of the world crumbled away. A light breeze threw the mist from the water back in her face, and she shivered. It was so strange to be here after all this time; it was nothing like she could have imagined. She'd been so absorbed in the journey; she'd forgotten the reason behind it. The reason why they'd almost been killed over and over. The reason why she woke up at dawn every morning. It didn't feel real.

Oviet should be here with her; the moment was disconcertingly hollow without her.

Now that she was finally here what was she supposed to do? The answer was in her head, but she didn't want to face it yet.

"Are you ready?" Lilianna asked and her armor dissipated. Mimie knew she meant more than just starting down the path.

"I have to be." There was too much resting on her shoulders to crumble the way she wanted to.

A small trail of switchbacks led the way down the cliff side in a decent that left Mimie feeling lightheaded. One slip on the slick rock, and it was over. She tried not to look down at the trees that were hundreds of feet below her. Couldn't the fairies have installed a handrail? The trail ended at a small cave hidden behind the violent cascade of water.

"This way," Lilianna motioned and led them inside. The small chamber had a thin layer of water on the floor that soaked into Mimie's shoes and splashed loudly as she made her way through it. Mimie's excitement was curbed by Koren's hesitant footsteps behind her. She took a deep breath and turned to face him. He was glancing toward the cave opening with a troubled look on his face.

"Lilianna?" he called uncertainly.

"Yes?"

"I was wondering if you could tell me something about…someone." Mimie knew then why he had spent so much time talking to Lilianna. He wanted to ask her about Emily.

"What I can tell you depends on what you want to know."

"There's a girl I want to find, but I don't know where she is, or if she's alive." Koren shifted his weight from one foot to the other as he anxiously waited for her reply.

"That's simple enough. Recall her image in your mind and focus on the information you want to know." Koren closed his eyes and wrinkled his forehead in concentration. Lilianna placed her palms on the sides of his head. She released him in surprise.

"Emily?" she asked in confusion. "She's been here for the last three years, visiting with her grandparents and helping with weapons training. She left a few weeks ago to join up with the rebels in dragon valley."

"Really?" Koren staggered back a step. He was so happy he was practically glowing. Jealousy burned in Mimie's heart like an open wound. Be happy for him, she grudgingly repeated to herself in her head. She rearranged her face into a smile and glued it in place. At least she hoped it was a smile, it could have been a painful grimace.

"You are welcome to the remaining provisions in my cube," Lilianna said and expanded it for him. "Mimie, please bring the cube inside after he leaves." She expanded it for him and disappeared inside the cave. Koren turned toward Mimie in surprise, as if he'd just remembered she was there. The smile wavered, only sheer willpower kept it intact.

When the doomsday scenario of this moment played through in her mind, she'd always pictured Oviet staying with her. Mimie realized only now how selfish it would have been to ask that of her. Oviet would have hated living in a cave. She needed open skies and besides, Octavious was in dragon valley. It was wrong to keep her from pursuing the one she loved just because Mimie wasn't able to. Even if Oviet had lived, Mimie still would have ended up alone.

Her feet dragged as she sloshed toward where Koren was standing over Lilianna's space cube. He took the supplies he wanted and dropped them into his cube.

"Are you sure you'll be ok by yourself?" he muttered.

"Yeah." It wasn't a lie exactly; she knew she'd be ok eventually.

Mimie raised her eyes to his. She was down to minutes now. The pain was waiting; ready to scorch through her like acid. The course was set, fate written.

"Good luck with Emily." She was grasping at pleasantries now, anything to slow her decent into the darkness that was threatening to swallow her. Koren held out her pack and Lilianna's space cube. Her hand brushed his as she took them.

"Goodbye, Mimie." The statement was so final. She stared at the little black box in her hand while she gathered the strength to say what she knew she must. Koren was anxious to find his beloved; her floundering for words was keeping him from that.

Koren pulled her into a tight hug. Mimie rested her cheek against his chest. His heart was beating faster than normal, lub dub, lub dub. She curled her fingers into the fabric of his shirt. He squeezed her shoulders and stepped back before she was ready to let go. Her arms dropped to her sides.

"Goodbye." The words burned her throat a little on the way out.

Moisture pricked at the corners of her eyes. Koren walked toward the edge of the waterfall and she imagined him climbing onto Oviet's back. The mental image sent a wave of pain through her, and she took a step forward before she remembered that she wasn't going with him. She locked her teeth together to keep from calling out as he disappeared silently into the mist generated by the waterfall.

He'd come back. If she stood there long enough she'd see a shadowed figure returning to her through the mist. She fell to her knees with a loud splash and watched the curtain of water roar down in front of her. The time passed slowly, carefully, as if scared to tell her that he truly was not coming back.

Sometime later, she staggered to her feet and headed deeper into the tunnel. Koren's smell lingered on her and it wafted around her like sweet poison. Moonstones embedded in the rocks lit her path and her footsteps echoed hollowly off the walls around her.

A tear welled over. She allowed it to dry stiffly on her cheek. Her balance waved as she teetered on the remaining pieces of her broken life. They fell one by one into an abyss below her until there was nothing left. She stood in a wide expanse of darkness with no ceiling, walls, or floor. Her mind was too broken to know the difference between truth and lies, so when the hollow darkness whispered, you are nothing, you are no one, she believed it.

The cave floor reappeared as she forced herself to push on. She followed the passage until it opened up into a flooded cavern shrouded in fog. Perched on top of the water was an intricate system of thatched huts, bridges, and walkways. It was busy, people hurried here and there in the bustle of everyday life. Pinpricks of light she assumed were fireflies glinted in and out of view in the perpetual night. Her old self might have called the quiet mystery of the place beautiful, but her new pain-hardened self barely glanced around. She wasn't here for the scenery. Unsure what the future had in store for her, or if she would ever be able to consider this place home, she hesitated.

Somewhere in her indecision, her stomach clenched. At first she thought it was from nerves but a wave of nausea washed over her. She fell to one knee, holding the railing for support. Her stomach heaved and a black substance spilled across the bridge.

Someone screamed.

The taste of bile mixed with blood hovered in the back of Mimie's mouth. She glanced at her arm and found the same black substance had started to ooze through the bandage.

The click of approaching heels hurt her ears. She lifted her head and her eyes crossed as she stared down the point of a sword.

"Stop!" Lilianna yelled.

"There's nothing we can do for her, she's been touched by darkness. You know what happens. If I don't kill her now she'll start attacking people." The voice was cold, unfeeling. The blade raised into a striking position.

Mimie lost her balance and fell against the bridge. The cold wood felt good against her feverous cheek. The sounds became muffled, voices tangled together to form a low hum.

Hot pain shot from her lower back through her stomach. She might have screamed, but her throat closed. Fear made her want to recoil, but she couldn't move. An ocean of darkness pulled at her, drowning her in it. She fought back. Her grip on reality slipped and she tumbled into the vast expanse of blackness.

To be continued...

ABOUT THE AUTHOR

B.H. Nelson is a lover of stories and all things fantasy. As a child she read constantly and would often get in trouble when her mom found her immersed in a book on the shower floor at 3 am on a school night. She attends the University of Arizona and is working toward a degree in Ecology and Evolutionary Biology.

www.ingramcontent.com/pod-product-compliance
Lightning Source LLC
Chambersburg PA
CBHW061942170626
46813CB00006B/2501